Scott Archer Jones

"Scott Jones has the imagination and chutzpah of a gifted circus promoter, and a great way with words. He is a born writer, full of humor and thrilling complexity, much compassion, and a great sense of crazy, tragedy, and everything in between. He can juggle plots like a gifted magician and keep you enthralled start to finish. *Jupiter and Gilgamesh* is funny, sad, original—I give it a hearty two thumbs up."

John Nichols, Author of: *Milagro Beanfield Wars*

"A novel that spans 4700 years is a novel with ambition and, shall we say, hubris. Yet Scott Archer Jones pulls off this narrative miracle with grace, wit, and bravado. No one writes this good the first time out, do they? *Jupiter and Gilgamesh* is more than a promising debut by a hugely talented writer; it is a compelling novel of the first order. Matt Devon's hermetic life goes public and all hell breaks loose. How does a man live an authentic life anymore? You'll find out on this exhilarating ride through Uruk and West Texas. Do yourself a favor, buy this book, get in on the secret before everyone else knows what you soon will: here is the future of contemporary fiction."

John Dufresne, Author of: *No Regrets, Coyote*

"Scott Archer Jones's *Jupiter and Gilgamesh* cleverly interfaces ancient myth with a story as contemporary as today's headlines about abandoned children, the tug-of-war of litigation, and the crossed wires of life and lust. The result is an evocative, entertaining, and challenging read."

Wally Lamb, Author of: *We Are Water*

Jupiter and Gilgamesh

A Novel of Sumeria and Texas

Scott Archer Jones

Published by:
Southern Yellow Pine (SYP) Publishing
4351 Natural Bridge Rd.
Tallahassee, FL 32305

www.syppublishing.com

This is a work of fiction. Names, characters, places, and events that occur either are the products of the author's imagination or are used fictitiously. Any resemblance to actual persons, places, or events is purely co-incidental.

The contents and opinions expressed in this book do not necessarily reflect the views and opinions of Southern Yellow Pine Publishing, nor does the mention of brands or trade names constitute endorsement.

ISBN-10: 1940869137
ISBN-13: 978-1-940869-13-1

Author Photo: Wende Woolley Photography
Front Cover Design: Taylor Nelson
Photo of Assyrian wall-carving in cover Copyright: khd/Shutterstock.com

Printed in the United States of America
First Edition
July 2014

Acknowledgements

I'd like to acknowledge the master class at the Taos Writers Conference led by John Dufresne—they helped me agonize through an earlier draft. The structure of the book changed significantly as a result.

I'd also like to thank my Taos editor and conscience Phaedra Greenwood, who carefully considered every word of draft 4B, whether it was pretty or not. We had so much fun, we're going to do it again with another book.

A charming friend and artist gave me the initial concept for the book cover, and for free—thank you Kathleen Ferguson Huntington.

I want to thank my mother for raising me on books and all the toasted cheese sandwiches I wanted.

Finally, I'd like to express deep appreciation to my wife, Sandra Hornback Jones. She was, as always, my first reader and my last, and she always reminded me when it was time to eat and to go to bed.

Scott

Jupiter and Gilgamesh

Prologue

In the third millennium, fifteen hundred years before Homer's *Iliad*, Gilgamesh was the stuff of legend. In fact, he was the first tragic hero. His dime-store novel was writ large on clay tablets. These were buried in the collapsed library of the last Assyrian king in the second millennium, lost for centuries, dug up, and liberated by the English Empire to be translated in the 1850s.

Gilgamesh's story deserved to be the first tragic epic. He rolled out of the desert like a raging ghibli, ripped the kingship of Uruk out of the hands of a council of old and weak men, and ruled the finest city-state of Sumeria for one hundred and twenty-six years. None of the hundred-plus years chalked up as easy for him, as he twisted history and the gods twisted him. For Gilgamesh, it was all about immortality. For the gods it was all about demanding humility.

Gilgamesh was born in the 2700s in a dirty little village outside of Uruk. His father was a womanizer and his mother a goddess who decamped soon after for more divine surroundings. They both abandoned a baby two-thirds a god. While still a boy, Gilgamesh ran away from his slave's life into the South Caucasus Mountains. After he had his fill of killing sheep and stag, he wandered home and took up the trade of soldier-of-fortune, hiring out his bronze battle axe to various Sumerian city-states. Returning to his own neighborhood just as King Dumizid of Uruk had a fatal stroke, Gilgamesh parlayed sociopathy and brawny charm into his own crown.

Gilgamesh hadn't picked up skills of kingship while a mercenary, and he soon fell into trouble with the locals for sleeping with their daughters. Gilgamesh as soldier had been the loner, the outsider. The

1

gods sent him a best friend, a Sasquatch-type fellow named Enkidu raised by wild animals. Enkidu lucked into some educational breaks: a golden-hearted whore (officially a temple prostitute) cleaned him up and took on his education. After a rocky start to their friendship, Enkidu gentled Gilgamesh and kept him out of the bedrooms of newly-minted brides.

A bored King Gilgamesh envisioned himself as a city builder, but he needed wood. The Euphrates Valley had been stripped bare of trees by humanity. He and Enkidu travelled to Lebanon to rob a Gorgon-like monster named Humbaba. Humbaba had defeated all, previous to this duo's arrival, and had his own version of cruise missiles—the seven splendors. Again the gods intervened for Gilgamesh. He and Enkidu captured and then murdered Humbaba in a morally awkward moment. Gilgamesh rafted the cypresses of Lebanon down the river and Uruk's building boom took off.

Like all great literature, things only got worse for the hero. Hubris, invented for Gilgamesh and still a major human theme 4700 years later for us, tripped him up. Gilgamesh and Enkidu tangled with Ishtar, a lustful goddess. She was deeply attracted to Gilgamesh and offered him the job of her consort, frozen in time in the heavens of the gods. Gilgamesh, all arrogance, detailed her savagery towards former lovers. He turned her down flat. He humiliated Ishtar: she went to war. Gilgamesh and Enkidu had to face off with her father's Bull of Heaven. They slaughtered this great icon of the gods and hurled the intestines at Ishtar herself. Someone had to die in retribution, and the gods chose Enkidu. Enkidu died in a startling and grotesque fashion, and Gilgamesh lost the only relationship he cherished. Worse yet, Gilgamesh now understood he himself was mortal, in spite of his divine bloodlines.

In despair, Gilgamesh cut and ran. He wandered the hinterlands searching for relief from his grief and a cure for his fear. He ended up at the door of the only man made immortal by the gods, the Sumerian Noah, Utnapishtim, but only after sailing across an ocean of lethal waters. Utnapishtim lived his unending existence in a sedentary and unchallenged way—a couch potato back when they made couches out of stone—but he had been granted immortality by an overkeen god who regretted the Great Flood and wanted to make amends to the man who would restart the world. Gilgamesh was enraged by Utnapishtim's

2

trickery and chatter, put off by the narration of the Great Flood, and childishly demanding in his desire for everlasting life. Utnapishtim tricked him one more time with a limited cure for death—a stinging sea-lotus that slowed the decay of the body to a crawl. Gilgamesh's judgment flew off target again; he left the lotus on the edge of a well and a local serpent gobbled it down. The snake then could renew itself by shedding its skin.

Gilgamesh returned to Uruk, having seen three versions of eternal life and having been saved from their toxic solutions to the mortality problem. Now he realized what his dream had been—to be the boy king, valorous, promiscuous, and warlike forever. He realized also that the boy king would never be human. As mournful as any supreme ruler could be, he embraced his approaching death and achieved his own humanity. He even achieved a fairly benign kingship. The city walls were completed, a Ziggurat and a half dozen temples added, and many hectares of gardens and orchards planted. He married enough wives to be troubled and oppressed and had many children. When he died, the lamenting people of Uruk diverted the Euphrates to build his tomb on the river floor, then returned it to preserve their hero king forever beneath the flood.

Gilgamesh had all the god-like aspirations, especially eternal life. Offsetting that, he had the seeds of his own history germinating within him. He was only a man, and as a man he left a legacy of children, grandchildren, and the eventual peoples of Europe.

***

But that wasn't Matt Devon's dilemma. In spite of his own bit of myth, the honorific of "Jupiter," he was childless, it was the year 2010, and he was sixty-two. He was convinced he was going crazy.

But Gilgamesh was about to help him out.

3

Jupiter and Gilgamesh

Chapter One: Jupiter's Hostiae

In the first light of the twenty-fifth of July 1989, Matt Devon rose from his marriage bed, looked at Sheila's small body beneath the sheets, her hair tousled oh so faintly by the air conditioning. Hovering over her, he relived the argument from the night before, played the video back in slow motion, and lingered over the ugly words.

Two doors down Jimmy Devereaux burst down off the front porch followed by his mother Estelle. She labored under the weight of four large paper bags full of craft materials. She dropped one, spilling a glue gun, rolls of crepe paper, and bags of plastic gems. She knelt. Jimmy wandered over to their mini-van and began kicking a rock up and down the driveway.

Matt poured coffee into the go-mug as he stood at his kitchen counter. He opened the briefcase on top of the counter and threw in the morning paper. He took the phone off its charger, thumbed the buttons, and checked for messages in the small screen. Yesterday afternoon's call from the fertility clinic was still there. He knew all about that. He deleted it with sharp little stabs on the keys. He clipped the phone to his belt. Reaching into the briefcase, he groped around until he found the antacids.

Estelle Devereaux placed all four bags into the back of the mini-van and slammed the hatch. She jerked the driver's door open and dropped a voluminous purse into the seat.

"Mommy's forgotten her day planner, Jimmy. Stay right here. I'll go get it."

Matt opened the door to the garage. It crawled up, rumbling like a dyspeptic gut. The sprinklers outside had just shut off, and the air in the

5

garage, already in the sixties, soared up into the moist seventies. He felt the first bead of sweat pop out of his forehead. High today in the nineties. The car chimed softly as he slid in.

The boy's bike laid in the grass at the bottom of his driveway. Jimmy shoved his hands in his pockets and kicked at the back tire. As he watched, lights flicked on and off in his house. He could track his mother's progress as she searched. Living room. Den. Now the front bedroom. Dawn came up strong from the east, and he could make out details of the yard. He dropped his schoolbag on the ground, grasped the handlebars of his bike and hopped on. The phone rang inside the house.

Matt's car ticked over quietly, its engine noise buried under the droning of the air conditioning. His coat laid on the leather seat beside him. He unclipped the phone and made the first call of the day, left a message. He turned on the radio, chose local news, and drowned out the internal noise of his life. The weather report claimed it was going to be a windy day and just under a hundred.

Jimmy sped down the sidewalk intent on making at least two laps around the cul-de-sac before his mother appeared on the front steps again.

Matt shifted into reverse and accelerated smoothly out of the garage. The sound of the bicycle as it folded up under his bumper, the clattering, scraping up under the car startled him, frightened him. He slammed on the brake.

Matt Devon had no idea what had happened. Among other sad and hideous things, he had finished off his marriage.

Child Of Sumeria

Chapter Two: Confessions in the Temple

March 25, 2010. Jupiter was alone. He walked in a place where no one could close in on him, touch him, jostle him, or breathe on him. His path took him where there could be no crush, no press, no one in the way, and nobody watching. He strode out into an empty early morning. No dead children here.

He found false spring was its own bitter reward. This morning he struggled. He struggled to keep up the routine walk in this biting season. This weather and time promised a beginning of new life with the stink of melting earth, but withheld it in the whipping breeze. He could tell a norther was on its way. The wind shifted around into his face and pushed thin drifts of snow in brush marks of white across the dirt road. Texas would get another week of freeze and thaw and then more winter—that was the wind he heard keening. He hunched his shoulders tighter.

Jupiter walked past the gates of the McCloskey farm, and the McCloskey dog he called White waited there, lying with his head on his paws. The dog lurched up, sniffed his knee in passing and trotted off, wagging his tail. White moved down the road leading the way, carrying out their familiar routine. Jupiter could barely see the course ahead through his wind-provoked tears, but he knew it well. Their route arrowed forward out into the farmland. The fields stretched under wire fences and girdled themselves with ditches and culverts. West Texas reached ahead of them clear to the North Pole and reached behind them to Tierra del Fuego. Down here on the ground, Jupiter lost himself on a walk with a dog and with his devils. Up there, on the grain elevator behind him, he ruled as premier of the plains.

Circling full round, boxing the square mile of his patrol, he shivered

8

his way back into the lot around his grain elevator. The wind pushed on his shoulder, trying to hurry him on, tacking him towards home. He allowed himself the smallest fragment of satisfaction for having made the four bleak miles.

In charge, White sniffed around an old pickup then nosed along the walls of the grain elevator. He cast about for the field mice that punctuated a dog's day. Jupiter let himself into the old office where the work floor stretched out behind the counter and the desks. He waited at the door and, in a moment, the dog appeared. He fed White out of a large sack of dry dog food. Then he took off the battered muddy boots he reserved for the morning walk and pulled on old trainers. Leaving the dog snuffling and grinding in his bowl, he plodded across the work floor to the ladder. He ascended the hundred and twenty feet hand over hand, as he did once a day in a ritual, ignoring the easy elevator that would have clanked him up quickly. There against the concrete wall, he clambered up through iron rings. They would supposedly stop a fall from killing him. He wondered if he could count on a preordained fatal plummet, saving him from decrepitude. As he pulled up and up, the concrete smell—the acid of Portland cement—hung in his nose and entered his laboring lungs. He moved quickly for sixty-two years but slower than he wanted.

At the top of the ladder, he entered the distribution floor, where the elevator had once circulated its grain up from truck to bin and from bin to train below. He walked past the chutes, the augers, and the metal strut work punctuating the floor's space until he came to the stairs leading up a flight to the head house above. From here on, he made this his region, a refuge set aside from the decayed industrial history of the grain elevator. He left his coat on as he ambled into his kitchen and fixed coffee. Then he strode through a door and outside again with the coffee in hand as it curled its heat up into the cold of the morning.

Anchored outside on the roof out by the rail, he stood in the wind shelter of the head house above him. He surveyed the southern and western ranges of his world. Amarillo spread rumpled across the skyline to the right, waiting for him. His own village of Aniline huddled below him on the south, pulling in on itself and marking time until spring and the life of tractors, seeding, and irrigation promised harvest. The old steel of the railroad split the plain below his grain elevator, covered in patches of snow and showing rust bands where the wind had excavated it. He could see a black figure walking down the tracks away from him, hunched up in the chill. Foreshortened by the great height, the figure was a dark ellipse, an implied human far away. The person threw away some orange wrapper, a snack bag that whipped away to the south.

Gazing down, he felt his aloneness wrapped around him, and he wore it like his old coat. Let the town attempt to dislodge him—he pretended confidence, at least this morning. He was confident he had made himself as fixed and as essential as this building had once been. He flung the dregs of his now cold coffee into the air below. The drops plummeted a hundred and forty feet to the ground. He imagined them freezing before they hit, imagined the drops, shattering out in brown ice fragments.

***

He strolled back in, pondering eremitic life. Even the hirsute, stinking hermits of the Gnostic desert had their routine, their domestic patterns punctuating their fervor of prayer and their round of abasement. He had his ritual.

He walked into his office, into a room fenestrated in glass on one side. Here he would practice his weekly deception. Flipping on a master switch, he brought the room to life. He waited as computers booted up and the overhead fluorescents popped on in succession, warming the cold blue light that came in through the windows. He used the computer to dial a number in Amarillo, and so started his weekly conference. The number rang, and he plugged in the headset.

The other end picked up. "Matthew Devon Associates, Jerry Douglas speaking."

Jupiter said, "Jerry? Matt here."

"Matt, good to hear from you. Where are you calling from?"

"Still up in British Columbia, a little farther north this week."

"Pretty cool, boss. How do I get your job?"

Jupiter grimaced, "Well, Jerry, a sabbatical is a sabbatical, not a job. How's the office?"

"Fine as usual, Matt. I have Tina and Art here to talk about a new campaign. She needs to tell you what she has in mind for the new client, and then I need to talk to you about a problem."

"Sounds good. I hope you have the numbers ready also."

"Sure. They're okay, like they have been for the last fifteen months."

Jerry delivered this cloaked dig, voiced to remind the boss profits and margins were perfectly acceptable in Jupiter's absence.

"Good, just what I expect from brilliant staff."

They consumed the next few minutes in professional practice; then Jerry ushered out the staff present on his end of the conference call.

Jerry worked around to the real point of the weekly call, the issue requiring Jupiter's intervention.

"We've got a problem with Billy Petersen," Jerry said. "His old man was always happy with our work, but Billy feels we're not doing enough creatively to keep his realty business ahead of the other Amarillo firms. He's making noises about taking his account to Bailey's."

"Well, it would be a real shame to lose the Petersens. They were one of my first accounts. What do you suggest?"

"We're fresh out of ideas here. Art's tired of real estate, kind of burned out, and I don't have anyone else to put on it. What do you think we should do, Boss?"

Jupiter smiled. *Another problem with no suggested solution.* "Hmm. We basically have two cards, and we better play them both. I'll help you with customer relations, and in return, you personally develop a couple of novel ideas to shake up the Petersen ads. I'd suggest you think about how to get some spin going among the media, some chatter about a clever new change in Bill's business. To do that we have to come up with a smart new slogan asserting the basic superiority of our clients over the other realty firms."

"I don't know," Jerry's voice was flat. "A house is a house, a lot is a lot, and a realtor is a realtor."

"Hmph, Jerry, you have a real winning attitude there. You call Mr. Petersen; offer to write him a couple of free radio spots. I'll call his father and take his pulse. In the meantime, get your head around this. I'll e-mail you a couple of basic ideas and maybe a story line over the next couple of days. I expect the same from you."

Jupiter knew his insight was simple—years in the business made it obvious what needed to be done. The right words to say sat easy in his mouth. He yawned at the idea of another round of client massaging.

Jupiter let Jerry recapitulate. Then inevitably they went around again, plowing the ground a third time. Before Jerry could start again, Jupiter rang off, saying he had to "check out and go down to catch the boat."

He had no fear his subordinate would catch his lie. He made the phone call through the Internet, and it could have appeared from anywhere in the world.

Deception committed, he sat and stared out his bank of windows, facing out to the west. The windows appeared as they had before he had started the restoration. His new rails and stiles mimicked the old form as he mimicked his old advertising behaviors. The moldings laid out a grid, three feet tall and twenty feet long, lining out a geometry superimposed over Amarillo. He interpreted the city as abstracted by the grid, rendered down into a static-bound graphic. He willed this impression to make Amarillo's image less powerful.

Over there, in a metroplex made diminutive by distance, he had made his splash and his money. Jupiter, recluse of the grain elevator, lived outside his own city and as closed up as an abbot in cloisters, not far from the scene of his triumphs and losses. He had run, and now, he hid. Even this place was not safe, and he might lose it.

***

When she picked up on the other end, he said, "Hello, Marjorie. It's Jupiter."

"Hey, Jupiter. Tell me, why do you use your real name with everyone except me?"

"Ah, you understand myth, now don't you? I admire that in a counselor."

"It's nice to be admired, even if I don't often see you to bask in said admiration. You know this isn't the regular time for our visit. I can only give you a few minutes before I have to lead a meditation session."

"I'll gladly borrow what time I can get."

Marjorie asked, "Where are you this time?"

"Perched in the sky east of Amarillo."

"Oh. I'll take that as poetic license. So, did you have a specific thing you wanted to talk about, or should we start where we left off?"

"I like it when you use technical jargon, like 'thing.'"

Jupiter could hear tinkling bells in the background. He pictured Marjorie sitting in her greenhouse surrounded by her Dao symbols and her incense mixing with the raw earth smell of the seedling trays. She would be round where her voice would have her thin, she would be dark where her words made her light, she would be puzzled where he wanted her to already know.

He said, "Sure then. Where were we?"

"That's right. 'Where' is exactly right. We were working on how you got to your 'where.'"

"Why, I was deposed by my own reticence. I was King of Amarillo, or at any rate a Prince. And with my predilection I've discovered myself exiled from my own court, a shaken man in exile."

"That's what you're calling it now, a predilection?"

Jupiter countered. "I also call it cultural claustrophobia."

"And again I ask, where is your 'where'?"

Jupiter halted briefly. "Literally, I have gone back to the farm to live rurally. It's a uniquely American story of solitary living. If I could have groceries delivered at the end of the lane, I would, and never see a neighbor."

"Doing a little myth-making yourself, aren't you? First you're a prince, and now you're a farm boy."

Jupiter laughed.

"I confess, I never grew up on a farm, though I'm a homegrown boy from the great prairie. So what if I'm not the Lincolnesque story? Maybe it's more European."

"Europe? I was so hoping for Tibet."

"No, definitely European, and ancient at that. My tale is flavored by the intrigue, the spices, the politics, and the mud and sewage of medieval times."

"Jupiter, you use feudal images quite a bit and you blarney a lot."

"Medieval seems right though."

"You amateur historians. If I might be bold, I would suggest you feel you're caught by fate rather than making it, born into your place, foretold to have these troubles. That's the medieval model."

"Would be nicer, wouldn't it? Then my dilemmas wouldn't be a function of my own actions and my own life. Not my fault. Yes, I quite like that."

"But it's not true, you know. You got here step by step, decision by decision."

"Marjorie, I never planned anything. It wasn't great strategy—I just blundered from opportunity to opportunity, seizing that one, charming this one, ducking the ones that didn't smell right. I was lucky."

"So you see yourself as an unguided fool. Well, how's that working out for you?"

"Not working well. Sticky and mortifying."

"Remind me. What decisions have you made lately, and how are you managing them?"

"I committed myself to a book, to writing a book."

"And I want an autographed copy. When can I have it?"

Fifteen months after walking away from his job and his firm, he still had not started.

He temporized, "I've got an old library table here in the office. On the table, I have piles of references and research."

"And what do you research?"

"The Sumerian, King Gilgamesh, subject of an epic. In fact, the first book about a man rather than a god."

"And you chose Gilgamesh because?"

What? An interrogation? "He's fascinated me ever since college. Tragic figure, alone and tormented."

"Like you."

She gets it. "Yes, but it works out for him in the end. So I'm researching him for a historical novel."

"But—"

"Uh-huh, I can hear you thinking. Little scraps of paper marking passages can't be pieced into a literary triumph or even a manuscript."

"So, if you're stalling, maybe you should ask why you committed to a book."

"Ah." He hadn't actually asked himself why. "Perhaps it's only pride to think I can start over with something new at my age. Still, it could be a great jump start, get my feet back under me."

"So your other decision was about your fear of people?"

He said, "I came to you because of my nervous tic, that nasty little uncomfortableness. How can I be me, the greatest ad man of all time, and get the shakes when I'm doing anything public—knowing everyone who's anyone, but sitting at home alone at night? Somewhere along the way I've become more and more crowded and closed in."

"Last time we talked, you said it was like being packed in a suitcase with your loved ones, somehow expected and yet all wrong."

"I've made up a new image. It goes like this: it's more a visceral allergy, a hidden shudder and frisson of fear caused by my customers, my ex-wife, my employees, and my friends."

"Nice. 'Frisson.' So what was the decision?"

"You know… to get better."

"And how do you feel that's going?"

"Getting a bit worse."

"We might make more progress if you didn't insist on doing this all over the phone."

As long as he was making confession, "Uh, there was one other decision."

"Something new?"

"Something I didn't tell you. I've been on sabbatical."

"Jupiter, you told me about that."

"Not entirely. It's a sabbatical with a secret; it's a solitary life lived in an unconventional place not far away from my previous existence."

"If it's that big a secret, don't tell me. What I truly want to know is why did you choose it?"

"I guess I'm remaking myself in my sixties and also finding a way to hide my condition at the same time. I've moved to a village that, despite its potential small town claustrophobia, is more spread out than Amarillo. The sweet touch is my house; I'm turning an industrial site into an eccentric home."

"You like eccentric?"

"I like you."

"Thanks." Her voice sounded dry, noncommittal.

"No, really, I was getting dull. Now I'm quirky and interesting."

"…and all grown up. How is the move working out, then, as a decision?"

"Basically not as well as I hoped. The local authorities don't appear to enjoy quirky and interesting."

"Three decisions that are taking you to your current 'where.' We'll have to talk more about this."

"Now? I've got the time. I'm on sabbatical."

"Listen, Jupiter, I've got to go. My people are coming in, and I should be laying out the rugs and the singing bowl. Let me leave you with something to think about. If you're going to beat this problem, you have to go to the cause, not mess around with the latest side effects. You have to take responsibility for who you are."

"Ah, the hard advice. Well, I'll call again in a couple of days when we're regularly scheduled."

"Not so fast. Here's your assignment for the week. I want you to go into a crowded place with someone you know. I want you to focus on that person rather than on the people around you. I want you to ask yourself how you feel about it before you leave, and I want you to write it all down to read to me when we next talk."

"Marjorie, I don't need to feel like I'm back in grade school getting assignments."

"Sure you do. Otherwise you'd stop calling." She hung up.

Sighing, he did her bidding and made a phone call. Jupiter called the one man in Aniline who made it all easy and smooth for him. He called his general contractor.

***

Jupiter enjoyed talking to Marjorie, especially when he felt well. Not seeing anyone in three days made him cheerful and largely happy. Or maybe, he reflected, the word should be un-anxious. He sipped coffee, smelling an echo of Marjorie's imagined incense. He gazed out over the prairie, turning the conversation over in his mind. He did much of nothing. He hoped his subconscious was at work on the big issues.

In all his heady mix of trouble, he prioritized his problems with the Aniline town councilmen at the top. He suspected they viewed him as a carpetbagger arrived from the big city, bringing a way of life that fought the balance of a small farming community. Aniline preferred not to change; those who wanted something different normally moved away. He couldn't resolve his problems by this piercing insight into the community. He needed to talk to Marjorie about it. He needed the town elders off his back.

As he sat there, the sky turned black and rolled past the tower, carrying winter back into the plains. He turned off the lights and went to stand at the windows. He watched God brew up a bitch of a day. A storm was just about right, a stand-in for his battle with Aniline.

As a young man he had appreciated black skies and trouble. He had experienced that extra pulse of life if he caught himself up in a bind. Now times had changed. Now he waited for inspiration to bail him out and for apathy to wane. He suffered from a missing invigoration. He wanted energy and inspiration. What he got was the sound of a car horn echoing against the concrete of his tower. He went through the office door to the roof and gazed below. A white truck was parked by his old blue pickup. A man in a coat and a ball cap stood there. He waved up. Jupiter cupped his hands into a megaphone and shouted down, "Hey, Dan! Give me a minute."

The man below cupped his hands and also shouted, but through the wind noise Jupiter only heard, "Lunch." He held up one finger, saw the man nod, and turned to go down below.

Dan Heldritch waited in his truck. Dan's business had improved because of Jupiter, so in contrast to Aniline's elected officials and their hostility, Dan liked him. In fact, quite a few workmen saw Jupiter, if not as a friend, then as a steady cash flow.

Jupiter hopped up into the passenger seat to escape the buffeting wind and said, "Hey, Dan. What's up?" He slammed the door.

"Too frickin' cold to work, especially outside. I got your message about lunch in town. Good chance to catch up on your projects. I have something to talk to you about anyway."

Jupiter perceived a hint of trouble, a sense it wouldn't all be smooth and easy. "Sure, whatever it takes. I need to go by the Post Office. Maybe you could stop there on the way to the café?"

"Can do. How you been?"

"All right. Getting some work done around the place."

They filled the time with small talk while Dan drove out of the yard and immediately into the outskirts of Aniline. They rolled past 1930s houses, porched and gable-hipped against the prairie's gales. There were '50s ranches sitting beside these older houses, pierced with ribbon windows, faced with cheap brick, and festooned with aluminum carports. There hadn't been much building in Aniline since the 1950s, but one or

17

two Amarillo-like new houses were sprinkled here and there. Dan's unspoken business sat in the cab of the truck with the two men, waiting.

Aniline's founders had laid out a main street two blocks long, leading off the square. It ended at the old highway, a road crumbled and pot-holed with neglect. The Post Office sat at the end of a strip shopping center, fronting the highway—the major sign of life for that eroded two-lane. Dan parked in a rank of trucks there and they hopped out leaving the motor running. Jupiter walked down the back of the vehicles, noting the plumes of smoke and the stink of exhaust. Going inside, the two men split apart and went to their respective mailboxes. In his, Jupiter discovered a yellow card with the date and his box number. He took it to the desk to collect his package.

The postal guy, cracking open his moon-shaped face in a grin, said, "Morning, Mr. Devon. How's it going?"

"Hi, Mike. Going fine for me. How about you?"

Jupiter handed over the card, and Mike, not replying to the pleasantry, went to the back. He returned with a nine by three envelope.

"Whoops, Mr. Devon, it's a letter from the Council. You gotta sign; they want to certify you received it. Hope it's not trouble."

There was not a lot of privacy in the Post Office; all was fair for the staff to comment on. Jupiter scribbled, "Devon," on the form, saying, "No, it's probably the zoning thing."

He stepped back, getting some distance away from Mike.

Dan leaned over Jupiter's shoulder, peeking at the letter in his hand, "Town chasing you, Matt?"

Jupiter turned to face Dan.

"Well, not for years of back taxes like you. I guess they want me to hire you to turn the grain elevator back into a ruin."

Dan laughed and answered, "I wouldn't complain about the restoration business, but I'd rather install a Jacuzzi and a pool for you."

They both glanced up to see the postal employee watching intently. Mike said, making a clear implication, "I thought you were living up there before the zoning laws got passed last year." By this nosiness, Mike let them know he understood what the town was up to.

"It was a close-run thing. I don't think I had my certificate of occupancy yet."

Dan said, "Time to get a lawyer I think. My brother's wife works in

18

a law office in Amarillo if you need a number."

"Thanks for the offer. I'll wait a little longer before I panic."

"You've waited too long now."

***

The café carried the name, Angie's, and it sat at the other end of Aniline's main street, backed up to the town hall and on a corner of the square. Its windows were thick with steam, and on the outside, streaming with condensation. There was blue tile from the sidewalk to the bottom of the windows, stucco up to the awnings, and board and batten faded to black from there up to the roof edge. Angie's had existed all through Aniline's middle age, and it had picked up patinas of style from each decade. It wasn't the woman you would marry; it was the comfortable older sister you went to visit.

Dan and Jupiter located a booth, sat down, and ordered coffee. Jupiter appreciated the booth—he had his back against something substantial, and anyone approaching him was held at bay by the table. He didn't see many people, and he liked that also. He enjoyed the smell of fried food, the noise of cutlery and banging plates coming from the back, and the voices punctuating the general hum. Angie's Café made him think he belonged in Aniline.

People wandered by as they sat there, saying hello to Dan and talking about the weather.

Both men were contemplating the menu when Jupiter asked, "So Dan, who is Angie? I've been coming here for months, and I've never met anyone named Angie."

Dan glanced up and answered, "Angie was Fredo's wife. You know Alfredo. He still drops in to see how his son is doing running the business. You've seen him—the fat swarthy guy who sits down at the end of the counter."

"What, did she pass away?"

Dan glanced around and then leaned across the table. "Nah, see she ran off. We don't talk about it much because Fredo gets upset. Doesn't think it's our business, and it isn't."

"How many years ago did this happen?"

Dan said, "Oh, years. Must have been in the late sixties. I remember

I was in high school. Fredo was too cheap to change the name and the sign, or maybe he believed she'd come back."

"Long time to still be waiting. Long time to be upset," Jupiter said.

"But you see, Angie ran off with a woman. That would hurt a guy's feelings. Amarillo isn't the only town with some strange goings-on. We get it all at one time or another."

"A woman?"

"Yeah, you'd have to ask my wife Sarah about it. She knew both women when she was a little girl, and liked them. According to Sarah's mother, Fredo had it coming."

Jupiter allowed a couple of beats then said, "I never knew, Aniline with its own counter-culture. Next thing, you'll have a rock band."

"You ain't the only one a bubble off ordinary, Matt." There wasn't anything to say about that, so Jupiter let it drop.

Lunch proceeded through ordering, frying, and delivery. None of the food they chose had any pretense of being healthy. Heldritch waited till the food hit the table to get around to what he wanted. With a fry in hand, he eased into his topic.

"You know that pump and the tanks you want us to put in?"

"Yes, I'm looking forward to it."

Jupiter didn't have town water pressure at the top of his tower. For half a year he had lived with a small pump, running on regular one-twenty volt current. It delivered an unconvincing amount of water on demand to the top. At first they tried to re-use the old fire system in the elevator to move water. That turned out to be fanciful. Heldritch had recommended a subcontractor who signed up to install tanks up on top and a powerhouse of a pump to move water up the hundred and forty feet.

"You know your plumber, Gary Hammet?"

"Sure. Haven't heard from him in awhile. He was supposed to be ready in the spring. Said he was working in Amarillo till then."

"Gary asked me to talk to you." Dan took a long pause. "Gary, he's got a bit of a cash problem. He needs to have the money for your equipment advanced to him. He also asked me if he could get half the labor cost up front."

"Times must be tough." Jupiter left a hole in the conversation to see what Dan would do to fill it.

"They'd be tougher if we hadn't had your elevator projects going. So how 'bout it? What should I tell Gary?"

"Hmm. I'll make him a deal. Have him order the equipment COD and have it delivered directly to the grain elevator. That way I pay the supplier myself."

Dan nodded, hearing the subtext. Then he asked, "Would Gary still get ten percent handling on it?"

"Sure. He has to do the paperwork, and it's his connections, his supplier."

"What about the labor? Can you front him?"

"His family lives here in Aniline don't they? His mom and dad?" Dan nodded yes. "Yeah, tell him I'll take the chance. Half up front. We can also do it time and materials so he's not so exposed. Tell him to estimate what time and materials will be plus a percent he names rather than the fixed bid. Then I'll write a check for half."

Both men knew Jupiter would pay less this way, and Hammet would run no risk of losing money.

Jupiter wanted to sound hard, so he added, "And he should start as soon as he can. I'd like a shower that doesn't just spit at me."

"Thanks, Mr. Devon."

Jupiter noticed Heldritch used his surname. The contractor acknowledged the favor and the relationship with a bit of formality.

***

Dan dropped him off at the base of the elevator. Jupiter re-entered the building through the old office and saw White had gone out as usual through the broken window, rather than hanging around. He walked back into the old tool room past a standard old-fashioned freight elevator and onto the work floor behind. A pile of burlap bags had blown out from where he had piled them and were nested up in a corner. He returned them to where he had stacked them. He piled an old paint can back on top again. Then he went further into the dark.

Here one of the attractions of the grain elevator, one of its toys, waited for him. He owned a man lift. He snapped an ugly electric switch, and it started up. The man lift was a belt with footboards attached twenty feet apart, set into a vertical wooden shaft. The shaft occupied the star-shaped space between four of the round elevator bins. Boards made flapping sounds down in the shaft below, swished past him heading up, and returned from the dark above into the pit below. The loose belt slapped away on the rollers.

He stepped onto one of the boards coming up at him and grabbed a wooden handrail fastened to the belt. The man-lift jerked him into motion, hurtling up at a speed he estimated over a hundred feet a minute. Within ten feet, it went dark, and he traveled up the shaft smelling the dust that always hung waiting. At the top, he stepped out onto the floor of the distribution shed without stumbling and turned off the lift using the antique sister-switch to the one below. The belt coasted to a stop.

Almost certainly, sooner or later, he would strike his head on the coaming of the shaft. He would be badly hurt. Let them come up with something this eccentric in New York. He dared them.

Chapter Three: Reading of Dreams

Jupiter shivered in the cold living room until it was too much. He went into his office. The library table squatted there covered with the raw materials for his book. His archetypical king awaited. He knew a way to avoid the table's accusation and the doubt he suffered; there were phone messages to distract him. He dialed his other house in Amarillo and accessed his old-fashioned answering machine.

"You have five new messages. Press seven to listen to new messages." Seven.

"Message one."

"Matt, this is Johnny. Listen, Irene and I were talking the other day. We were reliving the old days, like when you flew out for the big Ad Fair in Manhattan and stayed with us in Tribeca. Give us a call, or better yet, move back to town. We miss your arrogance and your inspiration. Later, guy."

"Press nine to delete this message, or...." Nine.

"Message two."

"Devo, this is Stanley Upchurch of the old Epsilon Gammas—I used to have the room next door to you. You'll remember me as the guy who bailed you out after that pissing-in-the-fountain arrest. We're having a big reunion this summer, and we were wondering if you would organize the Texans from your class. It's going to be a blast—give me a call; you've got my number." Delete.

"Message three."

"Mr. Devon, my name is Willard Monihan. I'm a Ph.D. candidate here at Columbia, and I'd like to interview you for my thesis. It's about viral effects in the media, and since you were one of the pioneers of cable television advertising, I'd like to get your views. Kind of a 'grand old artist comments on the new trends.' Give me a call...." Delete.

"Message four."

"Hey, Ad Monster! This is Freddy Johnson from the old days. You remember the campaign we did for condoms when we made that company rename their rubbers Jupiter? Well, I wanted to share how that great venture backfired on my own family. My daughter Julie was going through her daughter's room yesterday, and she opened the bedside drawer. Turns out the sucker was stuffed with condoms—I know, I know, my own granddaughter. But here's the thing—they were all Jupiters! Let's get together and do another campaign like that. I gotta admit, I've long ago spent all the money from the Jupiter push, probably on the first wife. In any event, let's get together for drinks next time you're in LA." Delete.

"Message five."

"Hey, Mattie. This is your ex-wife. Remember me? I called you to wish you a belated happy birthday. I know...I once said I hoped you would never make the next one—birthday, that is—but, gee, it's a really nice day here in Hawaii, and I'm feeling sentimental. No need to call back unless you want to." Delete.

"You have no more messages."

He stared down at the library table. It all appeared impressive, the piles of books with slips of paper sticking out and the tablets filled with notes. If there was only a single thread hanging out of that literary fabric he could pull, leading to the next and then to the next. He let out a breath and picked up a volume from a five-book history of the Fertile Crescent. He set it back down. There had to be a way to close in on this creatively. He could smell that particular taint of yellowed sun-bleached paper, and it evoked a memory of his old battered office in Manhattan. Now, there's where the creativity had burned a fire through his young life.

He dug around under one end of the table and unearthed a large portfolio, dragging it out from under the stack. He told himself he exhumed this bit of the past as an inspiration to get his attitude pumped up and his thoughts rolling. He opened up an old-fashioned set of storyboards that laid out three commercials from ad campaigns.

He glanced through them and settled on the last. Someone in his old New York office had scribbled, "Devon, Young Gun of New

Advertising" on the empty first frame. From there the storyboard told its tale quickly and explicitly. He smiled, realizing it had all been a success because he had reinvented sex. He had provided penises with fashion accessories and made the smell of latex a pheromone. He did regret, just the smallest amount, the way they had appropriated Holst's theme. Jupiter associated it forever with little foil packets full of lust and hopefulness.

He could reminisce about his young genius all day without relieving his old-man stupidity. He sensed only sleepiness.

***

Jupiter lay down in his bedroom on top of the duvet for a short nap. He slid off into sleep quickly; lately he slept more during daylight than at night. In the shallow doze of a stolen nap, he had the dream, or at least a variation of the dream.

He knew his name was Matthew Devereaux. He walked into a cheap tract house. Inexpensive hardboard paneling ran the length of the hall, leading to a faded pressboard-cabinet kitchen. She waited there for him. Her name was Estelle—the only Estelle he had ever known in all the world. He knew he had been married to her for twenty years, none of them much fun. Matthew could smell her perfume, thick and cloying. It made him sneeze, twice. He went to the sink, got a glass of water, and turned around. Her magazines were scattered out across the kitchen table—lurid things filled with loud, bright ads and stories about celebrities who were themselves advertisements for something he found faintly disgusting, even if he didn't understand it. He could feel his lip curl back in a sneer.

His mouth opened and hurtful words escaped, "So, I see you're doing good works again. Anything new with world's most famous movie couple?"

"Bite me, little man."

The magazines had turned into a checkerboard. She had three kings. He had none. "Always the witty answer."

With a heavy sigh, "So, don't forget that we are going over to the Trammels tonight. I've arranged the sitter."

"The Trammels. Oh joy."

There was a crumpled shirt on the floor. He kicked at it and noticed his foot was a hoof.

"Becky's a good friend, my best friend. You ought to try it sometime, having a friend." Estelle tapped a cigar box on the table. She said, "Keep your friends close."

"Okay, okay, you're right. They're nice people for smokers. Kind of needy though, always wanting to hear how great they are. Whose shirt is this?"

Estelle glanced back towards the hall.

"Jimmy's. Did he come in with you? I don't hear him."

He swung his gaze around. The hall was now a bright pipe, so bright it made him squint.

"No, he's still out front on his bike on the sidewalk. I left him for a minute to get some water."

At that moment they both heard the wailing tires—a car braking hard.

***

Jupiter snapped awake. He knew who the real Estelle and Jimmy Devereaux had been, and what he had done, what had happened in 1989.

He lay on top of the covers fully dressed. Heat boiled up off him as if he was about to burst into flame. The sound of the brakes had ripped him up out of the dream. He could sense the shock of that sudden emergence. His heart hammered clear through into his temples. Sweat soaked his clothes. His breath wheezed in and out of his mouth. He wanted to jump up and run. Or fight someone. The room resembled no room he had seen before; he didn't know if he lived there or if it was even his.

***

It was early evening, and he had wasted the day on his condition, on Marjorie, on Dan and Angie's. He made a meal. He grilled fish and added frozen peas to chopped, sautéed onions. He liked the smell of the lemon and the butter more than the eating itself. He cleaned up and left the drying dishes and the two pans on the drain board.

26

He pulled on a coat and walked down the flight of stairs from the head house into the distribution floor. Then he walked to the far east end. This was the top floor of the grain elevator. He passed eighteen of the great bins—six on one side and twelve on the other—closed up with their huge twenty-foot concrete covers. At the end of the building, the ninety-year-old windows faced the coming night. Out there in the gloaming he could see orange needles standing against the dark reflecting the sunset. These spires, luminescing in last light, were other grain elevators, dotted across Texas down the rail line—all except one. The exception was a cross shrouded in farmer tin. Its owners billed it as the biggest cross in the Western Hemisphere, and it anchored a truck stop and religious bookstore to the Interstate Highway. He had stopped there once and purchased a salt and pepper shaker set that showed a scene of Gethsemane. He admired good advertising, even from the Lord.

***

Dusk crossed fully to dark, and the beacons disappeared. He turned and climbed the steps. In his office he sat down and knocked out an advertising campaign for the Petersens. In it he spilled out blunt honesty, talking to the middle-class, mostly-white Americans of the prairie, in particular to beleaguered dads. His text said, "The right house in the right neighborhood isn't too much to ask. A house can't turn you handsome, save your dreams, or make you a success. It can't turn your life around or force your children to love you. It can, however, let you wake up happy every morning knowing you are in the right place—that you have come home. Petersen Realty…where we've dedicated ourselves to finding that right house for you. Petersen works on a better life for us all, day by day." He added a tag, for the billboards along the freeway through town. "Petersen Realty—The Right House—Even If Life is a Little Wrong. We Understand."

***

Time to start the book. Fearing his cluttered library table he chose the cold living room. It stood off his gourmet kitchen. Soaring two stories high, it reached up into the head house, where once cleaning

27

equipment had worked sieving the dirt of the fields from the grain. He supposed they had treated insects and mold with chemicals here. He didn't care about the residual toxins, even though he thought about them sometimes—he was already sixty-two, going on ninety.

He had installed two banks of glass facing north, one for each floor. He and his electricians had lit the other walls with sconces drilled into white-painted concrete. Waist high bookcases surrounded the room and separated two seating areas. In each, he had created a pit with leather couches punctuated on the corners with bronze floor lamps. On the bookcases he had placed old Lucite trophies, brass statuettes, glass pyramids, and bronzed customer products, including various awards for his work in New York and Texas. He had no decorations on the chalky-white walls. He knew he had built a stylized New York loft, a cliché possession for a metropolitan huckster. He liked the Texas twist.

He sat in one of his deep leather sofas, an urban cliché in itself, and swung his feet up. He opened a laptop. If he couldn't start the book, maybe he could do some background work; he could write a profile of Gilgamesh. But even this turned into a morass rather than a river of words. For many minutes he sat, his left hand starting to twitch. This didn't flow easily. Then he set his hands on the keys, one twitching and one poised.

"Why I Am Writing This Book?" He highlighted the text and made it bold.

"Because I'm vain."

"Because I'm afraid."

"Because I'm easily bored."

"Because Gilgamesh was the first real king we know about, the first to advance out of the darkness and have his story written down. And because he was as screwed as Alexander or Macbeth."

There, now he had an answer for Marjorie. It wasn't because Gilgamesh was his twin.

A profile had to start somewhere. He typed. "A Child in Sumeria."

He wondered what he would write next. Another wait—shorter this time.

"You were not born a king's son. You were not even born in Uruk. You were not a pretty child at all. If it is true your mother was a goddess, then she did not start you off with her heavenly looks. They named you

28

Gilgamesh although we had that wrong for some time. While your contemporaries called you Bilgames or Gilgamesh, we once believed you were named Izdubar. Of course you were also derisively called Little River Shrimp and Turnip Hair, so maybe Izdubar was not so bad. It was a very long time ago, twenty seven hundred years or so before Christ—Christ being a name and a story you did not know. Your religion was complex and your gods were rather human. Neither complex nor simple meant easy. Just as your later epic quest turned out to be simple but unendurably painful.

The sun was the defining force of each day. Even in winter, the sun rose hard, strode hot against the sky, and went down with a sudden bang into the horizon. The Sun God was named Utu, and also Shamash. The myth of where he went each night became part of your myth." He hit "enter" twice.

"It was a typical village. There was a short street lined by single-story houses. It ran perpendicular to the river. The houses were made of mud, and each year after the rainy season, the women would repair the cracks and re-plaster the walls. At the end of the hamlet closest to the river, there were fences made of thorny bushes, reeds, and sticks. The villagers kept goats and pigs in this feeble enclosure. Sumerians had not developed a prejudice against pork yet; the Semites would bring that into the area later. The ducks wandered loose and eggs were communally owned.

There was a ditch running down through the middle of the village. It carried those things no adult would want to get onto his feet, dripping the hamlet's meager sewage into the river right by the dock. Until you were three, you paid far too much attention to that ditch.

The dock stood barely above the water. They had made it of wattled walls and filled it with rammed earth. In spite of its modest construction, the humble dock touched the greatest element in your life—the river. The Euphrates gave you all. From the Euphrates came the water that made the food you ate and traded. Upon her, the boats of the Sumerian cities went back and forth, carrying food and goods to market. There were turnips, garlic, and onions, and also apples, wheat, and beans. There were even dates from the village downstream.

Your men carried water from a shallow lagoon at the river's edge up to the fields and poured it into small ditches that shared the water out abstemiously to each agricultural row. It was hard work, making those ditches and filling them with water. Young men hated it, and old men bent permanently into the stooping posture that mud-lined baskets inflicted upon them. Later, the hamlet would install irrigation that flowed from the river upstream. The river even gave you the earth in which your villagers planted their crops, overflowing her banks every few years and rolling out new carpets of lush organic garden soil for her people. That too was a mixed blessing, since not all of you could swim and not all survived a flood when it swept through."

With that last sentence, he hit a pause.

He went to a wooden cabinet in the corner. He fetched out a squat crystal glass and filled it an inch high with a glowing amber liquid. Then he sat beside the floor lamp on the couch with his feet up and cradled the glass. He stared into it for awhile as if he expected to see the next sentences floating up out of the scotch. When he pulled the laptop back into position, the screensaver cleared and the computer woke up. Just below his last words a new sentence had appeared. "What is my mother like?"

His heart rate rocketed up; he broke into a pant. He darted his eyes around the room, knowing full well he was alone. All of his choices for the last fifteen months guaranteed he was alone. He sheared a glance at the question, sneaking up on it. Then he slapped the laptop shut. After a minute, he opened it again, to check. Still there! He knew he hadn't typed it. He drained off his drink. The whiskey bit his tongue and throat; the smoke rose up into his sinuses.

He reflected, "Am I crazy?"

His ego answered, "Impossible."

Sure, he wouldn't sit in a conference room with a dozen people anymore or circulate through the crowd at a party. He couldn't sit still in traffic or walk through a busy mall. But he wasn't gaga.

He said aloud, "Where did the words come from?"

The room answered with silence.

Then he realized he hadn't asked the right question—Whose question is this?

He typed, "Whose mother?"

Then he snapped the computer's lid down and left it there on the couch.

He took himself off to bed. He wasn't going to sit there and wait for an answer like he had sent e-mail to God. God didn't exist, but he prayed regardless that all this would be gone in the morning. This had to be a glitch in the computer or in his mind. Maybe he had experienced a small stroke. Or maybe he was drunk, on a single glass.

He had made a mistake with the drink—with it in his blood, he couldn't take the Prozac. That could be the best explanation. Some cross between whiskey and yesterday's Prozac.

He lay in the dark, up in the rafters of the sky, waiting for sleep. Somewhere around four, he dropped off and dreamt of panicked birds flying up out of trees.

***

In the morning, he and White walked out into a frigid landscape around their four-mile route searching for half-frozen rodents and plausible answers. When they returned, he went straight up to the living room using the man lift and ignoring his vow of healthy living. He picked up the laptop from the couch and opened it. Blinking like a roused sleeper, it popped to life, showed him a screen saver, and then faded into the page he had left the night before. He had typed, "Whose mother?"

Below that question, the laptop now read, "My mother. The mother of Gilgamesh."

It laid on the couch all day hissing like the snake it could be as it spun its hard drive periodically. Madness waiting to strike, to poison. Late that afternoon, he noticed that it wouldn't wake up; he had run the battery down. He closed the lid. An hour later, he picked the laptop up with trepidation and plugged it in to charge. Then he called an old friend. "Trevor, Matt Devon here."

"Matt, good to hear from you. How's Amarillo?"

"Same old same old. How are things in Chicago?"

"A hundred and two straight days of subfreezing temperatures at night, so far, and we're not done yet. Be glad you live in the sunshine."

"Say, you used to be interested in computers, didn't you?"

"Enough small talk for you?"

Jupiter winced. "I had a techie question. Can someone make a PC

31

act like a teleprinter?"

"You mean one of the old teletypes? Anything's possible with code."

"I think someone maybe hacked into my PC."

"What do you mean 'into your PC'?"

"I'm getting otherworldly messages, and it's weirding me out."

"Yeah. Hmm. You'd need to have some badass hacker software jacked in there, and you'd need an Internet link. I'm not up to date on this, but my kid is. Let me go get him."

Time went by with some muffled thumps and shuffles and a murmured conversation.

"Hello?"

"Hi. I'm Matt Devon."

"Reggie."

"Well, Reggie, did your father explain my problem?"

"Some."

"So how could someone get to me here?"

Now the voice on the other end changed from teenage to confident, from sullen to expert.

"Most of this hack stuff is not conversational. I thought right away that you had a key-stroke logger on board…" The kid's lecture took quite a while. "…So if someone is playing ghost in the machine to freak you out, that's a new one on me."

"So how can I tell?"

"Open up your utilities and start your monitor program. Look for an application that's running that you don't know about."

Gingerly, he opened the lid and wiggled his finger on the pad. The words "The mother of Gilgamesh" appeared, and he went dizzy. "Where do I find utilities?"

"Point the arrow at your task icon down in the lower left corner."

Jupiter did as was requested and found the monitor.

"I see the usual stuff. Calendar. A word program. Clock. But there's a bunch of strange names that I have no idea."

"Read them out to me."

Jupiter did so.

"Those all sound normal, but a legit program could have been replaced with malware. Tell you what, pull the connection and see if activity stops in one of those programs."

"Connection?"

"Yeah, you're hooked up to cable or Ethernet right?"

"No."

"Then you're on Wi-Fi, right?"

"It's turned off. I don't have the icon showing."

"So unless someone stuck another Wi-Fi transmitter in your laptop, you're stand-alone. Awesome! Newish laptop?"

"Yes."

"Flip the laptop over."

Jupiter did so.

"There should be four screws or so, and if you've never had it serviced, they should be unscratched and have a spot of varnish sealing them."

"I see something shiny."

"Then I don't know what to tell you, Mr. Devon. I don't think anybody has hacked you."

"Thanks, Reggie. I guess that's good news. Would you put your Dad back on?"

Jupiter visited with Trevor for a bit. In the end, as he hung up, he had the distinct impression that Trevor thought Jupiter should get back on his meds. He leaned on one of his concrete walls, and he could feel the cold, creeping into his shoulder, making it ache. He mulled it over.

All day, the Sumerian message remained locked down because of its danger. He prowled past, like a cat in the zoo who knows he is being watched, but who doesn't understand cameras or one-way glass. He asked himself questions, some of which avoided the crisis, some of which resonated with risk. Why is this king, this five-thousand-year-old impossibility talking to me? Was a laptop capable of being possessed? Can a Sumerian type?

At eight he fled upstairs to bed, desperate to get away from himself, from circular thinking, and from the nagging fear of a meltdown. He dumped sleeping pills down on top of Prozac and slept after a fashion. When his eyes snapped open, he could feel the silver machine as it lay down there, humming.

***

He nestled the laptop into a shipper box, wrote his company's number on it, and took it down to the local pick-up bin. Problem solved—laptop in the hands of the pros. Three days later he found the package at the bottom of the elevator, left in the office by the man in a giant brown truck. Eagerly he ripped the tab and opened the bubble-wrapped box.

He read the handwritten note dropped in with an invoice. "We've de-fragged your disc, reinstalled your operating system, run virus scans over the entire contents, and have verified that there is no known virus, Trojan horse, or worm on board your system. Thanks for your business." The invoice demanded four hundred dollars.

He carried the silver enigmatic machine upstairs and plugged it in to charge. Flipping the lid back, he opened the Gilgamesh document. There was his text. There was the declaration down at the bottom, "My mother. The mother of Gilgamesh."

Below that was another line, "Hello? Are you there?"

So, he was crazy after all.

Chapter Four: Life is a Little Wrong

If anything, the weather was worse. He felt ice crystals abrading his cheeks and forehead. He liked the distraction. White rushed along in a traverse more than a hunt, wanting to get the morning circuit done and get to breakfast. As they approached the base of the elevator, he found the door swinging loose in the wind. He closed it behind him, and it clunked shut, solid as a bank. He rattled the knob. Scratching his chin, he took a tour of his domain, trailed by the unfed dog. Back on the dock, he found an empty orange bag of cheese puffs caught in the mouth of a lever-actuated chute. His brain pulled up an image of a small figure walking up the tracks. He remembered that orange bag sailing away. He stuffed this bag into his pocket and returned to the office, White following.

Puffing from the climb, he carried the laptop into the kitchen and eased it down on the breakfast bar as if it could blow up. He made coffee on autopilot, glancing frequently at the sleek device laying on the counter. While the coffee brewed, he paced up and down the kitchen, the laptop never out of his sight. When the gurgling stopped, he snatched his cup from the drain board and filled it. He opened the PC to expose the screen. He hovered on the stool in front of the laptop with his hands on the keyboard. The smell of the coffee made the room real, substantial, masked the strangeness. He stared at the last simple question.

After half a cup and some consideration, he typed, "Who are you?"

"I am Gilgamesh. You told me that I am Gilgamesh."

Jupiter jumped; the scrolling words alarmed him.

He scanned back through his own sentences. He had indeed been addressing someone named Gilgamesh. "Where are you?"

35

"In Uruk. I live above the river in a palace. The sun is bright. It was dark before."

"Before when?"

"Before you told me I was not a king's son."

"What is it like for you?"

"I just woke up. I am groggy, dizzy. It is early morning and the servants have not come in yet. Your voice is in my head."

Shit. A Sumerian palace created out there behind the PC screen, existing in the same "now" as Texas. In the past tense for him, though.

Jupiter typed. "How can I believe you?"

"Do you have a choice? Here I listen, because of you."

Jupiter considered. If it was a hoax, he could only know by going further. And the voice would wait, as it had waited for days. Still, he could feel his hands twitching, poised above the keys. "You can call me Jupiter."

"Jupiter. That is not a warrior's name."

"No, it's a god's name, but I'm not entitled to it. Maybe you would prefer ur-Jupiter."

"That has a strong sound. How old are you?"

"I am sixty-two." Right. Jupiter was sixty-two going on ninety.

"Are you divine then to live so long? Or a king?"

"No divine curse here."

"Then you have a secret for long life?"

Jupiter laughed. "Clean living. Lots of wine. Not your lifestyle at all, Gilgamesh."

"But then, I am happy. I suspect you are not."

Were all kings smug? "What do you want, Gilgamesh?"

"Tell me about my mother. If you know me, then you would know her. Maybe I will decide that you exist."

Or that I go mad. It felt real. He decided to pretend it was real. He typed. "She was named Ninsun. She was not an important goddess. Maybe because of her unimportance, she was much better looking than most of the divine crowd. They all came across as careworn with their constant infighting and desire to be big. All of them wanted to boss Ki the Earth and toady to the sky god Enlil...all except for Ninsun. She stood up much better on the beauty front. I think being a small god suited her." He stopped typing, and waited.

The words appeared across the screen. "Did I live with her?"

It was a test. Jupiter's hands shook, hovered over the keys. To reply would signify some contract or agreement with his correspondent.

Jupiter leaked a sigh and leaned forward towards the keys. He typed. "No, you lived in a small settlement up the Euphrates. On the days when she was on Earth, she lived in the city of Uruk, a few miles away. Your village was one of the hundreds that fed mighty Uruk, villages whose grain paid for its temples. Ninsun abandoned you in this small village."

"Careful. I would not have to wish you dead so early in our conversation. Still, what you say about my mother is true…mostly true."

An uppity delusion, threatening him. Jupiter scowled.

The words went on. "And your mother? She loved you better than Ninsun loved me?"

"She died about ten years ago. I left her and moved away, as children do, but in the end we both lived again in the same city." For that last while, he lived by her bed.

"Was she a goddess?"

Jupiter wanted to think so. "No, only a gentle, nagging-type person."

"But then, you never got to be King, I think."

"You remember being King, then."

"Of course. I am fully awake now. I remember being divine and being King. Tell me about my father and yours."

"We'll take you first. You had two fathers, and neither raised you. Before she appeared in your settlement, your mother had married a king of Uruk, Lugalbanda. You later took on Lugalbanda as your symbolic father."

"Lugalbanda. 'The Shepherd.'"

Jupiter wondered. Would Gilgamesh have been clean-shaven, or worn the ceremonial beard? If he asked this—this interlocutor—would it be truth or fiction?

Jupiter typed. "Let's talk about your real father, your blood father."

"Yes."

"The bad news is that your father was not much of a family man. The fellow who sired you was one of the important men in the village. He already had a family and some considerable wealth. His name was Lillû, which, surprisingly, means vampire demon, at least in some translations. He was known as both a fool and a bloodsucker."

37

"I barely knew him. What can you tell me of him? Was he a strong man?"

"He owned a lot of the village grain, according to the records, and he had children with several women, since some of his grain was portioned out to them. He did not work the fields which is why the other men believed him a fool."

"Your tongue puts you at risk, ur-Jupiter, speaking so harshly. I suppose your father was perfect?"

Jupiter snorted when he saw the words appear. "Perfectly absent. He left in the mornings for work before I got up. He came home late and ate with my mother after I went to bed. He loved me for playing sports but never made it to the games. Then he died when I was ten." There was a pang of anger at his missing father, followed by a wave of regret that he wasn't more loyal to his hardworking old man.

"You should consider yourself lucky, ur-Jupiter. At least your Father gave you his name."

Jupiter smiled, rueful. "Oh, I was lucky in a lot of ways. I didn't have to grow up half starved like you did."

"Yes, I was hungry… a lot."

Jupiter conjured a bronzed man sitting on a backless chair, oiled ringlets cascading down his shoulders. "Living with farmers in the most prolific farm belt in the world?"

"Seeing wealth and enjoying it can be two different things."

"I take it, then, that food was a big thing for you?"

"Big thing? You mean important. Hunger drives all men. Even for the best of us there was seldom meat to eat, except for dried fish, and everyone dressed much the same. Except on a god's holy day."

"I've thought about your feast days quite a lot." And Jupiter had.

The words appeared on the screen. "I loved all of the sacred days. I was an orphan of sorts. On a regular day I was treated like a pig or a duck and kicked out of the way. Not on a feast day."

Jupiter imagined a small boy with a goat fleece wrapped around his hips, naked to the waist, scrawny ribs showing, dodging the angry foot, the slapping hand. He said, "My theory is that people were nicer because they were depressed on feast days. Sure, they spent the day being polite to each other and to a god or two—but in truth, the relationship between humans and the gods was always shaky."

"The gods are not very trustworthy." Gilgamesh understood the tension between god and mortal.

"A feast day was a cleverly disguised form of blackmail by someone you did not trust and a payoff by someone who could not afford it. Sumerians, to thrust a sword in it, were quite cynical."

"Harsh and judgmental? The Elders would have had you taken up and gutted by now."

But Jupiter knew he was right. He typed, "From the Sumerian point of view, gods robbed you all your life, and then they destroyed you, one way or another. Their river tried to drown you. Their weather was bad and the crops failed. Misled by the gods' advice, your wife indulged in infidelity and the marriage soured. Then, if you were lucky, you died young. And everyone went to Hell. Everyone. By definition."

"Hell is only the End. You say it like it has other meanings."

True, the Sumerian Underworld wasn't for punishment, even if it was a sorrowful eternal existence. "We have special days, feast days too. We have one called Thanksgiving. We eat until we are stuffed like pigs ready for slaughter. Then we sleep for a while and eat again."

"I so enjoy feast days. Of course, it is all in a god's name, so you have the usual ceremony and prayer."

"We pray to the god Football."

"I do not know that god. Is it male or female?"

"Definitely male."

"I like the male gods the best."

I bet you do. He typed, "But don't you think that your life was supported by and moved forward by women? Mine certainly has been. I was raised in a blanket of love by my mother and her friends." *Suffocated also.*

"And I was raised by women in the village in a household of widows, divorcees, and cast-out daughters. Their age ranged from age fifteen, a grown woman, to forty, an ancient crone. Still, the crone was the sweetest of all."

"So, a poor house? The cast-offs of the village?"

"In the same dwelling of a normal family but crowded together like sheep in the pen. I was pressed in tight with a collection of females who had little to lose and little to look forward to."

Jupiter reflected on his own gilded, upper-class raising. "Tough."

"Not too bad. Charity came easy to these women because they lived close to hunger and death. They knew how the small gestures could soothe a brutish life."

"My women also knew the small gestures, and they taught me what was important... how to pay attention to people, how to learn, how to cook."

"Men do not cook."

Jupiter could hear the tone of voice behind the scrolling words, the condescension. "They do here. It's a form of priesthood. What did your women teach you?"

"They coddled me, disciplined me, and clothed me. They kept me out of the sewage ditch when I was very young. They showed me how to plaster, how to plant, and how to harvest. How to watch the goats and the sheep."

"And they fed you, maybe better than they fed themselves."

"True. There is one food for the poor I hate, bitter vetch. There are two things I like. I love chickpeas, in any dish I can get them. I also like emmer wheat, ground up and made into gruel with sheep or goat's milk. I do not eat it often now. It is a paste to fill the belly."

"Me, I like bacon. And pasta."

"What is pasta?"

"We mix flour, and eggs, and cut it into shapes. We use it as the bulk in a meal with some meat, under sauces, in soups, and to make vegetables appealing."

"Such a list! You worship your pasta, ur-Jupiter."

"Maybe. Those who are poor worship the belly even if they become rich."

"For a man who has never been a poor child, you know this well."

There was a long pause. Jupiter got up, fetched more coffee, and looked at the still screen. "Are you still there?"

"Servants came. I had to send them away. I told them I was thinking about a friend."

Jupiter had to ask. "Tell me about your land, where Uruk sits, where you rule."

"You do not know Sumeria? Greater Sumer is a bundle of feuding cities. We have been here a thousand years, here in a broad, hot land covered in sand and marsh with some remnant forest—a plain cut

40

through by two rivers. The Euphrates and the barbaric Tigris to the North link the far mountains of the West with the Gulf in the East. Here the farmers are kings, and the kings are farmers."

"I also live on a broad and hot plain, near a river, the Red River. Our rivers though cannot fill all our needs, so we have wells everywhere."

"I dug a well once. I would rather peel wool off sheep all day with a dull shear."

"We have machines to help with the wells."

"Then you confess to being soft?"

"Oh, I am as soft as any merchant, any scholar in the temple."

"Soft and old, then. But comforted by your friends?"

That was the crux of Jupiter's problem. "Oh, I don't see them much, now. I mostly stay in my rooms." And if he could, he would always hide there. "And you? Many friends?"

"No. Oh, a soldier has companions to drink and kill with. Only sometimes sides change and you must kill them. And a king, how can a king tell who his real friends are? When I was young, I had a friend. His name was ur-Bar."

"Tell me about your friend."

"He worshipped me. He had a limp because one of his legs was shorter than the other. I was the sole child in the settlement who would play with him, the only one who did not care about his deformity. He died of the fever."

Jupiter remembered a face or two from childhood, long gone.

Gilgamesh asked, "Surely you have friends?"

"I can tell you about it later." The simple promise of "later" made all this a deepening commitment.

"How did manhood begin for you then, ur-Jupiter?"

"I left my home for school."

He remembered that day clearly. He had been eighteen—how late that was for Sumerians.

"Then you were in the Temple?"

"A temple called NYC." He laughed—a joke Gilgamesh would not understand.

"Uruk, too, is like a temple, though it holds individual houses of the gods."

Jupiter choked. He typed, "Being a boy was easy. Going to temple

41

was easier."

"The beginning of my manhood was unpleasant. Five years of my life were sold to a man in the village who had fields in a good place. They were rich with marsh soil and close to the river but behind a levee. That was when I learned some of the things it took to be a man. Even a girl could watch goats, but a growing boy needed to be able to carry water hour after hour, to shake grain up into ricks, and to supervise women as they winnowed seed. A man knew how to take the wool off of a sheep. A man knew how to slaughter a goat for the gods, wasting none of the blood and using every part the gods would not want."

"Yes. Bloody business, sacrifices."

"I never minded the blood."

Jupiter stared grim and drawn at the screen. *The beast you killed was not you, so what did you care for its death? You could cut the goat's throat readily, without squeamishness, by the time you were six. It wouldn't end with goats.*

Chapter Five: Skirmish with the Elamites

Ensconced in his office before the monitors, Jupiter sent an e-mail to Marjorie.

"M, I've begun the book. Its shape is not quite the form I had foreseen, but it's zinging along. I had thought 'til last night it would be a literary work wrapped in a historical novel format. There are some new implications to my loss of writer's block—we'll have to visit about them next time I call."

The reply pinged right back. "Mplikatuns? Sent from my mobile device."

He considered, "It's turning out to be a talk with a dead king, kind of like sitting in a bar with him. The book is a dialogue with a specter."

"Spectr? Sent from my mobile device."

"My specter is the Sumerian king named Gilgamesh. The book is talking to me. Quite literally. It's asking questions like a reverse Ouija board."

"Really? Sent from my mobile device."

"Yes. Words appearing on the screen from the great beyond."

"Delusun?"

"Maybe paranoia. The true paranoid would believe his computer had been invaded and someone was watching and interjecting from out there in cyberspace."

He sent that off thinking that would cork it.

"Jungian conshusnes? Cnnected 2 al mnkind."

"Doesn't feel like a trance state. Questions are both plaintive and personal."

"Asume Dao til u talk me. Dont panic. Poss ur really talking to

Sumer king. Poss ur crazy."

She e-mailed right back with a final message. "Got2go. Even Dali Lama cant drive & type. I call 15 min, stand by fone."

He considered the consequences of his dialogue with this Gilgamesh. It had certainly stirred up Marjorie. He smiled at the thought of her sitting in traffic wondering if he had slipped over the edge. It was a kind of revenge for all the insistence on soul searching and for the homework assignments.

Nevertheless, he had started his book. The book prodded him along, focused by Gilgamesh on the other end, directed by the personality of his main character. Months of research convinced him he knew Gilgamesh. Still he could be muddling up the facts he had read with the fiction unwinding in his head. He had not revealed his own secrets to Gilgamesh yet. That was good. Things Gilgamesh wrote surprised him. That was bad. He could be inflaming his own madness.

Consequence—keep going in a drug-free state and crank out a book and fall off sanity's cliff. Option—start taking the Prozac regularly, and numb down to where Gilgamesh's pestering stops. Alternative—depend solely on Marjorie and hold her at arm's length, dropping into a type of purgatory. End Game—seek professional help, more than Marjorie, more than a life counselor, and tell all. Either be saved by confession or locked away until rehabilitated.

He couldn't even speculate as to what would happen next. Maybe the book would be a best-seller. Perhaps they would whip him into a psychiatric facility, and the Town Council would win by default. The book could become a best-seller because they locked him up. In that case, he'd like to run his own ad campaign.

***

Not even a self-styled recluse could stay in his cave all day every day. He went to town in his battered old pickup and stopped in at the Post Office. Inside, he noted the local government had made a posting on the community bulletin board. There would soon be a special election for Aniline's Town Council. Unfortunately, he was registered to vote in Amarillo, not locally. Someone had also posted an ad for old steel gates for sale—something he needed to close off the old truck shed at the

44

elevator. He tore off a tag from the ad with the phone number. He picked up his mail and sorted through it, throwing all the catalogues and credit card offers unopened into a recycle barrel. The next two stops were to be the local hardware store and then a late lunch at the café.

He purchased a can of insulating foam and a putty knife. Outside the hardware store he ran into the Mayor, a large man in a cowboy hat. He couldn't pass up the opportunity.

"Mr. Mayor! Cold day, isn't it?"

The Mayor paused in mid stride. He shot glances left and right and then confronted the man he was persecuting.

"Uh, Mr. Devon, isn't it?"

"That's right. Say, people are allowed to speak at the Town Council Meeting, aren't they? And get things on the agenda?"

"That's correct, Mr. Devon, but I suspect your item of interest would already be on the agenda."

"Well, I thought I might bring my lawyer and some documentation. But maybe I should work through it first with the Town Manager?"

"Yeah, why don't you do that?"

Jupiter bobbed his head. "Whatever is best for you. I wanted to ask your advice, Mayor Sharp, and do things the way you advised."

"Then I would advise you to formally reply to our letters concerning a zoning violation."

"Oh, but I have ninety days for a reply, and then I can request an extension for another ninety days. Then there is an appeal process." He pretended to consider, "Or I could file for a zoning waiver…either before or after the appeal."

"Look, Devon, you can do what you want, but sooner or later you're going to come down from that tower. Then I hope we'll see your tail lights in the distance." The Mayor grinned all smug, glad to rip off a witty saying.

"A poetic leave-taking? I was just getting settled in. I was thinking I'm getting so much from the community that I ought to start serving on some committees and charities. You know, give something back to the town."

The mayor's eyes protruded, often their natural state. "Committees?"

"Layton resigned from the Council, didn't he? Leaves a slot open for someone who wants to campaign. And your term, that finishes up next November too, doesn't it?"

"You can't buy City Hall. Not out here. And newcomers never get elected."

"If elected I would serve, etcetera etcetera."

"Huh. See you in Council."

Sharp strode on, a determined middle-aged man, carrying himself tall and proud. As he reached the bumper of his luxurious car and started the turn for the door, he slipped. His feet flung out and his large body cannoned sideways into the fender. As he bounced away with a grunt and fell onto his back in the ice and snow, the car alarm started wailing. With a heave, the Mayor attempted to sit up but succeeded only in thrusting his feet under the car. He appeared even larger than normal as he wriggled there attempting to roll over on to his front and get on his feet. He looked beached. Jupiter rushed forward and started pulling ineffectively at the Mayor's arm.

"Get off me, damn you!"

"Here, let me help."

In spite of Jupiter's best efforts to get his hands under the Mayor's armpits, the man was able to roll over onto his knees and hands. With a groan, Sharp heaved himself up and stood, clutching the fender. The alarm continued shrieking. Jupiter turned his eyes down and saw muddy knees and soiled hands.

"Well, if you're all right, I've got to go. Got some errands."

Jupiter fled the scene, shaking his head—that worked out well. Of course this escalated their modest war. *Did the Sumerian battles with the Elamites start like this, over small things?*

***

Down at the café things were slow, the way he wanted it. There in the warmth, swimming in the smell of French fries and burgers, he wondered if the primal hearth could really be a diner in Texas.

Jupiter ordered a BLT and a glass of milk. An attractive waitress named Kate hovered at the table; he delighted in his covert glances at her. Her youth cruelly reminded him of his celibate hermit existence. He knew what she saw when she looked at him, a short man, a silver mane

46

of hair, a big chest, and a little pot belly, to his regret.

Kate's last name was Heldritch; she was the daughter of his builder. He suspected she was nicer to him than she needed to be because of the steady work Jupiter had provided her family—a conclusion unflattering to them both.

Kate gave him the big smile, stuck her pencil into her mass of tangled yellow hair, and said, "It'll be right out, Matt. We wouldn't want to keep you waiting."

Jupiter watched her walk away wrapped in an apron, wearing those too-tight jeans. Whatever Kate ate, it wasn't the diner's fried food. He slid off into a reverie about showing her his house, doing the tour upstairs, handing her a drink in front of the big windows. When she swept by again carrying two plates in her left hand for customers down the counter, she set down a new glass of milk in front of him. Then she breezed off.

He shook his head, conscious of what the word "rueful" meant. Humiliation caressed him—he was thinking about chasing a young woman whose father was beholding to him. It was all improbable, anyway. Jupiter would fall apart with psychic tremors if he tried to talk with her. He wondered if her hair smelled of shampoo.

***

That afternoon, Jupiter answered the question the town had asked—what did he do all day? Down on the work floor, he hustled out the stored trash, junk, and old iron that Aniline citizens had dumped there for ten years—from the day of abandonment to the day of his purchase. He discovered steel wheels for a dozen sizes of vehicles, some with rotting rubber still on them. He also found naked tires and the counter from a store, broken up into parts. Would he soon locate tire balancing equipment and the rest of a tire store?

He concentrated on one side of the floor where trash-bearing trespassers had heaped junk against something he wanted to dig out, a part of the elevator that towered above the confusion. He dug his way towards one of the elevator's cyclones. Cyclones had removed the explosive dust from the air in the grain bins, but the giant cone and its workings remained mysterious to him. Why he was doing this manual labor in person was also mysterious. Exercise was good. This was certainly exercise.

Avoiding Gilgamesh was good too.

Much of the junk went into a dumpster he had asked Heldritch to deliver. The big green box sat on the ground right off one of the docks, so he could hurl everything down into it. He uncovered old signs from around town that someone had collected and then forgotten. Those were worth saving, so he moved them down to the dock at the far end of the floor and racked them neatly, anally, alphabetically. There, fifty feet away across the drive sat a late-century steel silo. It had been the final addition to the grain elevator complex and had already come in handy. In the first few months he had unbolted the large hatch in the side, had a double-car garage door installed, and now locked his car up there.

His back began to hurt with a bright series of small spasms, but he kept it up, shifting over to inspection rather than clearing. In the trash piles, he stumbled over TVs, a bar refrigerator, and three car radiators. Things continued to surprise. Under a mound of cardboard, he hit upon a church pew and then another beyond that.

After five hours of continuous work, he wasn't discouraged. *Maybe I'll be finished by midsummer, as long as I don't stumble on a lost city in here.*

***

Jupiter stood at the corner of his tower, leaning on the industrial railing up on the level of the distribution floor. The head house rose above him, white against the sky. Gazing south, he believed he could see all the way across the plains to the rivers in far South Texas, rivers that carried a sand load that choked their throats, girdled by oaks. Here below him, scattered about across the farmlands, lay ample evidence of far-spread civilization. It added up so thick and interwoven that he found it hard to understand how it all worked. It was possibly some illusion that would fall apart.

This part of Texas gave the world wheat and cattle, cotton, corn and milo maize, apparently out of nothing at all, from a landscape devoid of hills, mountains, or any other topographic interest. Only man and the occasional flash flood shaped this land. Here, using materials brought from elsewhere, the farmers pumped water from deep underground to huge wheels, irrigated the desert and brought forth the bounty that paid for the fertilizer, the steel for barns and sheds, the trucks and roads, houses, and the city on the western skyline. Nothing made of metal began here, no asphalt was mined here, and no wood was grown here. In reality, only the red and orange brick that rolled out of local kilns, fired by gas from not so far away, belonged to the plains. Even the cattle had first spread across this territory from Mexico, displacing the buffalo that could no longer survive in this modern world except as oddities. And now, he reasoned, Babylon lies to the west, Nineveh to the north, Baghdad to the southeast, and Ur lies down on the Gulf Coast. Our civilization is manifest; it is all fed from this productive plain.

Chapter Six: Finding Gotham

He opened the silver lid.

"Let me tell you another story about myself. Perhaps I should say, I can think you another story, since you are in my mind."

Gilgamesh's laptop—as Jupiter began to call it—posed the simple offer at the bottom of yesterday's session. Jupiter sat in his kitchen wondering what could be coming. The trouble with his delusion was that he couldn't help but participate.

Jupiter struck the keys. "You have the time right now?"

"I am in my bath. Soon, the simplest of meals will be laid in place for me, and I will eat alone."

"Why alone? You are King, after all."

"They all want my attention, a little slice of my time, my mind. It is a relief to sit alone in the quiet, to talk to the ghost in my head."

"What shall we talk about?"

"I have been thinking about something we mentioned last, about slavery. Subservience is one thing, but Uruk depends so much on slaves. I was a slave once."

Jupiter's delusion had a conscience. "You said. Five years of your life sold to a neighbor."

"It felt longer. But I did become strong as I toiled away for that master."

Jupiter created an image of a taller version of the jug-eared boy he had invented, thin with muscular arms and legs, veins that popped out, and the beginnings of a manly chest. "There must have been something redeeming about the work."

"Only one thing. It was thankfully over at nightfall, and I returned

50

home to our crowded little house. I used to sit in the evening before the cooking fire flexing my chest to make the muscles jump. A form of bragging. I thought it amused the women, and it did, a boy strutting around like a man."

"After my father died, I thought I ran our household. It was a lie both my Mother and I told, over and over."

"We were young fools, you and I."

"That's the truth."

"I also had a childish stunt I performed with a copper knife. I spread my fingers and pressed my palm to the floor and stabbed my knife between each finger from left to right and back. The women would shout and get angry. I would not quit until I had soaked up enough attention."

Jupiter conceived a view of Gilgamesh, up from his bath, alone over his dinner and half boastful, half rueful, remembering his childhood vanity. "Did you ever cut yourself?"

"Of course. But who cared? I did not like to work on the ditch, but bleeding was acceptable."

"The ditch? I think I remember. You mentioned the river and carrying water."

"This was worse. I was rented out to the village along with many others to dig a ditch—and what a ditch! A pox on the soul. Heat. Soreness. Raw wounds on my palms."

"There are vouchers recorded on clay in the granary that show day labor charges for many. Was the ditch for irrigation?"

"We did not have flowing water from the river. To compete with the next village, the old men determined we should dig from upriver and guide it down over a league to the top of the fields."

"A huge endeavor!" Jupiter could conjure up the King's nod, ringlets swaying in the rush light.

"One burning day at a time. One basket of earth at a time. One mattock swing at a time."

Jupiter could envisage Gilgamesh, seated on a mat, a bowl of cracked wheat and goat milk in his hand. He could picture the bitter smile. "Three miles is a long way."

"We started before the rains and worked through two summers. When we set the timbers for the sluice at the river, the time was right and we caught the river at its lowest point."

"Timber?" Jupiter asked. "Wood must have been very dear. No trees where you lived." Jupiter could visualize the hot barren plain cut by a river shrouded in brush and weeds.

"True. Trading for the timbers, all the extra food required, the manpower. The ditch was the biggest thing we had ever done."

And you hated it. "Did the slave Gilgamesh have any life of his own?"

"Besides the fields and the ditch? Oh yes. There was a woman named Danu in my house. She had been abandoned in the marsh as a baby, and the women had rescued her."

"Abandoned?"

"Danu had a withered arm, and besides, she was not a boy. Fathers want sons."

An old story throughout civilization. "She was your age?"

"Oh no. Much, much older. Fifteen perhaps."

Jupiter smiled. He knew Sumerian peasants grew up fast and died young. "She lived in your house, and you got together?"

"We hid it from the old women. I thought I was in love. After all this time, I am not sure what I could and could not do, what we did as we intertwined. I don't remember exactly. My pride wants to boast—you perhaps know how pride can make you a liar."

"And how did she feel?"

"I cannot with honesty say. I think she may have had pity or have been curious. She would not have wedding opportunities with that poor deformed arm."

"Your first, though."

"Yes, and the sweetest, in a way. There were others."

Sound him out. Find out if it's true. "The tales say you were a great one with the women, obsessed with sex."

"Perhaps. We have so few pleasures in our lives, even Kings. And I had more opportunities as a soldier than any bent-backed, splay-toed farmer. But Danu was my first woman, at age eight, no matter what happened or did not."

"What became of Danu?"

"She sold herself into slavery for the household and moved to Uruk to work in a cloth business."

What an act of despair and compassion. Jupiter sat silent, waited.

Gilgamesh continued, "She did not want to stay in a house where there was little food and only intermittent work. It made me angry, but then, I was half man, half boy. After Danu, it became merely sport to lie with a woman."

"What did the women think about this sport of yours?"

"You ask as if you do not know, ur-Jupiter. Do you have a lover?"

Jupiter thought of Kate Heldritch, the temptation, the fear of humiliation. "No one now. There is one unattainable girl that I might desire if I wanted the pain."

"Attack straight on, ur-Jupiter. Win her, bed her, and tell her she likes it."

Hmm, risk the affront. "You and I have different expectations of women, I think."

"Are you a man who lies with men, then?"

"No. Does it make a difference to you?"

"There was a man who loved men in our village. He was the best of all of us with a lance, but still no one liked him. He was like you, soft towards women."

Great. Competing with your basic jock with no way to win the pissing contest. "You should try it sometime. Women prefer gentleness."

"You and I have grown up differently, or you would not say this."

Jupiter nodded at the screen. "We definitely grew up differently."

"You had parents."

"Yes."

"You had food, and clothes, and teachers. You played games. You never slept cold."

"You've made your point, Gilgamesh."

"Your childhood made you soft."

Jupiter admitted it to himself but not to Gilgamesh. "Let me change the subject. What story were you going to tell about yourself?"

"You knew I started as a soldier?"

Jupiter smiled. Only now did he realize, Gilgamesh did not know about the Epic. Of course not! "A soldier and a wanderer. They say that from your mother Ninsun you received beauty, strength, and restlessness. They say her strength developed in you as you grew, her beauty turned visible as you moved from child to man, and her restlessness became evident when you first left the village."

53

"They? They say a lot, but you can hear what I say."

Jupiter grinned. Kings like to hear their stories but only the way they dictate. "I listen."

"All the cities make war to get what they want, so the soldier is paramount in Sumeria. Uruk herself makes war even to get the alabaster for the king's washbowl."

"Wasn't life based on trade?"

"Yes, but Triumph is based upon the sword."

"The sword made your neighbors angry, I bet."

"Oh yes. In particular, the nomadic peoples of the North. They lived on the march. Life made them hard, and they knew how to handle their weapons."

Jupiter asked, "What were they like?"

"They carried copper weapons, not bronze. They had toughened leather shields, and throwing sticks, and used the fire-that-clings. We never saw them except when they attacked. They squatted out there in the sand, below the low hills, lusting after the pillage and wealth we could provide."

"Were they raiders?"

"Yes, picking off travelers, ambushing villages. But they would also gather in great masses and attack Uruk herself. The threat of nomads gave me my first campaign and my first trip away from the village. Uruk's Council called upon us for duty because scouts had detected nomads massing in the desert. Uruk summoned us to man the walls."

"Exciting?"

"I could hardly sleep. Of course, no one asked me to swing a sword. I toted wheat and tents, and herded sheep for us to eat. Nearly all the men and boys marched off in one role or another."

"Leaving the village undefended?"

"Of course. Villages can be rebuilt, farmers replaced, but Uruk must remain untouched. Many of the women took fleeces to sleep in and carried baskets of precious grain out into the marsh."

"Home forgotten, but the Mother City defended?"

"But this is only natural. I have seen it many times."

"Tell me about this Mother you defended."

"My first vision of Uruk—like seeing a goddess. She rose up on the plain by the river. I saw the tops of the temple first, the Ziggurat. Next, I

54

spied the walls, and houses stacked up behind. I marveled at a giant wooden gate, more wood than I had seen in my entire young life, set into a twenty-rod wall. It was a wall of mud, with a parapet on top and soldiers walking back and forth, staring down on us. The unfinished Ziggurat rose above everything a hundred feet in the air, catching the light, centering the city. It was a man-made mountain in a place that had only low levees to break the view. It was the first mountain I ever saw."

Jupiter's memory flashed on a plane ride as a child, a shuddering small craft above Amarillo—an Amarillo stretched below like an immense blanket of humanity on the plain. "It must have been magnificent."

"We shambled up to Uruk at sunset, sheep and men strung out for half a league—quite dangerous. The walls shone orange and carnelian in the sunset. They ordered us peasants to camp below the walls the first night, sleeping beside our small fires. Fires indeed—the night laid on us moist and cold beside the river. In the morning, they brought us into the city. ur-Jupiter, we marched into the town through streets broader than our village path, five rods wide, and the houses formed walls that rose and hung over us towering two stories high. The village men deployed together on one of the walls. Dust, and noise, and confusion. There were more people than I had ever seen. They ordered me to keep the sheep organized below the wall and gave me skeins of wool to make string fences. The Elder told me how important it was to keep close by as shepherd and guard."

"A responsible job."

"Oh-ho. One I ignored. I was a pile of duck dung in those days. I left the responsibility to others and wandered off. What sights I saw that day—shops and markets, men with oiled, blocked beards and symbols of rank, oxen and their carts, and girls my own age. How clean everyone was, and how regal!"

"The first time in a city opens your eyes. You must have become used to it later."

"But never jaded. That day I walked halfway across Uruk, all the way to the main temple—to the temple of Anu himself, Uruk's principal deity. Anu shared Uruk with his great-granddaughter Inanna, the goddess of love and war—there is a story there, ur-Jupiter. As I said, I wandered all the way to the door of the temple, and through that door I could see the courtyard behind. I could not go in—I felt small, of no account."

Believable? Even at ten, Gilgamesh would not have been humble. "What was the real reason, Gilgamesh?"

"Ha...an anticlimax for my story! Hunger raged in my belly. I decided I should get back to my own people. I became lost and arrived hours later. In the end, they beat me."

"Not very pleasant." Jupiter imagined the fists, the flying feet.

"I swore then that it would be the last time anyone beat me. The next time it happened, I killed the man."

"Yes. That indeed is what the record shows."

Jupiter shook his head and murmured in the quiet kitchen, "Huh. Only ten years old. And at twelve, already a killer."

Chapter Seven: Behind the Walls of Uruk

Another rough night. Insomnia, his most constant companion, sat watching him through the long time before dawn. He conceived it as a real presence crouched in the corner, black against the concrete wall. Its breath surrounded him, stealing all the air, even in his empty and echoing head house. It was too cold to walk around on the roof in pajamas and a robe. There could be no escape.

In the dark before six, he swung by the McCloskeys to pick up White. The dog sensed his presence at the gate even in the moonlight and trotted up the drive out to him. He liked it that the dog asked no questions and took the situation as it came.

At the end of the four-mile patrol, he fed the dog. He showered and dressed for the city. He took his coffee in an insulated mug, descended using the freight elevator, and walked to the steel silo at the end of his grain elevator: his Amarillo car. He nestled into the luxury vehicle, drove through Aniline in the post-dawn light, and took the entrance ramp of I-40 going west.

The car held him in a cocoon, creating an unsettled sensation; the scenery moved rather than his machine. It smoothly made the pavement pull past and reeled Amarillo into view. The details displayed themselves as he rolled past the freight yards, the industrial sites, and the strip joint or two, and approached the malls and the upscale neighborhoods. The Interstate was chewed up in a few places, but the car preserved its illusion and made light of the potholes. Businesses big and small, shabby and glamorous, strung together as America's costume jewelry, fronting the access roads. He knew he would never walk into these shops, but they were all his—his market and his base. An idle thought swam by. To climb upon the battlements of Uruk, walk upon the fired-brick walls and exult in the strength of the city.

He arrived early, before the rush hour. In that distinct clear light of a winter morning, the town had a clean shimmer, a pop and an attitude. He knew Amarillo anchored itself in a cruder reality. The real city life included poor neighborhoods with trailers, with dives and juke joints, with second-hand car lots run by immigrants and patronized by illegals. The factual Amarillo included dollar stores, check cashing establishments, and the stinking feedlots out west. He did not see these things, or in any case he did not discern them. This was his capital, his urban love. He had made a name in New York, but he'd never had affection for that immense burg, not like the adoration he held for this small prairie city.

He turned up familiar streets through a neighborhood that had once suited him and drove into his place. The car automatically raised the door. He parked and strode through the interior entry into the kitchen.

The house was quiet enough that he could hear the clock ticking in the hall. They had decorated it in the usual upscale country-club way, all the choices made by his ex-wife. He wanted her to have this house in the divorce, but in the midst of the meltdown, she settled for money instead. She had wanted Hawaii and its beach-club lifestyle.

In the front hall he stepped into near-ankle-deep mail. He made three or four trips to the kitchen to get it all onto the counter. He then spent a satisfying half hour sorting it out, dumping most of it into the green recycle bin. He kept only the magazines and the personal mail. Bills didn't come here; they went directly to the accountant. There was less and less socialite mail coming to the house these days. He opened a letter from his ex-wife. It read:

"Mattie, you haven't heard from me for awhile because my health has been a little poor. I've got that neuralgia thing back again, and although I'm getting good homeopathic care for it, I'm starting to think I should try more conventional medicine. I have the insurance for it, thanks to you, so I might as well use it.

In other news, my partner Michelle has had her children visiting from the mainland, and to tell you the truth, I'm getting really tired of having these people underfoot. It makes me more appreciative of your idea of a perfect day, to be alone and quiet.

I'm considering a new car, what do you think? Maybe the Humvee. According to the news, they won't be making it much longer, and I always wanted one. Would it be possible to advance me the money for the SUV? I don't want to trade in the Mercedes; Michelle loves it and drives it all the time.

Bob sent the tax stuff to me to sign. He says you're claiming me as a dependent on your filing, and that affects my taxes. Is that the right way to handle it? After all, you did divorce me a long time ago. Oh, I forgot. I divorced you—and your job. Pity. I wouldn't mind still having your last name.

Thanks for the checks. Your loving ex, Sheila."

He folded the note carefully into quarters, then once more. He placed it in his wallet beside the tens and twenties of modern measurement.

***

Next stop, his general practitioner. Dr. Cransto kept his office in one of those squeaky-clean office parks invading the west side of town. There he administered expensive tests for the well-insured and gave out specialist referrals. Jupiter considered the doctor a good-hearted man, but he suspected Cransto couldn't stand the smell of poor people. In spite of that, Cransto went to the Yucatan every year and spent a week volunteering in a clinic there, and then lay on the beach for a week in the Mexican sun. This arrangement displayed a nice sense of rationalization, balance, and logic. In other words, there was guilt in a man too self-aware. Like Jupiter.

He had to wait in the sitting room for forty-five minutes. The room smelled of disinfectant and potpourri—he had the outlandish sensation he was in a medicinal Indian restaurant. During this time, he sat back in the corner, poised on the edge of his seat. It made the waiting easier if he leaned forward on his elbows with his hands between his legs as his knees drummed up and down. The other patients spread out through the room, each maximizing the distance to another human. Towards the end of the wait, a young mother with two children sat beside him. The youngest sat in her mother's lap and stared fixedly at him, hand thrust into her wet little mouth. Worse, the other child picked at the fabric of the cushion between them, as if he might start plucking at Jupiter's slacks. He watched the child out of the corner of his eye, ready to leap away. A sense of relief washed through him when a nurse came forth and called his name. He followed her down the hall and into an empty room. She didn't ask him to disrobe, and she didn't speak while she took his vital signs and entered them into her iPad. She smiled distractedly and closed the door without a word. He liked that.

Cransto ran further behind schedule, as usual. Jupiter spent ten minutes inspecting medical posters about heart disease and diabetes, wondering why the room had to be ice cold, and sneaking clandestine peeks into the equipment drawers. When Cransto bustled in, Jupiter gave a guilty jerk.

"So Matt, how have you been?"

"Good, Ben." The two allowed this first-name informality; they had played golf together for years. "Well, all right is maybe a better description."

Cransto peered shortsightedly at the chart. "This isn't your annual checkup, so I'm betting you came in to talk about the other thing."

"Yeah, the other thing."

"So, how has it been?"

"The usual. Night sweats and insomnia. Nervous in a crowd."

"How do you think you're coping?"

"Some of it is avoidance; some of it is just sweating it through. I prefer to do everything over the phone. I make up lies as to why I can't go to dinner or spend the weekend in Arizona with a supermodel."

"Is the drug helping? You need to be taking it every day, not intermittently. I suspect—says here you didn't call in for a renewal of the prescription."

He skated through this part. "I prefer to take the Prozac only when it's really bad."

Cransto shook his head and opened his mouth to protest.

Jupiter didn't want Cransto to start insisting on the drug's efficacy again. He cut him off, "It makes me nauseous and dizzy. But there's something new. I have the shakes. A lot."

"Really? When do you get them?"

"Any time. I get wound up, a little too focused on something. Then I start shaking."

"Just your hands?"

"Most of the time, but sometimes my shoulders shake too, as if I were really cold."

"Is it being around people?"

"Not always, although that can cause it. It happened a couple of times over the last two days, and I think it's because of a thing at work, an account that is going bad on us."

"It's just an account, Matt."

"An account—a patient. Same thing, huh?"

"Hardly."

"For me it's more how my agency is handling it."

"Okay, well the shaking…" Ben started into the adrenal reactions of the body and how they could be triggered by stress. Then he nattered on about lifestyle, stress, caffeine, and alcohol. He said he had a drug used to control adrenal overstimulation and fatigue—not an anti-depressant like the others. He gave him the contra-indicators and the side effects of the drug, and those didn't sound outlandish.

"All right, I'll try it. No guarantees it will be something I'm comfortable with."

Even though Jupiter had agreed to follow a recommended treatment, Cransto wasn't finished. "I know I've said it before, but I'll say it again. There are two things you should consider. You should be thinking about early retirement, and you should let me refer you to a specialist."

"Nope. Ain't going to turn either of those corners yet."

He hurried out of the office as quickly as he could and sat in his car for a few moments to catch his breath. He did a mental check on what sensations he could read. He felt good—confession and penance, and conditional absolution from Dr. Cransto. To his surprise he also felt hungry, but thinking about a restaurant made his shoulders tighten. He steered back onto the Interstate and headed for a drive-through burrito stand he knew on the east side of town.

***

The office at home hummed to him, a comfort of white noise. He unlocked a file cabinet and pulled out the top drawer. It was the Sheila drawer. In the front were the beginning years in NYC. He lingered over a

61

file partway back. A vacation in Belize. In the very back was the correspondence folder, correspondence after the divorce. He took out her letter, unfolded it, and placed it in its place behind ten years of notes, e-mails, letters, and photos.

He felt duty and gloom. Time to call the office and check on the Petersens.

"Hey, Jerry, this is Matt."

"Boss, good to hear from you. How did your talk with Mr. Petersen go?"

"Well enough. He wants to play golf as soon as the weather gets better and I'm back in town. As far as the advertising goes though, he was quite firm. He has turned all that over to his son. Still, he promised to say a good word for us, especially if we will do a 'shocker' as we had in the old days. He used phrases like, 'Blow the doors off the competition.' I think he's right."

"In any event, one Petersen is on our side."

"Oh? So tell me, what did Bill Petersen say?"

"Not much. We ran our campaign by him and promised him the original development at no charge. He said he'd let us know. He only gave us about a quarter of an hour, and then he lit out like he was on fire."

Jupiter pondered for three seconds. "So, Jerry, you're telling me you've lost this account?"

"No, I'm not. He didn't say anything definite."

"You showed him the stuff you e-mailed me last night?"

"Uh-huh."

"And you didn't use my pitch?"

"Boss, your stuff was way out there. And besides, you told me to get my head around this one, so I did."

Jupiter took a breath. He'd rather lose the account by stretching for something new than let it die of mediocrity. "Here's my take on the situation. I studied the video storyboards and the audio from your stuff, and I could barely stay awake. The only big change from the last two or three years was the color scheme, and that would cost Petersen a fortune if he converted over with all the lot signs and his office fronts. I'm really unhappy with our product. It's an inadequate effort."

"Huh. I'm sorry you feel that way...."

"Listen, Jerry. This is what you're going to do if you want to keep working for me. You're going to get an appointment at Bill's office for tomorrow at lunchtime. You're going to make a video storyboard of my idea, and you'll show up there with enthusiasm and a catered lunch from OHMS. You'll address him as Mr. Petersen, not Billy. Win or lose, you'll use my idea. Or if you say no, you can send your resume out there right now."

There was a whine in the voice, "Gee Matt, you're not letting us do our jobs here…."

"And further, I'm going to teleconference in. I'll call your mobile, and you can set it on speaker. Do we understand each other?"

"Yes, you're crystal clear."

Jupiter heard the brittleness in Jerry's voice but continued on relentlessly. "Let me know what time I should call."

He hung up to avoid any further discussion—he didn't need any escalation. His hands were shaking, and he tasted the bitterness of nausea in the back of his mouth. Conflict was such a great thing for his condition.

A Youth In Wandering

Chapter Eight: Fathers and Sons

There are laptops, and there are laptops. Standing at the window of his office he focused on the huge shadow of the grain elevator. The darkness laid like a block of night down on the train tracks and out to battered, abandoned industrial buildings. Not entirely abandoned—a small figure was wrapped in a coat that dwarfed it. It peeled back tin and slipped into one of the buildings. The weather was freezing out there. Some kid picking around in the ruins. Jupiter should lock the door down below, but then the entire work floor was open to the world anyway.

Squinting, Jupiter opened the laptop. Words laid in wait. Was any of this real?

"Who are you?"

The back of Jupiter's neck prickled. His fingers reached out, touched the keys, and retreated. He coughed. Why not? He typed.

"As I said, my name is ur-Jupiter."

"You must be more to be inside my head."

And you...you must be some strange split of my head. Or the dead king Gilgamesh. "Just a man. Someone who knows something of your life."

"Can this be so? Tell me why you have chosen me. Why are you in my story?"

"You were the first tragic figure in history and literature. You have an entire Epic dedicated to you."

"Wait a moment. I have to give all of my attention. I am deciding a case."

The moment stretched out. "There, it is done."

"Where are you, and what are you doing?"

"It is the Day of the Sixty-Four. Every sixty-four days I sit in judgment for those disputes among my people. They have sixty-three days to resolve them before they come to me, and sometimes that is threat enough for compromise."

Jupiter saw the hall in his mind—tall ceilings, a space crowded with square columns, stone facing on mud brick. There was a slab of alabaster with a simple bench for the King. There were scribes, a line of supplicants. "I can return another time."

"Do not be silly. It is only about wives, sheep, and oxen, and sometimes about the granary records. I have heard it all for many, many years."

Gray hair then, woven through the oiled ringlets of his beard and his hair. He wore robes of linen, a choke of lapis around the neck. Bronze cuffs. "I sat in judgment myself this day." How formal Jupiter sounded to himself: the cadence of the Sumerians, speech like Gilgamesh.

"Oh? This judgment was one of life and death?"

"No, just life. I have a man who works for me. He's become sloppy, jaded."

"Hold his oldest son as hostage. Or cut off a finger."

Jupiter grinned, thought what Jerry would say about sacrificing a finger to advertising. "Oh, I don't think it's that serious."

"Threaten him with a year in the fields. He will be most attentive then."

Not a bad strategy. "I offered him exile."

"That is very soft, ur-Jupiter. But I will indulge you."

"Thank you."

"How do you know me so well then?"

Jupiter typed, "We know from the Assyrians, the next wave of empire after Sumeria. To be specific, an Assyrian king named Ashurbanipal and his clay tablets. He lived in Nineveh, on the River Tigris. He collected every book he could get his hands on, read and wrote three languages. He studied you and considered your Epic the first management self-help book."

"I do not understand. He admired me?"

"Well, he admired your success, at any rate."

"Ashurbanipal failed as king himself?"

Jupiter wondered. How much ego did Gilgamesh have invested?

"Oh no, he wasn't a failure. Ashurbanipal made an empire far greater than you ever dreamed. He had many more cities under his rule than Sumeria ever possessed. In practical terms he owned all of the Fertile Crescent."

"Daunting. His halls would be over-run each Day of Sixty-Four. And the cities would consume the other sixty-three days."

So this Gilgamesh was a seasoned old king, not the young man who wanted to rule for the glory. "Large workload, to be a king?"

"Never ending. Does ur-Jupiter work hard?"

"No, my empire runs itself."

"Hah! No empire runs itself. The price of kingship is unrelenting vigilance."

Jupiter could imagine the laugh, the derision in that "Hah!" Still, Gilgamesh knew from his own experience. "You had a lesson in vigilance once when you fell asleep in front of Noah."

"Ah, yes. You refer to the seven days of sleep in the presence of Utnapishtim. Not one of my better adventures."

Jupiter conjured up an image of Gilgamesh poised on the edge of his bench, leaning forward towards the supplicants. In the image, Gilgamesh muttered to Jupiter, shook his head, and even smiled. What would the Sumerians think—that their King talked to himself over their disputes? He typed, "I never understood that part of the Epic."

"Oh, a simple thing. I failed on two accounts. First, I left my City and disappeared into the wilderness. Those were rather bad days; I lost my best friend, murdered at the hands of the gods. So I abandoned Uruk, or worse, left her to a pack of old men I charged with my trust."

Old men like you and I now are. "And the other?"

"What?"

"You said two failures?"

"Wait, I must be attentive. Two brothers love the same woman, and she wants neither of them. Unfortunately, she is already married to both. Now, my second failure was a disaster. I wanted the secret of eternal life from the immortal Utnapishtim. He, however, had no intention of conferring immortality on me, but he wanted a graceful way out of it. So he challenged me to stay awake as long as he had when he piloted the ark during the Great Deluge. I was bone tired, mortal tired you might say, so slumber overtook my vigilance."

"Our Noah, your Utnapishtim. It was a huge surprise for us to find one of our own stories in your Epic. God's punishment and the perilous seven days at sea."

"Yes, well, that was Utnapishtim's story, not mine. Tell me of my Epic."

"The Epic. Written and rewritten many times over, but the first version comes from you. If you haven't started it already, you soon will. We also know something about you from Sumeria's records. They're sketchy. We have a few dull accountant tablets that track your name and show you as part of village life and on various military rolls."

"When I was young, there was no one to write down my deeds?"

"You moved around a lot."

"True. And you—who writes down the life of ur-Jupiter?"

Jupiter's thumb caressed the space bar of the laptop, "Why, I do."

"How tedious, ur-Jupiter."

"I have a servant who helps. His name is Computer." It was nearly true. "We don't know how you got from your village to your life as a soldier. Tell me about that."

Gilgamesh tugged his ear, chuckled. "Very well. After my first military campaign—when not an arrow was shot nor a spear thrown—I trudged back to my settlement through the dust with all the others. It was such a tiny village after the mighty Uruk! In Uruk, I had wandered freely. In the village I was enslaved in the fields. I packed up a goatskin bag, slung it over my shoulder, and tramped northwest all night. By morning, my bondage laid far behind me."

Jupiter saw the small figure as it trudged across the desert. "What about your females, the women who raised you?"

"Yes, well, that is not something I am too proud of. To walk away was not the best part of valor, yet I was able to live by myself in the wilderness. After all, I had been trained to watch sheep, not to survive in the wild—so I was rather proud of myself. I hiked up into the mountains. Such stags and sheep! Such weather. Hunger and cold. Many days I thought I would die."

Jupiter cocked his head. He had been right—the wild had nurtured the future king, and Armenia had hidden him away. "But you returned to Sumeria?"

"Once I was fully a man. There was more glory in killing lions and men than in bighorn sheep. I enlisted in the army of Kish."

"I know about Kish, the Sumer City among cities, or at any rate, the first big powerhouse after the Deluge."

"Their army was huge, costly, built on the back of the people of Kish. I would never impose such a tax on Uruk, at least not now in my dotage."

"Did you stay with Kish?"

"No. After that city, there was Shurrapak and then Eridu. Advancement came easier by moving rather than promotion. If you stay too long, you end up in the slog of soldiering, the tedium between the days of glory."

"What was it like to be a simple soldier?"

"Why, it was the finest thing for a young man. I was a blooded soldier at fifteen, which earned me a place above the rabble. At that point, the girls thought me good-looking. I filled out even more by sixteen and received my promotion to Corporal. I was quite handsome, and I had cloaked myself in rumors of blood. This was most effective in impressing the daughters of my officers—another reason to move on. By the time I reached the rank of Sergeant, the women thought me beautiful and deadly. Why, there was none handsome enough to stand beside me without shame."

"Nice to look back upon now?"

"Those were glory days. Now I am not so comely, but I have the aphrodisiac of power—not that I pursue the opportunity these days."

Jupiter hesitated then typed his own revelation. "Much like me. I have a wife who has forsaken me for another. I pursued her to the ends of the earth but without success. Now I choose an empty bed."

"ur-Jupiter, I am embarrassed for you…to trail after a woman? Better to go out and conquer this other one, the one you said was unattainable."

"Sex and power. Interrelated, aren't they?"

"You understand, ur-Jupiter. You have an empire."

Of sorts. An ad agency in Amarillo. "Built from scratch."

"I won mine, much as my father Lugalbanda won his kingship of Uruk."

Jupiter shook his head, "It's never been clear to us that he was your father."

"I chose Lugalbanda as my father. He had married Ninsun, my mother, and we each ruled Uruk in our time. As King, I chose to make him a god and read the rites myself."

The Epic said Gilgamesh had been denied his real father. Jupiter's father had no time for him. Neither son had much luck. Would Jupiter have been happier at ten if he had been given a step-father? "Uruk and Ninsun, is that what you and Lugalbanda had in common?"

"Oh no, not just the City." Gilgamesh shook his head. "He was a wanderer, like me. He often led raiding expeditions out towards Kish, and I had a grudge against Kish. He fought the Elamites as I did. He was happy while hunting. I was happy killing. He ruled for six hundred years and more, and I shall do the same, may the gods help me."

No. Not six hundred. "You Sumerians, you count goats, count bushels, count the number of widows the temple feeds. You even count the number of styli used by the scribes. You don't appear to count years at all well, though."

"You are the scholar. How do you explain it?" Gilgamesh was grumpy.

"Your numbering system is based upon sixty-four, but you only have ten fingers."

"I take it then that you base your lives on ten little fingers. For us, we are carried by a bigger number, sixty-four abodes for the gods, sixty-four points of the compass, sixty-four plants and animals given to our domestic pleasure. A magnificent number, a number of size and strength."

Oh, yes, Gilgamesh was definitely irritated. "Sorry, I shouldn't be sarcastic. So how did Lugalbanda win his empire, and how did you win yours?"

"I cannot speak for my father's rise to the throne."

"Then speak of your own."

"Great things are decided by ironic turns."

"You lucked into it?" In his mind, Jupiter watched Gilgamesh pull his mouth down in a frown and hide it in the beard.

"Not quite accurate, but with some truth. Uruk held a festival, a five-day event at the beginning of the New Year. All of Uruk was determined to have a splendid time. Often at the beginning of the new year something horrible occurred, so the festival was the last chance for celebration just before the troubles."

"What type of horrible?"

"Floods, attacks by the cities of the North, sheep disease. This year though, the threat happened during the festival. A wind raged through King Dumizid's head. It left him frozen and bent, wordless."

Jupiter glanced over at his stack of reference books. But he already knew this. "Dumizid…, Lugalbanda's successor, your predecessor. He ruled for a mere century."

"But he ruled well. He had been known as the Fisherman. But now he was an old and feeble man, and he suffered the wind of the mind."

"A stroke."

"Certainly a blow. This impairment of the King was a major problem for the Elders. At the end of the five festival days there was to be a ceremony, a ritual that recreated the pairing of the city with the goddess Inanna."

"What ritual was this with the goddess of love and war?" Jupiter saw Gilgamesh spread his hands out, cock his head, and try to explain.

"The king takes the male role in this ceremony, and either a priestess or the goddess herself plays the female role. The priests and populace fill this ritual with charged and important symbols. The ceremony commemorates the time when rule descended from the gods to mere men, at the end of the great Deluge."

"You're not being very clear."

"The king lies with the Goddess and has communion of her."

"So Uruk can think of no greater way to celebrate humanity's right to rule than a good old-fashioned public copulation?"

"Yes. It is quite touching, really," Gilgamesh said with his head up and a defiant smile.

"How did this tie in to you?"

"I journeyed into Uruk from Eridu to compete in the contests. I dominated the wrestling. Even in a city the size of Uruk, I stood out as the man among men. It is not self-flattery to say everyone knew my name. When the King had the ill grace to die, the Elders of Election panicked. They needed to prevent turmoil and fear and to focus the people on the ritual of the next day. The Elect of Uruk needed business as usual and an admirable hero."

Jupiter laughed…a story so rich, so ludicrous. "So the old, terrified

71

men elected you king for a day, and you surprised everyone on the council of elders by how you pulled it off, how regal you were, a good performance in all ways? Neat trick—to parlay a pornographic moment into a full-time job."

"A sacred moment. And I was rather good. The people of Uruk spoke up for me, for the fair Gilgamesh."

"Oh, but the population is often fickle."

"Are they? Even where you live?"

"Aniline is a tiny version of Uruk. Yes, they love me, they hate me, and they pay me far too much attention. Like you, I have had disastrous beginnings in my new city."

Chapter Nine: In the Market Place of Uruk

March slid into April. The plan was an easy one—stay out of sight and out of trouble. Jupiter had until late April to ask for an extension on his zoning issue. In the meantime, no one except his contractors visited him. Of course he didn't follow his own plan.

Heldritch had long taken a heightened interest in the grain elevator, over and above what was required. He drove over to the elevator on a Saturday to help Jupiter with the cyclone, and brought three of his workmen. Between all of them, a large cart, and a front-end loader, they shifted the cyclone off the work floor and out through one of the docks. From there, they carried the fan into the steel silo and laid it down against the far wall. The silo was a large space, ringed in steel—room enough for the cyclone, the front-end loader, his car, and a small house if Jupiter had wanted. He liked this space bounded in its large circle.

Dan explained where the inlet and outlet ports of the cyclone were and drew a sketch in the dirt of the floor to explain how particles precipitated out of a circular "wind" in the cone chamber.

"So you get rid of the dust in the bins, and there's nothing to blow up. Of course you couldn't have had this dust remover back with the first elevators. They were built in the days of steam. It takes electricity to run a cyclone fan. Back then elevators blew up. But nothing is ever foolproof. Electric sparks caused a few explosions too. It wasn't normally the switches or wiring. It was the electricity in the motors for the conveyor belts and the cyclones that got 'em."

"What makes a bin explode?"

One of Dan's employees snickered. "What makes a person go postal?"

"No, seriously. I'd like to know."

Dan spread his hands out in a fan. "It's like a fuel-air bomb, the type we used in 'Nam. The grain gets hot because of all the weight pressing down on it. The dust heats up from the grain, and because the surface area of the dust is so high, a spark can make it ignite. It doesn't burn as much as it flashes all the way through and uses up the oxygen instantaneously."

"Blam!" Dan's youngest guy liked the idea, a bomb in a concrete tube.

Jupiter asked, "Did your family work here at the grain elevator?"

"Nah, we were just the farmers bringing grain up in wagons and later on in trucks. My great uncle, though, he was on the board of the farmer's co-op that bought the elevator—not the second cooperative, the first one. It was a local thing, and I don't think it had much leverage with the railroads."

Dan turned away from the cyclone to Jupiter's car.

"I didn't know you had one of these. The Germans, they can make some fancy vehicles."

He strolled over to the svelte shape.

Jupiter had bought the automobile in Amarillo where it fit in, suited the city streets, parking lots, and driveways. Here, it was an embarrassing car to own. "Well, it's not much good in Aniline, especially on the north end of town. I drive my old pickup mostly."

"Couldn't you buy the pickup version of this car? No, wait. Germans don't make pickups. 'Stylish pickup' would mean buying American." Dan snickered. "You're smart not to be seen in this vehicle—one of the councilmen owns our local American car and truck dealership."

"I don't drive it much."

"Yeah, and you ought to wash it more, too." Dan stooped to glance in the driver window. "Huh. Looks like someone appreciates this car better than you do."

"What?"

"There's a blanket here in the back seat and all kinds of trash in the floorboards. Candy wrappers. Chip bags. Loose cheese puffs. A soda can."

"You're right!"

Two of the other men were peering in the windows on the other side.

"Hey, guys," Dan said to his three workers, "scout around. It seems we have a vagrant living in this silo."

If Jupiter had an unwelcome guest, it could get complicated. He didn't want to be cruel, but he didn't want a homeless person with homeless issues camped on his doorstep.

From behind one of the stored advertising signs, a workman shouted, "Yo, someone's been taking a dump here and wiping their ass with the front page."

Dan slammed the back door of the car with his shoulder, his hands full of litter. He said, "So, how did your bum get in?"

"Well, guess I haven't been religious about locking up the garage door."

"Live and learn. I'd start being a little more careful."

"Yeah, like that hasn't occurred to me."

Dan shrugged. "I'll ask all the guys to keep a look-out when they're out here."

"Thanks. Hopefully nothing more will come of it."

"If you're lucky. How about lunch, then, Matt? My guys want to go on home, to get on with their weekend, but I've got time…and I figure you should buy."

"Dan, you're always going out to lunch."

"We can call it a second breakfast then. I do like going down to the café and seeing what's going on in town. Most of my work starts in the café. Besides, it gives me a chance to keep tabs on my daughter."

"She's a little grown up for you to still be tending her, isn't she?"

"Still lives in my house. Besides you don't know her. Kate's not bad, but she's wild. Always been her own person, doesn't stop to ask permission."

"You'd admire that in a boy."

Dan's voice dropped, making the conversation solely between them. "Maybe so, but she's pulled some real bone-headed stuff. Go-to-jail type stuff."

"You sound kind of proud."

"Of her setting fire to the middle school at fourteen? Or when she crashed a friend's car into Sarah's Buick? The time she jumped out of the cheerleader bus into the middle of the highway? Or the time I had to go down to Clarendon to get her out of jail? Maybe you'd like to hear about the semester she dated the worst hoodlum in high school?"

Jupiter said, "See, you do sound like you're puffed up with pride."

"At least none of it was cruel or hurtful."

"Must be hard living under the eyes of your parents. Maybe she's feeling the pressure of your, um, supervision."

"Like she cares what we think. Still, she wants out of this town real bad. You got any kids to go along with your parenting expertise?"

"No, timing was all wrong. Plus there was a divorce. I wanted kids though."

Dan waved his hand, dismissing Jupiter's alibi. "Children are funny. They won't ask beforehand, but expect you bail to them out later—even grown-up ones. I like to keep track of Kate's next train wreck before it happens. So how about it? The Café on you?"

"Sure, lunch is okay."

"I'd ask you to drive, but your car smells."

***

Jupiter winced when he saw the parking lot. The café was jammed. Dan loved it, greeting one and all. It took ten minutes to work across the room, searching for a seat, pausing to talk here and there.

When they slid into a booth Jupiter said, "Dan, you ought to run for mayor. You know everyone in town twice over."

"I don't think the current Mayor would like that, and I can't afford to offend him. He has a new development platted out on the west side of town and some serious partners. They're going to get rich off those Amarillites fleeing the big city."

"And?"

"I want to be one of the guys building houses for the Mayor and his buddies."

"The Mayor is Nelson Taggert Sharp, right?"

"Yes, goes by all three names and a two-banger title, The Honorable Mayor Nelson Taggert Sharp."

"I always had trouble trusting people who had three last names, or for that matter, three first names."

"Stay here long enough and Sharp will buy something you own, and

76

then you can trust the three names on his check. Here comes Kate."

Jupiter jerked his head around to see her. Kate wove her way towards them. She was a blonde young woman in a sea of gray-haired humanity. Jupiter inhaled; his breath caught.

"Hey, Daddy. Hi Mr. Devon," Kate said. "So Dad, which fat-fried thing on our menu do you want? Or should I have Ted sizzle up a heart attack and bring that to the table?"

"Ha-ha. Funny, funny, funny. You're scaring Matt."

"Oh, I doubt he scares easy."

She poured out coffee for them with the burnt-toast smell of a pot that had been on too long. "What can I get you besides our delicious day-old coffee?"

Heldritch chose the large burger and fries, and Jupiter ordered a Reuben, fried, with a side salad, iceberg. Kate rambled off with their orders and worked her way across the room dispensing coffee. Jupiter wondered if the young woman had influenced his order. It was ambiguous enough as a food statement. Jupiter dropped his eyes to the tabletop, contemplated his uncertainty and a snapshot memory of her breasts.

The door opened and closed, letting in another group of men and a whiff of the feedlot nearby. The café bottled up a dense press of humanity, and Jupiter could sense a tightening in all his muscles. A vein on his temple started to throb, a sure sign of a coming headache. He excused himself and hid in a stall in the men's restroom for five minutes. He swallowed a Prozac dry. When his chest wasn't bound tight and his eyes didn't feel like they were bulging out, he unlocked the stall, washed his hands, and left the restroom.

Kate was coming in from the back door there in the short hall running down the side of the kitchen. "Food up in a minute, Matt."

He caught her pattern. She called him Mr. Devon in front of her father and Matt otherwise.

He hesitated there in the hall, trying to think of something ingratiating to say as she rushed past him. Her hand tapped him on his shoulder, and her hip scrubbed across his zipper as she turned into the kitchen. It all seemed accidental. He couldn't breathe.

***

77

Later when Jupiter would think of Kate, he often had a subliminal flash of April somewhere in his mind's cortex, some vague elusive memory. It would be wind, or cold, or perhaps that strange yellow April daylight, felt but not really seen.

He took to fixing his own lunch and staying in and around the elevator. But there was only so much chicken soup a man could eat.

On a Tuesday when he was having, if not a good day, then an average one, he felt penned up in the elevator. Tuesdays were slow days for Aniline in general, so he decided a late lunch would be safe. He had something to deliver at Town Hall, so he had a good excuse to stop by the café and seize a chance to see Kate. She had been on his mind and sporadically in his dreams over the past month. He preferred to dream about the twenty-five-year-old woman much more than about a son named Jimmy Devereaux.

Even in late April the wind was cutting. He still wore his ranch coat inside the grain elevator where the concrete held the chill, down on the work floor in particular. The coat was brown canvas with large flap pockets, starting to get that broke-down, been-worked-in look. He was obscurely pleased to be wearing the right local clothes. Vanity on his part, or perhaps camouflage; he couldn't decide.

First, he went by Town Hall to hand in a letter. A woman behind the front desk asked, "Can I help you?"

She was thirty something, turned out perfectly, and good-looking in spite of the makeup and some extra weight.

His smile beamed out involuntary, spontaneous. "Yes. Is the Town Manager in?"

She glanced down at the flashing lights on the phone. "I'm sorry, he's on the phone right now."

"I'll wait then. I wanted to hand this to him personally."

"If you want, I can give it to him for you, Mr. Devon."

"Have we met?"

"Oh, most people in town know of you, Mr. Devon. As for me, I feel I know you personally since my Joe has been working for you off and on. He's Dan Heldritch's sheet-rocker."

Jupiter stuck his hand out. "So you should call me Matt."

"Matt, pleased tameetcha. I'm Krissy. So, this is about the zoning, or are you submitting the form to get on the ballot?"

"Zoning. I don't think I'll be running for councilman. So, how did you know about the zoning, and me maybe standing for election?"

"Oh, you know, talk around the coffee machine."

She leaned forward. "I wouldn't want this to get out, but my friend here, she's the recorder for the Council sessions, even the closed ones. She was sayin' they spend a lot of time talking about you."

"All good things, I hope."

She stared at him. "You got to be kidding."

"I'm a nice guy, Krissy. I can't understand it when somebody doesn't like me."

"If it makes you feel better, all the little people are rooting for you."

He ripped out a grin. "I think I'll take you up on that offer. Hand this in for me." He handed her the envelope.

"Yeah, I can be your witness it got to them on time. We got time stamps."

He laughed. "You have a good day, then. I'll see you around, Krissy."

***

Jupiter ran by the hardware store for some concrete patch. Only then did he drive over to Angie's Cafe and park in front. He took several large breaths before he climbed down from the cab of the truck.

The clock showed two when he entered the café and chose a table near the kitchen. He picked up the flatware wrapped in a paper napkin. His fingers knotted up in a cramp. No doubt a nascent anxiety that she wouldn't be there because it was her day off. He dropped the hand into his lap and started flexing the fingers, trying to straighten them. When she popped out of the kitchen and smiled at him, his concern switched. She was here, and he would be a fool. He felt a vast, frozen grin stuck on his face.

She appeared immediately at his table, there in the empty restaurant, and greeted him, "Matt, so good to see you. Where have you been?"

Jupiter wanted to read something into the smile and the hello but wouldn't allow himself the luxury of optimism.

He ordered chicken soup, but then, with a cough, reconsidered.

"Wait, I've changed my mind. I'll have the chili con carne and an iced tea."

"Don't know," she said as she inspected him appraisingly. "I've already written down 'Chicken Soup.' If I scratch it out and write 'CCC', will you change your mind again?"

"I do solemnly swear to stick to chili."

"All right," with a heavy sigh. "Beans or no beans?"

"No beans."

"Onions or no onions?"

"Onions." Was that the wrong choice?

"No date this afternoon, then. Cheese?"

"Yes."

"Bread or tortilla?"

"Tortilla." He grinned. Food was working out for him.

"Spoon or knife?"

"Why don't you decide for me? I'd hate to make another bad choice."

"Knife then. Very Texan, eating with a bowie knife."

She flashed him another smile before she turned away. She sauntered back to the kitchen, and Jupiter for the first time understood what the word sashay could mean. It certainly meant flirtation, if nothing else.

As he pushed the last of the chili around in the bowl with a shred of his tortilla, she strolled over and sat down across from him. Ah, time for some chitchat about the weather.

She leaned forward, giving him a peek down her T-shirt. "So you must like cooking if you live alone. It only stands to reason you would learn to cook for yourself... unless you're one of those guys that lives on frozen pizza."

"Hot Wraps, actually. Eighteen flavors. They're even available in strawberry and chocolate."

"So you don't cook?"

"I can cook. Mostly light stuff and a lot of fish. Also, my grandma was Italian, so I know how to do a great marinara and a chicken piccata. I can pickle nearly any kind of vegetable, and I know garlic is the true center of the universe. I also boil hotdogs and burn toast."

"Then you're really the man I want."

He stared at her, but her face held no expression except earnestness, with no suggestive hint. "It's nice to be needed, but it's good to know what for."

"I want you to cook. I don't cook, and I'm around cooking all day long, so I'm not likely to get keen on it. But I do belong to the Monday Club."

"Kate, you're way ahead of me on this one. What's the Monday Club? Why do you belong to it? Why do you need a guy who cooks? Why me?"

"Okay, okay with all the questions. The Monday Club is a bunch of show-offs who bring their prize dishes to lunch on Monday at the church and eat together. They're not a church group, but they use the hall and the kitchen. I belong because of who else belongs."

She paused, glanced sideways. Was this the beginning of regret? "Don't stop there." He wanted her to keep asking.

"The Monday Club has the usual women. Women started it and use it for socializing. On the other hand, there's always a guy around who has gone beyond barbeque, who thinks he's a TV chef. We have several." She halted again. Her eyes skittered away; she leaned forward to get up from the table.

He pinned her in the seat with a prompt, "And?"

"So, there's little Dell who used to run the pharmacy before he retired and a guy named Ed Chernowski who specializes in meat, meat and more meat. And Fat Bert and Anthony... they're both realtors here. In fact, they're the big realtors. I thought I might try to get a job with them as an agent, but I didn't want to start cold and end up a receptionist answering phones."

"Ah," he said. "Show-off cooking gets you to the table. Then you sell yourself. So this guy that cooks for you, does he have to go to the Monday Club with you, or do you drop by and get takeout?"

Now that the confession was out in the open, Kate was more direct. "Hmm. Takeout? I hadn't considered that."

"Careful. Sounds like exploitation of men."

"You're right. Of course as a waitperson, I understand being exploited. Every day, all day—that's our motto."

"And you think I might be your guy because...?"

She exhibited a miniscule vertical crease between her eyebrows.

"You appear to have the time. And you're from out of town, so you might have better taste in food than just chicken fried steak. And you said you could cook. And maybe because my Dad says you have a hard time saying no."

This made Jupiter's head hurt right between his eyes. Kate, a local community club, crowds, small talk. Only one compelling reason he could see going for it. And that could work out in humiliation.

She asked, "So, how about it?"

"Would I be a ringer? Would my little contribution be anonymous?"

"Oh, you can have all the credit. Just get us in the limelight."

"Gee, I don't know. Maybe."

She played it well, ducked her head and pulled her mouth to one side. Then she upped the ante, reached across the table, and patted both his hands. "Sure, I understand. I shouldn't have thought it would work anyway. Thanks for hearing me out."

She wasn't sashaying as she left the table.

***

On the following Monday, he called her family home; her mother answered, "Heldritch residence."

"Hi, this is Matt Devon."

"Oh, Mr. Devon. Dan isn't here right now. He had to take a trailer into Amarillo to pick up appliances for a remodel."

"Sorry, it's not Dan I was trying to reach. I was calling for Kate. Is she there?"

"Uh, sure, the diner's closed Mondays, so she's off. Let me see if she can come to the phone."

There was a thok, then a wait.

"Kate Heldritch here."

"Hi, this is…." He didn't know if he should say Matt, or Mr. Devon, or Matt Devon, or even Jupiter. He improvised, "This is Italian Takeout."

There was a pause. "I don't remember phoning in an order."

"And you didn't. We have a special offer this week we're talking up here in Aniline. We have a fennel purée soup with hazelnuts that is very popular. We also have a cauliflower sformato with Parmigiano-Reggiano cheese you might prefer to try. There's also cold pepperoni pizza from yesterday, but I wouldn't recommend that."

"I'll go with the first two things, even though I don't have the foggiest idea what they are. Is your takeout business really in Aniline? You must be going broke."

"We save money by not having a delivery service. You have to pick it up."

"Tell the chef to get his coat on. I'll be there in a half hour. I'm throwing out my macaroni casserole, so this better be good."

***

Jupiter didn't know what she meant by "coat," so he went with business casual. After dithering, it turned out ironed jeans, loafers, a shirt with an open collar and a blazer. Jupiter pulled his ranch coat on over all that, trying to hedge his bet. He stood uneasy at the bottom of his elevator where he could watch the front. He waited for a long five minutes. She parked by his pickup at the office. He trudged out with his stack of loaded plastic ware and climbed into her small Japanese car, settling it all in his lap. He seat-belted in and glanced over at her.

She was staring at him with a considering gaze—a formidable look, with an arched eyebrow, and that head of blonde hair thrown back. *God, I've got it bad. Please don't let this humiliate me.*

"Smells great—kind of like onion soup, only different."

"It's the fennel. Nice background aroma of licorice."

"Okay, Mr. Takee Outee. Ready for the Monday Club?"

"Let's hope they're ready for us. Cook and Driver. Smith and Jones. Stanley and Livingston. Batman and Robin."

"Matt, shut up."

He did, and they ground over the potholes in the gravel lot, humped over the train tracks, bumped over the rundown streets into town, and pulled up in front of the church. They clumped down wooden stairs into a basement where they found twelve people. The room was a typical church dining hall, with tables maybe for sixty stretching back into the dimness. It was expansive even if the ceiling hung low over their heads. Jupiter believed he could get through this one as long as he could make guy small talk and not get boxed in. People milled about making the space seem empty.

He hadn't reckoned on the biddy factor. The Angie's Café waitress had walked in with a silver hair, and the women wanted to know what it was all about. When he made his way back to reheat his soup, he discovered they had trapped him in the kitchen. He had his back to a counter, and the women, all except Kate, closed in, making diminutive fake domestic movements to show they were busy doing kitchen things. He couldn't get out without wriggling through and saying, "Excuse me" eight times. The Spanish Inquisition started its inexorable persecution.

"And you are, dear?"

"Matt Devon."

"Are you from Amarillo, dear?"

"Yes."

"Oh, how nice for you. Are you that new family that just moved to town?"

"No, no family."

"Oh, my, aren't you married?"

"No."

One word answers wouldn't satisfy. "How charming, the perpetual bachelor we all love so much."

"Sorry, married and divorced."

"Does your ex-wife live in Texas?"

"Hawaii." He was sweating.

"How interesting for her. And you're a new member of the Monday Club?"

"No, just here with a friend."

"And that Kate. Such a pretty young thing. Did you meet through her family?"

"I know her dad."

"Dan is such a sweet man, but he doesn't cook. Do you cook then?"

"Some."

"You're not a chef, are you?"

"No, only a hobby."

"Retired then?"

"No. Yes. Kind of."

"We're all retired here. But you're still in business?"

"Yes."

"And who do you work for? Or are you your own boss?"

"I own a company."

"A small intimate company, then?"

"Yes. Twenty employees."

"That's hardly small dear. That's quite substantial, I must say. Do you live here then?"

"Yes."

"Oh, in one of the new houses out south?"

"No, to the north."

"What's out north?"

"The grain elevator."

"You're that nice man who lives at the top of the grain elevator?"

"That's me. Well, my soup's done; I'll take it out. Excuse me. Excuse me. Excuse me."

While all this was going on, Kate wasn't standing close by to protect and support him. In fact, she had lingered in the dining hall by the coffee and the iced tea, talking to the men. Jupiter watched the men flocking about her.

Even the man Jupiter thought was Little Dell glowed with pleasure standing close to her. No doubt she was being impressed with his knowledgeable pharmacist ways. Three other men jostled for position. Jupiter cast the eye of a rival over the men. Voices murmured behind him, and he glanced behind him. He saw dismay and disapproval. Eight women buzzed quietly, judging and sentencing Kate. Still, he had escaped that crowded kitchen.

Once seated, he was flanked by two matrons and across the table from a man who had to be Fat Bert.

The behemoth handed across his business card and said, "In case things don't go well. In case you're looking around for new real estate."

The woman to Jupiter's left asked, "Why ever, would Mr. Devon be looking for real estate? Oh!" She slapped her hand over her mouth, all drama.

Jupiter smiled. "It's okay. I appear to have given the Mayor and the Council reason for offense. In any case they have misapprehended my small gestures of friendship."

Bert leaned across the table and said, "Oh, I think it was that interview in the barbershop—when the *High Plains* reporter was asking everyone what they wished for in the New Year."

Jupiter nodded, "Yes, that was unfortunate."

The woman to the other side of Jupiter said, "I was in Florida over the winter and didn't see the paper. What did Mr. Devon say?"

Really? Just to hear it again? "Please, call me Matt. So how long has the Monday Club been around?"

Her friend leaned across Jupiter and said to her, "It turns out, dear, most people said they hoped for higher grain prices, or for rain in mid-July for the corn, or for a Republican Senate in Washington. But Mr. Devon, well…."

Bert chortled, "Matt here wanted to replace the 'dead men on the Council with people who were new and vibrant and who didn't personally remember buying the first horseless carriages.' Or something like that."

Jupiter smiled weakly. "It was the aftershave the barber was wearing. It went to my head, made me tipsy."

He lay his fork down and pushed away Chernowski's antelope meatloaf. Up the table, three men laughed uproariously at something Kate said.

***

By the time she pulled up to his door, Jupiter was awash in weariness. Kate was quiet, pleased, and perhaps smug. He hesitated a moment before getting out with his stack of empty plastic ware.

"So, I don't think I made the sale. The Monday Club is tougher than I expected."

"We really wowed them, Matt."

"Maybe. Vegetables are non-threatening. Everyone can be nice about your vegetables. Main course, now, that's a commitment. That's where the competition gets mean. Nobody likes an uppity Swiss steak."

"I wasn't talking about the food."

"It was a lunch, you know. Potluck. We brought food."

"It wasn't food on trial today, you fool."

"Ah, that's what you mean."

"I heard some of the grilling you got over the Council thing. You had all the appearance of being cowed. I think I need to make it up to you."

She leaned over towards him. He sat rigidly still. His heartbeat thudded faster.

"Why don't I come over to dinner, say, Thursday? I'll eat for you, and all you have to do is cook."

"Well," he creaked out. "This is rather sudden; you're working so hard on my behalf. Thursday would be all right. Yes, Thursday would be good."

"Should I park out in front?" The question hung there.

"Might rain. Your car could get wet." One second. Two seconds. Three.

"Yes. It's been known to rain."

"There's a truck loading shed on the other side of the elevator, about halfway down. Park in there and take the steps up to the dock. Then walk back down the building to the freight elevator—if you want."

Her blue eyes were six inches from his.

She leaned closer and gave him a kiss on the cheek. Retreating to her side of the car, she asked, "Aren't you getting out?"

Jupiter wondered if Gilgamesh ever had this much trouble talking with a woman, or if the Sumerian king had ever skulked around, hiding a boyish courtship from the local chalcolithic crowd.

Chapter Ten: Fall of Kish

"Marjorie, it's Jupiter. Can you pick up?" He listened until the line clicked. "Are you there?"

"Jupiter! I didn't know you got up this early."

He sighed. "I haven't really been to sleep yet. Did I wake you?"

"Of course not. I try to do my prayers with the sunrise. It sets the day up."

"Prayers."

She laughed at his tone. "Pick a God, Jupiter. It doesn't matter which, as long as you pray."

"I'll stick to coffee, thanks."

There was a chuckle. "I'll check for you to see if the Hindus have a coffee god. We might have to adapt a tea god."

"You're way too cheerful, Marjorie."

"You should try it. What has you down, Jupiter?"

"The book, the woman, both…."

"Let's start with the book. You had some fun with me in our last conversation."

"Fun?"

"Well, this idea of Gilgamesh—it's both preposterous and intriguing. As a Daoist, I would love the idea that you are linked across the centuries to some kindred spirit. As your life counselor, though, I have to assume you haven't beaten the odds. It's more likely a message from your subconscious telling you that you need to see a psychologist. Not, as you insisted, an interview with someone who is undead."

"Feels real. Seems to be alive."

"What is real?"

Jupiter thought about the question. "Don't you believe in a mystic universe populated by unexplainable events?"

"You're ducking. It's my job to ask the questions."

She was right; he had flinched from the question. "I've got to play it out awhile. Maybe I have to do this to unlock the writing, do the Hemingway thing."

"Hmm. Hemingway didn't have a happy ending, did he? I have a friend. Let me give you his number."

"Not yet." There was dead space in the earpiece, a non-sound separating them.

Marjorie cleared her throat. "That feels done for now. You also said, 'The Woman.'"

"Yes."

"Go on."

Did he want to? "Her name is Kate."

"As in 'Kiss Me Kate?'"

"Yes," he waited for her response.

"Do you want to tell me about her?"

"Maybe."

Now Marjorie waited for him.

"Well, I better. She's half my age, and she's the most beautiful thing I've seen in years. She hasn't run me off, and she might even like me."

"And you're attracted to her?"

"I am practically incapacitated by my attraction."

"Is there a problem here?"

"Oh, so many problems. Her father is my friend. I'm over sixty and too dignified for such an elevated state of horniness. I want to see her every day, and I'm afraid to go close to her. What if she figures out what I look like naked? Or who I am?"

"It takes a long while to figure out another person, Jupiter."

"It takes a split second to change your mind."

"Or a few days of silence for interest to decline."

"So you sound like you're in favor of this."

"Why don't you find out if you are in favor of it?"

"I don't want to screw this one up." A machine-gun-like exchange.

She said, "That might not be up to you."

"You're right. So far, most of it seems up to her."

"Dynamic young woman?"
Dynamic? Jesus Christ. "A steamroller."

***

Daily he swam through lows and highs; afternoon was often low. Sitting on the couch waiting for a proper hour when he could stir together his solitary dinner, he fell into a dream, a deep, heavy-weighted slumber, self-aware but immobilizing. He sat there beside himself, a second person watching the first snore. The gray short man beside him lolled his head, snored some, and rolled his head back onto the couch bolster, his mouth hanging open and slack. Soon Matt might even drool, and he would have to watch that too. Jupiter could sense the dream starting in the brainstem and rising up through randomly firing neurons of the brain to lodge behind Matthew's forehead. It was Estelle. Matthew and Estelle were locked together in a pew. Both Jupiter and Matthew hated church.

Pity this man dreaming—the service hadn't even begun. No friends or acquaintances sat near them, so Estelle was speaking in a furious tone.

"It's irresponsible. You could have consulted me."

"Sssh, they'll hear you."

"God Himself hears it all anyway, Matthew. Of all the stupid decisions."

"He's growing up, Estelle. He and I know that. Only you don't."

This was the wrong thing to say. The ceiling in the church changed to the canopy of a gas station, raining down blue fluorescence. It was early evening.

"I know you don't leave a ten-year-old at home alone."

He observed how the light made her skin very shiny. "You got left home alone all the time. Both your parents worked."

A spider walked across her thigh, and he watched her brush at it in irritation.

Her voice grew sharper. "Ugh. I hate bugs. You did this to spite me, just to ruin the day."

"Sssh. Let's not argue here."

Three more spiders walked down the pew towards her—she squashed them with short brutal gestures. "As if you care about here."

90

She wiped spider juice off onto his pants leg.

She was right; he didn't care about here, especially since it was only a gas station. He had thought only to use the holiness of the sanctuary to deflect her venomous glare and angry head twitching, semaphores and signals to all the other church goers that she was angry with him. He was staring at a rack of oilcans. It was easier than gazing upon her anger. "Maybe we can talk about it later, after the service, after everyone has filled up."

"I like having him here, with me, in church. He kills the spiders for his mother. You decided it by yourself because you knew; you knew I would say no."

"Yes, that's true. You're right. Let's talk about it after the service. Listen, they're starting up."

But it wasn't the organ music or even pop music trickling out of the canopy speakers. It was distant sirens. In the dream, Jupiter knew with certainty where they were, those fire trucks. He stood up in the pew, turned to face his house. Right there across the dead grass, he watched it burn. He couldn't move. He was frozen in fear.

***

All Thursday afternoon, he was on edge, pacing back and forth. In the early evening Jupiter improved a bit because he was busy in the kitchen making up salads, throwing together an antipasto tray, and prepping the rest of dinner. Once that was done and the plates, silverware, and napkins lay on the breakfast bar—he felt the jitters coursing through his shoulders. This juvenile reaction would have been amusing and ironic if he didn't have a headache coming on. He felt the dampness of sweat under his arms, and took a sniff. He smelled more like a hardworking farmer than a cosmopolitan ad man. He scurried through the shower hoping she wouldn't arrive while he was washing, then hoping she wouldn't arrive while he was wet, then arrive while he was dry but naked, then while half-dressed, then dressed but not ready. What an idiot not to set a time for their dinner!

She called at seven. "Hi, it's me. I'm slipping out now. Be there in five minutes."

"Okay." There was a click in his ear.

"Slipping out" sounded so secretive, as if she was crawling out her window and hopping over the fence in the back yard, meeting up with the bad boy from across town.

When Kate drove up to the grain elevator, he was standing at the gate at the top of the freight elevator. He was trying to appear casual rather than eager—just there rather than hovering around. She arrived at the top, pushed the cage gate up, and glided towards him. He stepped forward. She leaned into his shoulder from a step away and kissed the air. Her hair did smell of shampoo and something else quite charming.

"You need some lights down there. Am I late? Did you miss me? Tell me I look good."

He stepped back and scanned her from head to toe. She was wearing a big black coat, but under that she wore a shimmery top, jeans, and heels. "You look really good, especially for a grain elevator. But the shoes make you taller than me."

"Yeah, I am taller than you, and don't you forget it. Let's see this attic you live in. The whole town is curious about it. Is it ultramodern, or did you go for the gothic vampire style?"

He escorted her across the bridge and up the stairs to the head house, through the steel door into the warmly lit hall.

"The floors are polished stained concrete. To the right is the kitchen. You'll see plenty of that later since I don't have a dining room. Straight ahead is the living room."

Kate gave a gasp as they walked in to a glowing white cube thirty by forty feet.

"As you see, I used the fact the room is two floors high. Or rather, there is a twenty by twenty cutout in the ceiling where the old equipment stuck up." He pointed. "There's a balcony running around up there on all four sides."

"No railings?"

"I haven't gotten to those yet. I might re-use the old ones."

"And, Matt, what are those?" She was pointing at the windows.

"We had to cut through concrete to set windows. I wanted north light, you know, artist light. I wanted them big."

"No, I'm serious. What are they?"

"Well, they're eleven patio doors I bought from your dad."

Jupiter flinched that he had reminded her about the extra

complications behind their dinner date. "He got them used from a contractor who had them stored away before he went broke. Six on this floor and five up there. I could have squeezed in seven each, but the balance wouldn't have been right."

"Recycler, huh? Let's hope the kitchen didn't get ripped out of an old trailer. I like your couches, and the bookcases are nice. What's this?" She picked up a Lucite plaque from the nearest bookcase.

"Oh, that's an award for the biggest ego in my class."

"No, it's not. It says here it's for doubling market share in the Tribeca Area, wherever that is."

"See, I told you it was for the biggest ego."

She set it down and picked up another one.

"This one says it's for The Francesca Launch—A Premier Campaign And A Singular Success."

"Francesca is a women's razor."

"I know what a Francesca is. We shave out here in the boonies."

"We opened in fifteen metropolitan markets simultaneously and sold twenty-five million razors the first year. It got bigger later on."

"You make razors?"

"No, I sell razors, and soda pop, health food, fat-saturated potato chips, and sour mash whiskey. Oh, and sexy underwear."

"My God, who would have believed it? You're a huckster."

"Not just any huckster—an award-winning huckster, with clients who have no faith in their own products. Who are therefore slobberingly grateful when they finally get some sales."

"Nice gig."

"You know it." Jupiter walked over to the wooden cabinet in the corner and said, "Would you like a drink?"

"And is this part of an ad campaign too?"

"I think it's more of a peace offering. I have wine, Scotch, bourbon, gin, vodka, and some horrible green stuff from Japan."

"Hmm, not Japanese. I'll have a red wine."

He uncorked a bottle, poured, and took it to her. "It's not Italian. Dinner will be Italian."

As soon as she had the wine stem in her fingers, he retreated to the kitchen, rechecked everything, got himself a glass of water, and returned.

"You're not drinking?"

93

"I have to chop parsley. I want to keep all my fingers."

He also wanted to keep his Prozac option open.

Kate walked to the far end of the room and halted to peer through the windows into the dark. Jupiter was standing on the far side of the room, alone in the space.

He coughed, "Would you like to see the rest of the place?"

When she nodded, he opened the door on the west wall leading into the darkened office and waited there for her. Kate sashayed across the room. She crossed very close to him and paused at the threshold. Then she stepped through into the dark and stood still. He followed, taking the opportunity to press lightly against her and hit the master switch. The room lit, clicked, hummed, and flickered its screens at them.

"This is the office. I purport to work here. Mostly I stare out the window at Amarillo."

"I know the feeling."

"That door leads to the roof. You can't escape that way."

"Good to know. What's upstairs?" She turned and popped back out into the main space.

Jupiter led the way up two flights of narrow concrete stairs. She followed him up. Off the landing he opened another steel industrial door.

"Here's where I keep the TV and other narcotics."

She stepped into a room without windows to find a leather couch identical to the ones below, a flat screen television, and a cabinet full of DVDs. He showed her the console with the rest of the equipment. "Sorry, no Danish B&O high-chic equipment, just Korean components from the mall."

Next door he and his contractors had built a guest bath and two diminutive bedrooms. "In case my children happen to visit."

"You have children?"

"Alas, no. But if I did, they would be younger than you."

His left arm jerked. Not younger by much, if at all. Why did he remind her?

"So you have many guests?"

"Actually not... not ever. You are the first visitor not carrying a hammer or a screwdriver, as you'll see when you sign the guest book. I think the bedrooms are here because we had the space."

"And the master?"

"Down a flight. Over the kitchen."

They clopped down a flight, walked around the balcony, and he opened the door. She went in to the center of the room and gazed around. Jupiter had stapled up a curtain of plastic, from ceiling to floor, to mask off the end of the room. He had placed a large bed against a blank wall. There was a door leading to the master bath and a closet. Stacks of books lay on the floor around the bed. He waited while she walked into the closet, shuffled some of the hangers, and inspected his clothes.

She said as she was coming back, "Interesting touch—the curtain. What's the space behind it going to be?"

She bounced the corner of the bed with her hand.

He was still standing in the doorway, ten feet away from her. "I don't know yet. Maybe a pawnshop. Maybe a dance floor."

He retreated to the living room, and she followed. Jupiter turned on some more of the floor lamps. She sat on the couch nearest the windows, and he perched on the armrest at the couch's far end and faced her.

She sipped her wine. "Funny, your coming here to Aniline now. You were nearly too late."

"How's that?"

"You could have missed me. I've been wanting to leave. In fact, I might leave Aniline this very night. But not this second. I'll wait to get my dinner."

The thought of her leaving already pulled at him; he frowned. "Another story about the young fleeing to the big city?"

"You fled. One of those plaques—the tawdry brass one over there, I think—says that you were something or other in New York."

"Everyone has a story."

"Give me the one-minute version."

She leaned toward him, ready to listen, inviting him in.

"I had a privileged upper-middle-class upbringing in an exclusive Amarillo neighborhood—all white at the time and very self-important. I graduated at the top of my class, which after all is not much of an accomplishment when someone has to every year in every school. Then Columbia in New York City where I partied my way through, but less partying than everyone below me in the list. After graduation, I stumbled on a job in Manhattan doing advertising. I started low in the company, Vice President, if I remember. Of course we were a three man firm

95

counting the receptionist."

"The receptionist was a man?"

"Yes. And gay. No affairs in the office I'm afraid."

Kate leaned back on her armrest watching Jupiter who had restlessly shifted across the room. "So you started at the top."

"And at the bottom, too."

"I'd like to start closer to the top than the bottom."

"The view is often better."

"Not much view in Aniline," she said.

"What view do you want? What's this flight reflex really all about?"

"I don't want to go to bed every night for the rest of my life smelling like French fries."

"Uh, good point."

Kate gave him the serious face, eyebrows drawn down and mouth resolute. "I tell you, Matt, I have to get out of this town. But when I go, I'm not going to end up waiting a counter somewhere or processing forms in some office. I have to become myself, not get lost in the machine."

"Helps to have a dream, Kate." That comment went both ways as advice and gentle sarcasm.

"Don't laugh. I think it's this real estate thing. I can get some credentials before I leave town. Mayor Sharp is starting a new commercial space next to his proposed motel—or at any rate he's applied to the Council for zoning waivers. That would be a chance to do more than residential real estate; the town followers will want to build all around him. But sometimes, I don't know. Realty. It seems so uncreative."

She pulled an ugly, minute mouth, then smiled to make up for it. "I've already done all the course work for a license, and it was horrible. Boring. And then what, driving people around to see lots while you smile, smile, smile?"

"Don't like smiling?"

"Don't like fake."

"Creative. What have you done before that you liked?"

"I went to school at SMU. School had some good patches."

"What was your major?"

"I won't tell anyone, not even you. I did carry a minor in Fashion and Decoration. I enjoyed that a lot, especially where I could pull things together, jam strange things side-by-side, and make your eyes pop."

Kate and he were also jammed side-by-side, disparate, vibrating. "Then maybe design, or graphics or even..." here he paused and shuddered, "...advertising. Just don't tell me you want to be an actress."

"Do you know anyone in design?"

"Yes. All are my age and running things. The men are fat-old-uncle types, and the women are fire-breathing dragons."

A timer rang in the kitchen.

"Come on in to dinner and I'll promise you interviews with them all, in return for eating my food and drinking my wine. It's a small thing to ask."

Once he had her in the kitchen, he sensed he was relaxing, perhaps. She settled at the breakfast bar, and he worked in the main kitchen space on the other side, so there was a bulky cabinet and countertop to protect him. He had something to do with his hands, and she had the antipasto. He opened another bottle of wine, a white, and fished out two glasses. He decided to give up on the Prozac and drained his first glass quickly.

Jupiter set out his opening salvo, a salad. "This is admittedly out of sequence. In Italy, salad should occur between the first and second main courses. But it's a Texas tradition to start with a salad."

"I like your dressing, scrumptious. Out of a bottle?"

"No. It's olive oil, white balsamic vinegar, and a bit of mustard for an emulsifier. Salt and white pepper."

"I don't dare ask what an emulsifier is."

"Smart. The details are boring."

He progressed her to a small pasta, fragrant with orange zest, and followed with a diminutive swordfish steak.

"Don't I get more than one thing at a time?"

"It's the only way I can delay your departure."

She held her fork out at him and stared over it. "What a sauce!"

"Good, or bad?"

"Definitely good."

He went then to the second main, a bit of veal under lemon. He opened another bottle of wine to go with it—a sweeter, rounder red. The room smelled like a bistro; he should have set out a red tablecloth and candles.

They finished with ice cream topped with raspberries, and he offered coffee. When she accepted, he brewed up two espressos and set one before her.

Kate reached across the breakfast bar and touched the back of his hand.

She said matter-of-factly, "Let's take these upstairs. And the white wine too—I really liked that."

Jupiter jumped up like the seat had ejected him. "Okay. Do we need a tray?"

"Nah." She had two wine glasses and a bottle in her hands. She turned away from him and jumped off the stool. He spilled half of an espresso over the counter and decided to leave it.

"Come along now," she instructed.

Jupiter followed her out of the kitchen and to the stairs where she went up ahead of him. He hadn't even touched her yet, not really, but here she was purposely walking into his bedroom. Things like this never happened to him. He was Jupiter, not Gilgamesh.

***

After, in the light that trickled in through the bathroom door, they lay facing each other.

"Not bad, Matt, especially for someone so old. I've had much worse evenings. I'd even rank you in my top twenty-five percent."

"Has anyone ever told you that you have a direct and blunt, even a rude way of talking?"

"Oh, shut up."

"No, really. Has anyone ever mentioned this tiny flaw?"

"My high school counselor. That was at the end of the session where she suggested I major in home economics, or as she called it, Domestic Education and Nutrition."

"Well, bear it in mind. The counselor was probably not the first, and I won't be the last to point out this characteristic."

"Speaking of lasting—care to go again?"

He replied, "Be gentle this time. I am easily bruised."

***

As he and Kate untangled themselves and dragged the sheets back onto the bed, the rain fell hard. Thunder, lightning, and an inch of downpour separated her from her own bed. After the midnight decision when she resolved to stay, she slept while he slipped in and out of consciousness and listened to the storm's aftermath. In the half-light, he watched her shoulders and the back of her head as she lay on her side. She had absurdly light and delicate shoulders, partially concealed by her tangled hair. He filled himself with a great affection for those shoulders and for the graceful back below. Sentimentality, a crush, a silly thing for a man his age. He didn't care.

Gilgamesh King in Uruk

Chapter Eleven: Top of the World Tonight

Unable to sleep, he left Kate behind and tramped downstairs. He retrieved the laptop and woke it up. Gilgamesh waited there, had started before him.

"ur-Jupiter, I summon you. Let us talk again."

Talk, to a dead king, or to a delusion in his own mind? "Where are you? What time is it?"

"It is in the one hundred and twentieth year of my reign. Of course, you may be asking a more unremarkable question. It is the hour before all others arise and begin the day. I have walked the roof of the palace and seen the Ziggurat rising behind, a deeper blackness. I sit in my room of scribes. A single bowl of oil burns to light the records and the work around me."

One hundred and twenty years; six more before death. "And you are alone?"

"Other rooms hold the royal family strung like beads along the corridor. My servants whisper in the hall outside the curtain, but the King is indeed alone."

"I am also in a room of scribes, before a table where I keep records of the fifth king of Uruk, read through many times."

"And are you alone?"

Jupiter cast his eyes up at the concrete ceiling towards the bed that held Kate. "Maybe more alone now than yesterday. The unattainable woman is here tonight."

Jupiter saw Gilgamesh drop his head, confer his approval with a sharp little nod.

"Excellent. The time of swordplay, of amorous battle and sighs of combat."

The warrior king—all life and love a metaphor of fighting. "The little death."

"We understand each other."

"I understand her less now than yesterday. I confess, women amaze and surprise me." And command me.

"I would not like the court to know, but I am also puzzled by women." Gilgamesh paused. "Let me tell you of one. She could have been the best for me, the one who knew my depths most perfectly."

"Inanna? Utnapishtim's angelic wife? Danu? Siduri?"

"The last in your short list, Siduri."

Jupiter could see Gilgamesh peer into the dark corner of the room, could see his forehead crease into three vertical slashes as he brought back a memory.

"She lived by the gardens of the gods, you know, beside the waters of death."

"I remember some of her story. She made wine and owned a tavern. She comforted all with that magical wine."

"It was sacred liquor made in golden vats and bowls. I have never tasted the like again."

Jupiter grinned. He and Gilgamesh, united in a love of wine, a puzzlement over women. "You didn't get along at first."

"Well, no. She barred her door. I had been in the desert for some time. I appeared at the gate with the stink of animal skins and the sweat of man, and hair like a thunderstorm. And she was young, half my age, made like the jewels in the nearby gardens."

Half his age. "Locked the gate, did she?"

"I must have looked like a bandit, a murderer from across the sands. But to deny Gilgamesh? I talked her into it. She unbarred the gate and took me in."

Jupiter smirked. "A woman's pity. Why do you say she was the one of all the women you have known?"

"We did not conjoin. Instead, she listened to me and held me through the night and the day."

Jupiter said, "All through your life, women have helped you and seldom have you heeded them or regarded them well." His words were harsh. He wished he were able to retract those words.

"Maybe I should have been softer, like you. It is true I did not heed Siduri. She heard my tale and comforted me. Enkidu, my only friend among men had died, leaving me bereft. Siduri listened through all my talk and grief and did not judge."

Judge. Jupiter stared at the word. Guilt. Gilgamesh was not alone in guilt. "You may gaze back longingly to Siduri now, but Enkidu was your true companion, your one great love, the wild man made for you by the gods."

"I was not a lover of men. Siduri understood that. Siduri carried away my guilt over Enkidu's life and his death. She was wise beyond measure."

Jupiter sat still over the keys. Not homosexuality—autoeroticism maybe. Gilgamesh loved himself in another. "And did she turn your life around?"

"No. I was blind. I saw Enkidu's death as the sign of the gods—I was merely mortal. I would die, will die. She could lessen the pain of his death but not the pain of mine."

Jupiter frowned. "It's the message of the Epic, Gilgamesh. But why did you desire immortality so much?"

"This is inexplicable to me also, now that I am an aged man. Perhaps... maybe I thought I, of all men, should have it. I was not just a warrior. I was not merely a king. My mother was a goddess, and I was two thirds divine myself. I deserved it. That is what I thought."

"Siduri couldn't talk you out of it?"

"No, though she was right. I am fated to 'eat, drink, and make love before Death overtakes me,' to live the best life man can have."

Simple love, family and duty are all the proper pursuits of a mortal. And was pursuit of Kate proper? "Siduri let you go then?"

"On across the waters of death to Utnapishtim and to failure. I always meant to go back, to ask her to come to Uruk."

"The perfect woman, lost to you?"

"Perhaps I understand the story better myself now that I have spoken it aloud. And what will you speak aloud to your unattainable one, ur-Jupiter?"

"I'll ask her to stay for breakfast. I'll ask her to make a small hole in her life for me."

"It is still night there in your world. Go back to your woman, ur-

Jupiter, if you will have her. You must win her—not settle for gnawing out small holes. Be the man, not the rodent."

Jupiter closed the laptop and held it between his palms for a moment. "It is still night in your world." Could Gilgamesh see into his universe?

Then he got up and shuffled back upstairs to the stranger in his bed.

Chapter Twelve: Ishtar

They awoke to a diluvium world. They stood barefoot and in bathrobes in a puddle on the roof, tousled by the wind from the backside of the squall. He was cold. They leaned on a rail, hips pushed together, shoulders touching. There wasn't much to see out there in the dark of a storm morning. The fresh smell of a clean sky whipped around them. He wondered why they were standing in the open, occasionally being spattered by remnant rain, but he didn't voice his doubts.

She said, "Now see what you did, too nasty to go out."

"Not grammatical and not fair. Even if I ran the weather, I was otherwise occupied, having my ego inflated."

"Inflated… that's what you call that physical reaction?"

"Tcha! No need to be vulgar."

"I thought we both did a masterfully good job of demonstrating vulgarity. You, in particular, were very vulgar."

"Fortunately, no one was watching."

"I was."

He said, "We could always turn out the lights."

"And miss the close-ups? Are you hungry?"

He was beginning to learn her rhythms or lack of them—the wild jump to the new subject, the right-hand turn into a non sequitur.

He gave what she wanted, nodding. "I can see I'll have to feed you breakfast. You're getting to be an expensive proposition."

She slapped him on the rear as she turned for the door. "More double entendre? You have a one-track mind."

"Regretfully not. Before your arrival last week, I had given up on my one-track and any chance for a romance."

105

He trailed behind her through the door into the office wondering if this "following about" would become a habit. "So should I get back on track and act the suitor's part?"

"Oh, hush up. Don't worry much about me. I'll let you know when I'm interested, and when you are, for that matter."

Yes, he was in explicit danger of tagging along behind her, waiting for cues. In the kitchen they both moved more easily than they had last night. She prepared coffee and poured out juice but made no move towards the range. After a moment's thought, he reduced the leftover raspberries into a compote and made waffles. It wasn't quiet, the click of fork on plate, the slurp he gave the coffee cup, but there was no talk during the food.

She wiped her mouth, "That was good. Better than Angie's. You ought to get a job as a short-order cook with us."

"That would take the pleasure out of it."

"You are focused on the pleasure side, aren't you?"

"A regular sybarite."

"Is that a treatable condition?"

He considered. "Sometimes the patient doesn't want to get better."

"Hmm. Terminal sybaritis, death by pleasure. Well, I better get home. I have to put in an appearance before work, run through the shower, and tell my mom it's none of her business where I was. You know."

"Can't say I was ever in your position when I was living with my folks."

"You got it backwards. They're living with me."

"Oh."

"I've got to get my clothes on. Come on up with me."

He followed her up the stairs. He lagged three steps back, stared up at her bare legs ahead of him, and watched her get dressed.

***

He lay alone in the bed, not wearing his usual paisley pajamas. He was cold, but pajamas weren't the right thing this morning. Outside, in the May of an emergent spring, water laid thick upon the land, flooding the ditches and drowning large stretches of the fields. He meditated idly

106

about getting up to see the sunlight on the water, but that would mean throwing off his indolence and pulling on some clothes. Sooner or later, though, he would have to get up. Jupiter dropped back into sleep and dreamt.

***

Jimmy Devereaux. James. Jim. Little Jim. Buddy. Bud. All his short life, Estelle and Matthew hadn't known what to call him. He lived as the ambiguous child in a black and white marriage. The slight, blond boy who always twisted away, always recoiled at the sound of the angry voices around him. Later they would remember him as scuttling down the hall, squeezed against the wall, ducking around the doorjamb to avoid them.

Matthew wanted to send Jim to pre-school. They were sitting in their living room, the hall running away into the house, framed by a giant empty TV shell. They both stared at the TV, arms crossed, necks pulled in. The TV showed Jimmy on his bicycle rolling down the hall. Three inches of water covered the floor. It was cold.

Estelle said, "No, let him stay here another year. Let him comfort his mother in her loneliness."

Matthew couldn't think of anyone who needed comforting less, and he said so. Perversely, feeling this was the moment he would lose the argument, he continued. "Jimmy needs socialization, needs to see other kids. He needs to get out of this God-forsaken house." He noticed that the house was more of a stable and that straw was scattered across the floor, soaking up the water.

"The House that Matthew built."

"C'mon Estelle, the change will do him good. And you can get out more, too. It will free up your day." He pawed his back hoof, clanging his shoe against the concrete beneath.

"I don't want my day freed up. I want my son."

"He's my foal, too."

"Lucky him. It's a shame I was such a good girl. Maybe Jimmy would have had a chance to grow up strong and tall if I had messed around and gotten him a different stud. Not every boy gets stuck with a Shetland as a father."

The insult laid in the room like a rotting manure heap.

Matthew needed to hurt her, but he wouldn't kick her. He raised his voice instead. "There she is again, the slut in virgin's clothes, trotted out for shock value. You may dream of a better man, Estelle, but you would never commit to another person long enough to get your clothes off, much less get up in the saddle."

"Not like you, mounting those broad-assed high school girls down at the parts store."

"As if I'd have the energy after my second job. But yes, I'd like to have a sex life, you frigid mare."

"You are a walking sack of disappointment." She held up a feed sack full of manure.

"And you're like your momma—the lowest form of life in the neighborhood, and a drunk on top of it."

Estelle screamed at him as she ran into the bedroom, and was still shrieking as she ran out with his .32 pistol. She waved it in the air between them as anger and bitterness poured out of her mouth.

It was his fault, he knew. He couldn't suppress the words that erupted next. "Go ahead and shoot, you stinking donkey. Anything is better than living in the same house as you."

The gun exploded. He cringed, expecting to be smashed by the blow of the bullet. Nothing happened.

The ringing in his ears subsided and the cordite dissipated from the air between them. They stared wide-eyed at each other, and her hand covered her mouth. The gun dropped to the floor, splashed into the water.

Behind him there was a burbling sound. Estelle's face collapsed into animal panic as she stared past him. Matthew didn't understand.

Jupiter woke up sitting propped against the headboard. Tears were running down his face, burning him. He understood what Matthew had not.

108

Chapter Thirteen: A Regular Sybarite

Pretending a healthy diet, Jupiter brought a bowl of dip and a bag of vegetable chips into the living room. He dropped onto the leather cushion and picked up the laptop from the table. The screen showed no new message from his hallucination.

He started. "You do know you had a problem with women?"

"Not enough women?"

"A joke, a forty-seven-hundred-year-old joke! No, you had a serious problem. You were a rapist."

Jupiter envisioned Gilgamesh flapping his hand. "That old story. All the kings in all the cities get bad marks for what is dutiful, occasional, and sometimes not enjoyable. I wasn't even around that often. I found it much more fun to take the troops out on a border dispute or irritate the ruler of Kish."

"Sorry to bring the bad news, but people preferred you out of town."

"You speak an ugly thought. This accusation of rape is about the king's right to the bridal night. Seldom exercised."

"Why not? Or why?"

"Perhaps it is different in your empire, but a king's sexual performance enhances his reputation. It helps him maintain his perilous grasp on power. I chose the brides who were the most attractive and from the most influential families. Some had already signaled their willingness. Some were taken by force, but it was necessary."

Jupiter considered this, sexual domination as power—hmm. This was unimaginable in his business, but elsewhere in Amarillo—of course. "So you avoided the unwashed and the lowly."

"Uruk is a large city. A king had to set his priorities."

Jupiter saw the frown, heard the defensiveness. "Let me point out

Enkidu didn't like your behavior either."

"That is certain truth. He challenged me his first day in Uruk. I remember it so well. Mid-evening had brought a coolness across the city. I felt randy, and I pursued my king's right. The inner court and I had gone forth to find the daughter of my chief scribe. We ambled down an avenue, then the girl's uncle—a gross sycophant, I would say—directed us into a street and then into a passage. I left the others hanging back beneath their torches. And there at the gate was no bridegroom, no bride, just a savage man from the savage out-lands."

"Enkidu?"

"Of course, who else? He spoke harshly to me, worse than anything you have said. Do not forget, I should have fed you to the vultures by now."

"You liked his brashness, didn't you?"

Gilgamesh smiled. "Oh, yes. But then, I did not think he would live long. Such a powerful clash, a heroic brawl. He was the Natural Man, strong as the meteor fallen from heaven, and I, I am the anointed of the gods, supposedly the Pinnacle of Civilization. I speak with all due irony."

"The Epic says you two destroyed the street, broke the gate and pushed over the walls. You 'cracked and overthrew the very pavement in your struggle.'"

"Very poetic. I did win, though, when I pinned him with a wrestler's trick. And I ended my visits to the brides thereafter."

"Less work for the King."

"I am at work now, ur-Jupiter. I tour the date groves of Inanna in a chariot. It is an annual event, expected of me. And you, you are hard at work?"

Jupiter glanced around his living room. It had come on dusk and the concrete walls glowed ghost-white in the dimming light. "I recline on a giant padded bench eating the equivalent of dates."

"Life is hard for the ur-Jupiter... and now you are entangled with your Siduri."

"More like your goddess Inanna. She may turn me into a mole like Inanna did her gardener." Or shoot at me, like Estelle. "Do you ever dream, Gilgamesh?"

"Kings are not exempt from the songs of dream or the nightmares that stalk us."

"I've been having a hell of a dream."

Gilgamesh's mouth turned down in a frown, and he gazed out over the orchards. "I too dream of Hell."

"Not quite what I meant, but your hell is something to haunt a man."

"To be dragged away by the taloned beast, then to sit eating dust, locked in the murky light of Hell's caverns for all eternity."

To tell him how he ends—or to wait? "I have to ask. Why, in your theology, does Hell turn you all into birds?"

"It is an inherited belief I have never questioned. It is a fitting image. The black birds live on carrion beneath the sun and are now locked flightless in the catacombs of the dead. And your dream of Hell?"

"Hell is what you have done, not where you go afterwards. At least for me."

"You talk, I think, of regret, or remorse."

"Oh yes. Black and ugly, something like an old wound that won't heal."

Gilgamesh inclined his head. "I am listening."

"We all have done things that shame us. I killed a child." *Unbelievable. He had just revealed it, to a phantom.*

"War spills over onto civilians, even children."

Jupiter shook his head. "No, this was just an accident. A stupid thing that didn't have to happen. If I had not been locked up in my own concerns, if I had been paying attention."

"How did the child's death become this Hell for you then?"

"Screaming women. The sound of screaming women."

The Coming of Enkidu

Chapter Fourteen: Hunting Lions

Kate arrowed in on it. "You basically don't know what's going on, do you? You think this is some great romance?"

He clutched the phone. "I don't know, maybe."

"More like an affair from my viewpoint, only you're not married, are you?"

"Hmm, killing a bit of time with me, Kate?"

He hated tense conversations over the phone a small amount less than he hated tense conversations in person.

"Listen, Matt, I'm certainly attracted to you. I even enjoy the sneaking around. Don't try to make it more complicated."

"You do know how to sweet-talk me."

She replied, "I give you better than sweet talk. A casual body bang plus the secrecy."

"Yes, I have to admit there is a thrill that comes with the fear of getting caught. Still, I'm not feeling noble about this—"

"What, you'd prefer noble? Let the town in on the secret? That comes with whispers and pointing fingers."

"Gossip isn't a fatal disease. Concealment, though, cuts both ways."

"Huh?"

"Are you ashamed of me Kate?"

"Are you conceited about sleeping with a woman half your age?"

"Less than half actually."

"So you are vain about it." She sounded triumphant.

"I'm vain about being with you."

"Ah, that's sweet. What are you wearing?"

She had turned right and accelerated away from him again. He was lost. "Jeans, a sweatshirt, sandals."

"No, underneath."

"What are you talking about?"

"Phone sex. I've never tried phone sex before."

This was not serious. She certainly didn't take him seriously. "Rather than making me drop the phone to check, why don't you come over?"

"When I get there, I'll stroll past you like you're not there. I'll go to the bedroom and take my dress off and lie on the bed. I'll close my eyes."

"What are you talking about?"

"You asked that before. Under the dress, I'm wearing silk shears. Everything is on display—everything."

He was already tumescent. His sex pointed down his jeans and felt increasingly constricted. Painful. "Are you coming over, then?"

"I don't know. It's called anticipation. Now shut up and hang up."

Maybe yes, maybe no. His whole body flushed with a painful desire when he thought of her casually pulling her dress over her head and strolling towards his bed.

***

Jupiter asked his life counselor, "Marjorie, are you comfortable talking about this with me?"

He personally was nervous about it—he sloshed a little coffee into his lap. Cold, fortunately.

Her voice carried into his ear from the telephone, "Oh, absolutely. This part is much less troubling than your belief in an undead king. Sex is all about relations, and that's my business. I would think, given your own comfort levels, you would be the one who was having difficulty talking about it."

"There is that."

"Listen, Jupiter, I counsel heteros and gays and lesbians on their sex lives frequently. It's all part of the human condition, all part of life coaching. Speaking of the human condition, how's yours?"

He mentally visualized her perched on one of her futons, bent forward intent on flushing him out.

114

"Strained to the breaking point. I like the relationship with Kate, or what is more germane, I need the relationship. So far the room doesn't feel crowded. Though I admit half the time I don't know what's going on."

"Happens to everyone, Jupiter. You just talk about it at strange times."

It wasn't their regular visit, but it was daylight, not one a.m. "Strange times?"

"You caught me on the road. I'm sitting in my car in front of the grocery store."

Not drinking tea on the futon then. "Oh. Have you already shopped, or are you about to go in?"

"Not important. You're talking about Kate. How she puzzles you."

"And...."

She waited. "And?"

He shifted his weight on the couch. The leather squeaked. "And I'm disappointed. Not with the woman. I thought this would change things."

"Change things."

"Good, great shrink trick, mirroring back my words."

She didn't say anything, so he plowed on.

"I thought all this would affect me positively. I thought the normality of—carnal coupling—would kick my anxiety, if not back to zero, then at least back to levels of average uneasiness."

"And it hasn't." She said it without inflection.

Let's boast a little. "Having sex frequently, and Kate likes frequent sex, should do something for me."

"Like what?"

"Oh, I don't know, reduce the headaches, the insomnia and the claustrophobia."

"Sex is all about you and Kate. The headaches are yours alone."

"Oh joy."

"Have you told her what's going on with you?"

"Are you kidding? I'm lucky she looks at me at all."

"This is the point where I give you the self-esteem pep talk, but I suspect you'd catch on. What does she know?"

"Not much. I've alibied the shakes by blaming too much coffee. She thinks I visit the café in the late afternoon to see her when she has more time, not because the diner is deserted then."

Marjorie moderated her voice, "So, you're relying on deceit to maintain the relationship?"

She had him. He ground the phone into his ear. "Still, the sex is astonishing, and my head doesn't journey off into strangeness during the act itself."

"Jupiter, you can't hide your problem behind this selfishness. You know the answer, so tell me."

"Marjorie, you are a demanding woman. What you want me to say is I can't be honest with myself unless I'm honest with her. Until then, the shakes aren't going away."

"Oh, Jup, you are a smart man."

***

Perhaps the ongoing adventure with Kate opened Jupiter up to being more impulsive, or stupid. He forgot to think about consequences when he goaded the Mayor once again. He had been mulling over the potential new Sharp real estate development Kate had mentioned, and he doubted he would like it. He figured a new motel close to the Interstate would be a standard cinderblock place, ugly even by Aniline standards. Then it occurred to him how to turn this his way. He downloaded the advertising brochure for the Quaker Square Inn in Akron and printed it out. He added a cover note on his stationary, writing, "Grain elevators make quite dramatic hotels, don't you think?" He signed it, addressed it to Mayor Nelson Taggert Sharp, c/o Aniline Town Hall, and mailed it off that day.

As the envelope left his hand and dropped into the Post Office slot, he regretted it. *I shouldn't have started up this skirmish. I don't need this complication. If the Mayor thinks he's in commercial competition with me, he'll squash me like a bug.*

Still, he chortled at the idea of the Mayor having an apoplectic seizure at his desk.

***

A new discovery, a new disaster. Jupiter had always had problems

116

with mice and bats in the old building, and he suspected he had other denizens as yet unknown, perhaps feral cats or even termites. Not all discoveries are that pleasant or work out well for the explorer. Later he wished it had been a cat.

At first, he underestimated the danger of this newfound wildlife. He was halfway on the journey before he saw the peril. He encountered the first signs at the grain silo next door where he parked his car. Jupiter now locked up his garage without fail. He believed he acted with cleverness, preventing some drifter from sleeping in his car. His hands were clean; he had no risk of confrontation. He hadn't thought of the vagrant being clever—until he discovered his invader had removed the bolts on a small hatch on the back side of the silo and leaned the lid against the coaming. Where did his vagrant get the wrench? Probably from his own toolbox on the work floor.

Interesting. He could have Heldritch recommend a welder and close the hatch permanently. He could lock the car to deny a homeless person any sleep on elegant leather seats. He could set out some sort of tests or traps to see how clever his drifter could be.

At that point, he decided to damp down his suburban white guilt about homeless people and do nothing. He told himself, *It's not so bad to have a poor person living nearby, and it would be cold-hearted to try and force that person to move on. Watching and waiting is doing something.*

Nonetheless, it made him uncomfortable. He liked being alone and felt jumpy with the idea eyes might be peering out at him from behind his collectibles and junk.

On a morning in late May, coming in from his walk with White, he caught sight of a small figure running out through the work floor away from the office. A child hanging around the elevator? Maybe a teenaged boy in an oversized coat and a ball cap? Distracted he got out a bowl of food for White and noticed the sack was emptying out quickly. He had been feeding his vagrant with mediocre dog kibble.

In a pensive mood, he climbed the ladder rungs up to the distribution floor, went into his kitchen, and made some coffee. Cup in hand, Jupiter thumped down on one of his couches to think. To the northeast the last part of the dawn lit some high, shredded clouds and turned them the impossible colors of a Renaissance painting. While Jupiter watched the color fade and the day approach, he sorted out his few choices. He could pretend there was no homeless teenager out there, and he could go on as before—the "blind-eye" approach. He had been using the blind-eye approach up until this point, and it wasn't working out well. The teenager could be dangerous to the elevator. Worst case, the boy could set fire to the work floor or the contents of the storage silo trying to stay warm. And burn up Jupiter's home.

There was a second choice—the path of legitimacy and good citizenship. He could inform the Chief of Police and cast this problem onto the Town. The "not-my-problem" approach. He didn't like this path. He could muster up the stomach to do it, however. Good fallback.

He could make another choice, the more interesting. He could take the risky route and try to make a connection with this adolescent. It would start with a conversation. He would talk to the boy and find out the circumstances. Then he'd call Child Protective Services. This depended on the teenager trusting him enough to be betrayed. He reasoned, *I could do that. Right up an ad man's alley.*

He went out to the loading dock at the end of the grain elevator and stared about. He cupped his hands and shouted, "Come on out and talk. I know you're out there."

This was casting a stone at random. He didn't know why anyone would answer the call. No response.

So, Jupiter would have to catch the boy, if he were to follow the risky third path. Bait and a snare. Once the child was caught, the responsibility for the boy would lie with Jupiter, if only for a while. All of the baggage coming with a vagrant underage runaway would temporarily be his. *You can't just keep a boy.*

He knew if and when others learned what he was doing, the situation would become volatile. Danger, Jupiter. They're going to think pedophile. No wife, no children, guilty even before the gossip started. Child molester. Christ.

There was also Kate. Would she oppose the scheme? She might fight the idea of a wild child metaphorically hiding in the basement. He suspected she didn't have a maternal bone in her body.

He wished he had someone who would talk him out of this impulse. Marjorie wasn't the one; she would want to delve into his motives and "where" he was today, not keep him from his own decisions. He considered calling his ex-wife in Hawaii—that was a horrid idea. Sheila's judgment hadn't proven to be that good in the past; after all, she had married him. He pondered discussing it with the Heldritchs, either singly or together. That could be embarrassing. He even considered calling his doctor, Ben Cransto. He already knew how that conversation would go.

Sorting out options could take awhile, and it might be a waste of time. He laughed, knowing he had already made up his mind. He went in the kitchen, made oatmeal, and poured a glass of milk. Taking an old saucepan and a saucer, he carried all down to the work floor and out to the far end, near the steel silo where the teenager had been sleeping. He set the bowl down on the loading dock, covered it with the saucepan, and set the milk nearby with the saucer on top.

That evening he checked but the food hadn't been touched, even though the milk had been turned over by something. Probably a rodent. The next morning he renewed the bait with a fresh breakfast. By noon it was gone. That evening he left a plate of sandwiches and a can of coke out under a soup pot. The next morning, he set the breakfast out inside the work floor between the first two grain bins. That third day, he spent a lot of time up on the distribution floor, doing little except listening and gazing idly out the windows. Two or three times he believed he heard rustling down on the dark work floor.

He and the wild one now shared a pattern. With each meal, Jupiter brought the food closer to the freight elevator. He shortened the distance to a minimum and set breakfast in front of the freight elevator. Now he was close to springing the trap. He went to town and bought some things. At noon, he took them out to his car and removed the ratty old blanket. In return he left soap, a toothbrush, toothpaste, a jug of water, a towel and a cheap sleeping bag. Jupiter also left a note, "The bathroom by the office works. There's no hot water, sorry."

The day after this gesture, he left no breakfast. Instead he placed a note under a rock in the freight elevator, "Come up for breakfast. I'll make waffles. No traps, no tricks."

Of course it was a lie. It didn't work, but the next morning, after missing two meals, his wild one walked into the trap.

Even though it was still a coolish morning in May, he left his house door open to the distribution floor. Jupiter sat at the breakfast bar with

119

his cereal and coffee and listened. Soon he heard the elevator clanking, then the squeak of the gate going up. Someone shuffled on the stairs. After an excruciating wait, he heard some movement in the hallway. A face peeked around the corner of the door, and seeing Jupiter, jerked back.

He said in an even tone, "I'll start the waffles now."

He stood up slow and, turning his back on his visitor, started pouring batter across a warm waffle iron. He took his time, listening to see if the boy had slid into the room. Working methodically, he made up a breakfast while giving the teenager time to get accustomed to the set-up and to him. Jupiter heard a bar stool scrape on the concrete.

When he turned around with a plate of waffles, a boy still wearing a long, oversized coat and a cap sat at his breakfast bar, watching him warily. He set the plate in front of the teenager, poured a glass of milk, and set down a bottle of syrup. The adolescent drizzled out the syrup, seized the fork in a rigid grip, and started eating. Jupiter sat down, picked up his coffee cup, and sipped. The boy chomped intensively, head down; only then did Jupiter finally stare at him. Dirty face, blotched with dust and yellowish in shade. A streak of bright orange ran from the left corner of his mouth towards his ear. Too much hair, chopped ragged at the ends. He was short and small behind the breakfast bar. Jupiter thought back to how the teenager had appeared in the doorway, about five foot two or three, dirty hands and black fingernails, nothing visible about the clothes except the coat. He had good teeth, white and straight, delicate features—wasn't going to grow up to look like a Neanderthal. He was nervous about eye contact with Jupiter; he kept his gaze averted, but Jupiter could see his eyes were blue. He twitched at every unexpected sound, including a coffee cup scraping on the counter. Could be from twelve to fifteen years old. Still, what judge was he of teenagers and their development?

When the boy had finished the plate and was sweeping up the remnants of syrup with his index finger, Jupiter asked, "Would you like another one?"

With his finger in his mouth, he nodded yes.

Jupiter stood up, took the plate, and made another waffle. Setting it down, he said, "Drink your milk."

The boy jumped as if he had been stung, but did reach out and take the glass.

Jupiter let him start eating the waffle; then he spoke quietly. "Here's the deal. I won't call the authorities. The door there, to the stairs, will be unlocked at mealtime. You can sleep anywhere you want except up here—the car is fine. You can clean up downstairs or up here. But…." He stopped.

The kid twitched his gaze from the plate to the wall on the left. "But what?"

"I want to know your name. Your first and last name."

The boy climbed off of the bar stool and backed towards the door. "No way."

He stood there in the door, half in and half out of the room, about to run.

Jupiter shrugged, "Think it over. You can tell me tomorrow if we have a deal. Sandwiches will be down in the office tonight."

***

The next morning when Jupiter returned from his four miles and struggled up the ladder, he discovered the kid in his kitchen. He first poured milk and orange juice, setting both down in front of the teenager. As he walked behind the adolescent, the boy flinched. Jupiter did too, hit by a strong smell of unclean humanity. Jupiter started his own coffee and then made breakfast: ham and scrambled eggs with toast on the side. During all the preparation, he kept his back to the boy as much as possible. He set plates down in front of both of them, and they picked up forks. The boy attacked the food, and as he shoveled in egg, he mumbled, "Bby, Inskt. Burby."

"What? I didn't catch that."

The boy stared past him at the wall, swallowed, and decided to trust Jupiter, just this little bit. Staring down at the counter, the boy mumbled in a high voice, "Bobbie Inskeep. That's my name."

"Are you going to school Bobbie?"

"That's not part of the deal. You said just my name."

"I haven't seen you around during the day. I need to know if I should feed you lunch."

"No school, not for a year or two."

121

"Too bad about that. I won't always be around for lunchtime, but I'll do what I can. Drink your milk."

The kid drank the milk, and the orange juice, and had another slice of ham and some toast. At the end, Bobbie stopped in the door as if waiting for information on what would happen next.

Jupiter played it light. "Come back up here at noon. I'll make you a hamburger and some potatoes. Today or tomorrow, we'll talk about whether you're going to keep living by yourself, and we'll talk about who you want to call."

"I'm not going back home." Bobbie's voice was surly and defiant.

**

About mid-morning, Jupiter called the Heldritch house. Mrs. Heldritch answered and said, "Oh, Mr. Devon, Kate isn't here."

"Uh, how did you know it was me?"

"Caller ID."

Of course. "Actually, Mrs. Heldritch, I was calling for you, not Dan or Kate."

She said, "That's nice. Matt, you better start calling me Sarah if you're going to be dating someone in the family. I think we should be on a first name basis, don't you?"

He watched her words fly into the air and drop to the floor. "All right. Sarah it is, then. I was calling for you because I understand you substitute teach in middle and high school."

"Yes, that's right. I can teach most grades and subjects."

"I was wondering what you could learn for me about a boy who used to be in your school. His name is Bobbie Inskeep, and he's between twelve and fifteen. I don't really know. Perhaps you could call a friend in the office and find out about, you know, parents and things."

Even to Jupiter, he sounded unconvincing.

He heard her laugh, "No need to call the school. I can tell you that one right up front. You got it wrong. She's a girl, Roberta Inskeep."

"Not a boy?"

"A girl."

Christ Almighty. "Fooled me."

"She should have graduated high school last year. I taught her when

122

she was a junior. You're right if you're thinking she dropped out. If you don't mind me asking, why are you interested in this kid?"

"Uh, ran into the teenager in town, and he—or she, I guess—looked abandoned, dirty, unsupervised."

He went on with the lie now that he had a story to sell. "She was in between two dumpsters, like that's where she lived. How old would she be, then? What about her family?"

Sarah considered. "Maybe nineteen, no younger than eighteen. No father that I know of. Roberta's mom is one of Aniline's failure stories, and Bobbie got the worst of it. Mom's name is Carol, lives in a trailer. Works mostly in truck stops down the interstate washing dishes and bussing tables. She's a meth head, Matt."

He could hear a spoon banging on a pan in the background. Sarah was cooking, then. "Meth head. Not much reason for the girl to be home then."

"The mom lives with her dealer the last I heard. I wouldn't know what Bobbie thinks about having the guy in the trailer, but I can guess."

Worse and worse. "So, do you think there's anything we can do for the girl?"

"Beyond shooting her mom and getting her into a decent family? That's a tough one, Matt. Bobbie had some other problems besides her mom. I remember she had learning disabilities, maybe dyslexia and borderline autism. Setting her up on her own would be tough, but we could do the church-mission thing, get her clothes, and try to work on her GED."

"But where would she live, while all this is going on?"

"Depends on if she's an adult. Also depends on if she's seen as competent by the state of Texas. If she isn't competent, the authorities would probably insist she stay with her family. Texas might be slow picking up on the problem here."

"And how do you see the problem?"

"Hold on a second. I need to get something out of the oven."

The phone hit the counter with a thok that rang into his ear.

"I'm back. To use teacher-speak, the fundamental issue is a dysfunctional family with a parent who is unable to maintain a role of support and control or provide a criminal-free environment. The parent isn't going to change."

123

"Oh."

"Sorting all this out could take some time. Bobbie can't stay on the street; she needs to go into the system."

"Is that such a good idea?"

"It's what we have. It's where we are. I can set up the first contact for you, or you can handle it. I wouldn't stall around if I were you."

He wasn't sure he wanted all this forceful opinion. "Maybe the dumpster is better than the system."

"You can't just set food out on the back porch, you know. Bobbie is a girl, not a stray cat."

He winced. "Hmm. Complicated. I was hoping for a simple answer. Maybe I'll say something to the Chief of Police. Well, thanks for satisfying my curiosity." Then he belatedly added, "…Sarah."

"That's okay, Matt. Call anytime you need the insider scoop. I'll tell Kate you rang. Or maybe it's best not."

She hung up.

Chapter Fifteen: Consequences

Jupiter thought through what he wanted to ask Gilgamesh. This was crazy, asking advice of a delusion. "You had a run-in with Inanna once, didn't you?"

"Yes, the goddess of love and war. Why do you ask?"

"You wouldn't know this, but Inanna will be reborn as a goddess named Ishtar. That's the name we know best."

"Soon you will have to come to the reason for your question."

Jupiter counted to ten. Gilgamesh was high-handed but right. "I think Ishtar is reborn again, this time as Kate."

"And is Kate your unattainable one?"

Jupiter could see the grin, knew he had amused Gilgamesh. "You guessed it. So tell me about Inanna."

"Inanna above all others is truly magnificent, but she is also trouble, and was trouble when we met—trouble inside a fire, brewing up a storm."

Jupiter's laugh burbled up. "So I understand."

"It is a tale that could take days, but I have only a small time. We are at banquet, and soon I shall have to speak."

Jupiter gazed out on the palace courtyard. Diners, cross-legged before food and tumblers, were arranged in a square. Gilgamesh sat his bench upon a plinth. A white flax cloth over his head billowed in the slight breeze and shielded the King from a warm evening's air. "Then get to the story, Gilgamesh."

Gilgamesh cleared his throat. "I met her right after my return from the Land of the Cedars. She appeared in my chambers after I had been bathed, oiled, my beard trimmed—but before the big festival."

125

"Kate appeared in my chamber after our own banquet."

Gilgamesh shook his head, "By all the gods, she was beautiful."

Jupiter nodded. "So far the same for Kate."

"She offered me dalliance. She declared herself quite overcome by my beauty."

"The same." Jupiter felt a twinge at the lie. No one would choose him in a beauty contest, especially over a young Sumerian in royal robes.

"She offered me marriage or as much a thing as the gods call marriage. I saw it for the trap it was. I would be her house boy, suspended in amber and on display, in the palaces of the gods forever."

"Well, Kate hasn't offered me immortality. Maybe my youth back. But why would marriage to Inanna be a bad thing?"

Jupiter could see the exasperated expression on Gilgamesh's face.

"ur-Jupiter, consider. A warrior king, two-thirds divine himself, at the beck and call of a woman? Perhaps that would be enough for you but not for Gilgamesh."

Jupiter flushed hot, red-faced. Beck and call? Kate's last telephone call. "So you broke it off gently?" Of course not. Gilgamesh had been an impetuous twenty year-old.

"No. I could have spoken with more grace. I cut her with sharp words. I reminded her of all those lovers ruined and cast aside. She became… unhappy with me."

"Furious in fact. A goddess spurned."

"You make her anger sound like a joke, ur-Jupiter. That bout of words built consequences near fatal for me, for Enkidu, for Uruk herself. I am less impetuous with the gods these days."

Jupiter laughed. "Lesson learned. I'll be careful around Kate, so she won't set the Bull of Heaven on me. I'll try not to offend her."

"As you offended Aniline's king?"

The words stunned him. Gilgamesh knew about the Mayor!

"ur-Jupiter?"

"Yes. I'm here."

Gilgamesh shook his ringlets. "You disappoint me. How could you compare that large soft man to the Elamites?"

The King stood and gazed down into a host of faces. "It is time for me to speak, ur-Jupiter. I will bid you an evening."

Jupiter tasted the metallic flavor of nausea at the back of his throat.

Much as he imagined Gilgamesh from his world, Gilgamesh could see into his life, maybe his thoughts. And Jupiter had believed the dialogue, the delusion, and the book to be under control.

Chapter Sixteen: Civilize the Wild One

Sleep gathered on his eyelids on the trip into Amarillo, weighed them down to the point of danger. The old need their afternoon naps. He wasn't comforted by this rueful thought. On the other hand, he saw no reason to be denied this miniscule pleasure. He pulled over in one of the Texas picnic spots and parked at the far end past all the tables. He reclined his leather-swathed German seat and surrendered to sleep.

***

It was the dream again. Matthew Devereaux was warehoused there in the yellow-painted institutional room in his wheelchair. His fellow residents surrounded him, castoffs of life waiting for their favorite shows like "Court TV," waiting for lunch, waiting for their children to visit, waiting. Matthew had a different attitude. He didn't wait; he lingered. It wasn't so bad.

His nose had always been a fine tool, an informant, and a sense that drove memory and mapped a hidden universe. Now it told him old men and women smelled, and disinfectant was its own mixed blessing. He caught no smell of urine however, so he knew his friend Dave hadn't let go yet and filled his diaper. The picture puzzle laid between them on the tabletop, with some of the edge in place defining the bounds of the problem. Some patches of an emerging still life laid in the interior. They had all the unclaimed pieces laid out around the puzzle, and the box lid was propped near Dave's elbow.

For the hundredth time, Dave said, "I don't know how you can work these things upside down like that. I have to see the picture right side up."

The lounge was also the office of his gas station, and a counter separated them from the aisles of candy and chips.

For the hundredth time, Matthew said, "The picture makes it harder because it hides the pattern the pieces are making. Upside down, you aren't fooled. Upside down, you just see the shapes."

The shapes were potato chips, and he noticed that he could break off little pieces to make a chip fit into the puzzle.

Dave craned his neck to view the clock, but he didn't have the flexibility to twist back far enough. He gazed instead through the glass to the driveway to see what car might be there at the pump. "What time is it? Is it ten? Are those the visitors driving up?"

Matthew glanced up from the puzzle. "Yes, it's ten. Did he call?"

"No, but you know he shows up sometimes without calling first."

"It's been a month, Dave. I wouldn't expect him."

"That's where your thinking is all screwed up, you old fart. If it's been awhile, then he's due to show up, overdue in fact. If my son had visited last week, that would mean he wasn't coming today. Besides, he gets the employee discount here, and he's bound to need a fill-up by now."

"Have it your way, Dave. But you don't believe it yourself; otherwise you would have shaved."

"What difference does shaving make?"

"You look like Gabby Hayes or someone bumming quarters on the street."

"Yeah, well you don't look so good yourself. You look like the wreck of Agamemnon."

Dave had taught English and world literature in high school. He enjoyed reminding his friends. But this was a bad simile, a sign of confusion.

"Agamemnon, Dave? A shipwreck? Senility has got you good."

"Not the boat, the King. He was a Greek. His wife was Clytemnestra, remember?"

"So?"

"Reminds me of Estelle. Clytee killed Agamemnon, remember?" One of the nurses was helping a customer at the register.

"Estelle never killed me, Dave."

129

"No, she killed Jimmy."

"That was the muscle car, Dave, and the way Jimmy drove it."

"And who bought him that car?"

"Why—if you want to bring up blame—I ended up paying for it."

"You paid all right." Dave liked his own punch line; he twisted his head back and forth as he sniggered.

"What is this, some vendetta against my wife? She passed, remember?"

"I never understood. You decided to hate cars instead of Estelle?"

"Cars are over-rated, especially when you're in the gas station business."

"No all-American male doesn't like cars."

"They take up too much space. Besides, I needed the time for Estelle. She was never the same after the boy died. Needed more taking care of, was harder for other people to be around."

"Admit it; you never liked her much—either before or after."

Matthew shook his head, pushed back on the table. "Estelle was no Clytemnestra and no Medea, either."

"You Catholics, or anyhow, you serious Catholics. You should have left her, had some kind of life."

Dave's imprecations faded off into a mutter. Then, as he glanced past Matthew, his face split into a broad smile. Dave's son was here to see his father, to do those things good sons do, to soothe the old man. Dave lumbered up out of his chair and hugged his boy.

"Dad, how are you? Morning, Mr. Devon." The middle-aged man tipped his head down towards Matthew.

"Good to see you, boy."

Dave tugged at his son's elbow. "Wait till I tell you. The nurses caught old Zevon in Miranda's bed."

He dragged his son slowly over to a cracked vinyl couch underneath the soft drink dispensers.

Matthew sat at the table, fiddled with puzzle pieces, and kept watch on the pair from under his shaggy eyebrows. The station's motion detectors dinged as cars drove in and out and the two on the couch talked.

They were good together even though the son visited infrequently. Dave's boy set his hand on his father's shoulder like a caress and leaned close to hear.

It could have been Matthew on that couch; it could have been Jimmy listening to an old man's complaints about food and nurses. It could have been possible. They could have had such a conversation. Even if Jimmy had left him in this home and gone his own way, it would be better than no chance at all. God rot it.

The usual wave of self-pity and resentment washed over him. It kept him warm and alive, as always. Tears stung his eyes. He was close to sniveling as he watched his friend talking to his son. Dave had a son while Matthew had a built-up anger, a rage that he would end alone in this home.

***

With a jolting twitch Jupiter sprang awake in the seat. He tried to suck saliva back into his dry mouth and rubbed clots of sleep from the corners of his eyes. Late afternoon had somehow snuck up on him. The disorientation of being catapulted into a cockeyed new world shrouded him.

He saw no point going into Amarillo now and facing the after-work rush hour. He turned the car back towards Aniline to hide in his grain elevator, hide from the memory of that rheumy-eyed, bitter old man.

***

"What if I did want to clean up? Up here?"

Bobbie stood in the doorway of the kitchen, half in and half out of his life. It had been a week since he had learned her name.

He had been a fool to think a twenty-year-old girl was a teenage boy five years younger. Sure, she slumped enough to appear even shorter than she was, and her wrists and neck were bird-thin. She might have been underfed for years. Bobbie wiped her nose on her sleeve.

Jupiter was making breakfast. He made French toast for her. It was the first time she had ever had it. They had developed some sort of understanding, but it was an anemic truce. "Well, there might be an unintended consequence."

"Huh?" She wrinkled her forehead, and her mouth turned down.

131

"You said I could. The water's cold downstairs." She had been flicking her eyes mostly in his direction, but now she stared off to the left at the floor.

What did they do to you in that claustrophobic little trailer? "Oh, you can shower up here. But if you actually wash your hands and dig the grime out from under your fingernails, then I would be inclined to teach you how to make breakfast. We'd split the duty, fifty-fifty."

"Okay. I can do eggs. And cereal."

"Eggs are good."

"Waffles are nice—I'd like to know how to do waffles."

He turned off the sauté pan and said, "Let me show you where the bathroom is. I'll wait breakfast, and you can take care of showering right now."

It was too good an opportunity to miss. He'd had no idea how he was going to get her sanitized and disinfected. The Epic had a similar concern. He remembered the lines, "And Shamhat rubbed down Enkidu's body, currying his mat of hair, and anointed his long locks with oil, and blocked his beard, placing upon him the guise of man."

The tangents were amusing, but getting out of control—he didn't live in Sumeria.

He guided her out of the kitchen and to the stairs. As they trekked up, she kept her distance from him, watching him all the way. They walked through one of the guest bedrooms into the Hollywood bath. He opened the linen closet and handed the girl a towel and a washcloth.

"There's soap on the counter there and shampoo. Here in a drawer I have some other things like a fingernail file." He showed her. "The water gets hotter as you turn to the right and the lever controls how much you get. Pull this knob up to get the shower."

Bobbie stood holding the towel fast against her chest. "Uh, my clothes. They're kind of grungy. Do I have to put them back on?"

Her jeans showed ground-in dirt, and her shirt hung limp and filthy, a rag in the making.

"I have some sweatpants and a sweatshirt I can loan you. Let me get them."

He went down to his room and when he returned, he found her staring out the diminutive window in the thick concrete wall.

"Here," he said, handing her the clothes. "When you come down,

132

bring your things and we'll wash them."

Bobbie dropped the offered sweat suit on the toilet seat and turned back to the window. He supposed she was flustered, for good reason. He didn't blame her; this was new for both of them. He turned to go, and he said as he left, "You can lock the door if you want."

When she shuffled back down the stairs, her hair was wet and plastered back. His clothes hung on her, though he was small. She had rolled the cuffs of the pants up by inches. This made her appear child-like. He blinked.

She eased the roll of her dirty clothes down onto one of the bar stools.

He said, "Step over here to the stove, and I'll show you how to make French toast. Use these tongs. See, you dip it in the bowl—this is mostly egg—then you nestle it down into the pan in a single layer. The heat should be about midway. Check every once in awhile to see if you should flip the bread. I'm right here," he said, pointing at a door in the back of the kitchen. "My washer and dryer are through there."

While he started the wash, he glanced at her clothes sizes. He was confounded to discover a bra even though he should have expected it. Figuring everything was colorfast by now, he lumped it all together on a sturdy cycle. He might run it twice.

She had breakfast ready. They sat down across from each other at the bar. The morning had opened up new territory for them, and they were both unsettled. His hands were shaking. He hadn't predicted this when he sorted through his options two weeks ago.

He asked, "Your mother is named Carol isn't she?"

She said, "That's not part of the deal." Her voice was sharp.

"What deal?"

"You don't check up on me."

"Just curious. Just asking. So, is she Carol?"

The alarm was subsiding. "I guess. I call her Mom."

"Do you want to see your mother?"

"I'm not going back."

What did happen in that trailer? "Even if your mother's friend wasn't there anymore?"

"She'd get another one."

"Do you have any other family? A grandma, a brother, a sister?"

133

"I have an aunt. She lives in Vega. She's all right."

"You like your aunt? What's her name?"

"Aunt Diane."

"What's her last name?"

"Dunno."

"Would you like to live with your aunt?" *Too fast.*

"Dunno. It would be okay, I guess. I haven't seen her since I was little."

"Is it all right if I talk to your aunt and see how she feels about it?"

"Maybe. She doesn't care about me. She hasn't been around for years."

"That doesn't mean she doesn't care."

"She was never there when Mom was getting really bad. She would have showed up if she cared."

Bobbie crossed her arms over her chest. She didn't appear to be simple; her vocabulary was good for a wild child.

***

Jupiter and Bobbie sat in the living room on a Wednesday. They had spread the *New York Times* Sunday newspaper around on couches and the coffee table. He sat at one end of the room and she occupied the other. They waited for some baked potatoes to finish in the oven.

"Do you like books?"

"Dunno."

"I assumed you'd know if you liked books." *Whoops, too challenging.*

She sat huddled on the floor working through the Sunday Supplement, the celebrity section. "Books are hard. I don't read much."

"If you have books at home you like, I thought you might pick them up and keep them here. I wouldn't mind having them around. If we went by your house, we could also get some of your clothes."

"I don't want to go back."

"Oh, come on. What's the worst thing that could happen?"

"They could catch me—that's what."

"Catch you."

"They caught me before and tied my ankle to the bed post. I couldn't even go to the bathroom. Mom was real mad when I… made a mess. Then he beat me."

"Did he hit you a lot?"

"Only when he could."

He thought about what she had said. The sarcasm must be unintentional. "All right, we won't go back there for anything, not until we can figure out how we could do it when no one is home."

***

Bobbie wouldn't stay in the head house after dark. He fed her about six, hours before the summer dusk. After dinner she slipped away. He tried not to dwell on where she went, but still it buzzed around his brain. *She's not keeping the sleeping bag in the car. She's out under a tree or in one of those derelict buildings, and she doesn't want me to know where.*

The early dinners had an advantage. He was alone and free in the evening for Kate's occasional visit. So far he kept all three of his lives separate from each other.

***

That separation disappeared Wednesday night. Kate drove up after dark, and after hiding her car, she rode up the lift. He met her at the top, always a pleasure. This time she brushed by him and started up the stairs speaking over her shoulder.

"Strangest thing… I nearly hit something down there in the dark. It was all gray and bigger than a dog. I was past it before I saw it. It nearly walked into the side of my car."

His heart jumped. "What was it? What did you see?"

"Beats me, but it scared the crap out of me. I need a drink." She went straight in and to the bar cabinet. "You need to restock. I've drunk all your red wine."

"I'll get you some white; it's in the kitchen."

He went to the refrigerator and hurried back. He knew what she had nearly struck.

"You know…." She started again, "You know, I am fond of you."

"Good. Now I don't feel so used and cheap."

135

"No, I mean it. I wouldn't like it if...." She had a way of falling off a sentence and not finishing.

"If?"

"Oh, you know, if you were screwing anyone else. I've left my scent on you, practically my brand."

"Darn. I'll call around tomorrow and cancel my engagements."

"Shut up! You're engaged?"

"Not to you. Can you imagine the announcement in the paper?"

"Nubile Young Woman Condescends To Sleep With Dry Old Fart."

That was too true. "Not to change the subject, but you didn't kiss me at the lift."

"I am struck by remorse. Get yourself over here and grope me while I open the wine."

He obliged, running his hands down her back, cupping her ass and then reaching around to hug her stomach.

"Higher, please. Damn, I'll have to use a pinot noir glass."

"Two months ago you didn't know what a pinot glass was." He continued to supply the requested attention.

"I didn't even know there was a grape by that name. Oh, that's good! Slow down; I want to eat first."

She plopped down on the couch, tucked a foot under her, and held up her glass. "Here's to the all-American grope. Long may it fumble around. Aren't you drinking?"

He glanced to the side as he sat down beside her. In the crevice between two cushions he spotted a cheese puff. With a stealthy reach he plucked it out, and turning his head away, popped it in his mouth "Um, we're eating German, so I'm drinking beer."

"What's that you're chewing?"

He lied. "A goldfish cracker."

"You piker! None for me? How about a bowl to set beside us, garçon."

He leapt up and trotted off to the kitchen, hoping he had cheese crackers.

***

Bobbie didn't enjoy fancy food, so he often made something simple and didn't eat with her—he sat quietly by. He gave her spaghetti and garlic bread, and watched as she ate. He wanted to take another step and ease the cage door closed a bit further.

He said, "You need some more clothes. You're going to wear out my sweatshirt and sweatpants."

"I thought you gave them to me."

"They were more of a loan."

"I have another pair of pants, and a tee shirt."

"It would be better if you had a week's worth of clothes so I don't have to do laundry as often."

"Can I have some more bread?"

"Sure." He painted some butter and roasted garlic onto a piece of bread and shoveled it into the toaster oven.

He asked, in a neutral voice, "So, would you like some new clothes?"

"Dunno. Couldn't hurt." She threw a glance up at him. "Would they be a loan?"

"No. You could keep them."

"Would we have to get them here in Aniline?"

"That wouldn't be a good idea, would it?" They both considered. "It would be best to go somewhere and try clothes and shoes on rather than shop online."

"Okay."

"Okay, what?"

"I'll do it."

"We'll go to Amarillo tomorrow. I kind of counted on it. On the chance you'd say yes, I called and booked you for an appointment. You're getting your hair cut."

"I don't know about a haircut. I cut my own hair with some scissors I got. What kind of haircut?"

"I'm a guy. How should I know? Guys only know afterwards if they like a girl's hair."

She wasn't rushing into it. There was a long silence. "Yes, I guess."

***

In the morning after a late breakfast, they took the car out of the

137

steel silo and drove to the city. On the way through Aniline, Bobbie slumped down in her seat. This suited Jupiter.

He grinned and said, "You can get a lot more invisible than that."

He and she left a lot unsaid, but there was some dancing around it.

Bobbie preferred to live out of sight, and he had his own secrets. Twice lately she had been in the head house when workmen rode up the elevator and climbed the stairs to his front door. He shooed her into the office and ready to pull the door shut said, "Shh, now's the time to be very quiet."

She whispered, "Yeah, like I'm stupid. I don't want them to know I'm here either."

Now in the car, she was quiet again, waiting miles before she spoke. Interstate traffic was light in late morning. His claustrophobia problem remained in the distant background. As Amarillo approached, Bobbie sat up and gazed around. "I'd love to live here someday—and drive around in a big car, talking on my cell phone, like her," she said, pointing at a passing car.

"I'd get a car that doesn't smell as if someone sleeps in it."

She frowned, serious. "You're laughing at me."

"Not really. Maybe your aunt will give you a bedroom, and you won't have to sleep in a car." He kicked himself. It was stupid to set expectations before he could deliver.

"I don't sleep in your old car, anyway. Not anymore."

They passed a billboard that said, "Petersen Realty—The People Who Can Get You Home, Even If We Can't Get Your Son to Talk to You. It's Going to Be OK—We Understand."

He flushed with a sudden rush of pleasure and then grinned, recognizing immaturity and vanity.

He drove clear across the city to the west side, to the tangle of malls planted in fields of parking. He found the right mall entrance and they traipsed straight into the store, avoiding the long galleries and aimless shoppers. He had chosen one of the more upscale stores, hoping for a smaller crowd. A soft gold florescence surrounded all, rained down on dummies in tweed and capes, expensive sports clothes, and silk ties. Fall fashions were already on the racks. A tight band clamped down across his forehead.

He said, "We have three hours before your appointment. Let's start with pants and tops."

They shopped for the non-controversial things first, for outerwear and for athletic shoes. Then, facing it square on, they went to Young Women's Intimate Apparel. Bobbie sidled away from him, peeking sideways over her shoulder.

She asked, "You're not coming with me are you?"

"No, I thought I would turn you over to this young woman here," and he cocked his head towards a sales clerk at the register. "I'll sit over to the side and only come along when you need to pay." He turned to the clerk and said, "We're here for underwear."

The woman replied, "Certainly. I assume it's for this young woman." She giggled.

He creased his forehead and talked past the remark. "She'll need a couple of weeks worth of everything. You two can pick out what works for her."

The woman simpered and, taking Bobbie's arm, wheeled her away.

He parked on a bench over near the boys' section and sat there clasping his knees and sweating. There weren't many people in the store, but there were enough. God, look how much stuff was in here! It was in heaps, piles, mountains.

Of course he had checked out the details of his cultural claustrophobia online, had spent an hour reading up on anthropophobia. It was ironic. Ironic indeed that he had a fear not only of people but also of their things, even the ones they might buy because of him and his ads.

It was only three quarters of an hour, and the clerk waved at him. He approached the desk with his head ducked. Fortunately, everything was in two large shopping bags, laying there on the counter. Bobbie had her hands protecting a bag's top, sealing its contents from view.

The clerk said, "The total comes to two-forty-two and eighteen cents."

He dug out his wallet and proffered a credit card. While it was being run through, he and Bobbie gazed at the counter, their shoes, the carpet off to the side, everywhere—except at each other.

***

He had chosen one of his old clients to cut Bobbie's hair, a woman

139

who had started with one small shop and now had a chain of salons promoted by his company. Eleanor didn't cut hair anymore, but she was doing this one as a favor. She and Bobbie chose a modified pageboy, short in back, with big side wings that swooped to points and framed the girl's mouth. Pleased, he and Eleanor stood behind the girl observing her in the mirror. Bobbie gazed round-eyed, working out how she felt about the young woman staring back at her. When she saw them watching her over her shoulder, her eyes skittered away. He understood her thought; now she was not a child. She was less concealed, more attractive and more vulnerable.

His client took him aside. "Once I cut through enough of the thicket, I could start seeing the shape of her head and face. It worked out really nicely. It's funny though. Maybe it's the black hair, but she looks so sallow. Better get her some sun, Matt—she's a little ivory ghost."

***

The car was a sanctuary, both for him from his phobia and her from all the changes that day. Before they left town, he stopped at his Amarillo neighborhood library.

"Come on, you. I have a card. You can pick out a few things to read, and we'll return them next week."

"I'm not sure I need a book."

"We can get art books. Not much reading in them. Besides, I need a book or two myself." A book on dyslexia. "After this, we'll swing through a fast-food place for burgers."

He walked her to the art books and left her in the stacks. After awhile, when he had the book he needed, he returned to her, locating her on the floor with her back to the main aisle, books open on the carpet and one in her lap. She appeared tiny, framed by the towering bookshelves. Tears sprang to his eyes, and he stepped forward. He reached out his hand and lowered it gently onto her head. She shrugged it off and bent closer to the book, away from him.

He backed up and sat at a nearby table to wait. His body was still, but his mind bounced, ricocheted hard. He dug out a crumpled tissue and after scrubbing his eyes, blew his nose loudly. So much for library silence.

When they left, she had two books clutched to her chest: *Poland, Window On The World* and *Famous Ballet Sets*. As promised, he drove her through a burger stand and ordered two fries and two burgers, one loaded and one plain. He tried not to flinch when she dripped grease onto the seat. The sun was low behind them as they drove east. Back at the elevator he whipped straight into the garage; these days he left the door open. He climbed out, leaving the headlights on.

"Bobbie, get the garage lights, will you?"

He went around to the trunk and pulled out the bags and boxes of clothes. When he straightened up, he stood alone in his big steel silo with the door to the outside facing him, empty and darkening into night. The evening wind was strange on his face.

***

Light from the north windows lit the couches and the coffee tables. Bobbie sat as far from Jupiter as the room allowed, slowly turning through the pages of *Poland*. He sat with a cup of coffee in his lap, both hands curled around it.

He observed. "You're becoming a fixture around here."

"What's that mean?"

"Means you're around a lot, at least during the day. Where do you go off to, at night?"

"Dunno."

"You mean you don't want to tell me."

"What does it matter?" Her shoulders drooped even more.

"Makes me nervous not knowing."

"Rough on you, huh?"

"No, I just don't want anything to happen to you at night." He slurped at the coffee.

"Neither do I. Besides, that girl is here at night."

"Girl?"

"Don't lie. Everybody lies." There was a whiny pitch to her voice.

"Okay. There is a woman who comes to see me."

"It's not a woman. It's Kate Heldritch. She was a few grades ahead of me."

"Yes, it's Kate." He felt short of breath, exposed.

"She's popular."

He was cautious. "Well, I would guess so."

Bobbie frowned. "Everybody loved her in school. She hung around the cool kids and the jocks and the geeks—everybody."

"Did you like her?" He regretted it the moment he asked.

"Not really. Everything went right for her."

"And not much went right for you."

"So, is she coming over tonight?"

He reflected. "I don't really know."

It all depended on whether mercurial Kate made up her mind.

***

June was tuning up a blast furnace of a summer, but Jupiter kept to the walk around the square mile. He talked his situation out to White the dog as they walked.

"It's a mare's nest, that's what it is. I need to locate the aunt and suss out what the possibilities are."

White shot a glance at him. All this talking was a new thing.

He nodded his head toward his companion. "No, I don't suppose you can help me out on the aunt. It's not a canine thing." He continued, "And there's Kate. Don't know how I'm going to square the Bobbie side of my life with Kate. She's her own person, and I'm not sure what I can talk her into."

He didn't know how she might react to a damaged young woman living on the grounds—Kate might decide to turn Bobbie over to the police. The dog shook his head, flapping his ears and his tags, and then trotted on.

"Easy for you to say," he called after the dog. "She's going to read me the riot act for this. Maybe I should keep on lying."

He deliberated about that for a quarter mile. White thought about rabbits.

Then he resumed, "Bobbie's got to see some specialists. She's had malnutrition for years thanks to her Mom. Maybe it's made her retarded. Mildly. She does have some type of reading disorder."

White, out of character, barked at him, one short bark.

"What? Yeah, I'm avoiding the real issue. She needs professional

142

psychological help. Some things happened in that trailer that aren't going away."

They turned for home. "In the meantime, I'm treating both of you about the same. I pour food out in a bowl on the back porch, spend a little time hanging around with you, and pretend I don't have any responsibility for either of you."

The Forest Journey

Chapter Seventeen: Sister City

Jupiter didn't have much trouble contacting the aunt, but getting what he wanted was harder. Vega is a community of a mere nine hundred, not counting outlying farms. He had depended on there being no more than one or two Dianes. He had started the search by checking a telephone book online. He was successful at first stab. The Yellow Pages supplied the name and address of a business, Inskeep Services; it was the same last name as Bobbie's. He telephoned and an answering machine picked up.

"Hello, this is Diane Inskeep. I'm out running errands or taking care of a customer. Leave a message at the sound of the beep."

Diane sounded like a formidable person. Her voice was without guile, artifice, or femininity. She sounded tired.

He left a cold lunch on the counter for Bobbie. He drove over to Vega to see who Diane Inskeep could be.

***

Her business was in a tin garage with an enclosed office, all locked up. He drove to the local diner to ask around. If that didn't work, he would check with the Baptist Church and then the police. But he spotted the truck on the Vega town square.

He knew it by the magnetic sign on the door that advertised Inskeep Services. Her vehicle was an ancient pickup that had been well maintained, better than his. He settled on a nearby bench in front of the lending library to wait and watched the town go by for a half hour. When she appeared on the curb and got in the truck, he was caught by surprise.

145

He'd had a different image for her in his mind. Chasing up to the truck left him short of breath, and he got there as she started to roll back. She was fifty-ish and wore job-site clothes—a plaid shirt, rough vest, and a baseball cap that advertised a lumberyard.

He caught her attention with, "Miz Inskeep, Miz Inskeep." She stepped on the brake but kept the truck running.

"My name is Matt Devon. I wonder if I could talk to you about a family matter?

She narrowed her eyes. "I don't know you."

"No, you don't. You and I both know Roberta and Carol Inskeep, though."

She considered, peered away, and looked back at him. Making up her mind, she pulled back in to the curb and turned the key.

"All right, the café there on the corner. I've only got about a half hour. Then I need to drive out to a shut-in."

He sat across from her in a booth. They both had coffee in front of them. It lay thin in the cup and had no aroma. Happily for him, the café was almost empty, and he would settle for bad coffee in trade for no people. She was brown-faced, sharp nosed, and had an incisor that sat proud of her other teeth. Her gray hair was caught in a ponytail that exited the back of the baseball hat and fell down her back in a sprawl. Lines trenched back from her eyes to her temples, losing themselves in the tight-drawn hair. "Mr. Devon, I think you said. What's your business with the Inskeeps?"

He was only going to get one shot. "To the best of my knowledge, you're the sister of Carol Inskeep and the aunt of Bobbie Inskeep. You're also the only relative, as far as I can tell."

"That much is true. I'll ask again, what's your business with my family?"

"Bobbie and her mother Carol are estranged, and Bobbie is living on the street over in Aniline. While I can't confirm it through first-hand knowledge, Carol, your sister…" Matt stopped. His hands moved back and forth above the table, fingers extended out to the Formica.

The vertical wrinkles above her mouth deepened as she knitted her lips. "There's not much you can tell me about my sister that will be a surprise. Just say what you came to say."

"Carol is a drug addict with a live-in boyfriend who is in the drug

146

business. I don't want to hurt you by saying it, but she's not likely to change at this late date. There are also some indications Bobbie has been sexually abused. Bobbie dropped out of high school a couple of years ago and now is a runaway, although she's still in the same town."

She flared her eyes, leaned back, and folded her hands. "I don't know you, like I said. This is pretty personal—you're hip deep in my family business. Do you have anyone who could vouch for you?"

She had just asked him for references! "Here's my card. You can call my business and ask to talk to my second, Jerry Douglas. He'll describe me, and you'll know at least I have a legitimate business. You could also talk to my doctor, Ben Cransto. He's an old friend, but I doubt if he would lie for my sake, being an MD and all."

"Anyone else?"

"I know the Mayor of Amarillo."

"Yeah right, like I would call her. Write the doctor's name on the back of your card. I'll go make a couple of phone calls."

Diane took the card and stood up. She clumped across the floor to the cash register to confer with a waitress. They retrieved a phone book and flipped through it together.

While she spoke into her mobile, she watched him at his table. He could hear her voice, "What business is this? And can you tell me who runs it?"

After a minute, she flipped the phone shut and consulted the book. The staff of the restaurant trickled by, conferred with the waitress, and stared at Jupiter. Diane dialed and spoke. She waited a long while and then listened, nodding now and then. Hanging up, she said to the waitress, "Guess it's okay. Hang around though."

Diane returned to the table. "Not an iron-clad set of references, but they'll do. Douglas was out, but the receptionist described you. I actually got to talk to the doctor after a bit, and he said you should call next time you want to play golf. You were saying something about Bobbie?"

"Runaway. Still in Aniline, living rough."

"How do you know all this?"

"Only by accident. I realized Bobbie was sleeping in old abandoned buildings in Aniline. Truth be told, she was half-starved when I met her, and I'm feeding her."

"That sounds about right for Carol, losing control of her family like

147

that. Carol always did make bad choices and never walked in the grace of God. This stuff about Bobbie though, that's all news to me. Carol's kid living off by herself in some tumbledown old house? So why are you here?"

"I think you already know."

"I can guess, but you tell me anyway."

"I'm trying to track down Bobbie's relatives because I think she needs some real family. Can you answer a question—how old is Bobbie?"

The way she stared directly into his eyes made him think she wasn't going to answer.

Then she peered up at the ceiling and calculated. "Oh, she'll be twenty this coming November."

"That's both good and bad. She's no longer a minor, so Child Protective Services can't help, or it would surprise me if they can. She can live where she wants with whom she wants. She says living with you would be all right with her."

Her breath leaked out in a long sigh. "So that's it, huh? Well, God gives us burdens. It would be hard, though, right hard. Bobbie still have those problems?"

"You mean, like not reading well?"

"Yeah, that, but also, she was always an obsessive, secretive thing. She'd do the same thing over and over again, like cutting up sheets of paper into smaller and smaller squares. She'd never look you in the eye, and she'd spend hours by herself."

"If anything, it's worse. I'd like to get her some professional help."

"You might as well know my job keeps me hopping, and I'm not home much. Bobbie wouldn't get much help from me day-in, day-out. And I'm uninsured. Paying for therapy—that would be next to impossible."

He let out his breath. He had advanced a long way tracking, catching, and taming his wild child. Now he believed he might lose after all and end up at square one.

He wasn't going to slink away without making all the right efforts. "Well, there might be ways I can help. What say—" he asked, "—what say you visit, see Bobbie, test out how you two get along? Then we can talk, see if we can work something out. You could even see your sister.

Make up your own mind whether she should be taking care of Bobbie. You could follow me over to Aniline."

She considered. "Bobbie is family. I'll have to come. I don't suppose you'd bring her here?"

"Why don't you go to her—it gives you a chance to check up on her situation."

She picked up her spoon, stirred the coffee, and tapped the rim of the cup repeatedly. "I got serious commitments this week. Someone's having surgery, and I'm watching out for her. With some telephoning, though, I could make time next week, Monday."

"Good," he said. "I'll make sure I'm there all day."

"And a week gives me time to check you out and get the scoop on Carol."

He took out a piece of paper and wrote out his name, address, and phone number. "I'm—working at the old Aniline grain elevator. That's the address."

He sketched a map showing the major streets. "You'll be able to see it on the skyline. You can't miss us."

"I'll come. I do need to check up on Bobbie, like you say." She was blunt. "I need to check up on you too, Mr. Devon. See how pure your motives are."

***

Jupiter heard the knock on the door while he was washing up breakfast. He said to Bobbie, "Wait here."

She sniffed disbelievingly, disappeared into the laundry room, and closed the door.

He would remember later that he was thinking about his steel front door, how he should paint the gray scarred inside, even if he left the outside rough. He had no foresight of who had knocked. He opened the door.

Dan Heldritch stood there, his fist cradled in his palm, his arms cocked up to his chest. The contractor took a step forward and hit Jupiter, one, two, three, times—in the nose, the temple, the mouth. Jupiter staggered back, lost his balance, and dumped onto the floor on his ass.

Heldritch stepped forward, stood over Jupiter.

"Damn it Matt! Just! Damn it!" He spun on his heel and clattered down the stairs.

Jupiter held both hands up to his face, cradled his head. His skull rang. Something warm was on his hands, his chin. He stared at his palms, saw hot, sticky blood. Struggling to his feet, he blundered into the kitchen to the sink, started the water, and held a dishtowel against his bleeding nose and mouth. The blood dripped out of the towel and splashed into the bottom of the sink. It spiraled around in the rush of the water and disappeared down the drain.

Bobbie, at his elbow. "Hurts, doesn't it?"

***

"Listen, it's Dan Heldritch."

"Oh." Jupiter moved the phone an inch away from his ear, as if it would punch him. After two days he still hurt.

"I called to, well, to apologize. I should have come by and done it in person. Not that you'd open the door to me."

"I would think twice."

"Listen, I know it's no excuse, but I blew up when I heard about you and Kate. And not even from Sarah. But…."

Jupiter cleared his throat. "I guess I should apologize to you too. About Kate and all." Not going well. Bad pitch to the client.

"How did you let it happen, Matt?"

"I didn't let it. It just kind of ate me up, and there I was."

"Huh?" Heldritch didn't sound so apologetic now.

"No excuses, then. She's half my age."

"No, you're twice her age."

Jupiter waited, silent.

"It wasn't right, me sucker punching you like that."

Jupiter could hear a faint roaring over the phone. Dan sat in his truck on a job site then, air conditioning cranked all the way up.

"I admit I'm impressed by how hard you can punch. You must have gotten some practice somewhere."

"Umph. Being a father is shit."

Maybe rougher to be the daughter's play-toy. "And a shock, I guess, to find someone older—dating—your daughter."

150

"Yeah, well. I'm pretty sure it wasn't you who chased her. She likes to lead when she dances, if you know what I mean."

Jupiter nodded. "Yes, I've kind of figured that out."

"Still this is so frickin' weird. And I'm not sure if you're a bastard or a loser."

"Let me know when you get to the apology part."

"Yeah I know. I slide back and forth from a desire to break you up into little pieces to feeling sorry for you. This will take awhile. So anyway, maybe you can find it...." He fell off the sentence and didn't finish it. Like Kate.

Jupiter whooshed out a sigh. "I accept your apology. Let's get this behind us, Dan."

"It'll be weird, Matt—you and Kate and all."

"It's been weird for a while now. You didn't know it yet, that's all."

"Okay. Not to dwell on that." The telephone line fell quiet, then, "So how swoll up are you?"

Jupiter momentarily forgot where it hurt. He pinched the bridge of his nose and flinched. "I'm paying my dues. The nose looks like a turnip, and one eye is blacked up."

"Wow."

"You shouldn't sound so pleased."

Dan chortled, "Well, I admit I felt better right away. I hope that you will too. Soon. Got to go." The line dropped into a hum, then a dial tone.

***

Jupiter let the phone ring and let the voice mail kick in. Sarah Heldritch's voice carried into the concrete room and bounced around. "Matt. Pick up. This is Sarah, Kate's mother. Are you there? Okay. I wanted to talk to Kate, and her mobile's off. Oh, and about Dan—he'll come around. Just give him some time. Tell Kate to call. And take care of yourself. Hanging around her is like being inside a twister. Bye for now."

Kate clattered down his stairs in high heel boots. From his couch, he focused on flashing legs under a mid-length skirt.

"Matt, your house is dark. Dark, dark, dark."

She waved her hand up towards the floors above. Now he could see the entire woman. Something this great couldn't be legal. Could it?

The corner of his mouth crooked up. "The walls are four foot thick. Installing windows is equivalent to hard-rock mining."

She snickered. "You're pretty quick with the excuses." She wandered over to the bar.

"I'm in advertising. I always have a glib answer."

"And there's no bathroom here on the first floor. Damned inconvenient."

"Pee over the outside rail, like I do."

"It's a wonder they haven't run you out of town for disgusting habits. Public display of genitalia, full frontal nudity from a very high place."

"Urinating in public is okay in Paris, France, but not in Paris, Texas."

She crossed over to him with two drinks. "Let me get a close-up here."

Thrusting the glass into his hand, she seized his chin, tilted his head, and cast a critical eye at him. "The bruising is getting better."

"That hurts. Your fingers are digging into me."

"Say it in French. It will sound sexier. Very seductive, that language is."

"Yes. You can get away with disgusting habits and a black eye, but only if you have the right accent. I see I'm to drink gin tonight."

"And glad of it. I checked out your fridge. You now buy milk two gallons at a time. That can't be healthy—what's with you and blah food lately? Milk, peanut butter, white bread?"

With a rush he plunged into another topic. "Your Mom called. Wants you to call back. She says she can't track you if your phone is off."

"Great. Like the CIA. Now I really need this drink."

Not the thing to talk about. That was enough of the Heldritchs. "So, how's the job search going?"

"Like crap. The last one I ran down was for hawking ads in Chicago. I wouldn't even get to design the ads, only sell them for a magazine. And such a magazine… something to do with commodities trading. A great looking woman like me, touting pork bellies? But thanks for asking."

He grinned. "I have to pretend to care. Otherwise…."

She laughed a self-conscious rueful chuckle, "I'd leave you dangling? Nah, I'm in it for the sex, not the ego boost. Besides, I like the solitude of your little tower."

Dangerous ground. "Well, I do get the occasional visitor. Someone's due to come by tomorrow."

"Right. If I believed that, I'd have to wear more clothes around here."

"I'll let you know when the coast is clear."

"And hang a sock on the doorknob if there is someone here?"

Jupiter thought about the mop and the bucket outside his door, the signal he and Bobbie had arranged. He considered telling Kate. He decided to wait. "What's your plan?"

"If there's ever a sock on the door? Besides murder you?"

"No. The plan for this evening." He definitely would wait to tell her.

"I've got to be at work for the breakfast rush, so I'm not staying the night. I thought you could whip up some gourmet snacks, and we could have them after."

"After what?"

She kissed him, hard. It made his lips hurt, throb across the splits. Her hands were busy. "Forget the snacks. We'll make them later."

Pulling him up off the couch, she marched him, arm in arm, towards the stairs, her hand still employed. "Say, what's with these dumb coffee table books? Polish buildings? Ballet?" She pointed to the books stacked on the end of the couch.

His tumescence retreated. "New account."

"Hey, don't take it seriously."

In a moment, before they ascended, she brought the situation back under her control.

Chapter Eighteen: Cyclone

Out on the roof, beneath the head house that teetered white above him, Jupiter surveyed the sky to the southeast and watched the July moon peer over at him. Hung low on the horizon, it waxed while he waned. He dropped the romantic notion of being tied to the moon and ambled inside.

Concrete echoed. And the smell of cement, sharp and poisonous, never quite disappeared, no matter how much leather he stuffed into the room. In the dark, he paused before he opened the laptop and stopped to contemplate the world out his north windows—while he girded his psychic loins. On to Gilgamesh, that brutal and charming figment of his imagination

"Your woman did not stay this night, ur-Jupiter?"

Not good. Gilgamesh was seeing more and more of his life. "No, she had duties elsewhere."

"Is she a goddess?"

"Or a queen? Hard to tell, really."

"I find her attractive. However, she is thin and her hair is a strange color."

Of course Gilgamesh could see into Jupiter's world. After all, he sprang out of Jupiter's head. Didn't he? "As bright as day."

"I prefer black like the raven's wing, but I would keep her around for novelty."

Jupiter drummed his fingers on the edge of the computer, "Can we talk about something else?"

"Tell me then, what problem bothers ur-Jupiter in all of his dominion?"

154

"I thought I'd ask your advice. Are you busy?"

"Not particularly. There is a parade of sorts, in my honor. We sit before the Ziggurat, and the young men drill in the square. I once enjoyed it, but now, I am old, and the sun is hot."

Once cued by Gilgamesh, Jupiter could see it clear in his mind. Gilgamesh sat on his backless bench beneath a canopy and hoped for a cool breeze. His court sprawled on the paving at his feet, some on pillows they had brought. He watched the young men of Uruk imbued with military fervor. They marched, turned, wheeled, all to entertain the King, but he had grown jaded over the last hundred years.

"Nice display of your military might."

"Oh this? This is not the military. These are only the youngsters who dream of swords and glory. We shall keep them safe a while longer. See how they are arranged by height, so each rank is uniform. The Chamberlain is very fussy."

Jupiter's mental image focused as sharp as the Sumerian light. Their bodies shone and narrow chests glistened with sweat above their kilts and girdles as they moved in serried ranks back and forth. "So, all this is for you, and you still have time to talk to me?"

"The ceremonies around a king are not for him, you know. You wished advice?"

"I'm working out how to civilize someone, bring her back into the arms of society."

Gilgamesh hemmed. "Civilization is not always the best. I lived alone in the wilderness myself for years."

Jupiter frowned. It was a wilderness of despair according to the Epic, a desert of fear for Gilgamesh. The King had a nostalgic remembrance of a bad time. "Let's take it for granted this person needs civilization."

"There are many legends of children raised wild by wolves or by the mountain bears, but I knew one wild beast that was brought into the pale of man."

"That would be Enkidu?"

"Yes. I was not present at his taming, but he told me often enough what it had been. Enkidu, created by Aruru, was left among the savage beasts to become a man."

"The Epic describes him as a magnificent creature with matted hair

155

and muscles like nothing Man has seen."

Gilgamesh grinned. "Oh, he was quite the animal. He ran wild among his animal friends on the plains. He was also quite a problem out there at the edges of the kingdom. He freed his friends the lions from our traps and filled in the holes we left for the aurochs and the horses. In the end, we had to tame him."

"You tamed him with a woman."

"Temple prostitute, in fact. What other charming form of treachery could work? Her name? Shamhat, which does not mean much since it translates to 'harlot.'"

Jupiter laughed out loud, "So, your golden-hearted whore, she used sex to tame the mighty Enkidu?"

"One of our largest weaknesses as men, I think. What shall you use on your uncivilized one, ur-Jupiter? What is her weakness?"

"She wants freedom and food, Gilgamesh. It's food I've used to tempt the wild child into my web of civilization."

Gilgamesh grinned. "You can't call your hermit tower civilization. Not on a scale of Uruk herself."

"Fair enough. Tell me how Shamhat trapped Enkidu and what happened then."

Gilgamesh waved a hand. "She possessed no modesty, none at all. She strolled out naked to where Enkidu grazed with some gazelle friends and there she took him, lying in the grass. Enkidu claimed they lay together for seven nights and six days, but I always believed it to be an exaggeration. Not even Gilgamesh as a young man could maintain interest that long."

"Does sound a little like boasting, doesn't it? So coitus continuous wore him down?"

Gilgamesh pursed his mouth. "The demands began soon after. She needed a tent to shelter her from starlight. She needed water—and a way to hold it. She wanted grain to be milled rather than chewed as seed. Shamhat sat down and civilized the poor fellow. She taught him to eat properly, to speak, to drink wine, and to think of himself as human. She bathed him and robbed him of his flowing, matted hair. In return for surrendering his bestiality, Enkidu grew softer and lost some of his animal strength."

"So I should concentrate on food, water, and bathing? I'm off to a

156

good start there. She has had her untamed matted hair cut back, and she has washed away the reek of life in the wilderness. She certainly eats my food."

"Your child will need clothing. Shamhat gave Enkidu some of her garments. The first time I saw him he dressed as a woman, having arrived that day in Uruk. A sore point later. He did not appreciate the reminder."

"Clothes, taken care of."

"And employment. Man must toil, must be broken to the ox's yoke... a woman even more so."

"Women work harder than men, don't you think?"

"There it is, that soft attitude again. Shamhat set Enkidu the task of guardianship. He took up the role of protector of the shepherds and shield of the flocks. Joyfully he killed the lions and the wolves who had been his friends, all for mankind and sheep."

"I don't think I can get my wild child to kill for a living. She does prepare the first meal of the day."

"You must obtain a loom or purchase some sheep for her to herd."

"Maybe." Jupiter doubted sheep would help.

"Do you own this uncivilized one then, ur-Jupiter? Is she your slave?"

That was the sticking point. Jupiter watched as Gilgamesh stood to return the salute coming from the close order drill in the plaza. How to answer...? "No, she belongs to another. And I am not king enough to take her into my care, either by law or force."

Gilgamesh, vehement, shook his head which caused the rank and file below him to jumble to a halt. He waved his hand and they reformed, continued. Feet stomped and raised puffs of dust in the plaza.

"You are enough like me, ur-Jupiter, to exercise power. I took the legendary Cedars of Lebanon for Uruk, took them in spite of the gods, took them in spite of a fierce monster who would have ground my bones on the mountain."

"Humbaba. The predecessor of the Greek monster Gorgon."

"The Greeks, those silly little fishermen to the North, in that little soup-bowl of an ocean—they will never kill their Gorgon, or build cities, or amount to much at all."

Jupiter snorted. "Oh, you might be surprised. But, talking of your

157

Humbaba, the Epic seems to believe conflict should end in death, even if through treachery."

"Never leave your enemies behind you. Take your situation. You have left your chamberlain to run your dominion as he sees fit, and he will have his knife in your back."

Jupiter chuckled. "Comparing Jerry to Humbaba? I wouldn't think so, but your point was I should take what I see as mine by treachery or force if necessary."

Gilgamesh tugged on the ringlets of his beard and frowned. "Gilgamesh has not needed treachery, not beyond the normal requirements of politics."

So delusional, Jupiter wanted to say. But kings rewrite their history. "I'll call you on that one. You and Enkidu slaughtered Humbaba after he surrendered to you, led you into his house, promised you fealty. Not the normal way to treat surrendered princes."

"Enkidu executed the monster out of loyalty to me and fear for my safety."

No, out of jealousy. Gilgamesh had soothed away the corrosion of this piece of history. "Humbaba may not have been the monster. He simply did as his god Enlil asked him to do and protected the Cedars with a reign of blood and fear. Simple mind, simple mission. But maybe I am harsh, so I apologize. The Epic thought it a great deed."

"Yes?"

"The poet of the Epic says, 'all glory to the great Gilgamesh, who slays Humbaba, who crosses the seas of life and death, who builds the great fired-brick walls of Uruk and provides the beams of the temples and the great gates that defend the city.'" That should take Gilgamesh aback!

"You should face your own Humbaba before you chastise me about mine. You will confront a horror of a mother for the sake of the wild one you have trapped."

158

Chapter Nineteen: Humbaba

"I don't like it." Bobbie pushed the plate of toast back towards him. Her hands dropped to her lap, folded, and she stared down.

Jupiter asked, "The toast?" She didn't bother with a reply. "We did talk about your aunt, Diane. Now I've set up a chance for you to meet her."

She mumbled, "You're always trying to change things."

The smell of the bread filled the kitchen, and the early morning was cool. Still, brittleness drowned it all out. "Or put them back together. This place is neutral territory. You don't have to talk much, not that you would. Just see what you think of her."

"She'll want to take me over or give me back to my mother."

"She may want to give you a place to sleep at night."

"I'm free now. I like it."

"Maybe she's free now, and she likes it. It's a change for her too."

"Who cares?"

He cajoled, "I promise. Just talk. No commitments."

She grumbled. He couldn't quite make out the words, but she didn't bolt.

"And maybe you could change out of that sweat suit and put on some of your new clothes?"

"Forget it."

This was going well. He was perspiring.

***

Diane arrived in the late morning, parking in the elevator lot by his

159

old pickup. He saw her arrive and started down the stairs from the head house to the elevator. By the time he walked into the old office, he had nearly lost her. He discovered a doubtful Diane backing out the door.

"It's fine," said Jupiter, gesturing her back in. "We're fixing the old place up, and we haven't gotten around to doing anything down here yet."

She looked at his bruised face. "What happened to you?"

"I don't suppose you'd believe I walked into a door?"

She shook her head, but let it drop.

He took her up to the head house; no surprise showed on her face.

"Nice," she said in a neutral tone as her gaze swept the place. Now if she could only grasp Bobbie's situation with the same calm. They found Bobbie in the kitchen.

The girl leapt up off her bar stool and stood there, arms at her side, not glancing up at either of them. Diane stepped forward and embraced her. Bobbie didn't recoil or hug back.

"Sit down, sit down girl. Let me take a gander at you. You remember me. I'm your Aunt Diane." The older woman swept on using small talk as lubricant. "What a cute haircut! Looks good on you. So here you are, all grown up. You could turn out to be a pretty young lady."

Bobbie didn't say anything. Diane glanced over her shoulder at Jupiter and gave him the face with the raised eyebrows. "Are you glad to see me, Bobbie?"

"I think so." Bobbie wiped snot noisily off her nose onto her sleeve.

Diane took it with equanimity. "How have you been?"

"I've been eating better because of—him." Bobbie twitched her head towards Jupiter who stood there with his best encouraging smile on his face. Even he knew it appeared fake.

"I went by to see your momma." Bobbie's eyes got round, and Diane said, "It's fine, it's fine. I didn't say anything about where you were. How are things, you know, between you and your mom?"

"I haven't seen her in awhile. I'm never going back."

"Well, she misses you. I'm sure she'd like you to come home. Wouldn't you like to see your mother again?"

"Dunno. Not where they could catch me."

"Why would anyone want to catch you, girl? Your momma and I only want what's best for you."

160

Bobbie narrowed her blue eyes. They contrasted sharply with her yellowish skin.

"Child, what do you think is best for you?"

He hoped Diane was ready for the girl's answer.

"It's not bad spending time here with—him," as she again nodded at Jupiter. "But I don't know." She paused.

Diane waited a bit then said, "I understand you've been sleeping in the old shacks around here. You can't do that forever."

"I like it. No one hurts me."

"Maybe we could do better. Where do you want to live?"

"If I could live down below, that would be fine. I wouldn't want to actually live up here." Bobbie shrugged a single shoulder. "Living with you, that would be okay. Maybe."

"Maybe I would like that too."

"Could we live here, in this town?"

"Why this town, child?"

"It's, it's...." Bobbie stalled out.

Jupiter said, "She didn't run far."

Bobbie turned her face to the wall. "I know where to hide."

The talk dropped away while Diane sat mutely holding the girl's hand. After a minute, Diane glared at Jupiter.

He got it. "I'm going into the living room. We can chat later. Come out when you and Bobbie are finished talking here, finished with the visit. Bobbie will stay here. She likes the kitchen best of all."

***

Diane and Jupiter sat across from each other, each on separate couches, a gulf between them. She leaned back with her shoulders rolled and her wrinkled thin arms clasped across her chest. He poised on the edge of the cushion, leaning towards her.

He said, "I can't see her going back—in any event, not for years."

"Yes. That trailer, that's a bad place for Bobbie to be. I hardly recognized my sister. There was drug stuff everywhere. The place was filthy, and there was a man living there, as you said. It took awhile for Carol to even acknowledge me. She started out angry and loud. I'm sure she was high."

161

"If you don't mind me asking, what did you and Bobbie visit about?"

"She told me about dropping out of school—about how mean the kids had been. She also told me about living in the trailer. It wasn't much of a life. Not much food and a lot of dangerous people around, doing meth in the front room."

"Did she say anything about…?"

"No. She shied away from talking about men, even the boyfriend. Even you. It's unfair, awful she's brought to this."

"Bobbie sleeps rough every night out there somewhere, you know. I wouldn't encourage her to sleep up here, because, well, you know how it could look."

"Yes. I can guess what people would say. Is there any truth in what they would say, Mr. Devon?"

"None at all. God forbid. Besides, she wouldn't spend a night up here. She's a long way from trusting me, I think. She may trust you."

"That's what it boils down to. She needs to trust me, and I want to trust you. Bobbie and I might be able to build our own little family of two. But it would be so hard, and she would have to live in Vega."

"Tell me how would it be hard? Maybe I can help."

"First off there's my job, my company. I inherited it from my Mom and Dad."

"What do you do?"

"Short answer? I take care of old people." He nodded and she continued, "I clean and I shop for them, and I do repairs that are needed on their houses. Some of them are shut-ins, most are sick or semi-disabled. None of them are independent anymore."

"Bobbie couldn't live with you because of your job?"

She considered, "Assuming we could get her to Vega, then there would be a room for her in the old house. But I work most days of the week, all of it outside the house. I'm always running around taking care of something, and I always have emergencies to tend to. She'd be alone. It's not much of a home-life; I don't even eat there often."

"I think she could be happier there, away from her mom, in a safe house, with a room to call her own."

"Raising her like Boo Radley isn't the answer." She continued to think of the hurdles. "And then, there's the money. Bobbie is going to

162

need some expensive help if she's ever to grow out of this."

He felt he was interviewing a client. "Your business sounds like a great service to the community, hard but rewarding."

"Hasn't been very rewarding lately, at least financially."

Yes, this was discovering what the product meant to the owner before he invented the ad campaign. "This what you want to do, how you see your life?"

She smiled. "Oh no. I was going to run a bookkeeping firm. I had one and was doing well when Dad got sick. I shut it down and joined the family business. You kind of get roped in, you know. The obligations and the expectations can pile up."

"Why didn't your sister help?"

She waved her hand dismissing the idea. "Oh, she was already long gone."

"Could you sell your current business and start over?"

"Maybe. There are a couple of girls in town who like the work, who have stepped in for me when I was sick. But what would I be selling—a client list? That wouldn't give me enough money to start again."

Now he cranked up the sell. "Still, it would give you a means to walk away. You wouldn't have to feel guilty about your customers."

They didn't speak for a while there in that cavernous room. She drooped on her couch, eyes wide and mouth turned down. He searched for a way out, irritated he was blocked. An ad man always had a path forward, even if he took a lot of turns in order to get to his goal. A glimmer of an idea. "Could you do bookkeeping now?"

"Oh, it never changes that much. I've kept my certifications up. I know the new rules for small business because I am one, and I do my own books. I suppose I could go to work for one of the big firms in Amarillo. It could be difficult, getting hired in at my age. But it would be eight-to-five and out of town."

"Could you run your own company? Do you have those types of skills?"

She laughed. "Honey, running a company that only produces paper, why that's easy compared to running Inskeep Services. I'd rather worry about customers' payroll taxes any day than trying to make small repairs, using scavenged parts for no money, just because one of my old dears is broke."

163

He walked over to the windows and stared north at some black birds wheeling against the sky. Tumbling, spiraling, like his thoughts. He turned back to her.

"Here's a proposal. We'll partner and you set up a bookkeeping company for us. I'll supply a hundred and fifty thousand up front and an office. Better yet, you work out of your home, and I'll supply the house here in Aniline. The first year or two, you won't have many clients, so we'll run off of the money I invest. When you get on your feet and start making some headway, you can start buying me out."

"What are you talking about?"

"We can even get the medical insurance handled all right. We can get it from my company if our partnership is under its umbrella."

She shot him a glance of deep skepticism. He knew he made it sound easy, but she saw it as a big thing, an enormous leap. He understood she didn't know him. If she really knew him, she wouldn't have enough confidence to try this new life.

"You have that kind of money?" She sounded disbelieving; he knew he better not make it sound too easy.

"I would have to sell something, a lot of somethings. It might be better to borrow and charge the interest against the business. But yes, I effectively have the money."

"You're making it sound like a zero interest loan."

"Oh, I would charge you a terrible fee. You have to pay me back by taking Bobbie in as your own. Otherwise, Carol could challenge Bobbie's competency and force her into her own custody."

"I'd make a more likely guardian if it went into court." She was considering it. "It's easiest that Carol give Bobbie up voluntarily; otherwise it could make trouble. And Carol'd be right across town and Bobbie would feel threatened if her mom was still part of her life."

"I agree. Sooner or later, Carol would be on you asking for money, even if she presents no other problems. We'll have to figure Carol out. We'll find out what Carol wants and sell it to her in return for legally giving up Bobbie. Maybe it's a monthly stipend, maybe we pay her bills so all her own money goes into, you know, the drugs. Maybe it's a fresh start in another town. Maybe it's rehab. You'd have to talk her in to it, although I think I can help. The trick, I've learned, is to get her to ask us for what we want as if it's her idea." He was babbling.

164

She went on to the next problem. "You'd make me leave Vega."

"But that's an advantage, you see. You'd get away from Inskeep Services forever. If you stayed, you'd slip back into that life, wouldn't you?" He sensed some guilt about this argument. He was not sure any of this part was true.

"What if we never made money? How much bookkeeping does Aniline need?"

"I'd be taking the money risk as an investor. I'd be betting on you, and I'm ready to, based on what little I know. You take the life risk; you'd be betting your way of life, a way of life you're not too keen on right now."

"Too big, too fast."

"Come on, Diane. You always wanted to be a bookkeeper. Take the chance."

"I want to think about it. I want to pray on it. I can't give you my answer today."

***

She called two days later. "Mr. Devon, this is Diane Inskeep. I'll do it. It's family, so I have to do it."

"Good," he said, with great satisfaction. "You get a lawyer, and I'll start on partnership papers and getting the money together." He was fixing it just like his dad would have—throwing money at it.

"Aren't you forgetting something? Bobbie has to be convinced also."

"Oh."

"I'm not going to move away from Vega only to have the girl run away from me in Aniline."

"She's already close. She almost agreed."

"Yes, but that was hypothetical. Just like your offer two days ago."

He saw the hole in front of him, at the edge of his feet. "I could talk to her."

She was unsure. "Hmm. If it's right, then God will guide your words. Give it a try."

"Okay, I'll let you know how it goes. Get started on your end. I want to do this fast."

"So it's really going to happen."

"I'll call you tomorrow late, and we'll see where we are. Good-bye for now."

He found the diminutive teenager paging around on the TV up in the third floor, hunkered down into the couch.

"Hey, I just got off the phone with your Aunt Diane."

Bobbie continued to stare at the muted television. "What did she want?"

"She was telling me she's moving to our town. To Aniline."

"Why?"

"You might be part of the reason."

"I didn't say I'd live with her."

"She's going to start a business here. I think that's a lot of the reason."

"You never listen. I didn't say I would do it."

"You've got time to think about it. And you can always move out. You moved out of your mother's house."

She kept clicking through the channels. "If you want to call it that."

He let time stretch out. "Diane couldn't be any worse than me."

"Are you moving away?"

He saw it was about stability as much as safety. He thought back to that afternoon in the library, to the firestorm in his feelings. "I won't lie. I might have to move out of this place, but I'll stay in town. I'll be close."

"Not too close."

"No, not too close."

She pressed the mute button, and as the sound popped on for a wildlife program, she said, "Tell her okay. I'll try."

Fast was for his sake also. He wanted to have this handled before Kate uncovered his plot, or before the police discovered his runaway, or before Carol the Demon Mother caught the girl.

***

"Dan, this is Matt Devon."

"Mr. Devon. Give me a second to pull over. You caught me in the truck…so what's up?"

"I wanted some advice. That is, if you're talking to me."

166

"Time to get on with life. Let bygones be bygones, right?"

Jesus, buddy. You hit me, not the other way around. Oh, and I'm screwing your daughter. "Hopefully. I need an inexpensive house as part of a business venture. I thought I'd get some ideas from you and maybe a realtor's name.

Dan's voice was a little warmer. "What are you looking for?"

"Nothing fancy. Needs to be on a major street, adequate parking. Three bedrooms so that one of them can become a home office. I don't mind a fixer-upper at all, but we'd have to have a move-in within a month at the latest."

Jupiter could hear Dan get into it, lose his close-clipped response for a more swinging cadence. "Is 'cheap' one of your requirements?"

"How did you guess?"

"Listen, I could give you a realtor's name, but…."

"But?"

"I know most of the housing stock here in Aniline. If you go back far enough, I swung a hammer on the build site, and a quarter of the newer stuff is mine anyway."

"So, you're offering a tour?"

"More like a first pass. Would a foreclosure be all right for you? Best price that way."

"As long as we can get clear title."

"Then I know about five possibilities. I'll come get you, and we'll do a drive-by."

"Weren't you on your way to do something when I called?"

"Yeah. Guess what?"

"Second breakfast at Angie's?"

"Uh-huh. Be downstairs in ten."

"No problem. And Dan."

"Yes?"

"Thanks."

"Thank me with breakfast."

***

The third house they checked out was located on the east side of Aniline, near the square and as far from the freeway as could be found in a small town. Jupiter stared at the front, seeing empty windows and a yard rank with weeds. The carport had collapsed. "Looks pretty beat-up, Dan."

"You can't tell much from inside the truck, Matt." Dan jumped out and Jupiter followed. They walked around the house peering in the windows. "The carport needs to be ripped off entirely; it was a cheap add-on. The roof and soffits look okay, but we need to check in the attic for leaks. Brick is good, except for some repointing needed on the side here. No cracks in the concrete yet or the brickwork, so the foundation might be a hundred percent." Dan kept up a running monologue as they went.

They could see through dirty windows that the previous occupants had abandoned their belongings, leaving them strewn through the rooms, overturned and shoved aside in haste. Jupiter didn't blame them for abandoning all this—these symbols of a life lived in hope and lost in financial despair. Of course, he wasn't about to take on a sad case like this unless the fundamentals were sound. "Did you build this one, Dan?"

"No way. Any problems you find later have nothing to do with me."

"Seems like a possible. What do you think?" Now that he saw past the yard's sadness, he was encouraged.

"We've got to inspect this old thing closely, see if she's just tired or needs to be put down. Given that nothing major is wrong, I've got a crew that can work it for you. Repairs, paint inside and out, carpet, and a spruce up of the bathrooms and kitchen—it's all doable. Do you want to get in and see?"

"Yes, I like this one better than the others, especially for location."

"All right then." Heldritch walked out into the yard to the realty sign. He dialed the number emblazoned in red.

"Hi, this is Dan Heldritch. Can I talk to Rick? Hey, Rickie. This is Dan. I've got a friend who wants to tour your foreclosure on Third Street. —Oh, legit. No waste of time on this one. —Well, maybe I'm the guy that gets to fix it up. —Sure. —And the combination for the realty lock is? —Thanks, Rick. I'll call you whichever way it goes." Dan hung up the phone. "He thinks you're an angel from God above, Matt. Let's go see what this old beast looks like inside."

***

In the end, Jupiter inspected ten foreclosures over two days, but they returned to this third house. He did a walkthrough with Dan Heldritch and an appraiser, and used Dan's subs to diagnose and bid on plumbing, wiring, the roof, and the HVAC. When the risk was low enough to make the house a good gamble, Jupiter e-mailed off photos to Vega. Diane bought in to the choice, so he went down to talk to Rick. Rick worked out of a local real estate agency that handled the property for a distant bank.

Jupiter offered twenty thousand and Rickie nearly leapt over the desk to shake his hand. Jupiter offered Heldritch another twenty to make the house habitable. Dan and his workmen had the carport, the weeds, and the trash cleared within a week, started painting the outside, and went on to interior work. The project moved along swiftly, and he realized he was becoming smug about it.

He had already made his big mistake when he had chosen the house, but he figured it out only late in the game. Bobbie would make the house an impossibility.

On a Saturday morning after breakfast he took her the half dozen blocks from the grain elevator to the house, wanting to show her where she and Diane would live. Jupiter pulled up in the drive, and they both climbed out of his truck. He walked to the door and got out his key while Bobbie stood in the front yard scrubbing her toe in the patchy green grass. He opened the door and stepped in to the smell of new paint. The girl followed him at a distance. They walked through the house and he pointed out details. One bedroom was in the front off the living room. This would become the office. Of the two bedrooms in the back, one had a door to the outside, showing it had been retrofitted as a den at one time. She walked over to the outside door. "I'd like this room."

When he pointed out the bathrooms, she shrugged her shoulders. "Okay." They stood in the center of the living room. "Where will the TV go?" The kitchen got more interest. "It's not all awful shiny like yours. It's smaller too. I can see out the window when I do dishes."

When they visited the backyard, she jumped down the step from the back door into the yard and stared to the East, into the scrappy development and farmland on the outskirts of town. Shaking, she pointed at something—a trailer. That's when she collapsed, while he was looking

169

away.

He heard her hit the ground and he turned, but he was slow to understand. The idea jumped through his mind that something had knocked her down. He ran the four steps back to her and rolled her over on her back. She convulsed continuously, but not with the bone-jarring jerk of a *grand mal* seizure. Her eyes were open but glazed. Drool ran out of the corner of her mouth. He realized the sound he heard was the heels of her sneakers thudding on the ground. He pried her mouth open with his left hand and she bit him, hard. In spite of the pain, he continued to wedge her teeth apart with his injured hand. He thrust a stick from the grass across her teeth and tongue. He prayed this was the right thing to do. The fit lasted a full, horrible, interminable minute.

As her eyes focused once again, Bobbie realized she was lying on her back, and he was kneeling over her with her head cradled in his hands. He could see the panic coming up like a wave, the alarmed round eyes with flaring eyebrows. He jerked his hands away and fell over backwards to give her some space as fast as he could. The young woman was frightened and disoriented, but Jupiter—all of the muscles in his flabby abdomen were tight as iron bars, bending him over in pain.

She sat up and began sobbing loudly, uncontrollably. He didn't touch her; he only sat there turning the mistake over and over. Jupiter hadn't bothered to find out where Carol Inskeep lived.

***

It took awhile and a lot of thinking. Jupiter paced back and forth, alone in the head house with no idea where Bobbie had gone. He did know she'd be huddled in the dimness of a refuge somewhere. She would wait for something inside to say she could safely venture out. She would also decide whether she could trust his promise to "fix it."

Jupiter had options. The easy one wouldn't work. Bobbie wouldn't be fooled by a fence or by a row of trees.

Other options were nastier. He could dump the house back on the market and start over, considerably poorer. He could get Carol Inskeep to move away from the house and preferably out of town. He could get Carol locked up. He could get her dead. He had four ways to go and no clear choice. And he could probably think of some more, equally bad.

170

He picked up the phone and called Vega. At the familiar Inskeep Services message, he said, "Diane, it's Matt; pick up if you can. Are you there? Call me when you get this message. It's important."

Diane called back in an hour, and he still had not made a choice. He told her about the house and trailer and then about the seizure. He let it soak in.

"Dirt and damnation, Matt! This is a really awful thing. I should have driven over and looked at the house myself. How's Bobbie?"

He lied smoothly. "Not good, not bad. Locked up in the TV room distracting herself." It looked like lying was what he did well.

"You didn't take her to ER?"

"And how well do you think she would do there?"

"What do you think we ought to do?"

He took it as a positive sign that she had said "we" rather than "you." He asked, "First things first. Is there any history of epilepsy in your family?"

"None I ever heard."

"Did Carol ever say anything about Bobbie having seizures?"

"No. Believe it or not, Carol was always a real squeamish mother. I think she would have tried to dump Bobbie back on my Momma if she'd had epilepsy."

"Now for the kicker—how attached to your sister are you, Diane?"

He could hear her breath over the line. "I love her, if that's what you mean. I also think she was the tribulation of the Inskeeps. Inflicted by God on my parents as some kind of test. She came close to ruining all our lives, and I'm not talking about just shame."

He said nothing.

"I think Carol hates herself and that's the sad part, makes it kind of hopeless."

"But how far would you go, Diane? Would you want her out of town or in jail? Would you ever want to see her again?"

"What are you saying? Carol, shall we forsake thee?"

"It's not biblical, Diane."

"Sure it is, Matt. Everything important ends up being biblical." Diane asked, "I think what you're saying is—Carol has to—we've got to make her move away?"

He pointed her away from the mother towards the girl. "Bobbie

171

can't live in the house if Carol is in the trailer."

"Are we ruining my sister's life for a house, then?"

"We talked before about a solution to Carol and the other problems she poses, you remember. This is just moving the need to the front—moving the timeline up." Matt tried to control his voice, to sound calm and reasonable, but he could hear that background quaver in his words.

"Years ago my parents had to get Carol away from the family. They bought her a lot and a trailer in Aniline and told her to never come home." Matt waited for the woman to speak, and he waited awhile. "If it was best for Bobbie, I would agree to never see my sister again. Out of town is acceptable. Even jail is acceptable. It could either finish her or set her on God's path. Living the way she is now, it will kill her sooner or later, won't it?"

"I haven't met Carol. I'm not a doctor or a policeman, so I don't know, but I think so."

"Do you know what to do?"

Like a bonfire in his head, he could suddenly see the basic idea, the shining idea of what he would do. "Let me work something out and make a few phone calls. I need to talk to someone. If I can get it organized, then I'll call you. You might need to drive over here for awhile to help me make it happen."

"Tell me sooner than later, Matt. But what about the fits?"

"Only one fit, and caused entirely by her mother."

"You're ducking it."

"Delaying, maybe. Call your doctor; talk it over. It's got to be serious, but it's not immediate."

"Let's pray it's not immediate."

***

When Jupiter heard Bobbie in the kitchen, he felt the sob in his throat but caught it before it broke through. He went in and made a small tomato sauce and cheese pizza for her dinner without saying a word. He sat with an iced tea opposite her at the breakfast bar, watching his hands tremble with small jolts and jerks. She ate at it savagely, leaving a smear of the grease on her cheek.

"Bobbie?"

"Hmm," she said, around the final mouthful of pizza.

"You said you didn't want to see your mother again."

She didn't like this topic. Her glance slid off into the corner and then down at her plate. She hunched her shoulders.

"Your Mother is sick. She's addicted to drugs, and that's a disease."

"So?"

"So she might never get better. She might go to jail. She might die from this disease."

Bobbie nested her hands in her lap and stared down at them. "Let her die."

That's what Jupiter needed to know.

***

First Jupiter called his lawyer and asked him a couple of guarded questions. Next call he made was for some preliminary arrangements. Then he drove down to the police station and asked to see the Chief. A civilian clerk ushered him into the Chief's office. He sat down gingerly on a chair in a room full of clutter. A hundred flyers and memos nailed with their thumbtacks hung from a bulletin board. The desk sergeant could see him through the glass, so he sat still and didn't poke around inspecting the piles of things on the desktop. In a minute, the Chief bustled in and threw himself bodily into his chair. He was not armed. "Mr. Devon, I was wondering when we would meet."

The Chief gave Jupiter one of those sizing-you-up looks, but that was fair. Jupiter was inspecting the Chief himself, checking for clues to the man. Jupiter saw a short guy in a dark blue uniform, perhaps fifty, with a heavy tan, a balding head. The Chief had a walrus mustache, thin eyebrows, and a strong chin. Jupiter tried a smile and held his hand out.

The Chief's shake was vigorous and short, and he threw Jupiter's hand back like it was a fish.

Jupiter answered, "Yes. I thought you and I would meet when the Town Attorney sent you over with relevant paperwork."

"Not today, but we can still look forward to that, can't we?"

"Hmm. I have months left in the appeal process. I also have a Council meeting ahead, I think, and I could get an injunction maybe in civil court. We're still a ways off from an eviction."

"So today isn't about a grand departure from the grain elevator?"

"No, this isn't about my *home*." He cleared his throat. "I wanted to sound you out about crime here in Aniline and your views on a couple of things."

"This isn't a reporter thing, is it? Or are you running for office?"

"No, I just know of a situation that is affecting a couple of my friends here in Aniline. Do you know Carol Inskeep? Lives out on the east side of town?"

"Now, before you start demanding we take action, I have to tell you we've done everything we can legally do at this point. Come to think of it, that's true in your case too." He smiled, blurring out the sting some.

"I'm not here to make demands. I understand Carol is a drug user."

"So who are these friends of yours, and why do you have an interest?"

"I have a business partner named Diane Inskeep. Diane is Carol's sister. She's worried about her new business if Carol is here in town. It's also hard to have a sister around who is a drug addict. It is true Carol is a user?"

"Certainly, most obvious thing in Texas. Just so you understand me, we have to apportion our resources carefully, so I would never be using police officers to chase her around. She's a victim of her habit, but we've never heard she breaks the law to pay for the meth. No, the thorn in my side is the drug dealer that lives with her."

"I don't think I know his name."

The Chief pursed his lips, inhaled, then answered. "The alleged drug dealer is a gentleman of no evident financial support named Henry Lovato."

"Is there anything else I should know about him?"

"A couple of suspicious deaths near him, including an old girlfriend."

"And?"

"To date we have searched his car four times during DUI roadblocks and had probable cause once to get a warrant to search the trailer. We've had no positive results."

"Is there a way to get them to move on?"

"You mean, get a landlord to evict them? No. She evidently got the property from her parents and owns it fair and clear."

"Seize the property? Condemn the trailer?"

"As far as condemning the trailer, it's not a restaurant or some other public thing. Trying to use a claim of a health problem—that's a dead end. 'No' on seizing the property; somebody always pays the taxes. All I can do is send a patrol car by there every once in awhile."

"I take it you would find it…" Jupiter paused searching for the words, "…ah, consider it in the best interests of the community if Carol was to move on, or if Lovato could no longer use the trailer as a base."

"It may be selfish to say, but I'd wish them on any other community as long as they were out of mine."

"I'd like to make it worthwhile for Carol to either move on or to go into rehab. I don't think she will take her sister or me seriously, though. I was wondering how far you would go to bolster our position. Maybe I can provide you with something in return."

"I'll listen, but I warn you not to propose anything illegal."

***

Diane stood in the yard while Jupiter ascended the wooden steps and knocked on the trailer door. They waited. He knocked again. He heard shuffling. The inside door opened. Through the screen, still closed against them, Jupiter could see a woman who appeared as if she were forty-going-on-seventy and dying of some wasting disease. Carol was both blonde and gray, pale and discolored the yellow of smoke, thin and flabby around the face. She had a cigarette in her hand with one arm clasping her waist, one arm cocked out. It didn't come across like the old Hollywood vamp pose. "What do you want?"

Diane spoke from the bunch grass and the dust, "It's me, Carol. Can we come in? We'd like to talk."

"Nothing much to say, Diane. Henry isn't here."

"What we have to say is for you, Carol, not for your—for Henry."

"I guess." Carol pushed the screen door open with her foot, and Jupiter caught it. He held it for Diane who entered first. As he passed Carol, he could see her teeth—rotted black stumps, decayed and diseased. The teeth of a dragon, a stench of breath from the Underworld, and tangled hair of the Gorgon.

A wave of smell, the tang of rotting garbage packed his nose. A large new TV dominated the tiny room. All else was faded, dirty, and worn. In the shag carpet at his feet, he saw glass splinters; it was a smashed meth pipe woven into the loops of the rug. On the coffee table with its burned and scarred surface, there were two or three crushed-down soda cans with perforations ripped around their rims and burn marks in their centers. The leatherette seats were sticky with blotches of food. He heard a crunching and realized he was standing in caramel corn spilled out across the floor from an open bag.

As they had agreed, Diane took the lead. "Carol, we talked about this last time I was here. I'd love to see you get rid of this life, move on to something else, something more Christian."

Carol perched on the couch edge, hunched her shoulders, and hugged herself. She squinted up at Diane, gusted a cloud of cigarette smoke out of the corner of her mouth. "Diane, you always were ready to run everyone else's life. Don't give me any of your holy-roller shit."

Carol's hands jittered, skittish, touched this and that and moved on. Her mouth twitched and her eyes were dilated. Jupiter whispered to Diane, "Well, what were the odds we'd catch her between highs?"

Diane tried again, sat opposite her sister, leaned forward and touched her knee. "I thought maybe you were ready to think about what's best for Bobbie."

"She's got a place here if she wants it. I'm doing fine—she would too."

There was the sound of tires on gravel outside the trailer. He stood up, moved to the window, saw that the Chief had done as promised. With relish, he said to Carol, "Excuse me for interrupting, but I think the police are outside."

Carol jumped up, peeked out the window, and headed for the bedroom. Diane leapt up from the sofa and started to follow, but he held out a hand and stopped her. In a moment they heard a flushing sound, and Carol ran back into the room to peer out the window again.

He took over from Diane, acting as the bearer of bad tidings. "What you see outside are two squad cars with their lights flashing. They have a warrant to search here. But you're not worried about that—not now."

Carol smirked. That nasty little curl of the lip signaled her confidence.

"What we came to tell you is that they've had wiretaps in place for

176

some time as part of a big operation. They've been eavesdropping on Henry. He's about to get swept up and arrested as part of a major bust."

Carol jerked her head and stared at the door. "Shit!"

"Tell me, Carol, do you think you'll go down with him? Or do you think you'll only lose your free meth?" He felt elated, buoyed up by the sheer pleasure of lying. Guilt free. Extravagant lying backed up by squad cars outside.

Carol skittered partway into the kitchen and darted back to the window, then back to the center of the room.

"Carol, sit down." He nudged her to a perch on the couch and then leaned forward. He projected the comforting image of a friend. "The way I see it is that you have a few options. Maybe you can run. You know, leave town. Let Henry take the fall along with his business associates. Or you could stay and go to jail with him."

Carol said, "Maybe they won't arrest me."

"But if they do arrest you, you could roll over on Henry. If you choose to cooperate with the police, and if you give them something big enough, they'll let you walk."

Maintaining eye contact, he gazed into her dilated eyes; he knew she was having trouble following him.

Carol flicked her eyes first at him, then Diane, then back to him. He went on, "If you run, we can help. We can send you some money each month. We can pay for rehab if you'll take it."

He glanced over at Diane, and she stared amazed at him, her mouth open and working like a fish. He hadn't let Diane in on all the details of his scheme—after all, she wasn't the great liar.

Carol's face flashed from scowling to wide-eyed frightened staring, to slack defeat. She was overwhelmed. He plowed on, narrowing the choices for her. "If you cooperate with the police, if you roll on Henry, either the State can pay for rehab or we will. We can get you help."

He glanced over at Diane, checked to see what her state of mind was. She had slapped her mouth shut. Her forehead wrinkled up, and her eyes narrowed.

Carol's mouth worked, opening and closing. "If they arrest me? Henry?"

"You would know more about that than me. What do you think?"

"I don't know anything to tell them about Henry. I just—I just let him live here. He gives me what I want, but I never have to move his drugs. I don't know anything about his business."

Diane took a breath and made up her mind about his lie. "So you have nothing to trade the police? You'll have to serve time." She handed it back to him with a nod of her head.

Carol pleaded, "Don't let the cops in! I don't know what to do." As if on cue, they all heard footsteps at the door.

"You have to decide now." He marched on, piled it on top of her. "It's jail or run. Or you can sit here, and let Henry decide. After he's arrested but you two are out on bail, that's when he'll decide. He might worry about you, about what you would say to the police. You know Henry better than we do."

She made a quiet despairing sound like a kitten mewling.

He kept pushing. "What's it going to be, Carol? What do you want to do?"

She cracked, gave the snap answer of an amphetamine buzz. "I'll run—I'll get away."

Diane leaned forward. "Right now. Go pack. I'll get Matt to send the police away." Carol scurried into the bedroom with Diane shooing her on.

***

He stuffed both women into the back seat. He leaned in the window on Diane's side.

She demanded, "Where are the police cars?"

"I did in fact send them away." He dropped his voice, "We'll drive her to Dallas this afternoon to rehab. I've made the preliminary contacts. I had the paperwork faxed to me. It's there in the car beside you. We can finish filling it out as we go. You should be there to help check her in."

She murmured back, "Yes, I see that."

"Tell her rehab is her best bet; keep saying that it was her idea." He rubbed his eyes. "We've done the right thing. Henry has killed at least one girlfriend." He dug in his shirt pocket, handed her two Prozac pills. "If she needs calming down."

Diane regarded him levelly and said, "I agree, and I've helped you, but I have to ask forgiveness for the way we did it."

178

"Don't ask her for forgiveness, Diane. You'll confuse the issue."

"I meant the Lord, not her."

He went back inside and collected all the paper in the trailer—scribbled notes, an address book, phone records, utility bills, airline frequent flyer reports, letters, a pile of unopened mail, and a day planner. He found a manila folder hidden in a foolish place, taped to the bottom of a drawer. He poured everything into grocery-store plastic bags. He collected three mobile phones that lay on the counter.

He drove to a public park they had passed on the way in. It was in full view of the road and was sprinkled with picnic tables. Leaving the women in the car, he walked to a table and left the bags weighted down by a rock. The Chief would be by soon.

Ishtar and Gilgamesh,

and the Death of Enkidu

Chapter Twenty: Fighting Before the Gate

Divergent pieces of Jupiter's life collided at the last of July like a meteor shattering hard earth. It happened because he had given Kate a key to the head house, because he had not told Bobbie that Kate was coming over. It happened because he wore himself out...because of his long day of travel to Vega, the meeting with Diane Inskeep to sign final papers and the travel home through Amarillo traffic. When he arrived at his elevator, his anxiety was flaming in like a comet. He took a Valium and lay down in the bedroom. He fell asleep. Afterwards he was never sure whether he saw the whole episode in his tranquilized mind or if he pieced it together from Kate's words. A Daoist drug haze.

He lay in bed dreaming. He saw Kate arrive at five, bringing a bottle of wine and some cold fried chicken from the café. Jupiter's responsibility included vegetables, coffee, and after-dinner brandy, but he couldn't move. When she walked into the head house, Kate went first to the kitchen where she set her groceries on the bar. She saw an empty banana skin, a juice carton, and a hair barrette laying on the counter. She picked the barrette up, bounced it in her hand, and dropped it on the counter. She made a little *moue* of her mouth. He recognized that expression, the thought.

Coming out into the lofted space, she hesitated, listened. She could hear water running. Creeping up the stairs, she followed the sound to the guest suite.

Jupiter was right behind her at the door, and he was also lying in bed.

Kate stole forward into a bedroom. A pair of pink sneakers lay by the bed. Kate glared down at the shoes and rolled one over with her toe.

181

She turned the doorknob of the bathroom. It was locked. She smiled and ran her hand along the top of the doorframe. A metal pin fell off. She used it to unlock the knob.

He tried to speak, to stop her—nothing.

Stepping into the steam, Kate pulled aside the shower curtain and said, "I don't know who you are, but come out and show yourself."

Kate peered into the steam. A great deal of noise, screaming, and panic boiled out of the tub and made her step back. She retreated back into the bedroom, closing the door on bedlam. She was soaked down her front from her breasts to her ankles.

He knew that look—she was poised, expectant, nearly gleeful. He saw her drop to the bed ready for the door to open.

In a couple of minutes, the bathroom door flew back. A small woman, barefoot and in a sweat suit, sprinted past for the bedroom door. Kate caught a glimpse of sallow skin and short jet-black hair, a frightened face. She laughed at the wide-eyed, open-mouthed appearance and the shrill sounds the mouth made. The girl never glanced her way. A second later, Kate and he could hear feet slapping on the stairs.

For a moment Kate sat there on the bed, swinging one foot in the air. She stood up, went in the bathroom, and toweled out some of the water in her clothes. Then she marched off to find Jupiter. He lay in the dusk, curled up on his side in the bed, and he also walked with her to the master bedroom. She flipped on the light, perched on the edge of the bed and roughly shook him, "Matt. Matt! Wake up!"

His eyes jumped open. He had been deep asleep. Groggy, he stared up at her. The valium made the light around her head flare into a rainbow surround.

"Matt, you'll never guess what I discovered. I found a woman in your bathroom. Think of that, another woman." Her voice sounded artful and wondering.

He sat up. He had visualized a different moment when he had rehearsed telling Kate about Bobbie Inskeep. "Did you frighten her?"

"I sure hope so! She scared the hell out of me."

She didn't appear frightened to him. "Hmm, that's not good."

He shifted towards the edge of the bed, towards Kate. She reached out and touched his cheek.

"Not good I discovered the other woman? Or maybe I am the other

182

woman." Her hand, which had lain softly on his cheek, curled up in the warning scratch of four nails.

"You're the only woman here in this house. She's a special case. Let's go downstairs. I'll pour you a drink and tell you about it."

"Oh yes, I think you had better do that."

She stepped back, and he got up. They went together down the stairs, a stranger's distance between them. As they descended, he began. "Do you remember the name Roberta Inskeep?"

"Uh-huh. About six or seven years behind me in school. That makes her high school about now, high school, Matt."

"She's not my Lolita, Kate. She's a runaway. At first she was just around. Then she became my charity cause. Your mom knows about her. Well, kind of knows about her."

She sat and waited while he poured two white wines. When he approached her with the glasses, she nodded and bid him set hers down on the table. He figured this might be one of his toughest sales.

"So tell me about your naked runaway."

Loaded words. "I became involved because she was hanging around the elevator starved half to death. I thought she was a boy. She was sleeping in the steel silo. At first I thought about calling the authorities...."

"Now, that would have been a good idea."

"And I would have. Maybe should have. But they would have chased her down if they caught her at all, and I didn't like the idea of that—cops in squad cars chasing a kid."

She nodded—a small victory. "That sounds nearly plausible. Nobody likes the police, but it is their job. You should have called."

"I decided it would be best if I could talk her in from the cold and call Child Protective Services myself."

"They're not called that any more."

"What?"

"They're called the Texas Department of Family Services."

"Oh." He had trouble starting up his defensive patter again. "Well, I lured the girl with breakfast. I bribed her with food to get her close enough to talk—to learn her name. That's where your mom comes in to the story. She tells me I have a nineteen-year-old girl on my hands. Bobbie isn't a minor."

"Uh-huh, barely legal." She picked up her wine glass.

"Your mom says that Bobbie's mother is a meth head, which you might already know. I was able to locate her Aunt Diane. She's moving here from Vega to take over the girl."

"Take over? But you said Bobbie isn't a minor, so she can do what she wants."

"Well, no. Bobbie has some extra problems. She's more homeless than a runaway. She eats and cleans up here, but she sleeps out there somewhere where she feels safe."

"So?" Kate waved her hand in a come-on gesture, urging him to say something to the point.

"I haven't gotten to the extra problems yet. From what I can tell, she has dyslexia or some other disability. Uh, and she should be under psychological care because she's probably been sexually abused. And she occasionally falls down and has a fit."

Kate plunked her elbow on her knee and her forehead onto the side of her wine glass. "So you've got a naked teenager living in your house who needs a shrink and who can't read and who has fits?" She shot him a look, the look he knew.

He made a placating gesture, pushing down with both hands. "No, she merely eats here, and I've never seen her naked. Listen, I could call the aunt, and she'll confirm what I'm telling you."

She stared up at him in challenge. "Fine. Call her."

He retreated, searched for the phone, and ducked her stare. He found the wireless phone buried in one of the couches and called Diane in Vega. She was there, for once, and he blurted out, "Diane, it's Matt. I've got another problem."

"Is it that Lovato? Is he causing trouble? Does he want to know where Carol is?"

"No, it's not your sister's boyfriend—point in fact, it's about me and someone I've been seeing."

"At your age, Mr. Devon? You continue to surprise me."

"Uh, right. But now I'm in a jam here, and I need you to explain in your own words...." This was awkward.

Diane finished the sentence up for him, "Why you've become involved in a young girl's life and how it's all platonic?"

"That would be good. Here, I'll put her on." He handed the phone to

Kate. "Here's Bobbie's aunt."

Kate took the phone, holding it down to her side while she flicked her eyes over him. Then she held it to her ear. "Hello, this is Kate Heldritch. To whom am I speaking?" She listened for a moment only. She asked, "And you're Bobbie's aunt?" Kate waited through a short answer, then said, "I think you should tell me all about it. —Uh-huh. —Right. —Here in Aniline? —And her mother? —Is she unstable? —And you're sure? —Sure about Devon?"

The conversation went on for some time. In the end, Kate said "Thanks" and handed the phone back to him.

He held the receiver to his ear and asked, "Diane?"

"Don't worry about her, Matt. Our Lord above knows you're a good man."

"Be nice if she knew it, too."

"She's about half convinced, I think."

"When are you moving?"

"Need a little protection? The van is scheduled to move me next Tuesday."

"Good. None too soon. I'll see you then." He walked across the room and set the phone back in its stand, took a breath, and turned back to Kate.

"For a saint, Matt, you sure look like a sinner."

"Not a compliment, I think."

"You're either a pervert or the stupidest man in town. You appear quite stupid, so I think we may let the pervert part go. On the other hand, I'd welcome more confirmation." Kate slugged down the rest of her wine. "Where is Bobbie now?"

"You saw her last."

"Don't get uppity, Matt. When I last saw her, she was wet but dressed and running like hell."

He bobbed his head. "I'd guess she's hiding in the work floor or is out in the steel silo… if she didn't run further."

"She's barefoot."

"Then she's still here. Rocks. Stickers."

"Will she trust me?"

"Dunno." He felt woozy-strange answering with Bobbie's own two syllable reply. "She trusts her aunt, so maybe it extends to other women."

185

"I'm going to try and find her and take her home to my mom. If I'm successful, I'll call once I get to the house. Otherwise, I'll come back up here and wait."

"For what?"

"For the girl…to take her home. Jesus, Matt, wake up. You know I'll ask her about you if I can."

"I hope you do."

"If it's a good answer, then I want to see you tomorrow night, to talk all this out. Otherwise…." The threat hung there.

"Ah."

***

Kate called two hours later. "Matt. We're on for dinner and that talk tomorrow. It also looks like you need a permanent keeper. I'll see you about six."

"Bobbie is with you?"

"Yes, not that you're entitled to know. She remembers my mom; it's working out and she's calmed down."

"You're taking over?"

"Right. Like you did so well on your own?"

Any defense would be deadly. He was quiet.

"You still there?"

He asked, "But, this is only till Diane gets here, right?

"Leave it to the women, Matt."

"So we're okay?"

"Oh, shut up." She slammed down the phone.

He was so relieved he went into the bathroom and vomited. He had forgotten how acrid puke smelled once it was backed up in your nose.

***

Jupiter should have known better than to try to sleep when he was upset. He also shouldn't have been sitting in bed, propped up by pillows, because it gave him the illusion he was awake. In the dream, the lights were on in the bedroom, as they had been when he had clambered into bed. But in this dream, he had left the door of the bedroom open, and that open door let in the sound of woodblocks, of a woman's clopping shoes. He knew that stride, the sound of that walk. Estelle Devereaux appeared at the foot of his bed. This Estelle was not the dumpy supermarket checker he had married. She was Sheila, his porcelain suburbanite. There was a hint of perfume, a really good fragrance. Her haircut was one of those two-hundred dollar manes. Puzzled he asked, "Sheila, aren't you in Hawaii? Why are you here?"

She clopped again, her hooves ringing on the concrete. "Sheila, huh? No one I know can afford Hawaii, Matthew Devereaux. You're talking crazy. Who's this broodmare Sheila?"

"Sorry, Estelle. I—I just had a mind glitch."

"Not the first time. And don't think I won't figure out who Sheila is."

"Not tonight, Estelle. I'm too tired to fight." He rustled in his bed of straw, slight motions of burrowing in and rejection.

"Even divorced, I still don't like the idea of you screwing around." She tossed her mane and her nostrils flared.

"Honest, there's no Sheila. It's the truth."

"I guess there's a first time in every marriage." Estelle stepped back. "Let me start over, Matthew. I wanted to talk about Jimmy." Matthew felt a jump in his heart, a lightness. "He's a senior this year." She turned her head and smiled, showing large yellow teeth. Her ear rotated, twitched away a horsefly.

"I know, Estelle. I may not live in the house anymore, but I keep up with Jim. I do call. I'm coming to the graduation, you know."

"I admit it. You were a crap husband, but you're an okay dad."

He was alert to the danger. The thought dropped into speech before he could stop it, "You must want something."

"Not for me, Matthew. I want Jimmy to go to college, actually to the University of Texas on the Austin campus, in September. Then Vet School."

"I'd like that too." He noticed her flanks were perspiring, as if she had been running a long way.

"It's not a matter of liking. It's a matter of paying."

"Ah, I knew this day was coming."

"You've got to do it, Matthew. He's your son. He needs you to sign the papers that guarantee the tuition. Then you have to pay it."

"Even at a state school, tuition will eat up most of my income and yours too. Empty feed bags."

"That's right." She plunged on. "You're going to have to sell it."

He knew what she meant. "Sell what?"

"It's just a run-down farm."

He lay there watching the large fly buzz past and go up to the ceiling, circling. "It's my dad's farm. It's the last of my Dad."

"It's for your son."

"That's right. That's right. It would be for Jim." They stared at each other, she standing there tawny and magnificent, he lying in bed under a disgraceful old horse blanket—as usual.

"So, are you actually agreeing?" She laughed a quiet whicker.

"I'll do it. My dad would see his way clear if he were still here. He'd do it for his only grandson."

Estelle stood tossing her head at the bottom of the bed, far away, but closer than she had been in years. They would send their son to college.

***

Jupiter slid regretfully into wakefulness, grasping at the slippery dream as it got away. He weighed it up. He'd never drive Jimmy down to Austin, never take him to freshman orientation. Never help him carry his possessions up to a dorm room. Jim won't go to college. Jim will never appear here in this grain house. He had killed Jim in 1989.

His real life was a gray version of what he wanted, and the dream was the truth within him. He felt a stinging in his eyes.

He picked up the phone, and he called Marjorie.

She answered, "Hello, Marjorie here."

"Marjorie, its Jupiter."

"Ah, that's the trouble with working out of one's house. Your clients call all hours of the day and night, any time they want. Luckily I'm up."

"I wouldn't bother you this late if it weren't important."

Her voice went from banter to professional. "What is it, Jupiter?"

"I've lied to you for awhile—by omission. And I've lost my son."

"I didn't think you and Sheila had any children."

"No. That's true. Can I come to see you about it?"

"Actually talk to me in person? Drive straight over."

188

"I'll be there in forty-five minutes."

"I'll make the tea."

***

Even in the dark, her house was different than any other he had seen. On one end was a glass geodesic, lit from within like a jewel. Marjorie met him at the door and took him back through the dim-lit house, past tapestries on the walls, past futons and bookcases, to the dome. From within, it framed the black night in triangles, reflected the candles' flames over and over. On a rug-strewn floor, she sank into an open lotus. He hunkered his way to the ground, folded his legs, and felt the first twinge of pain in his knees. Between them was a flat stone, and on the stone was an Asian teapot and two English bone china cups.

"It was good of you to see me tonight, Marjorie." He stared at her calm round face and tried to discover any irritation on her part.

"No problem. Can I pour you tea?"

"I'd prefer Scotch."

"I think, maybe, you're working up your nerve for something." A quick smile flashed out of her brown face. "The drink wouldn't help, you know, not for anything this serious."

"How do you know it's serious?"

"You came to me." She waved her hand across the room. "This is not the phone."

"No, it's not the phone."

She poured, and in the silence he could hear the nearly metallic gurgle. He picked up the cup, cradled it in his lap, and felt it heat up. She waited.

"Marjorie, I'm in more trouble than I've told you."

"At least that is the truth." She smiled, robbed the words of harshness.

"You know about... my fear of people."

"Hmm. Real and visceral enough. You're sweating right now, because you're with me."

"And I've told you about my conversations with Gilgamesh."

"Yes. On a computer."

"There's more."

"Jupiter, I will gladly listen, but I am not a professional psychiatrist or psychologist. I'm your Life Coach."

"You minored in psychology."

She waved her hand. "Sometime soon you must listen to me, and trust me more than you trust yourself. It's time for professional help. It has been time for a while."

"You don't even know what it is."

"It's worse than your Gilgamesh delusion, or you would have told me."

"Maybe."

She sipped her tea. "When you're ready. The tea will help. My family ships it to me from the Philippines. It has always soothed me."

He slurped a bit. It smelled of flowers, sweet and tart together. The taste was thin and bitter. "I've been having nightmares, variations on a theme. I'm married in these dreams, to someone else... not to Sheila."

"Another woman, or a man?"

"Woman."

"How long have you had these dreams?"

"Several years. Before the anthropophobia."

"Sex, death, mortality, humiliation?"

"All of those." He ducked his head. "How did you know?"

She waved a hand. "How do you know this is a dream and not a daydream?"

"Sometimes I'm a horse."

"And you think the dream means something?"

"Yes."

"Jupiter, you're making me interrogate you. This is your story."

"Ahh." He cleared his throat. He sipped on the tea, and gazed into the dark behind her. "I dream that I am married to a woman named Estelle. I dream that our son dies—in various ways. The dreams are terrifying. All except the latest one."

"You had better tell me about them, as many as you can remember."

***

After he had said all, Marjorie reached across the stone and took his hand. "You've built a horror of a dream life and submerged yourself in it,

190

again and again. You keep going back through that gate because there's something there that you need. You're fighting it."

"Is that what the Daoist says?"

"No, the humanist. There was a chance at a son, somewhere in your time, and you must deeply regret missing that chance. There is also some major guilt, because this imaginary son keeps dying while in your care."

"Sounds facile to me, Marjorie."

"I'm sure you're wrong, and I may be right. Dreams are never facile. Nightmares peer into our truer selves."

"God, I hope not."

Chapter Twenty-One: Dreams of What Could Have Been

Jupiter lay in a nest of sheets and blankets, in the slight stench of self-pity. After his last Jimmy Devereaux dream, he was afraid to sleep. His body ached; his eyelashes were clotted with the sand of eye mattering, irritated.

He heard chiming and a tinny burst from an alarm—a tintinnabulation. In his head? Downstairs. He crawled out of bed and felt the hard, dusty floor on his bare feet. Jupiter crept down the stairs and shuffled towards the couch—of course, the laptop. Still, he could have imagined the chime and also—the conversation that was about to come.

"I would speak to my friend ur-Jupiter."

Jupiter replied, "Here I am. You seem the most awake when I am the most asleep."

"I am, after all, on the other side of the earth, and the sun Shamash rides in the sky. I thank you with all sincerity for convincing me the earth Ki is round."

"How did you make the laptop chime?"

"Your mechanical scribe? I have no idea—I only thought to summon you."

"No problem. I hadn't gotten to sleep yet. Tell me where you are, what you are doing."

"It is a day of prayer on the Ziggurat. I have one or two priests with me, but I am alone for all purposes. The sky is veiled with gray between us and Shamash. My form casts little shadow. That would be a foretelling or symbol if I was a poet or singer—or a priest."

192

With a jolt, Jupiter actually saw him now. On the screen, Gilgamesh surfaced up through the text. Gilgamesh knelt on a rush mat high above Uruk, facing the door to the top chamber. Inside, a large block of alabaster formed the altar. Gray light, squinting bright, radiated from a flat ashen sky. Gilgamesh looked exactly as Jupiter had expected. "Casting no shadow? You sound reflective, maybe even depressed."

Gilgamesh gave him a sad grin, extended his hands to the sky first, and then to the altar. "Yesterday was the Day of Births. All my progeny gathered around and we celebrated the King's lineage. We pretended all are born to the same calendar day. ur-Jupiter, I have great-great-great-grandchildren now fully grown. Age creeps up on this king." He bowed his head to the altar and then rocked back on his heels.

"We're both getting older."

"I wheezed like an old auroch by the time we reached the pinnacle of the Ziggurat this morning."

"And I couldn't kneel like you're doing, at least not for long. What shall we visit about?"

"Speak to me of your wild one and her Humbaba of a mother."

Jupiter paused. Gilgamesh had predicted the conflict. "I have confined the mother in a place far away."

"So I see. But you should have taken the sword to her. She is a threat at your back."

The image of Bobbie in the midst of her seizure leapt in. "She threatens my wild one, not me."

Bending, Gilgamesh lowered his head to the stone, spread his hands as far apart as they would go, and placed his palms on the pavement. From the position of supplication, he said, "Humbaba is not the threat to the child. Like Enkidu, the gods concern themselves with this one. You must be on guard against them, for her sake."

Great—now Gilgamesh was laying out prophecy. "And you know this how?"

"I dreamt of it."

Jupiter twitched his eyebrows. "Then I'm not worried. You and Enkidu both interpreted dreams, even though you knew only the women of Sumeria had the true skill. Your Epic details how often you got it wrong."

Gilgamesh grimaced. His priests brought a copper bowl, and he washed his hands, drowning his bronze bracelets and his sleeves in water. "That is most true. All of the dreams before the battle with Humbaba should have sent me home in panic. If Enkidu had not created such positive meanings for each, I would have given up. And, rightly interpreted, the dreams were nearly true in their doom and gloom. I would have been charred flesh on the mountain if Shamash had not sent the four winds against my demon Humbaba."

"Enkidu interpreted his own dream after the battle with the Bull of Heaven."

The priests removed the bowl and gave Gilgamesh a towel of linen. He dried his hands and clambered to his feet with a grunt. "Enkidu was right about his dream. Death sat in the room."

Jupiter watched Gilgamesh bow to the cardinal points, sixty-four—a slow progression around the compass. "A vivid and hideous dream."

Gilgamesh finished the circumambulation and rubbed his back. "His death was horrible. I sat beside him the next days until the worm crawled up through his eye. The dream foretold this."

Jupiter had dreadful dreams about death too. "Is it possible Enkidu convinced himself he would die?"

Gilgamesh stepped into the gloom of the chamber. The altar was before him, the goat bound and waiting. "I have asked myself that also. Is it possible ur-Jupiter convinces himself he must be alone? No children, alone in his house—is that his desire?"

"How did you know the house is empty?"

Gilgamesh picked up the bronze dagger and cradled the leather-bound handle in his palms. "Do I not see you clearly? Your wild one is with your Inanna, kept from you by the woman whose strength astounds you. You are alone in your tower as you prefer."

Not quite. There was bittersweet quiet, a lukewarm relief in the freedom. "Kate will be coming to the house tomorrow—or today. It's after midnight."

Holding the animal's head back, Gilgamesh ripped across the throat. The blood jetted into the copper basin. "Poor little goat. ur-Jupiter, I say treasure this Kate while you can. She will leave you as Inanna left me. You are only a stop on her journey."

That was clear. Bitter in the mouth, but clear.

The Search for Everlasting Life

Chapter Twenty-Two: Ishtar's Offer

No nonsense. Jupiter had a distinct impression of no-nonsense when Kate arrived that evening.

He had the shakes all day, even after he resorted to Prozac and the new anti-adrenal. Bobbie didn't show for breakfast or lunch. He hesitated to call—but it meant that she didn't live at the grain elevator anymore.

The same thoughts collided in his head, banged against each other over and over. When would the drug's sensation of well-being and numbness start kicking in? Why did he feel shut out? What was Kate going to be like?

She parked not in the truck shed to the north of the elevator but in the lot by the office, in full view of the street. She rode up the freight elevator, and he met her on the stairs leading to the head house. Both of them faltered. He let her take the lead; she stopped there at the bottom. Jupiter could see her make up her mind. She ascended two steps to where he stood and gave him a light hug. Then she gave him a soft hit on the shoulder. Some tension drained from between his shoulder blades. *At least she's not about to scream and screech.*

She spoke, "Shut up, you. You think too loud." She stepped around him and led the way into the kitchen. He caught the faint, dreamlike smell of shampoo and makeup, of clean clothes, and maybe the hint of a fragrance. "Shall we start where we were, yesterday? You didn't eat my chicken, did you?"

"No, and I didn't drink your wine, either." Sotto voce, he said, "Though I considered it."

"All right then. I'll do the waitress part." She swept open a cabinet

196

and started setting their places at the counter. "You do the cook thing."

"We're having eggplant with avocado cream, and I have potato cakes in the oven." To stall, he hemmed, "Mmm." He wanted to ask a question but didn't know how to start. "I noticed you parked in front."

"Standing out there watching for me, huh? I decided I provide a good alibi for you. I'll focus people's attention on standard gossip rather than cradle robbing and pedophilia. Besides, if I'm going to be supervising you more closely, I can't be sneaking around in the background."

"So, you're taking us out of the closet?"

"That's a gay phrase, Matt. Let's say we've been flushed out into the open."

"How's Bobbie?"

"She's doing fine. She likes my Mom, and she's spending her time in my room. Bobbie is nervous around my Dad though. That's a bummer for him—he hasn't been allowed to eat with us. He hangs out at the other end of the house. Sends his regards and thanks for the situation, by the way."

"Is she sleeping outside?"

"No, no! Inside. How many weeks did you let her sleep out there, Matt?"

"More like months in reality. At first I didn't know who I was dealing with. Later, I was waiting to learn what she could be comfortable with."

She sighed. "Wait no more. She's comfortable with me. When does the aunt… when does Diane move to town?"

"This Tuesday. She and Bobbie will need some time to get used to each other, but Bobbie said she was ready to live with her aunt."

"I'd like to help them settle in. I can help move Bobbie from one house to the other and maybe spend the first night there with her."

"And you don't want me around?"

"Not at their house, not for awhile."

He opened the wine and brought out the eggplant and the potato. He explained his potato cake—it showed good faith through domestic activity. "It has minced zucchini and onion in it, sautéed up before I make the rosti." They settled down to a relaxed meal, a quiet one. Jupiter started to feel better overall, even lightheaded. It was probably the wine

197

banging up against the Prozac. As they reached the end of dinner, he asked, "This isn't the quiet before the shock is it?"

"Oho, do I ever have a shock."

"Well, let me have it."

"It's not about Bobbie. I wanted to let you know I'm giving up my job here and moving to Dallas in September. I've got some contacts at the big Market Center, some old friends who stayed in the design business after school rather than waitressing or digging ditches. There are also a few graphics houses there I might interview. By then you'll be out of the woods with this Bobbie thing."

"Oh. It seems kind of sudden." It was sudden; it was like smacking the wall.

"It isn't like we haven't talked about it before."

"Sure. It sounds like the right thing for you. You need to see if that's the life you want to lead." This was true, a truth that stuck in his throat.

"If I stay, Matt, it's all very well for you, but I'd end up getting stuck as the princess of the diner—for the rest of my life."

He fished around. "What about Fat Bert and Anthony? Weren't you going to start into real estate with one of them?"

"It didn't work out. They wanted to get into my pants, but they didn't want to give me a job."

It was a done deal then. "Uh, like I said before, I know some people in Dallas. You have to make your own impression, but I can get you in the door in a couple of places."

"Good. I was hoping you would say something like that. I'm grateful for any help you can give." She waved a graceful hand from her knees to her collarbone. "Just as you should be grateful for all the fantastic sex to date." She stood up. "I'll do the coffee."

She made two lattes, and they took them through into the living room. He fetched two brandies from the cabinet and joined her on a couch. She moved over so their thighs touched. Jupiter didn't object, even though he didn't possess any undue expectations. They shared a silence as they stared out the window into the early evening.

"Listen, Matt, I want you to move to Dallas with me."

This confounded Jupiter, and he gave a huge twitch, one that strained his neck and sent a pain shooting down his back. Great. He had a new symptom of his predilection. "Kate, I'm knocked on my butt. I thought you were dumping me."

"Still don't know what's going on, do you? We break up when I say we do—and we get serious when I say we do." She inclined her head with a smile.

Yes, she loved being in charge—if she could only make up her mind where they were going. "Felt serious to me. At least the sex was."

"You do like jumping my bones, don't you?"

"And nice bones they are, too. So, let me get this straight. Up to this point, you've been using me for my manly virtues?"

"Mostly the cooking and the wine."

"No marriage, no children?"

"Hah! Like that would happen."

"So why are you thinking differently about our fling?"

"Things have to change for me, so they may as well change for you too. We're good together. Dallas would be a lot of fun, and you need to start getting out of the house in a major way. Besides, it's essential I keep an eye on you so you don't screw up. Like by adopting a gypsy family or marrying a serial killer."

"But what would I do there?"

"Matt, what do you do here, besides get in trouble? We could take a house together, waste all my new money on restaurants. I don't know, go to the opera. They do have an opera, don't they?"

"I know they have a Cow Palace."

"That's in California."

"Well, they ought to have a Cow Palace." He fell silent.

She wanted it resolved. "Give me a break, guy. This is not the marry-me-and-have-my-baby proposal you mentioned—much easier, much more palatable."

Disappointing—what if it had been a proposal to have a family? At sixty-two?

She said, "I'm not asking for anything besides setting up house and living pleasantly for a while. You know how to live pleasantly. Besides, you're going to get evicted here, most probably."

"Ouch!" Jupiter reflected on how best to answer. He gazed out over the prairie while she scrutinized him, half-turned on the couch.

He said, "Dallas will be great for you, and I'd like to help set you up there and start a life. What's good for you, though, would not be great for me. I have a certain—claustrophobia—these days, and I'd prefer to visit the great metropolis rather than live in it. Dallas would squash me."

"Tcha!" she said. "But I'll take what I can get. Maybe we can trade hot weekends for a while. I'll set up a closet for you where you can keep your stuff. After a short time, you'll snap to your senses and realize the incredible offer I've made. I'll certainly make you crawl to get another chance to move in with me. Idiot!" She thumped him on the forehead with the heel of her hand.

"First, let's get you a job. Your confidence is huge and inspiring, but there are beginning steps to get through. And you might meet someone your age who—"

"Oh, please, you're not going to make that tired speech, are you? Let's go upstairs and tear each other's clothes off. I haven't got much time. I'm in the mood, but I have to get back home before Bobbie's bedtime."

***

The sidewalks of Aniline were awash with slow moving idlers in midsummer's moist air. Anyone at work was hunkered under air conditioning, while those with leisure time swam back and forth through the town, seeking shade, any shade. Jupiter found his way impeded more than once by some slow-finning person, acclimated more than he to the heat, the damp, and the sheer treacle of a Texas summer. He felt a wave of nostalgia for the Amarillo air-conditioned culture. He tried to get from his truck to the post office but couldn't push past the sidewalk stream and its trickling rill of pedestrians—people he knew who wanted to visit barred his way. They saw no point in going anywhere, so they stopped to chat, in the shade, under awnings, in doorways. By the time he reached the counter to pick up his package, he had visited with his barber, two carpenters, Sarah Heldritch, and Krissy, the clerk at Town Hall. Too many people, too little Prozac.

The package had been mailed in Cooperstown, Ohio. Considering the contents, he liked the irony of its origin. Back in his idling truck, he sweated as anemic air conditioning spat condensation on his knees, as well as the smell of must and damp. He opened his package. Five hundred baseball cards, all in mint condition and each shrouded in its

200

own prophylaxis of plastic. They dated from the fifties onward and spanned a large piece of American sporting history. Jupiter had seldom played baseball and found it appallingly tedious to watch. The cards cost him four hundred dollars. They weren't for him.

A tap came at the window of Jupiter's truck. He glanced up. The Chief of Police stood there beside the truck. A small wave of panic rose, as if he had done something wrong and gotten caught. He rolled down the window. "Yes sir?"

Aniline's police chief bent down into his window, with sweat on his forehead and vast black rings under the arms of his dark blue shirt. "Chief Dodd, Mr. Devon. You remember we had some conversations a bit ago, concerning Carol Inskeep."

"Of course I remember, Chief. I meant to drop by and thank you for parking those two squad cars at the trailer, but I hadn't quite got around to it."

"Oh, it was a pleasure. The guys like these strange offbeat assignments. So, did it work out on your end?"

"Better than expected. Carol Inskeep is in rehab in Dallas. By all accounts, she is doing better. We're hoping it will stick."

"On our end we lucked into some information regarding Henry Lovato. It turned out he had some interesting phone numbers and call logs. There was also a delivery schedule of sorts, though no locations. We arrested a couple of guys, but Mr. Lovato disappeared on us. We guess he left town because he knew we finally had some leverage on him. He's had quite a few airline tickets to LA over the last year—perhaps he's immigrated to California."

"Well, that's good news."

"Yes, nice the way things worked out. It's never perfect in law enforcement, but sometimes it gets close."

"Well, thanks for letting me know, Chief. I'm sure Diane Inskeep will be relieved."

"I wonder if I might visit with you on another item, Mr. Devon?"

"Shoot."

"We've noticed your grain elevator has a rather commanding view of northern Aniline."

"The view from my home—" he stepped hard on the word home "—is one of its many advantages."

The Chief nodded, but stayed focused. "Would you agree to a surveillance team spending some time with you? We have a house we're watching, and the grain elevator would be a good observation spot to track comings and goings."

"What's in this house? Is it close to my elevator?"

"The 'what' is probably marijuana. The 'where' is three blocks away from you. Luckily, it doesn't have anything around it; the neighboring houses fell derelict and the town tore them down long ago. So the view of the house and the street should be quite good. The angle would be practically straight down. We won't be able to see the front door, but we'll be able to see the back yard, and anyone parking on the street."

"How long do you think you'd be up there with me?"

"Just long enough, I think, to establish probable cause. Then we can get a warrant and do a search. Maybe three days. Maybe a week."

"I suppose I have to say yes. Public duty and all that."

The Chief stood up straight, nodded decisively, and got out his mobile phone. "Good then. Are you on your way home now? I could have a couple of men meet you there in a half hour."

***

Jupiter nestled blocks of the Cooperstown cards around a baseball glove sitting on one of the living room bookcases. He had a vague idea about one of Heldritch's finish carpenters making a wooden box to hold them. Over the last month, he had become attracted to the artifacts of boyhood. He was slowly acquiring things that resonated with the idea of fathers and sons.

Like his namesake, Jupiter, the god of jollity and happiness, he wanted to celebrate the rituals of coming of age, even if at a distance. He might even discover a liking for baseball through these talismans. He went back into the kitchen to start dinner and to kill time until the police arrived.

The squeaking of the elevator and its noisy gate announced the officers. He showed them working, unbroken windows on the south side of the distribution floor, and helped them to set up their cameras and scopes, card tables and folding chairs, junk food, and a cooler of cold drinks.

While they were settling in, Kate's car arrived. From the great height, he saw boxes protruding from her trunk.

***

She leaned against the car. "I was hoping you'd show up to help."

"You brought me something?"

"I brought you the best. This is lawn furniture for the roof outside your office. I need some place I can laze about. The swimming pool wouldn't fit in the car; you'll have to send someone over to pick that up."

"Oh, straightaway. And what do we have here?"

"Two loungers, a table, and a freestanding umbrella. It's your job to provide the white wine and the bucket of ice." Kate nodded towards the ugly American sedan parked in front of the door. "So we have company?"

"Loosely speaking. The police chief did me a favor concerning Bobbie's mother awhile back. Now he's asked for a favor in return."

"Oh?"

"Yeah, they've set up an observation post on top, down on the end. Shouldn't be around for more than a week."

"We have the police living with us?"

"Well," he said, "living with me. But you'll hardly notice them."

"Who are they spying on?"

"A nearby house. It's a marijuana stakeout, I think."

"You could have asked me." Her mouth was a gash of a line.

"Kate, what's going on here? You once chided me for not going to the police about Bobbie. Now that they happen to be here, you're mad at me."

"There's a reason your generation called them pigs. I don't like having them anywhere near us."

"Are you seriously wound up about these cops?"

She was. Her beautiful face contorted in ugliness. "Hostile, more like. Matt, you are always picking risky people to associate with."

"The police, risky?" The world was wobbling.

"You don't know what a small-town cop is like, Matt. He'll abuse his power any chance he gets. Here they are, using our place to spy and probably prey upon some poor teenager or other, all over a couple of bags of weed."

"Is this somehow personal, Kate?"

"That's my life, not yours, Matt Devon. In other words—none of your business."

"You had some run-in with the law when you were young, didn't you?"

"They ran in to me."

"What happened, Kate?"

Storm clouds were gathering. "Get them out of your house, Matt."

He shook his head and held his hands out. "I'm afraid it's too late to back out. It would be less than gracious, and I don't feel good about going back on my word."

Lightning struck. "Damn you for a toad-sucking dog then! Here's your goddamn furniture!" She jerked the boxes out of the car and splayed them out onto the ground.

"Wait. This is silly. Are you leaving? Stay and we'll talk."

She jumped into the driver's seat and jerked the door shut. She raced backwards, ran over the corner of one of the boxes, slammed on the brakes, and shifted into drive. She sped away, bouncing through the potholes.

He stood there in the settling dust, wondering what had happened. He mulled over the story of Ishtar cursing the gardener. "When she heard his answer, she changed him utterly, into a silent, blind mole burrowing beneath the garden he had once tended for her with all love."

***

August heated up the plain, crisping the few trees so that their leaves curled and went brown. Holed up inside cool concrete walls, Jupiter reflected on a month of change. He had crawled out at last from a long tunnel. The grain elevator stood silent and empty once again, except for his own footfalls. True, he talked to Diane nearly every day, and Kate dropped over when it suited her. She refused to talk about their argument, and he still didn't know what it had been about—about a right to a private history. Don't ask; don't pry. Don't think about September.

Office issues had abated. He enjoyed spinning out the fictional sabbatical—the narrative said he had progressed north to Alaska. All his worry over Bobbie Inskeep had disappeared. He had de-cluttered his life by spending lots of money. His hands had stopped shaking over three solitary days. He reveled in his solitude.

To stay in touch, he called the Inskeep house. "Diane, this is Matt. Checking in on how it's going."

"Fine. You know, I never believed I'd like Aniline, Matt, but I'm beginning to, in spite of myself. The church here is really great."

"Good, I'm happy to hear it."

"Don't suppose you'd like to come with me Sunday to services?"

He shuddered. "How's Bobbie these days?"

"Dodging the bullet, huh? Bobbie is pretty good; she's tired a lot, but she's settled in. She's spent every night here with me and hasn't snuck off once to sleep under a bush somewhere. She keeps that sleeping bag you gave her ready to go, but she's not using it. We're getting a routine started we both like. She makes breakfast, and I make lunch and dinner."

"I'm glad to hear it. Does she run errands with you?"

"No, she's not ready to be out there with other people yet. I normally take her over to stay with Sarah Heldritch when I have to be gone any length of time; they get along well. I've left her alone at the house a couple of times, but you know...."

"Yeah, makes you nervous doesn't it? She might not be there when you get back." He paused. "Does she ever ask about me?"

"She asked what your name was the other night. Fancy, all that time together, and you never told her your name."

"It didn't come up."

"Say, you know we now have our first customer? I'm doing books for the auto parts store. They had a big fight with their accountants in Amarillo and decided outsourcing to the big city was a dumb thing to do. The Lord provides."

The Lord, and of course his own telephoning around. "That's great, Diane. Soon you'll have a fortune and a house in Barbados."

"I'd settle for paying my own utilities. You know the medical insurance card hasn't come yet, even though we filled everything out in July."

"Tell you what, I'll call the office manager, Ellen, in Amarillo. I can get her to phone the insurance hotline and shake the cage some. We both want Bobbie to see the specialists as soon as she can. In the meantime, has she been in to the doctor here in town, the GP?"

"Matt, that's not going to work. I went down to the clinic, and the doctor is a guy with a wooly beard and an attitude."

He could hear the disgust in her voice. "Do they have a nurse practitioner?"

"I'd rather get her into a women's clinic. There's one in Amarillo that's on the insurance network, but I need the card."

"All right, we'll pursue it. Do you still hear from your sister?"

Diane made a grunting noise. "She calls about twice a day asking me to get her out. She thinks it's unreasonable we stranded her there without money and a car. Still, she sounded better yesterday than the day before, and she hasn't called another addict to drive down and break her out."

"Once she's dried out, then we'll set her up, but not in Aniline. Till then—"

"Yes. Tough Love. I'm going down to see her this weekend."

"That's great. Listen, got to go. I'll call tomorrow or the day after."

***

Jupiter always read the minutes of the Council meeting in the local paper. He liked the section where they reviewed recent building permit applications. Projects of any size had to be discussed in Council before permits could be considered—it was the Aniline way. Jupiter thought if he could get partnered with a councilman or two in a development project, the Council might start swinging towards him.

While he read between the lines for possibilities, the phone rang. "Hi, Mr. Devon. This is Rodney Barco, the surveyor."

An image of the short, stumpy man, face burned brick-red, swam up in his imagination. "Rodney, good to hear from you. Are you still eating heart-attack food with Dan Heldritch?"

"Sure. It's the only game in town as far as I'm concerned. How's that thing with the Town Council going?"

"Oh, you know, I haven't really got it fixed. I only arrange various stays of execution."

"I don't see how you do it. They make the rules up to suit

themselves, and you seem to be making the rules work for you instead."

Jupiter admitted, "It's all subterfuge and bureaucracy."

"Better you than me. Listen, Dan said you were interested in what was going on around town, keeping a pulse on projects. Especially projects by councilmen."

"Can't hurt, Rodney." This was great; he was getting allies among the tradesmen.

"See, I'm laying out foundation lines for some high rise condos. You know the city lake Aniline installed two years ago, with the playground and picnic area?"

"Sure, driven by it a hundred times."

"But see, the mayor owns the adjacent field."

"Interesting." The town had built a park next door to the Mayor's property. "You said high rise condos?"

"Ak'shly, three story. They're going to overlook the lake all right. The idea is to build living space for young professionals out of Amarillo."

"But why here in Aniline? And why condos?"

"Clean living in the country, bicycle paths through the fields, a farmer's market. Low-maintenance relaxed living for the busy professional. And only minutes from the same shops, bars, and restaurants they're using now."

"Sounds like you've heard the talk. And what do you think, Rodney?"

"I think that the Mayor and his partners pay me, which I like, and they take all the risk. I like that part too."

Jupiter pursed his lips. "I haven't heard anything about this in town."

"So far it's just plans and fancy architect sketches. See, we're going to mow the field and do basic surveying. Then the Mayor will bring the investors out to walk the property, kick the dirt."

"And he waves his hands in the blue, blue sky promising a successful scheme."

Rodney chortled, "Something like that."

"I owe you Rodney. This is fascinating stuff."

"Buy me lunch sometime. Listen, got to go."

***

City Hall smelled like linoleum with an undertone of mildew and ozone from the AC. Jupiter ducked through the glass door, smudged over with fingerprints, into an empty lobby. He checked out the US and Texas flags that flanked photos of the Mayor and Council, and noted the water stains on some of the ceiling tiles. He approached reception and leaned across the counter. "Hey, Krissy, remember me?"

"Hi there, Mr. Devon." She stuck out a plump white hand, and he shook it. "For a guy we're always talking about, you don't make it by Town Hall much."

He shrugged. "Probably not a healthy place for me to hang out."

She grinned and leaned forward to whisper, "You can hide in the employees lounge with us."

"Maybe I should do that. Bring lunch; see what's going on down at Town Hall."

"Certainly catch all the gossip."

"Krissy, you work with the Permits Department some, don't you?"

"Oh sure. All part of the daily grind."

"I've gotten all my permits through Dan, you know, so I don't know anyone in that department."

"Head man is Stan Lurton. Real nice guy."

"So he'd be the person to talk to, clue me up on what's required for unusual projects?" No real project. She doesn't have to know that.

"Yeah, that's right. Here's the number and the extension." She handed him a yellow sticky folded in half. "So are you going to build that swimming pool for Kate Heldritch?" That stopped Jupiter cold. "Knock, knock. You still there, Mr. Devon?"

"Uh, yes. No pool this year."

"Sorry, didn't mean to tease you Mr. Devon." Her face said she meant it.

"Say, do you know this new condo project?"

"Sure, big talk around here."

"What do you think?"

"Well—" She glanced to the left, to the right, and arched an eyebrow. "My Joe says it's another one of Taggert's pipe dreams. He says people don't move out of the city to live in a glorified apartment building. They buy a house."

"Sounds like Joe got it right."

"Except for you, Mr. Devon. You might do anything. Most people wouldn't be turning a grain elevator into a castle."

"I've got an excuse. I'm so old I'm getting a bit funny."

"You're not so old. Just ask us women in town."

"Why, thank you, Krissy. I'll take that as a compliment."

She gave him the arched eyebrow again. "Let me be clear. I wasn't flirting. Kate wouldn't like that." Krissy got a ledger-like book out of her desk and set it before her. "Say, Mr. Devon, how do you feel about the PTA?"

"Good. I feel good. Parents should work with the teachers for the kids." He nodded his head and tried to appear wise.

"I'm happy to hear you say that. Our PTA is selling raffle tickets."

***

The compulsion to cause trouble ran strong and hot in him. Again he downloaded and printed inflammatory material, this time realty brochures from the Silo Point condos in Baltimore and the Calhoun Isles condos in Minneapolis—two developments that had repurposed grain elevators.

He again attached a note, this one reading: "I've been thinking about multi-family housing here in Aniline, and the market looks promising to me. If you're interested in a joint venture that would turn the grain elevator into a really exciting twelve story complex with commercial and residential space, give me a call." He signed it, "Respectfully, Matt Devon," and mailed it off.

***

Jimmy Devereaux occupied more of his mind these past weeks. One of the guest rooms had morphed into the boy's bedroom, and Jupiter bought a bedspread with a giant glove and baseball imprinted upon it. Daily, Jupiter wandered into the room to poke through the stuff piling up on the dresser, and he always tried to add an interesting rock or other artifact to the growing collection on the short desk. He knew this was bent. Somewhere a piece of his mind said the boy was real and another piece said fantasy. Jupiter wanted the room to be just so, in case Jimmie walked in. There was no harm done in playing around with it. But it was something to keep from Marjorie.

Chapter Twenty-Three: Enkidu's Jeopardy

Languorously splashed across the couch, Kate waited for him. Two etched glasses and an open bottle stood sentinel on the coffee table. "So, have you been sneaking around on me, tomcatting in the alleys of Aniline?"

Jupiter had barely gotten back from Amarillo, where he had consulted with his lawyer. He now understood that the legal fees he had paid, and would continue to pay, stank of futility. Lawyers couldn't prevent his eviction from the grain elevator. Too depressing to talk about. "Nothing that exciting, I'm afraid. I see you've made yourself at home."

"Waiting is hard work. I had to take a little rest here after I wore out, pacing back and forth, thinking about your potential infidelity."

"What happened to our open relationship?"

"You mean the one where you wait at home for me to call, while I date a professional football team?"

"That's the one."

She flapped a hand and dismissed the notion. "As for that, what I say I want and what I really want are two different things. Let's go out on the roof. It's a beautiful day. Pity I didn't get to work on my tan much this summer." She didn't mention the broken lounger.

They wandered out through the office onto the western roof and into the warm afternoon light. They leaned over the rail, gazing at the view. Standing side by side with this young woman was comfortable, comforting. The strain of the day trickled away. Comfortable could soon shift over to aroused.

She said, "You know, I'm off to Dallas next week. I got that design job in the graphics firm." She peeked up at him from under her blonde hair to watch her bombshell explode.

"Kate, that's great! I'm so happy for you." He felt that plummeting sensation and knew his smile came off strained.

"Thanks to you, I got to talk to the bigwigs."

"Yeah, well."

"Don't be modest. If I'd gone through a regular interview, I'd still be down at the café pouring coffee."

Instead of packing. He could taste the bitterness, like metal filings. "You still might have to fetch coffee. You'll be junior to everybody."

"Tcha!" She smirked and delivered another surprise. "They're sending me off to a techie school at SMU's Computer Department for a couple of months. It turns out I have great color sense, an innovative way of blocking mass and shape, and a great ass. But I'm computer illiterate by their standards."

"They told you all that?"

"Admittedly not the cute butt part."

"Next week? Huh."

"Yes. It's occurred to me you haven't maximized your opportunities with me here. You should use your time more wisely."

Jupiter sipped his wine. "Well, why don't you come observe while I make you a frittata Florentine style."

"What's that mean?"

"I'll add in spinach, also some herbs and a dash of Italian political intrigue to whisked eggs. By the end of the meal, one of us will be Pope."

"Sounds good. A woman Pope?"

"Happens all the time. Well, at least once."

"Would I have to dress in drag?"

"With the robes, who could tell? Grab the bottle, will you?"

"Shut up! I opened the wine; you should carry it."

***

They learned about the crisis as they sauntered across to the kitchen. The grain elevator's phone rang as Kate's mobile buzzed. She swished a finger to answer. As his landline jangled on, Jupiter watched her eyes widen and her mouth hang open. He picked up his own phone.

212

"Devon here."

Diane's voice quavered in his ear. "Matt, it's me."

"Is something wrong?"

All in a rush, Diane tumbled out her words. "The medical insurance card came in the mail, so we called for an appointment at the women's clinic I told you about. I took her in right away, about the fit, the possibility of epilepsy."

"Good. I've been worried too."

"That wasn't it, though. When they saw Bobbie, they were concerned about her skin color, the yellowness, you know, and they asked her some questions. Her joints have been hurting, and her urine is dark, and we've been here for a day and a night. She had been vomiting, but she didn't tell me. I should have noticed. I didn't know she was feeling bad. I'm afraid I let it go on too long."

"Diane, where is here?"

"Bobbie is checked in to the Northwest Hospital. They think it's liver dysfunction."

"Liver—what does that mean?"

"It could be hepatitis or lupus. She's in ICU. She could die."

"Have you been there the entire time?"

"Yes."

"Have you had any sleep?"

"Just in the chair."

"I'll ask the Heldritchs if they can help."

"I've already called Sarah. I think she's coming."

Of course. He would be the second or third call. He pressed the phone deeper into his ear. "Diane, I'll take Kate to your house, and she'll pack some things for you. How do I get into your house?"

"There's a key under a pot on the back steps."

As Matt rang off, Kate touched his shoulder. "That was my mom. We have to go to Amarillo."

"Sarah filled you in?"

"Bobbie's got liver disease. Diane thinks she's dying."

"We'll take Diane some clothes. I think we should pack bags for us too."

***

213

Jupiter could smell the hospital AC, a breath green and stale, life preserved by chemicals and their airborne taint. Bobbie lay behind glass, in a bed far too big for her. Her matted black hair was splayed out on the pillow. The flush across her skin showed dark yellow under the bluish hospital light.

Jupiter asked, "Do we know what she's got?"

Diane turned from the glass, her eyes tremulous with waiting tears. "Not lupus. They're sure it's hepatitis."

Three women and Jupiter were hovering outside the room. He cajoled them to chairs that lined the other side of the corridor. The women clung to each other. He sat on the end.

***

Women and men in scrubs swept into the room and checked the monitors and the bags. They strode out, nodded at the quartet slumped in chairs against the wall, and scuffed down the hall. Nurses changed shifts, moved the life of the place along while patients and visitors waited frozen, locked into little boxes of concern and fear.

The strange hours of the pre-dawn arrived, when the hospital hushed even as the business of sickness and death ground on. The two Heldritch women slept, heads dropped forward. Diane and Jupiter leaned into each other and waited for first light.

"Matt, I really messed this one up, didn't I?"

"Because you're not a doctor? Ever been around hepatitis before?"

She shook her head.

"Then I don't see how this is your fault. Or mine. How bad could it be? What's the worst?"

Diane said, "The ugly form of hepatitis, Hep B. There are two stages: the acute and then the chronic where it won't go away. I don't know much, but the acute phase can either run its course, or they can fight it with drugs. There's a chance her liver won't come back from this attack."

"What about liver transplants?"

"Not a preferred option. Doable, but the new liver would be infected with the virus after awhile. But if the old liver is dying...."

214

Kate asked, "How do you get this kind of hepatitis?" Awake after all.

Diane said, "Sex with an infected person or dirty needles. That's the likeliest way. That would mean Henry Lovato, or one of his friends, injected drugs into her."

Kate shook her cloud of blonde hair. She asked, "How could they do that?"

The obvious question. Diane glanced at Jupiter. He shrugged.

Kate muttered, "Goddamn them."

He said, "We *should* be angry. I am. Diane is." Jupiter patted Diane's knee. "We'll get through this; she'll be all right. Everything that can be done will be done."

Diane shot a worried glance at him, "If we had only been a year earlier."

A year earlier in Bobbie's life. Slumped down into the vinyl chair, he sighed aloud. He wished he believed his reassurances. He reflected. *Gilgamesh has made the kings and princes of the earth kiss Enkidu's feet, has placed him at the King of Uruk's left hand, but it avails not. Enkidu lies fallen upon his bed with his sickness upon him, and his eyes are blind with weeping.*

***

Strong light came through the venetian blinds at their backs; orange streaked across the floor and into Bobbie's room.

Jupiter straightened up and touched Kate on the knee. "I'll be a half hour. I want to get us all rooms at a motel. We need a place to nap and shower."

"Diane won't leave. I'll find her a place in the hospital where she can clean up."

So much for taking charge. "All right. I'll get her bag from the car. Then I'll go get us two rooms and be back."

On the return from the motel, Jupiter fretted over debilitating disease. He brooded over the death of the young. Swinging past Marjorie's house, he knocked on the door. When she answered, plump and calm, he ducked his head. "Do you have some time?"

"For you? Always. Come in." She led him back to the patio, sat him

215

on a large flat rock, and brought a stool over for herself.

Strange, Daoists wear faded, tattered jeans like everyone else. See how she folds her hands in her lap, how her knees kick out to the sides. What can be said? "I need you to coach me on death, not life."

"So that's your 'where.' Life and death are scarcely separate. But they do manifest differently. This death is specific, isn't it?"

"It's my wild child, Bobbie Inskeep. She's very ill. She may die."

Her face drew down in a display of concern. "Oh, Jupiter. I am so sorry."

"We're over at the hospital waiting to hear." The concrete smell of hospital despair still choked his nose and hung on his clothes. He couldn't pick up the smell of incense.

"By we, you mean you and the aunt?"

"And Kate—and her mother Sarah."

"Tell me about it."

So he did.

***

Much later Kate said, "There's always a scene in the movie with the doctor."

He frowned. "Just in chic flicks."

"Except this is real. The nurse says the doctor is on her way. Diane and Mom are in the cafeteria. I'll go get them." Kate strode off down the hall and returned with the other women in tow.

Jupiter asked Diane, "Did you eat anything?"

"Shhh, here comes the doctor," warned Kate.

The physician was a striking woman who had made the decision to look overworked rather than beautiful. Jupiter thought medicine was the perfect career for her to accomplish this goal. She sat at the end of their little line of chairs and inclined her head, professional—grave. Jupiter stood up and shuffled around to where he could see and hear.

"Hi, I'm Dr. Branson. I know Ms. Inskeep here. Are the rest of you friends or family?"

Three of them replied, "Friends," but Diane said, "they're as close to real family as the Lord has provided."

"So, Ms. Inskeep, you have no objection if they hear this?"

216

"None at all."

The doctor took a breath and reached out to hold Diane's hand. "We've confirmed Bobbie has both Hepatitis B and D. They're transmitted through blood exchange, so we call them serum hepatitis."

Diane's voice trembled, "Does 'blood' mean it's worse or moves faster?"

The doctor cradled her hand. "Not really. Serum means how you contract it. Adults get Hep B from dirty drug paraphernalia or from sexual intercourse. Hepatitis D is a companion viral infection with B, and the two together make it much more likely Bobbie will suffer liver failure. Bobbie is in the acute phase of the disease, which she may have had for weeks, months, or even a year. She is definitely immunocompromised. That means she doesn't fight off disease well."

Jupiter shuffled closer. "Is she HIV positive then?"

"No, there's no indication of that. She could have a compromised immune system for reasons like genetics or malnutrition. We've all noted Bobbie is seriously underweight."

"What are you doing for her then?" asked Kate.

"We're fighting the viruses. We're searching for a liver through the transplant list. We're controlling the side effects, like vomiting, through a secondary drug regimen."

Jupiter asked, "How bad is this?"

"Liver function is way down. We have to feed her through IV, but the liver stopped producing what she needs for digestion—the bile—and it isn't breaking down glucose. Her toxins are way up. The liver isn't working for her anymore."

***

Jupiter sat in the chair beside the bed deep in the night and deep in his brooding. Beside him, above his shoulder level, Bobbie huddled under the sheets, machines attached to her and a box with a nine-inch scrolling display hanging over her on the other side of the bed. A single florescent was lit on the wall behind the bed. In the yellow light, he could see the backs of his hands, a couple of old-age spots, a fine web of crackle where his skin was surrendering to mortality.

"It's you."

Bobbie had spoken! After sleeping for twenty hours, sliding ever closer to a deeper sleep, she was awake. "Yes, it's me."

Drowsy, mumbling, she said, "I've been thinking."

He leaned forward, bringing his face over the sheets closer to her. "About what?"

"I want to be normal just like everyone else. I never got to have the dumb problems." She rolled her head and stared at him with blue eyes, the black pupils open so wide the color was a thin ring.

He said, "You never appreciate the dumb things until you're looking back."

"Yeah. I could have had girlfriends, worried about algebra, had zits. Instead, I got my mother."

Jupiter had seldom been this close to the wild child. "We can make up for that some, I think."

Her eyes suddenly swam. Taking a tissue from the bedside table, he dabbed in the corners of her eyes. She didn't recoil.

She said, "High school. I never finished high school."

"Would you like to go back?"

"No, no!" She insisted, emphatic even in her weakness. "I know there's something called the GED you can do at home. I'd like to do that. When I'm over this," and she waved a hand over the bed and her form. The tube taped into the back of her hand followed the gesture. "When this is done, I'll need to get a job."

"Bobbie, I think that's great." He prayed to God they got the chance.

She yawned a little. "I want you to help me study. You know things, and you don't shout."

"I'd be honored."

Her mouth turned down. "Now you're laughing again."

"No, I assure you. I'd like to be your tutor, very much so." She was done with the conversation—got what she wanted. Her eyelids sank closed.

Jupiter said, "Go back to sleep. We'll talk more tomorrow."

***

He slept in the hall chair again; pain woke him. Knots had tied themselves all through his calves, his back bent rusty and broken, and his

218

shoulders were locked in an unnatural hunch. "Why is she on a respirator?"

Kate rubbed his back. "They put her on it about an hour ago. She's developed pneumonia."

"Oh, Christ. Why didn't you wake me?"

"What could you have done? Besides, she hasn't been conscious for hours. She's slipped from sleep into coma."

"Where is Diane?"

"She's on the far side of the bed. You can just see the top of her head. Mom's in there with her."

"What should we be doing?"

"We're doing it now. Come on; let me buy you some breakfast. We can be back in twenty minutes."

"But what if she…?" No way to fix this one. He couldn't massage this crisis away with money. His father's way.

"Her heartbeat is strong, and she's getting help breathing. It's still early yet."

***

Jupiter stood at the end of the bed and stared down at her. Needles impaled her veins, tied off with little strips of blue cling gauze. She lay with her arms out to the edge of the bed, wrists up, a geometry of supplication. Diane held her hand, and Sarah leaned close. Kate stood on the other side with her head down. Kate's hair created a shadow that hid her eyes, her thoughts.

The monitor showed a heart beating soft, slowing, irregular. The respirator rode her like a large plastic crustacean, masking her face, biting. Jupiter imagined how it would be if he lay there with plastic shoved into his mouth, pushing air. He gazed down on the little figure in the bed.

He backed up. His heels touched the door. He felt behind him for the handle.

Chapter Twenty-Four: Tower

The laptop sat on the kitchen counter beside a cold toasted cheese sandwich and a pickle—a pickle that had bled its green juice onto the plate and into the bread. Jupiter slumped on the stool, head in hands. The shining freezer and refrigerators, the six-burner range, the two ovens were all a waste. Brushed steel surfaces bounced the light, tinged it the faintest green under the fluorescents. Two a.m.

The laptop flashed, black to white and spelled out. "Should ur-Jupiter be alone?" Delusion calling.

Jupiter exhaled, slow, wheezy. He pulled the computer over in front of him. It bumped a hair barrette, and he pushed that aside. "I'm always alone."

"There are those who talk to you, reach out to you. You have isolated yourself, but you are not alone."

"The women of Aniline." How could he face them? Even be in the room with them?

"I like these women. They own your world." He was a Sumerian king, living a Texas life vicariously.

"So you see me in my shiny kitchen, waiting for the perfect life in the perfect house to start."

Jupiter could see Sumeria there on the screen, Gilgamesh's sleeping chamber. It was a half-lit room with an oil lamp guttering on the floor near the door. Gilgamesh was on his bed, and a woman had an arm draped across his chest. She looked young, absurdly beautiful. "You're not alone."

"Regrettably, she is asleep." Gilgamesh pushed at the strands of her black hair, smoothing it back from her face.

220

"Why the regret?"

"In my youth I would have woken her. Now days, it seems cruel. Besides, she is beautiful to watch, even as she snores."

"The perfect time to talk to me." Maybe if he just closed the lid, shut Gilgamesh out.

"ur-Jupiter, now is when you need a friend."

"I lost her, you know."

Gilgamesh shifted out from under the woman's arm, slowly, gently. "The wild child. Yes, I saw. A cold and heartless place to die." He sat at the edge of the pallet with his bony knees up in the air.

"It came so quickly. We didn't know, and then it was too late to bring her home."

"A bed surrounded by wailing women."

"I wanted to take care of them, to make it right. To say the right things over Bobbie after she had slipped away." *Always want to make it right, whether it's a child murdered or a wife driven away.*

Gilgamesh nodded. "As I wanted to speak the right words over Enkidu to save him from Hell, to bring him back."

"But I—it was—I froze, back to the door, wanting to run, unable to say anything."

"You haven't grieved yet. You must cry."

"It's the Sumerians that cry, not Texans."

"I have cried, and my tears honored the gods. I cried for help from Shamash to defeat Humbaba. I cried when the snake took the sea lotus and immortality from me at the well. I cried for Enkidu. It is a natural state for man, in a world of loss."

A single tear, then another, ran down Jupiter's nose and dripped onto the keyboard. And suddenly, there was a deluge of salted tears, a gathering film of mucus on his lip below his nostrils.

Chapter Twenty-Five: Return to Uruk

"You don't want to talk about her?"

"No." Back in the geodesic dome awash in heat and humidity. The potting soil smelled a little rank, like compost still curing. He could see the yard lights of the next-door neighbor, stars in the black.

"You can't get over your grief if you bottle it up."

"I don't want to get over my grief. I don't want to get over any of it."

Marjorie nodded, solemn. "So what do you want to talk about?"

"My incipient madness."

"And we're proud of it, aren't we?"

He ignored the barb. "My unraveling started with the onset of the Gilgamesh delusion. Before that, I kept it all together."

She grinned, a crooked grin, and poured more iced tea into his glass. "Jupiter, you had plenty to complain about long before Gilgamesh started talking to you. I always thought therapy would be good for you in general. Gilgamesh was only the break-over point where I thought you should consider intensive help."

"But I was holding it all together." He stared at the cascading vines, their flowers closed for the night. It was better than looking straight at her.

"I remember several panic attacks that led to migraines, and once you threw up at Rotary. You've since descended into a state of retreat and deceit."

"Booger. Somehow I wish it all sounded grander. Trust a matter-of-fact Daoist to remember the vomiting." He swirled the tea around in the glass and listened to the ice cubes.

She tilted her head to the side and pressed on. "Confess, Jupiter. You're not troubled by reality here. You like the 'Book', and you like Gilgamesh."

"Maybe the idea of him...." It did sound ridiculous, said out loud.

"No, you like him personally. You're hanging on to him as much as you hang on to anybody. He amuses you. You enjoy the patron role you're playing."

"Lately Gilgamesh plays my patron rather than the other way around. And he's reading my tea leaves, making predictions that come true. But that's flat-out crazy, isn't it?"

"I rather hold on to a small hope Gilgamesh is real, and the book constitutes a tantric prayer to raise him up in his next rebirth. But that doesn't happen very often, does it? What's *more* indicative of losing your grip is this lost son you never had."

"Is that tantric stuff Daoism or Buddhism?"

"It's difficult to define Daoism. Daoism is like Jazz, at the root of all things. You changed the subject on me, didn't you?"

"Yes."

"Naughty." She waited.

"I'm nostalgic for Amarillo. Amarillo doesn't seem half bad as a life compared to what I'm going through now."

"We Daoists have a concept called *Pu*. It means to see things as they really are, without the cloud of emotion, prejudice, or even knowledge. Something tells me that your Amarillo wasn't so great, and isn't so great. You haven't seen clearly, seen with Pu."

"Tell me something new. Listen, Marjorie, I have to go now. I have to meet a man very early tomorrow about a dog, or in this case an audit. I just wanted to touch base with you, let you know I'm still loose and wandering the streets."

She walked him to the door. "You're a lovely man, Jupiter. It's a shame you don't know that. Good-bye for now, and let me know when you're serious about getting help."

***

Jupiter had requested the usual independent audit on his company and it arrived, complete with a tall, fat man to explain it all. For him, the audit existed as a normal piece of business, something he had to pay for every three years as good practice. He didn't want the auditor in his grain elevator, so they met at the community center on the old highway—a rehabilitated grocery store—and borrowed one of the rooms.

The room smelled a little dank. The auditor wore old-fashioned bay rum cologne. He began with pretentious tones ringing out. "It's the old story. I have good news and bad news." His name was Audrey Tompkins, known to his friends as Mr. Tompkins.

"Give me the good news first."

"Good first. Now of course, Mr. Devon, reporting on business strategy and success or failure of that strategy is not in our mandate. We're hired purely to determine if the books of the corporation are being maintained in a fashion compliant with FASBI accounting standards and proper procedures are in place to ensure legitimate information for tax preparation and corporate reporting. Additionally, we examine procedures and protocols for items like workman's compensation payments and quarterly tax payments." Jupiter narrowly avoided crossing his eyes. "I will say, however, the overall health of the concern impressed us. Margins are well within what we expect for your type of enterprise, capital expenditures are minimal, cash flow is more than adequate, and expenses on a per employee basis are within the expected range."

Jupiter worked hard to stifle a yawn. "Glad to hear I don't have to file Chapter Eleven, Mr. Tompkins."

"Of course, you will want to read through all the details." The auditor handed over a two-inch-thick bound file. "Now the bad news: there is one minor thing I would like to especially point out, summarized on this page," said Mr. Tompkins, sliding a piece of paper over to Jupiter. "As you can see, convention and conference costs are up sharply over the last two years, particularly for one employee, and the company has leased a rather expensive car, also for that employee. You may be surprised to learn the employee is your Jerome Douglas. He signed his own authorization for his conferences and car. Fortunately, none of the other employees receive these types of expensive benefits."

"So Jerry has started living well during my sabbatical? I'll have to have a word."

The big man took a deep breath for dramatic effect. "I'm afraid I have another item to bring to your attention, a much more serious issue. As you know, you have separation of procurement and disbursement in your company, but I suspect as in most firms your size, these functions are in reality quite informal. The people carrying on these two roles know each other quite well as colleagues and friends. Additionally, your accounting procedures are very lax. Nearly anyone can book journal entries and set up accounts in your books. Nearly anyone can approve invoices. As a result, you have a nasty round of embezzling going on."

"Embezzling?" Jupiter's attention snapped on.

"Please, let me finish." Even now, in the dénouement, he pontificated. "Two vendors have been established as service providers in your books. Invoices have come in at a regular rate, and they've been authorized for payment. Unfortunately, no actual services have been provided to your firm by these vendors. Further, a check of the papers of incorporation for both vendors doesn't show officers that we can trace. Addresses on the filings are empty lots. Mailing addresses are post office boxes. They don't appear to be anything more than paper corporations with bank accounts."

This news, presented with a flourish, brought Jupiter to a standstill. His first thought—he was amazed. Dumbfounded. A Sumerian would already have expected some calamity. But he was an optimist, forward-looking, except for anthropophobic tendencies. A hermit, a delusional writer. A victim.

Jupiter seized one of the thoughts that rocketed around in his brain and shaped it as a question, "How much has been taken?"

"A hundred and fifty this year and eighty-five for the previous accounting year." Mr. Tompkins glowered down at his notes. "To be exact, for the two years the amounts are 154,872 dollars and twelve cents and 85,413 dollars and twenty-seven cents. We are reasonably sure there are no other thefts. We are also reasonably sure no other accounts are fraudulent."

"Who paid money out to the fake accounts?"

"We don't know that for certain."

"Who authorized the invoices?"

"All invoices are destroyed after journal entries and payments are made. There's no paper trail."

"It's got to be Jerry." Jupiter's fist rapped up and down on the tabletop. He stared beyond Mr. Tompkins.

"We cannot confirm that."

"So Jerry has skimmed me for, um, a quarter of a million dollars? Give me a second. I have to catch my breath here." The strong sensations of betrayal shoved him into a desire for retribution and revenge. He was hot, flushed, and angry!

"Are you all right, Mr. Devon? I know this is a shock."

"I lost a quarter of million and still had a great couple of years? What a piece of work Jerry is! He could have asked anything for such sterling performance while he was my second. Instead, he stole what is really a small amount—for something that could wreck him!"

Mr. Tompkins smirked. "Not quite a quarter of a million, by the way. Assuming you are correct as to who the perpetrator is, I would say that he is a poor criminal. He doesn't understand how to balance risk and reward." He drummed his fingers on his ample belly and coughed in a superior, knowing way.

"Probably didn't expect to get caught. Zero risk, he'd think. All for a measly...," Jupiter glanced at the sum, "two hundred and forty thousand." He slammed the file shut, opened it again, and riffled through it.

Mr. Tompkins shook his head and took Jupiter to task. "I wouldn't call the loss a paltry amount, by accounting standards, or by normal small-business terms." He said all this with arching eyebrows. "And to the criminal mind—arrest, incarceration—all unlikely possibilities to the nefarious."

"The devious little shit. He calculated what my profit expectations were from the firm's goals, and he delivered just enough." Jupiter thought for a moment. "Of course, he stole most of the money from his fellow employees, not from me. A lot of the money would have gone out as bonuses at year end."

"Yes, we see by the books your recruiting and retention are based on bonuses." Mr. Tompkins's pudgy hand patted his bound volumes of paper, as if the very words he spoke resided there. "But let me caution you; there is no proof Mr. Douglas is your embezzler."

Jupiter gazed down at the fat man's quick moving hand, "Do you have any advice?" He nearly added—advice that doesn't sound like preaching?

"If you intend to press charges, then our firm is already contracted to present the facts for you during the investigation and in court." Mr. Tompkins' face glowed. Perhaps the idea of the public stage intrigued him.

"I hate to have it known on the street I was robbed, and robbed so easily." Jupiter felt his mouth turn down in disgust and embarrassment.

"Yes, firms and owners often feel that way." The auditor released a disappointed sigh, vented it out into the space between them. "Then I would suggest you use the threat of criminal proceedings to leverage a return of any remaining funds. You can declare the rest as a business loss."

"I'll need full documentation in my hands. I'll have to bluff, and Jerry might be intimidated by the stack of paper." Time to show decisive leadership.

Mr. Tompkins relished the moment and flashed out a confident beam. "We have those materials, and I've brought them with me today." The auditor handed the voluminous files over. "You'll want to go carefully through the evidence. If you have questions while you read through it, here is my cell number." He handed over a business card.

Jupiter sighed. "Looks like I better drop into the office tomorrow or the day after."

"Indeed. Time to man the ramparts."

***

September at dawn was so benign, disconnected from human affairs in its magnificent display of color, riffs through thin torn strings of clouds, red and pink wash forgiving the jet contrails streaked across its brow. He halted by the silo to let the sun warm his face, then, low in spirits, he drove into town, into conflict, into perdition.

He hoped for an hour or two of quiet before the battle. Unnamed caretakers had arranged his empty desk just so, with pens and a ruler squared up on a blotter. The regimented conference table was another matter. They had stacked the mail, arranged by topic in a dozen labeled piles, and in the middle sat a large box covered in brown paper. Jupiter opened that. Tearing away the paper, he uncovered a leather-bound case. A round cylinder girdled in leather lay inside; he removed it with care.

An iron spindle and a chain with a weight were also nestled in the box. He assembled the pieces and made the tantric wheel once again a working artifact. The wheel carried a mantra imprinted many times around the cylinder. He gave the spindle an experimental flick of his wrist. The chain and weight circled around, propelling the drum into a spinning prayer.

Inside the box he discovered a note from Marjorie. "Jupiter, I'm sending you my Mani prayer wheel. I have the feeling that 'where' you are, you'll need it more than I. While you use the wheel, aspire to the Bodhichitta of Enlightenment. Perhaps the good karma will help you in your relationship with Kate. P.S. I would have sent this to your new home, but you've not confided that address to me—yet."

Again he held the wheel level and snapped his wrist. The chain swung out and carried the drum around a half dozen times. Jupiter nestled the wheel back in its box and that into a desk drawer. In a little while, he would be praying, but not for enlightenment.

The room crowded in on him even while he was alone. His imagination filled the space. He concentrated on deep breathing, holding the headache at bay, and keeping his shoulder muscles loose. The phone rang; the receptionist was on the line. "Mr. Devon, Mr. Douglas has arrived and is on his way back just as you asked." The call, the beginning, broke Jupiter's concentration, letting a wall of headache sweep over him.

The door flung back. Jerry bounded into the room with a large grin of welcome on his face. "Matt, you're back! You look great! How was the Arctic Circle?" He hesitated at the desk, as if he smelled something in the room.

"Jerry, as always, have a seat."

Jerry sat down in the chair opposite Jupiter.

"Critical business brought me home, Jerry. Bit of unpleasantness, I'm afraid. The audit is back."

Jerry stopped smiling. He adjusted himself in the chair. "Yeah, the auditors were a real pain for the CPA and our office manager. The usual three days of requests for this and that, all the time making us feel incompetent, especially poor Ellen. Nothing serious, I hope?"

"Turns out someone has stolen…," Jupiter glanced down at a slip of paper, "two hundred forty thousand, two hundred and eighty-five dollars, and thirty-nine cents. I want it back. You're the thief, right, Jerry?"

"Matt, are you crazy? What are you talking about?"

Jupiter patted two very large file folders. "We unearthed your dummy vendors. Charges came in and got paid by someone who knew the system. Handled like regular pieces of business, but it wasn't regular business, was it?"

"Dummy vendors? I know all our vendors, most of them personally."

"We paid them neatly by electronic transfer. No one here need ever have met them."

"Well, give me the two names, and we'll contact them, sort it out."

"You know the names, don't you Jerry? And you just told me there were two of them."

Jerry's face wrinkled up in puzzlement. "If there's something wrong, Ellen must have done it. As office manager, she organizes the books. I never mess with the small stuff. I just run the projects and supervise the staff."

Jupiter's left hand started to twitch. He clamped down on his muscles to stop the shakes, and that aggravated the tremor. He shoved the hand down in his lap. "No good, Jerry. The proof is here." Jupiter tapped the folders again with his right index finger. He bent forward as his left hand jumped in his lap.

Jerry stared down at the folders, then up at the ceiling, avoiding eye contact. He composed his face and stared Jupiter full in the face. "I don't know what you have there—"

"Yes, you do, Jerry. This is the paper trail you left as you embezzled from us, and now it's the paper trail that can get you locked up. All your own careful work, and you know every page of it."

"I'd never steal from the firm. You can look at all my personal accounts. The money isn't there."

Jupiter's vision narrowed—shrunk down to a tunnel, a spot of light surrounded by black. "I don't need to prove where you hid the money, only that you took it."

Jerry's face relaxed. His smile shone out, toothed and carnivorous. "Well, Mr. Devon." He made the "Mister" sound snide. "I don't think you can prove anything at all."

"I want our money back. I want your assets if you don't have it in cash."

"Is that all?"

"No. I want you off my payroll. I want you out of my building, and I prefer you out of Texas, but I'll leave that up to you. I want you out of advertising. I can do that too. I'll make sure my circle of acquaintances knows I fired you for malfeasance." A metallic taste of bile rose up in Jupiter's mouth—he might be sick.

"Is that the deal you're offering then? The money for not prosecuting me? And slander and the end of my career on top of it all?" Jerry paused. "Well, I've got news for you. You can't prosecute me because there's no proof. You can't threaten my reputation because I'll sue. You can't fire me because I quit. I was going to resign on the first of the month anyway."

"Resign?" Jupiter's stomach surged. He clamped his mouth shut.

"I've opened up my own shop, Matt. The space is rented. The staff is hired. And even better—"

"Your own company?"

"Damn straight. And the sweet part—I'm taking a third of your accounts with me. No money returned, fewer customers, and no way to get back at me. Bend over, Matt. You're getting screwed."

He's right. He does have the upper hand.

Jerry jeered, "I've waited a long time for this moment, old timer."

"At least I can get you out of my building. Your secretary, Glennis, has packed your personal things, and they're waiting in front. After you're gone, we'll see what recourse we have." Jupiter asked himself, Now, who's bluffing? He reached for the phone and punched the button for reception.

Jerry got up, planted his hands on the desk, and leaned forward. "Don't bother, old man. I'll see myself out."

✳✳✳

The door had closed on Jupiter's silence. He hunched over in his chair. He waited for the nausea to subside. In a moment, he finished the call to reception. "Lisa, this is Matt. Has Jerry Douglas left?"

"Yes, Mr. Devon. He sailed out the door just now. Left his boxes and said he would send for them."

230

"In a good mood, was he?"

"I'd say so. Real chipper."

Jupiter made some meaningless, friendly sounds and hung up. Then he pushed the button for Jerry's office. "Glennis, this is Matt."

"Mr. Devon, I finished packing Mr. Douglas' things, and we carried them up to reception. I, I just…."

"Yes, this is a sad day. Glennis, you need to know up front that Jerry's leaving doesn't hurt your job here. In fact, you'll be coming over to work for me as my personal assistant if that's agreeable with you. Think about it, and we'll talk later."

"Oh."

"In the meantime, is Tom Wicket in today?" Wicket ran his computer graphics section. "He is? Please ask him to step in. Then, in three minutes, I need to see Ellen Dunn."

**

Six hours later, he sat alone at his desk in his agency, hoping for redemption and forgiveness for neglect. Reaching forward, he turned off the desk light so the room turned gray and still. He considered that his life has been longer and darker than he had known while he lived it. Sheila was gone. Eight years of emptiness, and then two years of running away. He'd crawled for miles. Like the Epic said, "the path ahead was constricted, knotted on itself, until only a serpent could traverse it." Gilgamesh's journey beneath the mountain, in the dark and in despair— Jupiter understood that path.

Breaking out from dark into the light would not be terrific. He had to end his sabbatical; he understood that. Time to pay back.

He picked up the phone and called Glennis to make sure they would talk the next day. Jupiter couldn't do anymore right now; he made excuses and left. With his audit and vendor files stuffed into an oversized briefcase, he paced out to the car. The case's weight rubbed against his leg and bent him over lopsided. He sat for a few moments, hands on the wheel, eyes staring out the windshield. He thrust on sunglasses and then started the engine. Rolling out of the lot, he fled from his Amarillo problems towards his Aniline troubles. Jupiter, driving down the Interstate, thought; *Why should the face of Gilgamesh not be drawn and his cheeks hollow, his visage burned black with the sun and etched with a long journey? His heart is filled with despair.*

The Story of the Flood

Chapter Twenty-Six: Days and Nights of Rain

He wanted escape into delusion. Jupiter asked Gilgamesh, "What do you see?"

"Behind me I see whitecaps that run ahead of a squall, a rip of white in front of a mass of boiling black. The water itself is a brown gray and reflects a woeful sky. There is a beach, a slash of dirty sand barely a dozen rods wide."

A shiver ran up Jupiter's neck into his hair, tingling. He could actually see the scene like last time, the words now scrolling at the bottom of the page. It was nearly a horror.

The view swung wildly as Gilgamesh continued. "Turning the other way I see a fertile plain, grass to the knee, stiff spine-laden trees, and thorny bushes. Across the plain a square sail approaches, held aloft by servants in black with two figures in white shaded from the sun. A troop follows the two and behind that a rabble. The sun is hot, orange, and unkind. This is Qurnah, and Qurnah both welcomes and burns us."

Jupiter could see the scene clearly, complete in all detail. "It could be Texas. Port Aransas, even. Tell me why you're at the sea."

"We've come down the Euphrates to meet with the King of Dilmun. I have four boats filled with silver, tin, and wool. We expect exotic woods, lapis lazulite, and pearls in return."

"Wasn't Dilmun where Noah, your Utnapishtim, lived forever with the gods?"

"Of course you would know. Close, very close. But I shall not venture there again. Qurnah is close enough. My time of questing for

234

immortality is long over."

Jupiter paused. "You have children. That's a form of immortality." He thought about Bobbie, dead, waiting at the funeral home for her burial today.

"Ah, the old myth. Your people have that myth too? You see yourself reflected in the face of a child, your child. You watch him do the things you did, play the games you played, live through the same little heartbreaks you had. You are fooled into thinking you live on in the little child."

Jupiter nodded. "Exactly."

"A fallacy. The child is his own person and will go off to become his own man. My sons are not Gilgamesh, nor my grandsons, nor my great-grandsons. I would not even wish such a burden upon them."

"Always the romantic warrior."

Servants brought Gilgamesh a linen fly to shield him from the sun and a tripod on which to sit. He sank onto it and waited for the King of Dilmun. "You chide me for my realism, but I will admit there is a romance in children. These little beings, sparked in a moment of passion and sweat, a mix of man and woman, old times and times coming, blood and learning. They will spread out across the earth even as I reach my own end."

"Sweat and passion. I miss Kate, you know."

"The unattainable one? I suspect your real regret is that you did not pin her to your life."

"You mean marry her."

"Just so. You want to have a child."

"Of course not. Kate is so much younger than I am. It wouldn't be right to saddle a young woman with an old man, to start a family so late in life."

Gilgamesh held his face up, his beard oiled ringlets gone gray. "Look at my age. Yet my wives are young. Most of them."

"And if I should die?"

"ur-Jupiter, you said your father died when you were young. You survived. So would your Inanna and her child."

"Maybe." *A marriage was required before a child—doubtful. She would laugh.*

"A birth is the best counter to old age, unless you can have a little war."

"I'm not very good at war." *After all, Jerry had won, hadn't he?*

Gilgamesh waved his hand and denied Jupiter's point. "You don't have to be good at war, just inspiring. Take my war with Kish. When I returned to Uruk, I was sick with disappointment. After all, I had lost two chances at immortality, my last chances."

"Your return to Uruk is in the Epic, but I don't see what it has to do with perking up our old age."

"I will explain it. Do not be fretful with me. In my absence, Aga of Kish had taken to demanding tribute. Uruk had sunk so low as to supply men to clean irrigation ditches and dig new wells in Kish."

Jupiter sighed—another self-aggrandizing story from Gilgamesh. Still, this was the King's Book. "Go on. See if you can tie it all together."

Gilgamesh chuckled. "Oh, I think I can. I took the troops into the field, chose a place outside the city walls where Kish lost her numerical advantage. Aga came out, straggled out through his gate. I attacked in a pincer movement. We beat Aga of Kish soundly."

"And so the war gave you a new boost of life?"

Gilgamesh held up a finger and cocked his head. "It did several things. First, the war made up to my people for my abandonment of Uruk." Gilgamesh held up another finger. "Second, the win released Uruk from Kish's fealty. Third, leading it settled me down into the daily details of rule. And fourth, battle gave the young men their time of glory with only a few of them dying. A pleasant little war."

"And it made you feel young again?"

"Why, I *was* young compared to now. That was a hundred years ago, approximately. But you yourself find conflict invigorates you. You choose conflict often enough."

"I didn't choose a war with Jerry." *Nor the humiliation of a loss.*

Gilgamesh shook his head. "Your negotiation with your Chamberlain—you cannot call that a war. Theft from the granary? Veiled threats?"

"So you know about that? Of course. You warned me twice."

"Eternal vigilance, the price of rule."

Jupiter grimaced. *Smug old bastard. But he was right.*

Gilgamesh tugged at his beard. "My words don't please you, but you expected nothing less. You will never recover what he took, and so you must focus on the thief."

"What would you have me do?"

"Disembowel him in front of his sons. Send them into exile. Salt the earth around his house and burn it."

"I think perhaps I can hollow out his life instead. Leave him a gray world where his name has been destroyed." *Poison his triumph, his reputation.*

"A petty plan. A king charges forward rather than slithers under. But you do need to enact a revenge—on the mother of your wild one. Avenge death."

"I'm busy saving the mother's life."

"She should at least pay with exile."

Chapter Twenty-Seven: Story of the Flood

It took only a week for Jupiter to realize he had lost his company and then gotten it back, even if it was poorer than he left it. Bobbie had died ten days ago. Drained dry by turmoil, Jupiter shuffled through each day. Sumerians thought in sixty-four's. He couldn't see that many days ahead.

Kate swung by the elevator to say goodbye. Jupiter peered into the little car. She had packed it to the ceiling, but still it wasn't much. "Is that all you're taking?"

"I don't have an apartment yet. I'll live in a cheap hotel on the north side until I've got a place; then I'll make my Dad move my stuff down."

"What about furniture?"

"Hmm. You've got a lot of couches in your living room—way too crowded."

"Let's go upstairs for a bit and visit your couches. It might be awhile before you see them again."

In the freight elevator she leaned against him and ducked down from her height so her head could rest on his shoulder. *The time might be right. I might ask.*

He brought her an espresso and opened a can of diet soft drink for himself. On the sofa they spooned, him in back and propped up against the leather arm. Gazing past her hair, a tangle of blonde pushed into the side of his face, he saw one beautiful cheekbone, the edge of her lovely nose. He stumbled into it. "You know, I—well—see it's this way. Why don't we have a kid? And get married? You and me?"

She sat up, flipped around, and faced him. Her legs were crossed, her face concerned. She reached up and caressed his cheek. "What's this

238

all about?"

"I thought we're so good together, we should have a family."

"Poor old Matt, clueless. I'm moving to Dallas, gonna be a superstar, direct my own movie where I have a beautiful, scintillating life. You already said you wouldn't come."

"You can still go to Dallas. We can see each other on weekends, travel together, all three of us, on holidays."

She cocked an eyebrow at him. Here it came. "Shut up! I'd be a single mom in the big D, raise the kid myself while I also have a day job?"

"No, no! I'll raise him here. I can take care of him."

She did laugh. "Are you high on something? By the time he, or she, is in high school, you'll be eighty years old. You can't handle me, much less an eighteen-year-old."

He felt tears spring to his eyes. Shit, death rising up on the horizon. "Maybe I could move to Dallas." That was stupid. That wasn't going to work.

"Matt, I'm real sorry, but I'm not going to pump out a baby just because you're feeling your oats." She patted him on the cheek, dismissive. "I tell you what. We'll put you in a sperm bank account for me. When I'm forty-five, I'll reconsider your proposition. I might make a withdrawal then."

"Well, that will be a lot of fun."

She leaned in so close he could only see her eyes. "Tell you what; would you like to make a deposit now?" She tilted her face and kissed him, hard. She had trapped his lower lip across his teeth, grating. This was her solution to every problem.

***

It was two days short of a week since Kate had packed her car and headed to Dallas. He didn't believe an absence could be so manifest, so physically difficult, so debilitating.

He rang the bell. When Diane opened the door, he asked, "Okay to come in?"

"Yes. I've got someone on the office phone. Go on through into the kitchen. I'll be there in a minute and make you some coffee."

239

Diane's kitchen table was straight out of the thirties: a deck of linoleum and an apron of chrome that looked like three stacked tubes. He slumped into the chrome chair; its vinyl complained with a squeak.

"You look tired," Diane said, coming in behind him. It was she who looked tired, wrung to the ground.

He jumped up and took her hand. "How are you bearing up?"

She smiled, but her eyes filled up with tears. "Oh, I've got my faith. It helps."

Neither said anything. They busied themselves with the coffee pot, cups, and spoons. While it perked on the gas stove, she sat opposite him. "We haven't seen you since the funeral."

"Oh, I've been driving in to Amarillo a lot. I'm not used to working for a living."

"I think it's good for you. Idle hands, devil's playground. You need to be kept busy, out of trouble."

"I like trouble."

"No, you don't. You like to think you can handle trouble."

"Yes, ma'am." All the women in his life told him what he thought and when he thought it, even Marjorie and Sheila. "How's the business?"

"Oh, fine. Not very busy, but I'm doing the daily reckoning for the auto parts store now as well as the weekly books. I go down to their place about five." She brought the coffee pot from the stove and placed it on a kitchen towel on the table.

"That's good."

"You seem distracted."

"Oh, you know, the company. Kate. Bobbie. Tell me, Diane, do you think revenge is an acceptable act."

"I think the Lord would say revenge hurts the actor as much as the recipient."

"Hmm."

Diane leaned across the table and refilled his coffee cup. "You know you dropped by to ask me something."

"Yes, I did."

"So ask it."

"Are you going to return to Vega? Quit here?"

She rotated a spoon on the table top and gave it her concentration. "I don't know. I don't think so. When I first moved here, it was for Bobbie,

240

but now I have a baby business, some friends, and a new church. Vega—there's some guilt there—all those old dears who needed me. But I gave that business away."

"So you'll stay?"

She glanced up. "Day by day. The same way we get along after a funeral."

***

It was still hot during the fall days, and the pickup had gone to full burner in the parking lot. Jupiter squirmed on the vinyl seat and wished it wasn't burning him through his khakis. He sorted mail, stacking it in a good news pile and a bad news pile. His head snapped up as he heard a metallic knocking on the hood. It was Heldritch coming around to talk to him. "Morning, Matt. How are you?"

"Good, Dan. And you?" Jupiter reached up to touch a nose long healed and suppressed the impulse.

"Oh, fine, fine."

Jupiter made small talk. "So, beautiful day. Feels more like summer."

"Yeah, the farmers might get another alfalfa crop if the weather holds."

"You look like a man with something on his mind. It's not alfalfa you want to talk about, right?" He watched Dan's eyebrows twitch, the smile break out.

"My foreman Julio is going to kill a pig. It's a big annual thing for my work crews. We do all of the butcher work on a Wednesday morning, and on Sunday the families arrive for a pig roast. It's a last-of-summer thing, and it fits in with a football party." He made a passing motion with his hand like a quarterback stepping back to throw.

"Wow, sounds like you're keeping the old traditions alive."

"Nah, if we were doing that, we would still be killing Indians and re-fighting the Civil War. Not to mention gunning down men who are sleeping with our womenfolk."

"Oh." Jupiter touched his lip with his index finger. No answer possible.

"So, are you up to it?"

"Dan, I've always been a supermarket man."

"Yeah, so?"

"My pork arrives from the store on a Styrofoam tray, with plastic wrap over the top." Jupiter had a sudden image of a grungy six-year-old with a fleece cinched around his waist, pinning a sheep between his knees, drawing a copper knife across its throat. "Maybe it's time I got closer to the food I eat. Sure, I'll come out and watch you butcher the hog." He nodded his head vigorously. It was the gesture that convinced him.

Dan grinned. "Sounds good. If you can get through the bloodletting without—you know—puking, then we'll get you to scrape the bristles off. And then you're up for the picnic?"

Jupiter pictured a backyard full of men and women, dogs and kids—mass confusion in a holiday atmosphere. Maybe tolerable. But a crowded, jammed-up living room full of screaming and a blaring TV? It made him clammy with sweat just imagining it. "That's harder. I have to run into the city on Sunday. Got some real estate business that's already scheduled. Okay if I pass this time?"

"Sure, means more for the rest of us. The pig kill starts at nine on Wednesday and the picnic at eleven on Sunday. If you get back from Amarillo before five, drive over for a beer and some pork."

"No promises, but I'll try." He stuck his hand out; Dan shook it.

The contractor spun on his heel. "Gotta go. See ya Wednesday."

He dug out his phone. He tried instant messaging Kate. "Your father invited me to picnic."

"B4 U go on ur txt crap—try—Ur fthr invit me 2 party."

"Cant we use English?"

"K. Dad said wood invite you 2 pigkill 2."

"Yes."

"Going?"

"Yes."

"Wy tl me?"

"Weird."

"?"

"Dan younger than me."

"O th father n law act?"

"Yes."

"Brace slf. Xmas nxt ROTFL."

***

Dan's one acre had cars strewn down the driveway. Jupiter parked on the road and strode down around the house. In the back they were getting started. The hog's back legs were tied, and two men were winching it backwards across the ground, then up into a tree. Dan's foreman whipped a twenty gallon galvanized tub underneath the pig's squealing head. Then he cut its throat. A short scream trailed off to gurgling. Blood cascaded down. The foreman opened the belly. Organs spilled out into the immense tub—and the smell. Jupiter grew nauseous, barely in control.

"Yo, look at la niña, sitting on the ground."

"Gone all white."

Dan warned the guys. "I'd step away until his color changes back."

"You okay, man?" A grinning face thrust down into his.

Jupiter smiled the brave smile. "Yeah, I'm better, thanks. I was supposed to do something with the bristles."

The faces around him were laughing, but without cruelty.

"Chure, you think you up to it." A man, burnt by sun nearly to ebony, handed him a machete. "We use this; I ground it off flat. See, put it on the skin; slant it this way." He showed Jupiter the art of bristle scraping and commented continuously on Jupiter's form. "No, no, don't cut the skin; it's harder to peel later. That's good."

***

Jupiter felt his stomach jump the same way on Sunday. This time casual, sleek women and well-dressed men surrounded him at an open house in Amarillo. Glennis had arranged this real estate event, in his own house, signifying the place was on the market. They hadn't planned this for realtors, however. Glennis mailed out invitations to his friends and business acquaintances of years past. It commemorated all the parties and dinners once held under this roof.

Jupiter planned to make the speech at two, since he calculated the crowd arriving and departing—but mostly arriving—would have taken on enough to drink by then. He stood in the living room backed up against a bookcase. He wondered if drops of sweat were going to run off his forehead for all to see. Glennis caught his eye and tapped her watch. When he agreed with a nod, she clanged her champagne glass with a salad fork.

He stepped up onto the fireplace hearth, outwardly all charm and urbanity, inwardly sweating and panicky. "Can I have your attention for a moment? What a worn-out, senior-looking crowd! I'm sure most of you are here for the champagne." A loud babble from the room agreed with him. "I'm hoping some of you are also here house shopping." Again the people in the room made a noisy response, including raspberries. "And no, I'm in no hurry to sell, so I'm not going to mark it down two hundred off the asking price. At any rate—not this afternoon." Loud laughter made him more comfortable. The pitch was going okay. "I just wanted to thank you all for the wonderful times we've had here, you and me and my ex-wife Sheila, who couldn't be here today. We did invite her, Glennis, didn't we?"

He heard from the crowd, "So where's she?" "We want Sheila!" "We want the Babe."

"Sheila Yes, Matt No! Sheila Yes, Matt NO!"

He waited for the clamor to die down. "I say this both without a doubt and with no small pride, this old house has seen some great times. It has also seen some embarrassment, like Johnny over there throwing up in the fireplace after too many margaritas." He paused long enough for John to receive his kudos. "Selling the place is a symbol I guess, not that I'm leaving the greater Amarillo area or my job, but this is to let you all know I've moved over to Aniline. I'm doing a renovation there because… well, because I can. It's got a killer view. So you'll still have me to kick around, but you'll have to drive further to do it. That's it! Enough speech. Drink up, and remember the good times as you wander through the house."

Jupiter escaped as quickly as he could, slipped out the side gate, quick-stepped to his car parked on the street. In the front seat beside him there was a plastic bag. In it, he had a pig's foot wrapped in a rag. He'd carried it around since Wednesday. The beginning of a good stink filled the car. Jupiter thought Jimmy might like it; it was both fascinating and disgusting—if he could only figure out how the devil to dry it.

***

It didn't take long to drive from his Amarillo house to Dan and Sarah's. Traffic had dwindled during the weekend thanks to football season and televised games. The buildings, the parked cars and trucks, and the power lines slid past gracefully, dreaming. It mirrored the Epic— *I have traveled as much of a journey as three times sixteen days in thirty minutes.* A shame tomorrow wouldn't be like this.

As Jupiter drove across Aniline, he noticed dark, challenging clouds rolling in. He was going to a pig roast, something he would have never predicted. He had waited, nonetheless, as late in the day as he decently could. He discovered the party had thinned out to four people in the kitchen. They drank beer and reminisced about things that had gone badly on one job site or another. He ate pig fritters. His hands didn't shake. He got a good beer buzz.

***

It rained for four days and four nights, hard. Aniline wasn't used to it. At first in the neighborhoods, ditches adjacent to the streets handled the flood. The water finished filling the ditches and hid the potholes in the roads. Rain then brimmed the streets over, making Aniline into Venice. It eventually spread out in the low spots in the driveways, invaded lawns, and crept up towards the house foundations. People wandered into the café with squelching boots and comments ranging from philosophical to querulous. Then the weather broke. They had two intensely hot days. Banks of mist rose off the saturated yards and fields. The roads drained, and a blanket of mud covered the pavements. As if all this wasn't enough, a super-cell thunderstorm rolled towards them to give them another taste of violent Texas weather.

Jupiter sat in his living room with the lights off. This was one way to break a ten-year drought.

Though it was mid-afternoon, it was as gray-blue as dusk inside and out. He watched the huge thunderheads brewing their own turmoil out there, and he waited for a descending curtain wall, a rotational cloud indicating a tornado. While he observed the sky breathing up a monster

245

of a storm, he plotted simplification. He wanted to cut down on his number of rubbed and raw places where the outside world ground up against him.

First, he decided to get a driver for the daily commute to and from Amarillo. Then he decided to make some of his meetings with Kate at lake resorts instead of in the heart of Dallas. He still hadn't nerved up for Dallas week-ends. When resorts got old for her, they might fly out somewhere for the weekend—if he could stand the airplane.

Then he cast his mind to Carol Inskeep and her rehabilitation. It now appeared possible she would exit rehab clean and sober. He had no faith it would last. She was coming back to Aniline to her old hangouts and ways. As Bobbie had once said, "She'll just get another." That was a complication he wished he could head off, for Diane's sake.

He had a brilliant thought, an idea of charm, magic, and criminality; something that charged out of his subconscious and ran smack into his delight. He hurried to the closet and grabbed a waterproof coat. He ran out into the beginnings of the storm, where huge raindrops struck around him like incoming artillery. He jumped into his pickup and drove the eight blocks to Carol Inskeep's twenty-year-old trailer. It was deserted now and seedier than ever.

A key sat under a flowerpot, like Diane's house, but this flowerpot held only dead twigs. Once he unlocked the door and got inside, he opened every window and looped the curtains over their rods out of the way. He opened the vent in the roof. He pinned the front door open with the coffee table and ran back out to his pickup in the driving rain. A strong wind blew past, laden with water like a wave. *The gods don't like noise, do they? And they don't like trailers either.*

***

September had slipped away with its minor triumphs. October arrived as a bird of prey plunging into Jupiter's life. His brooding over the elevator continued full and unabated, sinking talons into him. Kate lived far away in Dallas, called less often, but texted him once a day—often to ask him to drive down for the weekend. He didn't think of himself as an instant message guy, but his thumb dance improved week by week. He was now playing with the idea of a dog, just to make the head house less quiet. He rather suspected he liked the idea of a dog more than the actual animal, the commitment. Besides, he was more of a cat person. But cats had litter boxes. On further reflection he had White, the dog he borrowed each day from the McCloskeys, still getting a second breakfast down in the elevator's office.

***

In mid-month, Kate drove into Aniline for a weekend and moved into the elevator, rather than going home to her parents. She greeted him at the stairs to the head house with real estate brochures in hand. "Look Matt, I'm house shopping! Absolutely amazing—moving out of my daddy's house and a month later ready to buy a house of my own!" She hugged him hard and then swept by him into the head house. When he got to the living room, he learned she had dumped her suitcase first thing at the bottom of the stairs and was spreading out house ads on a coffee table.

He parked himself beside her. "Good to see you too."

"I couldn't wait to get here and show you these. Look at this one. It's got a pool, and it's only a half million."

"Kind of rich for your first house."

"It's not your first house, though."

That was ominous. "Anything in blue? With a relaxed fit?"

"Get a load of this one—I like it; it has a low-maintenance yard and sprinklers."

He glanced at it. "We're having chicken piccata and oven-roasted vegetables." Return to normalcy.

"Uh-huh. What do you think of this one?"

"I own that house in Amarillo, and I'm trying to sell it."

"Oh. What about this one?" She waved a brochure of a hideous 1950s brick at him.

"After dinner, I thought we would take a drive out to the lake and drown ourselves."

"Okay, whatever you think. I don't really like that one. Do you like brick or siding?"

"Or we could round up the tanks and have a blitzkrieg into Poland, take Warsaw, and be in Gdansk by morning."

"What? You're not paying attention at all. This is serious stuff, buying a house." She laughed, and he caught himself on the edge of a smile.

He asked her, "So, you've been employed as a designer, what, six weeks?"

"Uh-huh. And I'm a natural at it, too." She threw her blonde hair back and struck a pose.

"And you think you have serious banking credit, after six weeks?"

"No, I have a job and some money. You have credit." She grinned at him and nudged him with her shoulder.

"I fail to see what my credit rating has to do with you, young lady."

"We'll buy it together."

"Don't we have to be married or something first? Otherwise we can't get a mortgage."

She snorted. "Matt dear, you really are an old fogey. Now days you only have to be domiciled together. That's polite talk for 'shacked up.'"

"So you're not proposing marriage to me, just advocating the kidnap of my credit rating." He dropped his head for effect and assumed the hangdog posture.

She patted him on the leg. "I know you're not ready for marriage, yet. I can wait. Probably longer than you can, considering your age."

He turned the idea over in his mind. Kate, shacking up, then maybe marriage? Aniline, Dallas? It didn't appear half bad. It was a stupid idea. He decided to keep his mouth shut and not to commit one way or the other until shoved hard. "Well, it is nice to be asked."

"I figure by summer next year I'll have you in tow."

"You have me in tow now." That was true. Piteous.

She flapped a hand and dismissed his confession. "What do you think about this one? It's a cottage on Morningside." She was pushing another brochure at him. "We can take a tour online."

"Will they let me keep goats?"

"Matt, grow up. You don't want goats."

"How do you know?"

"Because I just told you so."

They made dinner a minor triumph, with both of them talking busily away at each other. Later, as they tussled on the bed, she complained, "You've got your knee on one of my brochures. You're crunching it all up." When she left Sunday night, the head house echoed, empty. Solitude versus loneliness depended on who had just walked out the door.

***

Fresh baked cookies filled the air, smelling better even than they tasted. "We're bleeding money, Matt." Diane was not happy.

He pushed his coffee cup across the 30s table towards the pot at her elbow. "You mean we didn't make a lot of money."

"I mean there's more going out than coming in." She refilled his cup and plunked it down on his side of the table.

"Diane, no problem. We talked about this. I've got a business model that says we take losses for two years during this recession and then have a slow return to prosperity. Along with the rest of the country." He took a cookie off the plate and nibbled it reflectively. The chocolate chips were still gooey.

"So I bleed you white for two years. Doesn't feel good. Feels rotten, actually."

"Do what I do. Ignore it, pretend it's not there."

"I'm a bookkeeper, Matt. That's what I do. At the end of the month, I sit down and subtract expenses from income. It's a red number right now." She tapped a forefinger on the tabletop. "Red!"

"If my supposed indifference doesn't help you, what will?"

"Paah." She narrowed her eyes and thought. "Tomorrow I'll go door-to-door, talk to every office manager and owner in town."

"Want to make the ad in the paper bigger?"

"Now, that would cost more money, wouldn't it? Sometimes I don't think you're listening." She stood up, leaned forward, brushed at the crumbs on his paunch with a paper napkin, and thumped back down in her chair.

"I always listen. Sometimes I don't cooperate, that's all."

"Call it what you will. Say, Artie at the hardware store said there was a moving van at the elevator. What's that all about? Are you sneaking out of town?"

"No, I'm trying to sell a house in Amarillo. I'm storing some of its contents on the empty work floor of the elevator. I want to give it to charity, but I thought it would be nicer to give it away locally."

"You might save them for a house in Dallas."

"Jesus Christ, Diane. Are there no secrets in this town?"

"I wish you wouldn't use our Lord's name that way, Matt. Besides, Kate mentioned you haven't given in yet."

***

In spite of the likelihood of his eviction for zoning violations, Jupiter chose to continue work at the grain elevator. Heldritch had brought over a finish carpenter who was applying interior muntins to the windows of the living room, restoring a 1920s exterior style to the sheets of glass. Once again, Jupiter liked the grid imposed upon the sky as he gazed out. He stood there with Dan Heldritch and his carpenter staring up.

Heldritch picked up where he had left off. "Like I said, I showed up today for our walkthrough on both the bedroom and the old office downstairs."

"You haven't started on the office yet."

"Yeah, but me and the boys need to know how authentic you want it. You know, a lot of the old woodwork has to be replaced because of water and bug damage. We can do it cheap, or we can do it nice, or we can do it authentic."

"Let me guess which is the most expensive."

"Not really knock-you-down expensive. It's cheap compared to a custom kitchen."

"You have relieved my mind." The carpenter snickered. "Bedroom first, since we're up here?"

"Sure." They went from the kitchen to the upstairs, clumping up the concrete steps talking about the weather.

Jupiter smelled that rich paint reek soaking the air. Dan walked through the bedroom to the new half. "Both the ivory and the red paint took fine, I think. Jim is great at edging in with a brush. Hope you like that color—it would be a bitch to cover over." Dan waved his hand at the carnelian wall.

"It's fine. You may not like red, but I do. Fantastic shelves; they worked out really well. And this library table—your guy does excellent work, beautiful oak."

"You know, Matt, I get it for this end. I even kind of like it. It looks like an old Victorian office."

"It looks like George Smith's office in 1866."

"Who's he?"

"Translated Assyrian cuneiform."

"Poor guy. This red end of the nook though. Whoa Nelly! The backless couch and the table with the hammered copper tray! That's the most custom thing we've ever done, and I've got Custom Builder on all my business cards."

"It's a Sumerian room—kind of a bookend for the office on the other side."

"We figured that out from the museum prints leaning up here—we're not stupid. You have strange hobbies, Matt."

"Beats an addiction to football."

"Hey, no need to get personal. What's Kate think about this?"

"Hey, no need to get personal yourself. She's comfortable with it. I sent her a phone photo. She called it 'fanciful and wicked.'"

They thumped down the stairs to the kitchen. "Want some coffee? Or orange juice?" Mid-morning light crowded through the small window in the kitchen wall, across the breakfast bar and onto the range behind.

Heldritch said, "OJ would be great!"

Jupiter got out two glasses and then pulled the carton from the refrigerator door, kicking the big stainless steel slab shut with his heel. Dan accepted the glass and cradled it lovingly in his hand. "Sarah doesn't let me have orange juice very often."

"Why ever not?"

"I got an acid reflux thing."

"That sucks. What do you think causes it?"

"Either customers or a daughter—take your pick."

"I could be a partner rather than a customer. We could convert this whole thing to condos."

"Who lives in condos out in the country? No thanks. I'll keep working on the place until you run out of money; then I'll move on to working for the Mayor."

"Has he hired you yet?"

"No comment. I'm breaking ground on a spec house and hope to get the concrete work done before winter weather slows us down."

***

Success was a problem. So was the pressure of growth. Jupiter resisted the easy answer, to replace Jerry with a new second-in-command. As a result, he started each day by getting into the passenger seat of his own car and letting a silent local named Carl take him into work. On most days he would leave by three, but he was bringing home a briefcase full of materials. The head house office, seldom used for work before, became more and more an extension of the firm in Amarillo. Maybe Glennis could come over a couple of times a week.

Somehow, through good staff, friends, or an offbeat reputation, the shop now had three new major accounts based outside of Texas. In years past, Jupiter had become spoiled. He had worked in local markets for people he knew. Now he was back in the big time. Business had become so good, or bad, it appeared he would have to send staff to Chicago next month—all because his firm was bringing ballet back with a vengeance.

He even had an approach from an international oil company who wanted some reputation management. Jupiter thought about resurrecting his gravedigger campaign from the early seventies, how it might be reworked as an oil shocker. He had the campaign in his mind, one that would be quite effective, but hard to sell to the client. He closed his eyes and watched it on the inside of his eyelids: We make it. You buy it and burn it in your car. Then we all breathe it. Don't you think it's time we did something together rather than wringing our hands and pointing fingers? We're the people with the green gas stations and the dirty secret. You're the drivers with insatiable needs. Visit us online at Cough.com, a commercial alliance for change.

***

It could have been an old horror movie where his hand committed terrible crimes. He couldn't stop that hand. Jupiter watched it write out a third note to Mayor Nelson Taggert Sharp: "Mayor, I would like to discuss the possibility of a limited partnership. My idea, one I am sure you will see value in, is to renovate the industrial buildings around the grain elevator as destination office parks. It's quite probable that I can provide an anchor point for the development, a first major client. The claims division of a regional insurance company has expressed strong interest in office space in the elevator. I'd like to meet with you at your convenience to discuss this possible joint venture. Yours sincerely, Matthew Devon." He received no reply from Sharp, a man who perhaps didn't deserve Jupiter's abuse. But it was delicious.

The Council informed him by certified mail that they would review his zoning status at the December meeting—delaying until the new council was sitting. In his heart he knew his own pettiness, his teasing of fate, would spring back on him. Just as Gilgamesh's effrontery with Ishtar had led to a threat—a threat pointed at the core of Uruk.

***

Sharp's third mayoral campaign was in swing. Jupiter was following it closely through the café and the newspaper.

The Mayor discovered he was in a political pinch. Three other people had announced their candidacies. All three had no experience in politics. Jupiter knew two to be well-known cranks in Aniline, running out of some sense of whimsy. The third was a serious contender—Ralph Stroud, a rancher who had a certain standing in the community.

All things happened in Aniline either in Angie's or in the parking lot of the Post Office. Jupiter drove in, skirting an immense pothole that had eaten the best parking space and was approaching the curb of the street. His eyes flicked back and forth, searching. Yes, there it was. He pulled in beside a pickup with a cracked windshield and a headache rack; it was Sarah's truck. He dropped down out of his seat, circled around, and clambered up into her passenger seat. He waited for quite a while.

Sarah strolled out of the building, crossed in front of him, and stopped dead, staring at him in her truck. Then, with aplomb, she settled her packages in the bed, got in, and turned to face him. "Matt, is anything wrong? Is Diane all right?"

"No, there's nothing wrong. I only wanted to visit."

"From out of the blue? This from the man who won't even come to dinner?"

"I'm beginning to understand where Kate inherited her gentle manners."

She jabbed her keys into the ignition. "Smooth, Matt, very smooth. Flattery gets you everything. What do you need?"

"I can't visit without needing something?"

She laughed, took the keys back out of the ignition, and dropped them farm-style on the dash. "Let's say it's doubtful. If I remember right, I did offer the insider scoop any time—so I suspect you're here to take me up on it."

"Guilty as charged. What can you tell me about Ralph Stroud?"

"Pillar of the community. His great-great-grandfather helped found this town. Big family guy, has six kids, four of them boys. Has ten thousand acres under cultivation and a substantial payroll for a farmer. Dan built his house. I don't like him at all."

"Really? Why not?" He was thrilled—this was why he had chosen her.

"Ralph led the informal opposition to school bonds four times and got them voted down." She arched an eyebrow. "You'll remember I'm a teacher?"

"I remember something about that."

"Plus he left his dear old mother living alone in the old family house—and I mean old, both the house and Mom—and moved across the road into his own Dallas South Fork."

He pursed his lips. "Not nice to Mother. Dearie me."

"And he's a bigot who passed it on to his kids. Half the fights the teachers break up in school are between a Stroud and a black or a Hispanic. Stroud is so opposed to change, he makes even the Mayor look like a left-wing, bleeding-heart liberal."

"Wow, Sarah, you're carrying a crush for this guy."

"Laugh if you want. Aniline isn't really about family farming anymore, and it isn't about grain shipments out of your old elevator. If it isn't about something soon, then Aniline will die like all the other farm towns are dying. We need development and, God help us, we need Sharp—or in any case someone who isn't Stroud."

"I think I understand what you're saying. Even though you always sugar-coat it."

Sarah laughed. "Here's another bitter pill for you, Matt. You're coming to dinner on Saturday with Kate whether you like it or not. Kate's driving in from Dallas this weekend, and we'd like to see our daughter for a change, rather than getting phone calls from your house. She and I are agreed on this, so there's no getting out of it. She's bringing you over in handcuffs if necessary."

"I surrender. No need for cuffs."

"Good-bye, Matt. Get out of my truck. I need to go." She waved out the window as she drove away. "See you Saturday."

Chapter Twenty-Eight: Return to Amarillo

Gilgamesh had left his demand; it pulsed there on the laptop when Jupiter opened it. "ur-Jupiter, unlock your scribing machine. Good. Now I see a new room. You have heaped it with documents. They are not clay but flat white things. Linen, and quite thin."

Marjorie was right. He really did enjoy talking to Gilgamesh, even if it was all madness. "This place is Amarillo. Soon a scribe will come in and bully me, take me away from this chat with you."

"All I see is strange to me. Can you explain this place?"

"If I turn my machine away from my worktable, you can see through a window. There is lush green up against my building, where we have created a strip of garden out of the desert, then parking—a plaza of sorts many cubits wide. Those shining things are chariots. Close by, another of our buildings rises eight stories. They built it of concrete, a masonry Sumeria has not invented. Our sun beats down on us even though winter is on its way. 'Amarillo' means yellow, which is appropriate. The sun, your Shamash, has bleached our city to the color of old bones. Nearby, I can see a riot of activity on a road swarming with those who keep our commerce in motion."

"It is the same scene in Uruk." The screen flicked green and blue; then up flashed Gilgamesh in the soft light of dusk. Gilgamesh leaned on a brick balustrade and stared down into the busy streets below even as Jupiter showed him I-40 in Amarillo.

Commerce created traffic jams whether made of aurochs or semi-trailers. "The more things have changed, the more they repeat."

"I have been thinking. I have been puzzling over what happened between Utnapishtim and me."

256

"The immortality thing again? With our Noah?"

Gilgamesh shook his head. "My friend, I have lost all. I have lost immortality, and I also face the rest of my short life without my friend Enkidu. Your own distress over the wild one has reminded me of the old troubles."

"Can't help you with the heartache and the loneliness. I can suggest a comforting way to look at mortality though."

"Comfort. A linen coat made from a pig's skin?"

"Hmm. Mortality is a gift. Shamash, Siduri, and Utnapishtim each warned you of disappointment, but you didn't notice that they shaped it as a promise rather than a threat. Mortality is your gift from the gods, and all things mortal belong to you, including death. The trick is to think you possess death instead of it possessing you—then you can be a great king and know there will be a trope that rounds out your reign."

"Trope? I am a warrior, not a scholar. I don't know that word," Gilgamesh said.

"A final graceful word or figure. In your case, this means a great ceremony and a conference of the gods. A glorious end."

"Yes, I have always been greedy for glory, haven't I?"

"For a king, not remarkably so."

Gilgamesh stared out off his rooftop. He gazed towards the river. "It has occurred to me; you have read the entire Epic."

Jupiter thought of the piles of reference in his grain elevator and all the translations of the Epic he owned. "Yes, I studied it."

"Then you know how I end, and you know what my final reputation will be."

Jupiter nodded, "Yes, friend."

"A good reputation?"

"The best. The first reputation preserved as part of our culture. We study you in our schools and argue about your lessons. Our great writers fictionalize your life and bring it into our age."

"You know when and how I will die?"

"Would you like to hear about it?'

Gilgamesh paced back and forth. "I do not know. Man is mortal, but he is free of Death until Death takes him."

"Umm. Good point. So you would rather not know?"

Gilgamesh stared directly at Jupiter. "I shall consider it. Your hints of glorious ends and a name that continues on—this knowledge could be a joy, or a plague."

Jupiter stared back. "Tell me when you decide. I'll abide by what you want."

"We shall play the tale out for awhile. You have your own story to finish. When I returned to Uruk, I promised prosperity. A new temple, new date trees, and gardens that would stretch for a league each way, more people and commerce."

More one-upmanship? "Yes, a great king, a good shepherd for your people...."

"You are also a shepherd and a king-maker. You will soon install a puppet in your city-state. You will set him on a pedestal, and he will not recognize his benefactor."

Gilgamesh liked ending on a prediction: this time a prophecy of political intrigue and a reference to stewardship. Gilgamesh had not been the only one to promise prosperity. Jupiter dwelt on it, on what he must do there for his company, until Glennis knocked and brought him his next customer.

Chapter Twenty-Nine: The Bull of Heaven

Jupiter could smell bacon. He hovered in the door of the Inskeep kitchen, there to cash in an invitation to breakfast. Around the table sat his three Aniline women. Diane took the head seat. She was wearing half glasses, dressed in jeans and a flannel shirt. Kate sat at her left deferring to what the older woman said, nodding her head in time to Diane's words. Sarah, blonde by choice but clearly her daughter's mother, leaned her cheekbone against her fist with her elbow on the table. The sound of the TV seeped in from the living room; the gray light changed color as it came through the kitchen curtains.

In this last week of October, he experienced a mirage of near-contentment. The walls of the small kitchen didn't close in on him. He could breathe, and his head didn't throb. He tried out a belief that the predilection had subsided some, but then smiled at his self-deception. This wasn't improvement. He had only found another place to hide. His dinner with the Heldritchs still lay ahead of him. There would be plenty of opportunity left in the weekend for his condition to exercise itself.

Kate shot him a sideways glance while she dabbed at some syrup in the tangle of hair near her mouth. "Are you okay? You look shaky."

"I'm fine, just too much coffee." And not enough concealment. *Pretend it's a casual question.* "So, if the Mayor is defeated in the election, will that improve my chances to stay in my home?"

The women glanced at each other, a little secret message. Diane answered first. "One of our new bookkeeping customers is a councilman. He's irritated at how long all this has drug out. He voted for the zoning ordinances in the first place. I don't think he'll cut you much slack."

Sarah folded her arms on the table. "If Stroud wins, you're in worse

259

shape than with Sharp. He probably hates everything you stand for. You're a city slicker playing around in his town—in a town full of decent hard-working people."

"I work hard," Jupiter protested.

Kate hammered the nail into it. "Yeah, you work hard selling soap. That's not a job a real man does. A real man farms, or fixes trucks, or builds houses. Mom is right; you're a big-time dilettante gracing us hicks with your sophisticated presence."

"And you're a graphics designer. You're no better than me."

Kate gave up with the napkin and flicked her hair back from her face. "Oh, shut up. I'm younger and better looking, and don't forget, I had to move away to be a designer."

Jupiter glanced around the table. "The women in town like me."

Sarah said, "I like you. You're okay for a man even if you're not good enough for my daughter."

"So, maybe the women on the Town Council will take pity on me."

Sarah pointed out, "You know there aren't any women on the Council. I can't remember if there ever has been a woman on the Council. It's just not the Aniline way."

"So the Council will rule against me even when the newly-elected members join. I can fight it in court after that." And he would most likely lose.

Sarah made a little *moue* with her mouth, very much like Kate. "Even if he's sympathetic, the Chief will have to evict you. You'll have to find a place to live, while you're waiting on the courts. More French toast?"

Bobbie had liked French toast.

***

Jupiter deserved a miracle, and it was Angie's. Each day, in the morning or late in the afternoon, he deployed his cunning, his eyes, his ears to Angie's, searching for the edge. A steady diet of Prozac won the day, and he sat in the center of the room.

Dead ahead of him was a table of the serious breakfast eaters. They wore brown overalls and dirty crumpled ball caps, bandanas, and goat-roper boots. As they shoveled in food, they turned over their employment chances. From a man wearing sunglasses above the brim of his hat came, "When this job is done, I get laid off. They already asked me to look around."

"At least your boss let you know," his friend in a ranch coat said. "The last time I was let go, I found out at five p.m. The day of."

"And that was?"

"Four weeks ago. Now I'll probably lose this job."

The other two denizens of the table continued to shovel in food. "Hurry up," one said. "Joey don't like us to be late." They shed dollar bills on the table and took their restaurant checks up to the register.

As the hammer swingers and the tractor jockeys left the café, the second wave, the social coffee-drinkers trickled in. He watched them float through the door as if on the tide, up against the counter and around the booths, settling at the high water mark. From behind him, he overheard, "Stroud, he's got it sewn up." He sneaked a peek over his shoulder—two gray-hairs, also a fat man with a walker—about forty years old. A fourth, the one talking, wore an old-fashioned cowboy hat banded with turquoise. "Ralphie, he's got a plan on how to save money in the local government."

A gray-hair asked, "But will it save me money?"

Cowboy hat answered, "Shit yeah."

"That's good. My social security check isn't stretching as far these days."

The man with the walker chimed in, "Or my disability check."

Jupiter shifted his attention to a booth across the way by the ice machine. Its periodic clatter made eavesdropping harder. There were only three men there, all retired or on their way. One man lolled back, hat on the back of his head, while the other two leaned across towards each other, co-conspirators.

The smallest, though he had the most nose hair, insisted, "We got to vote Stroud in. I heard Stroud will outsource our waste management, getting it cheaper out of Amarillo. He'll have to sell the trucks and fire some people for sure, but it will keep property taxes from going up."

The loller replied, drawling his way through it, "Crap, Herman, you don't own anything anyway. You rent."

Herman continued, "I thought his idea about the roads was interesting. Ralph claims you can maintain gravel better and cheaper than you can maintain blacktop, so he wants to rip up some of the outlying streets."

It was doubtful, very doubtful that could work. Jupiter scribbled a note anyway.

Herman's disbelieving friend said, "As long as it's not my street."

Coffee-drinker three, leaning even further over the table, stabbed his finger at Herman for emphasis. "What's more, he promised to reduce the town government by twenty percent in each department. Across the board cuts."

Herman wrinkled up his eyebrows, drawing them down onto the top of his nose. "Well, I don't much like that. My boy works in Human Resources." Jupiter scribbled another note, added another piece of sentiment to the list.

"Why Mr. Devon, good to see you!" He glanced up in surprise. One of the waitresses leaned over the table to refill his coffee cup and flashed huge cleavage at him. He saw her name tag perched on the awesome bosom. Darlene. "How's Kate doing these days?"

"Good, Darlene, good. I think she likes Dallas. How have you been?"

"Fine, Mr. Devon. Things don't slow down in Angie's like everywhere else this time of the year. Well, see ya." She took her broad beam across the room with the coffee pot.

Jupiter shifted his attention to a third table, two guys and a girl. They had on name tags, and with a little secret peering, he was able to make out a real estate logo.

Guy one said, "I heard he's going to get rid of all the town's special events or at least, farm all those things out to the Chamber of Commerce. Not that they'll be able to handle it."

Guy two scowled at the first speaker. "For someone who never goes to the meetings, you got a real low opinion of the Chamber."

The girl asked, "What special events are those, Harry?"

"Oh, the ones Sharp is planning—an antiques festival and a big barbeque in the square."

"That's a shame. I always like looking at antiques."

Jupiter scribbled. Outside money. Foot traffic.

Dan Heldritch burst in the door and clumped over to the table. "I saw your truck out in the square."

"So you thought you would buy me breakfast?"

"Not this time. I'm going into Amarillo for some plumbing. Want to ride along?"

"Why not? It's Saturday. Let me pay my check."

***

Out on the Interstate in the truck, Dan was rhapsodic about bowl games and his favorite college team. "I think that the way things are going, we got a chance to play UT in the Cotton Bowl. But I forgot. You don't like football."

"Not particularly. Politics are more interesting." Jupiter watched a little cardboard pine tree swing beneath the rear view mirror; he smelled its pine cleaner fumes.

"Well, we got that in spades right in town. No need to go to Washington to see the best and the worst." Dan glanced over with a grin.

"And who's the best?"

"Not a real good choice there." Dan said, "I favor Whiffey. He's a crackpot, but at least he's harmless. It's my protest vote. Sarah's going to vote for Sharp."

"And the worst?"

"A certain knuckle-dragging idiot of a farmer. Ask Sarah what she thinks about Stroud." He thumped his fist on the steering wheel twice. "She'd run over him if she could."

"And what do you have against him?"

"He doesn't pay his bills. It took months on the house I built for him. The Mayor, now, never gets a project off the ground. No bills to pay."

Curious on both counts. "So, who do you think Stroud's base is?"

"You tell me. You're the one who'd be a demographics expert."

"Well, I don't have the luxury of a poll. I'd say Stroud's political base is probably made up of town inhabitants on fixed incomes and pensions. They're the ones who want lower taxes at any cost."

"Right! They're the old farts who want cheap and cheerful during their last years, even if the town fades away."

"Careful, Dan. One person in this truck is an old fart."

"But you're not fading away, even if the Council wants you to." Dan snapped a glance out his window at the left wing mirror and changed lanes for the fifteenth time. He sped up, again.

"So if Stroud's base is the living dead, then…." Jupiter stuck his hand out towards Dan handing off the comment.

"Sharp's base should include anyone still working for a paycheck or trying to run a business."

"How's that working out for him?" Jupiter heard a whisper of Marjorie's questions in his own.

"Over the last two years he's pissed me and many others off, over and over again. Even the Chamber hates him."

"Then it's really too late unless something genius happens?" Will someone save the Bull of Heaven from the swords?

***

The billboard ads started going up that week. Billboards with decrepit and flaking advertisements were resurrected with brand new ads. One read, "Re-elect Mayor Nelson Taggert Sharp. He Loves This Town More Than Anybody. After All, He Owns Half of It." Another billboard close to the square promised, "Mayor Sharp Will Help Aniline Grow—He's a Large Man Who Looks Slimmer in a Big Town." It wasn't to be a one-shot campaign. Days before the election, ads in the paper read, "Mayor Sharp—Obviously He Supports Big Times," and "Vote for Sharp—He's Never Starved Himself, And He Won't Starve The Town." On the day of the election, another ad boasted, "Nelson Taggert Sharp—You Can Trust His Rapacity to Make Us All Healthy, Wealthy, and Wise." And at the bottom of all in small print, "Paid for by the Committee to Irritate the Mayor."

***

Jupiter didn't see voting day. His fortunes, getting better every week, surged as the West Coast called. A team he named the "Gang in Black" called looking for their Super Bowl ad. More than a year away, and they were looking for something that would shake the world. His little agency wouldn't make the spot; why, that would be ridiculous to think. But thanks to his reputation for quirkiness, he could build the idea that would be put together by another firm and filmed by another outfit and edited by a fourth. And it could maybe reset modern consumer spending. On the phone, he paced his living room and stared hard into an alternative universe, one based on ad space.

He said, "We'll make it all about the Generation of the Gypsy. Here's your gypsy—hip clothes, a small roller suitcase, a device in the pocket that takes care of all communication needs, and untethered travel. A totally mobile workforce—living this month in Prague, next month in San Diego. It's year 2014, and your phone is your personal assistant, your concierge, and damn near your family. The phone has to talk to you, has to have a personality—a proxy person. Can you do that?"

"Done. Been in the works for awhile. We like the gypsy idea, and we also want to talk about your first idea, the Revolution. 'He' will want to see you, and so will the head of design, to talk visuals with you and the director. Can you come out tomorrow?"

Flying. Airports, crowds, a seat where someone was pressed up against him. Sweat, shaking, nausea. "Can we do it by phone conference? I'm involved in some politics out here in Texas."

"No way. Face to face makes the process so much quicker. We only have fourteen months to get this ad ready to air. We'll send a plane. If we make it an evening meeting with 'Him,' then we can hammer the rest out in a week and be done with the design."

To his surprise, he found himself clear across the house from where he had started the conversation. He hung up the wireless. The timing could work—but all those crowds in LAX. Stop it.

Imagination was a raw thing and sometimes a liar. The airports would have executive lounges, and he could get a cart and driver for transport through the crowds, and he was riding in their corporate jet— and he did have the Prozac.

***

Less than a week later, Jupiter said good-bye and returned to his city, fleeing in the dark towards a new day. The dawn rolled its way as quickly towards him. As Amarillo appeared below, he gazed down and imagined: seven wise ranchers laid the foundation of this city, and many kings built its walls up towards the sky. Amarillo stands forever upon its

265

brown plain beneath the hot sun.

Carl picked him up at the airport and dropped him at the office door of the grain elevator, without speaking more than five words. Jupiter let himself into the elevator's refurbished office, through the door fitted with a dog flap. A rug with two stainless steel bowls lay below one of the windows. He refilled one of them with water. After, he went upstairs riding up in the freight elevator. He wandered into Jim's room. Going over to the desk, he fished a paper bundle from his pocket. He unwrapped it revealing the starfish he had bought in the hotel gift shop. He left it there on the desk beside the catcher's mask and the metal dump truck. He scratched idly at his arm as he left the room. He had rashes on both elbows and his knees.

***

Mayor Nelson Taggert Sharp had been re-elected by a landslide. The election had a high voter turnout and was carried by regional news, showing up on television as far away as Oklahoma City. Jupiter asked his inside sources about it; he met the Heldritchs at the diner, this time for afternoon pie. He ducked in the door, into the steam of an overheated room, and let the aluminum and glass door strike his back. In the corner at the far end of the black and white tiles, Dan and Sarah sat together in a booth. Jupiter slid in opposite them, asked, "What's the recommendation?" He shucked out of his ranch coat.

"Apple with ice cream." Dan had a slice in front of him.

"Pay no attention to him," said Sarah. "Banana cream. It's excellent."

"So, the run-up to the election. What was it like?"

Dan shook his head. "Man, people wouldn't quit talking about it. Just as the chatter was dying out, a new sign would go up. At first folks believed it was Sharp himself doing it, but he was way too angry to be the one."

"And not smart enough to make himself a laughing stock," she added.

Dan said, "Or a whipping boy. Once the town figured out someone else was doing it, they were overjoyed. Folks went around cornering the sign guys, trying to get them to say who was paying them. They told

266

people they worked for a company in Amarillo and to call their office. The office refused to talk, of course."

Sarah broke in. "The staff at the newspaper, they were the same, but I think they didn't know themselves who was paying for the ads. They printed an editorial saying 'Political discourse should be public and not anonymous,' but they ran the ads just the same."

Jupiter frowned. "Some of the billboards feel cruel to me." He held up a hand and got the waitress' attention. She came over with a cup of coffee; he ordered banana cream.

Dan chortled. "Yeah, everybody likes a laugh at someone else's expense. Vonnegut said humor was based on cruelty, you know."

"Vonnegut? You're reading Vonnegut?" Jupiter leaned on his elbow and gazed admiringly at Dan.

"We don't all do our reading in the bathroom like you, Matt. But you know, those signs had some truth to them, and after you repeat the joke to your friends ten times, you start paying attention to the words."

Sarah put her hand on Dan's arm, shoe-horned her way in, "Like you and I talked about before. Stroud's idea was to turn off the lights and sit in the dark to save money, and the Mayor's was to build houses and strip malls. Fill 'em up with people paying taxes."

Dan stared at her. "You two have been talking about this?"

Jupiter said, "We bumped into each other one day at the Post Office."

She patted the back of Dan's hand. "It's okay, dear. You don't have to know everything." She swiveled back to Jupiter. "Of course, the employees down at Town Hall kept playing up the differences between the two front runners, but they had the most to lose, didn't they, with their jobs on the line? Still, people started talking about growing the town, not just saving it. Even the farmers were saying Aniline should be more than a feed store. The last billboard was the best."

"What did it say?"

Dan jumped in. "It showed a giant balloon, a blimp like at the football games, you know, and it read, 'Behold the Blimp's Big View— It's Sharp to Believe in Aniline's Future.' It may not have been the best ad, but now the Mayor is called the Blimp." Sarah shook her head while the two men shared a guffaw.

Jupiter got his pie, spooned in a mouthful and said, "You were right,

Sarah. This is sin on a plate. So how is the Mayor taking it?"

Sarah took her turn. "I think the poor guy is schizo about it."

Dan leaned back. "Yeah, but he's got real investor money now he's won the election. He's going ahead with all his development plans—anyhow those with me and with a couple guys I know. Sharp is also still the lord and master of the Town Council. But, he's touchy and he acts, well, subdued or even ashamed sometimes—when he comes into Angie's, for instance. The room will get quiet and there might be a laugh or two. Then he hurries over to the counter, sits down, and orders. He's not such a big stick anymore. He might end up being one of the rest of us."

Darlene came by with refills on the coffee; Jupiter remembered her name in time. "Darlene, how's it going?"

"Why, fine, Mr. Devon. Nice to have you back in town. Sarah, good to see you. Dan, you want another scoop of ice cream on that?"

"Shoot yes." She snatched up his plate, wheeled gracefully, and charged back behind the counter. "I like Darlene."

Sarah laughed, "You'd like anyone who gives you extra ice cream." She squeezed him in a hug and left her arm laying on the back of the booth.

Darlene swooped back with Dan's freebee, accepted thanks with poise, and took herself off to other customers. Dan said, "You know, she married one of my guys recently, Stevie Martinez. God knows how they'll sort out her children and his."

"How did Darlene know I was out of town?"

Sara answered, her face bland and innocent. "No idea. I heard it from Diane."

Dan muttered, "I might have mentioned something."

Jupiter pushed his plate away leaving only a crumb and a smidgen of meringue. "Well, it's a big relief to be back."

"You went to Cupertino? For a week?"

"Yes, about a week. Business." Jupiter picked up his check and snatched theirs.

"Hey," Dan protested. "You can't afford that. That embezzlement thing, and you're broke from the elevator anyway."

"There are no secrets in a small town, are there?"

Sarah laughed at the idea of secrets. "Especially not about money.

Or ex-wives."

"Does Kate know? About me being married?"

Dan rolled his eyes. "Haven't you told her? Afraid she'll have a fit about you being married back in the Dark Ages?"

"Hmm, no, I haven't told her. And, no, I don't know if she would care one way or the other."

Sarah tried on her teacher voice. "Kate lives in the present, Matt. Maybe she doesn't even think of you as 'older' since your early decades occurred 'Before Kate.' She didn't see them happen. Dan and I haven't talked to her about your ex-wife—"

Dan interrupted. "But then, we're not allowed to talk to her about you. She laid down the rules on that."

Jupiter sighed. "That's something, at any rate."

***

Jupiter's truck tipped downhill into the curb in front of the hardware store. He rolled up one sleeve so that he could get at his elbow to scratch. Through the big windows, past the specials and prices pasted to the glass, he could see a queue. He wasn't going in until there was some breathing space. He counted his way through the people leaving. He counted the days since he had seen Kate. Like picking a scab, he counted years of marriage to Sheila. Fifteen customers gone now, back in their vehicles and driving away.

He went over to the paint counter. Diane, wrapped in the orange smock of the hardware store, dropped a can of paint into the shaker, screwed down the clamps, and flipped the switch. The shaker shuddered vibration into the floor, into Jupiter's head. "It'll be just a minute," she said to her customer.

Jupiter rubbed his forehead and raised his forefinger to get her attention. "Diane, I heard you were here."

"Matt, good to see you. What do you think about my new wardrobe?" She flipped her hand at her own body like a TV host showing off the prizes.

"Very stylish." The woman buying the paint smiled secretly and glanced at both Diane and Jupiter. She didn't step away. Accidental eavesdropping—never a crime in a village.

"Can I get you anything Matt?"

"Hmm, I actually came by to see you. We haven't talked since I called from California."

"Been back long?"

"Just long enough to hear I went to California—and what I did there."

The customer leaned in closer. Diane gazed appraisingly at him. "Why, is that a complaint I hear, Matt?"

"Is there somewhere we could visit?" His eyes pointed at their audience.

"Sure, let me settle up here. The manager's office is empty today. Bill is at the other store."

***

The manager's office was a booth open to the space behind the counter, stuffed with shipping orders, invoices, and inventories. Diane dropped into the boss' chair, put her hands behind her head, and leaned back. "Have a seat," she offered.

"You are too kind." He took a box of jumbled hardware off a rickety chair, dusted the seat, and eased down onto it.

"We have a lot to catch up on." She sat forward with a bump.

"Diane, what could happen in ten days?"

"I have three new customers, which is the good news. The bad news is the auto parts store sold out to a chain, so we lost a customer. Still, I can charge a nice transfer fee for that one."

"So, all together we're ahead by two clients."

"Yes indeedy, Matt. The glass is half full."

"I'm sure it will start picking up, Diane."

"Frankly, I got bored. I've fixed up nearly everything I can around the house without spending any real money. I've never much liked TV. Not enough for me to do."

"Diane, I'm not sure what you're saying. I'm your partner, but I don't think I need to worry about your leisure time."

"I haven't had leisure time since I was seventeen, Mr. Partner. So to keep from being driven crazy, I went out and got this job. Part time, not leisure time, that's the motto."

"Looks like a good fit."

"The Lord knows I bought enough hardware in my life; I ought to be able to sell it."

"Diane, that's great, as long as you're sure." Not great at all. Not the plan.

"Oh, don't worry, I'll still be looking for customers for the bookkeeping."

"I wasn't worried." Mind reader.

"You should be. You're far too easy to take advantage of. The boss here, Bill, is letting me keep my business cards on the counter. So this means I can take care of the grocery bills now by myself, the gas and insurance, and some of the utilities."

"Let me know when you get a raise; then you can start paying for my groceries."

"As if that would happen. Whoops, better get back to it. Customer at the counter." She bustled away before he could answer.

The Death of Gilgamesh

Chapter Thirty: Council and Rule

Jupiter could see and hear the instant the screen saver cleared. He had now perfected his delusion. He saw a Sumerian council chamber heaped with tablets scribed with cuneiform. He saw Gilgamesh and his clerks around him, as they waited to take down the King's decisions. Columns everywhere supported the ceiling, closing the room in. People stood or squatted on the stone floor in a long line, held in place by the majordomo until the King could see them. Gilgamesh glanced up at Jupiter and spoke. Jupiter heard him clearly, though the King murmured in an aside for Jupiter alone. "There you are. You catch me as I care for my flock."

"You use a lot of clay tablets to run a kingdom."

Gilgamesh shot him an exasperated glance. "Admiration and adulation come with responsibility. Easy glory turns into long work. I carry no sword, only the symbolic one of politics."

Jupiter thought of his own appointment calendar, gone from empty to chock-a-block. "There's a certain pride in the sacrifice, though."

"Enough of small things. Let us take a rest. We have things to say." Gilgamesh spoke to his chief scribe, rose, and paced from the room. Jupiter's view caromed after the King at first and then steadied out. Jupiter followed him down the hall, as Gilgamesh peeked over his shoulder. Gilgamesh ducked under a curtain into a small room and took his place on a wooden bench. One oil lamp burned. There were no windows to open up the claustrophobic space.

Jupiter's view dropped down as if he had found his own bench and sat. They stared at each other, disconcerted by the new tangibility of their meeting. Jupiter waited.

273

Gilgamesh coughed. His head swung up towards the coffered ceiling above and then dropped back to Jupiter. "I have decided. I can be a better king if I know when and how I die. I can at least plan. Uruk should have a better succession than Dumizid gave her."

"You care about kingship, don't you?"

"I could ask you the same question. But I know that you do. I see it every day."

"So, shall I finish the story now?"

"We will not be disturbed."

Jupiter cleared his throat. How to begin. "In all, you reigned a hundred and twenty-six years. You have six years left if the Epic is correct."

"Six years." Gilgamesh laughed. "Not a long time. I can live with that. Or die by it."

"In these last years, you will create the first version of your Epic. You will write out your tale of the quest for immortality and the meanings and lessons behind it. One copy you make available to the people through the scribes who guard Uruk's literacy. Other copies you will send to the cities over which Uruk has dominion. You also will bury tablets in cedar chests within the fortified walls of Uruk."

"That I like. It will be a hidden library in the one place that is mine."

Jupiter smiled, quizzical. "I don't understand."

"I share my dominion over the temples, the palace, and the plaza with the priests and the Elect. The fortifications belong to the King."

"Ah. So, in addition to the public copies, you will bury your thoughts deep within Uruk so they may be discovered once the city has passed away."

"Will Uruk pass away?"

"Yes and no. The city survives for two thousand years, but in the end, the people destroy the countryside that supports Uruk. Irrigation will make the farmland salty and the sheep will eat the brush that prevents erosion, so the gentle hills themselves melt into the rivers. The people will move west into a land we call Europe. Once the people are gone, Uruk becomes an immense hill as the mud bricks dissolve. The appearance of Uruk that I know is a soft, shapeless memorial by the river."

"How sad you make me. Even my city will not survive?"

"Not even the stars live forever. But in my time Uruk is revived. My people dig Uruk up, and many of them spend their entire lives learning how your people lived and loved, ate and drank, worshipped and died. Uruk exists again in the imagination of my people."

Gilgamesh blinked. His mouth worked, "You are the curators of our dreams and memories, and we will never know you."

"I hadn't considered it that way. But you will have had more than a century of rule. You took on the role of King and father, Lord and husband, Ruler and lover, and you enjoyed those things Siduri had said should be yours. You took the hands of your children and led them in dance; you stood upon the steps of the Ziggurat and offered homage to Anu and Enlil. You drank and were merry, you feasted and were full, and you gave bounteous celebration days to your people. The Elect of Uruk granted you power supreme, and you exercised it wisely."

Gilgamesh scowled. "I am not dead yet. The eulogy does not have to begin."

"You wanted to know. You die well, noble, and strong to the end. The Epic says Death will pin you to your bed like a gazelle caught in a noose, and that you wrestle Death like a lion. You succumb only because he is inhuman, a beast without hand or foot but with claw and talon. They say you are unafraid and unapologetic at the end, even though you know you will not rule again in Uruk.

Afterwards, the people of Uruk will make obeisance to twenty gods for you and declare you the heart of Uruk. They will set out bread for Ereshkigal the Queen of Death and for the seven judges of the dead, for the kings Dumizid and Lugalbanda."

All the names, memorized with such difficulty, rolled off Jupiter's tongue. "Priestess and priest will measure out libation for Anu and for Enlil himself. They will lay out a feast for the god of feasts, Shulpae, because he must be present. Such Sumer names, such glory, so hard for me to pronounce."

Gilgamesh pulled at his beard. "By the gods, ur-Jupiter, I do love a feast, even when I don't get to attend."

"Then the city will gather together to entomb their beloved Gilgamesh. The people of Uruk, the young men, the temple prostitutes and the priestesses, the mothers and the fathers—all of Uruk will work to divert the river. Imagine it, Gilgamesh, turning the river aside for you!

There in the hollow of the Euphrates' course, they will build your tomb and place you there. Then they tear down the levees and bring the river back to blanket you through all time and keep you soft-nestled and protected below the Euphrates, warm in the earth."

"Very poetic. And then it is over? I am just dead and buried? Clay in clay, hidden beneath the river?"

"No, there is a last twist on the tale. The gods will meet and talk once again about the fate of the great Gilgamesh. The lesser gods will speak. They will say you should be granted the immortality you sought so hard as a young man."

Gilgamesh dropped his chin and gazed down to the floor. "They will be wrong. All my years of being king are about being a mortal."

"Don't worry. Ea, god of wisdom, will show your years after Dilmun and Utnapishtim upon the heavens for all to see, and the gods will see your reconciliation to mortality. To force immortality on you would be to sail against the wind of your soul. Then Anu will speak. He will declare you the judge of the Underworld, elevated above all others there. He will grant you light and meat there in the Underworld and a return of your relatives and your beloved brother Enkidu. These are not things given to any other dead before or since. You will serve as the judge of the Anunnaki gods. You will deal honorably with the dead, to represent the good who are now voiceless, and to punish the bad who have carried their evil into the Underworld itself, where evil can be contained."

"Friend and guide, I will be a mortal man even in the Underworld. But you said I would have immortality. You said in the end, I would understand you, understand what you meant by immortality."

Jupiter wanted to pitch this right. He wanted to repair that hole of disappointment deep within his friend. "Yes, Gilgamesh, immortality is yours because you will take the essence of man, the mortality and the experience, and you will write it down for all humanity. You have seized knowledge, and when you record it, you will make knowledge into wisdom. Wisdom that is still with us and that has made you immortal."

"What is this wisdom you speak of?"

"Why, it is the Epic of Gilgamesh, the Epic scribed on clay. Fragile, smashed by time and pillage. Pieced together. Immortal in the world, brought to us in our own languages."

276

Jupiter leaned forward, and with Gilgamesh so close, Jupiter could distinguish the old-age spot on his forehead, the craters of his pores. "The Epic is about good and evil. It is about tyranny and beneficent rule. It is about hubris and obligation. It is about love and loss. You can rest easy; you are the first hero who is a man and not a god, and you are first among our heroes. 'Oh Gilgamesh, King of Uruk and warrior of the Fertile Crescent, to you all praise.'"

Gilgamesh held out his palms and shrugged. "I am to be reduced to words?"

"No. More important. Think through your life right now. Think from the riverbank, the village to the city, to the arrival of your beloved. Think of your long quest through to your return. Think of your century of Kingship. Think of how that message, a life, comes to us."

"Perhaps. It has been a surprising passage, at least to me. My name will still live." Gilgamesh's voice caught on the last word. He paused such a long pause. Then he slapped his knees. "I am content. As you have said, I will come no more to this earth. This will be our good-bye, then, ur-Jupiter."

Chapter Thirty-One: To Be Wise

Jupiter leaned close to the window, peered through the Venetian blinds, and kept as far away from the six people in the room as possible. Virginia wasn't a dream visit in late November. A leaden sky sat outside the office and started to spit cold and damp down. Outside on the mall between the buildings, figures scurried for cover turning collars up. Umbrellas appeared—held aloft between humans and Enlil, gloomy god of the sky. Lord, he missed Gilgamesh, even if he might not have been real.

Across the table, Robert Tunston demurred. "It's a strange project in a rural location, during a down economy."

Jupiter turned back to the room. "It's been done before. You all have one up in St. Paul on the Mississippi River. What do you need to know in order to come see it?"

"Describe it to me, describe this cachet, this drawing card you're promising."

"History. Unique use of an agricultural site. Huge media coverage for creative re-use at a time when architecture is all glass boxes on the Interstate." Three people perched immobile, waiting for their boss to decide. A fourth pushed back, unconvinced. A fifth was already sold.

"Details?"

"It started as a country grain elevator. It evolved with each change in the agricultural system. They built the first elevator all out of wood, and it held less than twenty thousand bushels. That one burned down. They built a second one on top of the old foundation, made of four by four by tens, lined in iron, and covered in tin. It's still there."

Tunston spoke with a dry voice, "Sounds rustic."

"Oh, it gets better. When the time was right for a subterminal elevator—"

"Subterminal?"

"Preliminary staging point for grain before the railroad took it up to the final big complexes—in places like Buffalo and Duluth...." Jupiter's temples pulsed with each beat of his heart. It was a wonder the others couldn't hear it.

"So there's no flour mill sitting beside it?"

He was a cold, demanding bastard. "Too far away from the cities. About ten years before the First World War, they poured the concrete for the modern elevator up beside the old one. They slip-formed the new elevator in a continuous pour, raised all eighteen big bins, and the star-shaped interstitial bins, over a twenty-day period. All of this is very photogenic, and we have the photos. You could make giant displays in the lobby."

"Imposing size, I hope?"

"The big bins themselves are each one-hundred-and-twenty feet high and twenty feet across. They held about six-hundred-thousand bushels apiece."

"Wow!"

That impressed even this guy. "Yeah, a lot of breakfast cereal. The bins sit on their own reinforced columns above the ground floor, which is called the work floor. They were emptied or accessed from there and monitored for moisture and heat. The builders also slip-formed a rectangular one-hundred-and-forty-foot tower capped by a head house. The head house acted as a cupola between the new grain bins and the old wooden building." Maybe he was turning this guy around.

"What's that mean?"

"It means they attached the old elevator to the new with chutes and conveyors, kept it in use. Waste not, want not."

"What's on top of the bins?"

He had raised some interest in spite of Tunston's hard-shell image. "A long rectangular building. The distribution floor on top is a single-story shed running eighty feet along the top of the bins and then forming a bridge to the head house. It'd make a nice restaurant with a view, and there's space for decks and outside seating. There are vertical conveyor legs down on both sides, to the road and to the tracks. There's even a ground shed with a grating in the floor where belly-dumper trucks discharged the grain into the ground and augurs took it up to the top."

"Is this standard enough to be a nostalgia thing for guests?"

Smart question. "Pretty standard. They built one every fifteen miles down the rail line. Thousands of them have disappeared now."

"What about insurance?"

That was a really strange question. Tunston was jumping around. "Just a concrete building now with no risk of a grain explosion. It's standard stuff."

"Any other facilities come with this deal?"

"There's parking and an acre that could be used for theme-oriented outbuildings. During the 1991 China boom, the co-op added a forty-foot high, fifty-foot round steel silo on the end and connected it into the distribution floor through a boom. It's a great utility building. The original scales, some of the cleaning sieves, and two cyclones are stored inside."

"What's a cyclone?"

The rash on his legs was itching dreadfully. "I'm told it took the dust out of the air to prevent explosions. And if all this isn't enough, a Pentecostal church occupied the work floor for five years. The parishioners cut the bottom out of one of the bins. They utilized it as a hundred and twenty foot high altar."

"Now that's creative reuse!"

Tunston was interested in spite of himself.

"Yes, it was a great concept. The pews extended out into the work floor itself, and we still have them. It must have been something—a twenty-foot wide shaft of light streaming down like God himself from far above. The baptismal fount is still there; that's a concrete bin that once held insecticide."

"Insecticide?"

"Yeah, they probably scrubbed it out first with bleach and thought they were fine."

"Glad I wasn't dipped in that! Hmm, does sound like something with history and a name, something we could develop. Close to Amarillo?"

"Yes, fast growing city, lots of market share. Also don't forget Dallas, Oklahoma City, and Tulsa are close by. Medium driving range from Albuquerque and Kansas City."

"All right, enough of the voice-over. Give my aide whatever slide talk and photos you've got prepared. I'll want to bring them into my board meeting next month."

"No glossy presentation. I can give you a prospectus on the financials." Jupiter pushed a leather-bound notebook across the table. "I'll go you one better than a dog-and-pony show. Why don't I buy you three airplane tickets? You bring an engineer and a photographer and see what you think. I'll book you into a hotel in Amarillo, my expense. You'll get ground truth rather than a PowerPoint presentation."

"Huh…" Tunston grunted. "You caught me by surprise."

"Yes." Jupiter relaxed. He had seen Tunston's pupils dilate. "No strings attached, instant gratification."

"Listen, we didn't expect this meeting to work out, and I've unfortunately got another scheduled for now. This needs some thinking. Where can I reach you?"

"I'm at the Sofitel in D.C., across the river."

"Let me call you there this afternoon, and I'll let you know."

***

In the cab on the way back, Jupiter msg'd Kate. "Good and bad news."

"Gd 1rst."

"May hve savd elevatr."

"Holy shit impossbl!"

"Accept yr congrats."

"Bd nws?"

"No Dallas house. $ tied up for awhil."

"Wat?"

"Svng elevator."

"&U didnt ask?"

"Aftr all is my $."

"Fck u old frt."

He tried two more times to text and call—nothing. Ishtar was angry beyond all measure. Would she listen? Or would she release the Bull of Heaven upon him?

***

On the way through Washington National Airport, Jupiter bought Jimmy Devereaux a pewter version of Lincoln's Memorial.

Chapter Thirty-Two: Prologue of the Epic

There was a mélange of perfume—floral, woodsy, citrus, sharp, overpowering, blurred. He could think of a hundred adjectives for the stink. It hung in the hallway, floated through the scarves, hair, and dresses of the women waiting to get into the room. Jupiter stifled a sneeze with a tissue and wiped the corners of his eyes. Outside the Council Chamber, the walls were lined with photos of past Council Members and Mayors, arrayed like bas-relief of gods on the side of a temple, but the frames were chipped gilt, and the effect would have been more magnificent in terra cotta. The photos looked like tarted-up death masks. The ranchers standing in front of them projected a tougher reality. He found her waiting for him near a copy machine down a corridor.

"Marjorie, how did you know I'd come down here?"

"Look around. How many people do you see?"

"Four. Six, counting us."

"How is the skin problem?"

"Oh, that. Cransto has that under control with topical steroids."

"Treating the symptom rather than the cause?"

"Marjorie, please, not today of all days."

"Of course, dear. 'Where' are you today?"

"I've got a chance to win today. Or to lose. Either way, it will change things."

"Good luck, Jupiter." She floated off down the hall, waving a graceful hand over her shoulder. "See you inside."

Jupiter knew he appeared ill at ease, if twitching could be defined as "ill at ease." Tunston, who had saved him a seat, leaned around to eye him narrowly, "Are you okay, Devon?"

"I think I might have a touch of the flu. Don't worry; I won't breathe on you." Most lies are designed to keep people happy.

They sat in the second row. People filled the room to overflowing. He inhaled the multi-layered scents of close-ranked humanity, with that extra pungent smell of cow shit brought in on someone's boots. The buzz in the air sounded of baritone hornets, made up of all the small talk going back and forth. The high-pitched greetings of women who wanted to be heard above the crowd punctuated the hum. The townsfolk had turned out in numbers because they had heard this was the showdown—the Council had at last brought Matt Devon to judgment on this day in mid-December.

Jupiter was wet with sweat, yet he kept his old-style ranch coat on. The perspiration on his forehead had nothing to do with room temperature or coat. Fundamentally, he wanted to keep his local uniform on display. The bulk of the men were dressed in jeans and boots, good go-to-town hats, and their rough and ready coats. The Councilmen, on the other hand, were dressed in slacks, golf shirts, and blazers. Jupiter knew where his market niche existed, and it wasn't with the blazers.

The meeting ground along, crawling its way toward the agenda item that brought him and others here. He sat sandwiched hard between Tunston and a well-padded grandmother, with his knees touching the back of the chair in front of him. He noticed it was difficult to get his breath, and he heard ringing in his ears. He supposed the drug was causing the tintinnabulation. He hoped it was the drug.

Tunston touched him on the knee, indicated the dais. "Look at them. They know something's up. They're squirming." Focusing on the Council helped. The Mayor, reincarnated man of three surnames, sat somber and dark, communing with himself. Elsewhere among the council, they buzzed back and forth, handing each other paper documents too thick to be of help at this late date, making little supportive gestures. The size of the crowd was disturbing.

At long last, the Town Manager announced, "Item Seven. Commercial and Residential Zoning, the Devon Household."

The Mayor signaled to the man who sat beside him. Sharp had chosen the local banker who sat on the Council to act the heavy. Jupiter considered him with jaded eye. His nemesis. He was a thin man, a man with a dramatic widow's peak, an Elvis bang—a man with a bronze knife.

With that black shock of hair hanging off his forehead, the banker took the podium. He set out index cards and leaned up to the mike. He asked, "Can you hear me? Testing, testing?" The crowd sat stolid in their minimal seats and regarded him with hostile expressions. This he took as his cue, clearing his throat. "Before we hear from Mr. Devon, I'm going to reiterate, for the record, how the town policy and regulations affect this agenda point." He glanced down at the cards and rolled one over. Someone in the crowd snickered.

He began reading, at first slowly, then accelerating. "While the current zoning laws were voted into place during Mr. Devon's alterations to his grain elevator, they still affect Mr. Devon. The regulation is clear—nothing north of Fifth Street can be residential. From Fifth to the town limits is duly zoned as commercial-only. While Mr. Devon may wish to contest this in court, due to alleged ambiguities in timing between the zoning vote and his occupancy, the Town stands ready to enforce its policy in the interim. We are actually required to evict Mr. Devon by statute, using local law enforcement if needed."

The councilman went on, "There has also been some discussion about multi-family development. While the zoning regulations don't directly address condominiums or apartments, it is clear under our policy and regulations. The Town would not allow the grain elevator to be renovated for multi-family dwellings, since that would be residential. Such repurposing of the elevator would also be after the date the zoning regulations went into effect, so we do not expect this could be legitimately—" he repeated, "—legitimately contested in court. Now that the agenda item is in context, we'll open the floor for discussion."

Jupiter raised his hand, and the Town Manager said, "The chair recognizes Mr. Devon."

Jupiter stood up, turned to face the crowd, and placed his back to the council. Cowardice. Defiance. He couldn't actually focus on most faces, but there was one—a short round woman buried in the back row; he recognized Marjorie's Filipino features. He raised his hand slightly to her in a concealed greeting. He rubbed his sweaty hands on his jacket and took a shuddering breath. Now he felt better. Now he was doing the pitch.

"I thought I would let you know up front, I will not be competing with other residential developments here in Aniline, nor will the grain elevator continue to be a personal residence owned by me." The room erupted in amazement.

A sigh gusted free on the dais behind him. They had him now. He had capitulated without reservation!

Jupiter smiled. "I'd like to introduce the gentleman with me. His name is Robert Tunston, and he is with the National Trust for Historic Preservation. He'll be here to answer specific questions, but I'll give you my overview. The grain elevator has been registered on the National List and so is now a protected structure. More importantly, the elevator is also now a National Property and has an endowment for its upkeep and maintenance. With that, I'd ask the Chair to recognize Bob here." He practically spun and sat down as if the chair could swallow him.

The Town Manager, mouth hanging open like a fish, nodded, and Tunston stood up. He played to authority and faced front, but his voice carried strong across the room. "As Mr. Devon said, I represent the National Trust. We have decided to accept the very generous gift of the elevator and the endowment that comes with it. We completed the paperwork yesterday to transfer ownership. The Trust intends to turn the elevator into a museum to celebrate American agricultural business and the key role grain elevators have played for two hundred years in communities like Aniline."

There was a shout from the crowd, "Hot Damn—Yes!" The audience vibrated like a wasp nest gone mad. The Town Manager gaveled furiously.

Tunston continued, louder now. "Just some details. The Pentecostal Sanctuary onsite will be preserved and restored. Likewise, the original wooden elevator will be preserved. The name of the company that built the concrete elevator and first owned it will be repainted on the head house. The name of the first farmer's co-operative to own the elevator will be painted on the north side of the bins, and the name of the second co-op will be painted on the south. The name of the museum is yet to be determined. The entire grounds will be committed to the theme of agriculture with the elevator as the show-case."

Tunston raised his voice over the increasingly agitated crowd. "The legal staff of the Trust has examined the zoning regulations of Aniline in detail and is satisfied its museum will fit the commercial zoning requirement. Moreover, the Trust has agreed a caretaker should live on site for security and to supervise work. The zoning regulations do not disallow us to make any arrangements for security we deem necessary. The Trust has agreed in writing that Mr. Devon can be that caretaker until such time he chooses to resign and vacate."

A hush rolled across the room like a wave, except for one cracked voice that asked, "What did he say?"

Tunston leaned towards the old man who had spoken, "I said, Mr. Devon stays until he wants to go."

Now it was the Council that was buzzing, but Tunston bore on, speaking above their muttered consultation. "Gentlemen, I believe I have the floor. Of course, the Trust does not wish to be responsible for the Museum forever, so we visualize the establishment of a local Historical Society that would receive the museum from us as a free and clear transfer."

He cleared his throat and continued. "Now, Mr. Mayor, I'm sure you're thinking about the economy. As to the impact on the community—that's something we always try to project. You can expect there will be a boost to employment with the work in creating the actual museum space and its displays—that should be considered no more than a short-term advantage to the local community. The Trust anticipates it would employ four to six staff full time once the museum is up and running. We would be willing to lease space to a commercial venture for a coffee shop or a restaurant, but that might take some time. Elsewhere in Aniline, we could expect increased traffic in town: museum visitors from such places as Amarillo, Dallas, and Oklahoma City. In summary, an improved business climate. That's all I came to say, but I can answer questions after the meeting if there are any."

Mayor Nelson Taggert Sharp jumped to his feet and nodded to Tunston. The Council was mute and bewildered, but not the Mayor. "On behalf of the Town of Aniline, we hereby accept, and we thank the generous donation and hard work of our very own citizen, Matthew Devon." There was a "boo" from the side, and a man in a baseball cap made a farting sound up into the Mayor's face.

The Mayor remained standing, Tunston sat down, and the buzz and shuffle mounted, spiraled up in clamor. Then Sarah Heldritch stood up and slowly started clapping. She picked up the pace, and another person started, and another, till the room thundered. It was the most perfect thing.

Scott Archer Jones & Siena © Wende Woolley Photography

About the Author

Scott Archer Jones is currently living and working on his fifth novel in northern New Mexico, after stints in the Netherlands, Scotland and Norway plus less exotic locations. He's worked for a power company, grocers, a lumberyard, an energy company (for a very long time), and a winery. Now he's on the masthead of the Prague Revue.

A new writer for such an old guy, he has received an honorable mention in the E. M. Koeppel Short Fiction Contest, and been a finalist in a Glimmer Train Fiction Open and the SouthWest Writers Annual Contest. He's been published at Blue Lake Review, Bookends Review, Circa, Copperfield, Eunoia, Faircloth, Fear of Monkeys, Foliate Oak, Infinite Press, ken*again, The Life As An [insert label here], Piker's Press, the Prague Revue, Rusty Nail, Stepping Stones, Synchronized Chaos, a Thousand and One Stories, Thrice Fiction, Whistling Fire, and Wilderness House Literary Review—and soon at Glint, Literary Orphans, and Thought Collection.

Scott cuts all his own firewood, lives a mile from his nearest neighbor and writes grant applications for the community. He is currently the Treasurer of Shuter Library of Angel Fire, a private 501.C3, and desperately needs your money to keep the doors open.

https://www.facebook.com/ScottArcherJones

www.scottarcherjones.com

www.ingramcontent.com/pod-product-compliance
Lightning Source LLC
Chambersburg PA
CBHW021506240626

47154CB00002B/527